F BEN
The Bermuda key
Bentley, B. R., author.

THE BERMUDA KEY

BY B. R. BENTLEY

Suite 300 - 990 Fort St
Victoria, BC, Canada, V8V 3K2
www.friesenpress.com

Copyright © 2015 by B.R. Bentley
First Edition — 2015

Editor – Nicky F. Spires
Author's Photograph – Dr. MJ Bowie

All rights reserved, including the right to reproduce this book or portions thereof in any form whatsoever.

This book is a work of fiction. Any references to historical events, real people, real objects or real places are used fictitiously. Other names, characters, places, objects and events are products of the author's imagination, and any resemblance to actual objects, events, places or persons, living or dead, is entirely coincidental.

No part of this publication may be reproduced in any form, or by any means, electronic or mechanical, including photocopying, recording, or any information browsing, storage, or retrieval system, without permission in writing from FriesenPress.

All excerpts from *The Cross* – Copyright © 2014 by B.R. Bentley – with the permission of the author.

www.brbentley.com

ISBN
978-1-4602-8007-2 (Hardcover)
978-1-4602-8008-9 (Paperback)
978-1-4602-8009-6 (eBook)

1. *Fiction, Crime*
2. *Fiction, Mystery & Detective, Historical*
3. *Fiction, Religious*

Distributed to the trade by The Ingram Book Company

THE BOOK THAT STARTED IT ALL

The Cross by B.R. Bentley

After nearly 400 years, an emerald-encrusted gold pectoral cross belonging to the Catholic Church is discovered by two salvage divers off the coast of Bermuda. Carried by an Augustinian friar on the ill-fated Spanish galleon *San Pedro*, the cross contains a priceless hidden key.

The divers want it for the money. The Bermuda government wants it for its historical value. A group of cardinals known as the Silenti want it for the key hidden inside.

Displayed in the Bermuda Maritime Museum from the time of its discovery, it is not until Queen Elizabeth's visit to the island many years later that the cross in the museum is found to be a fake.

Inspired by one of Bermuda's greatest unsolved mysteries, fact and fiction are cleverly woven together throughout this debut novel from author B.R. Bentley as the protagonists conspire to achieve their aims.

"The true story is so extraordinary it hardly needs much additional dramatization. A fast-paced thriller that's difficult to put down." – *Kirkus Reviews*

Website: **www.brbentley.com**

Table of Contents

ACKNOWLEDGEMENTS iii
PROLOGUE v
CHAPTER 1 1
CHAPTER 2 9
CHAPTER 3 12
CHAPTER 4 18
CHAPTER 5 19
CHAPTER 6 22
CHAPTER 7 24
CHAPTER 8 27
CHAPTER 9 31
CHAPTER 10 35
CHAPTER 11 36
CHAPTER 12 42
CHAPTER 13 44
CHAPTER 14 54
CHAPTER 15 56
CHAPTER 16 59
CHAPTER 17 61
CHAPTER 18 63
CHAPTER 19 70
CHAPTER 20 73
CHAPTER 21 77
CHAPTER 22 79

CHAPTER 23	85
CHAPTER 24	87
CHAPTER 25	94
CHAPTER 26	101
CHAPTER 27	103
CHAPTER 28	106
CHAPTER 29	111
CHAPTER 30	113
CHAPTER 31	115
CHAPTER 32	122
CHAPTER 33	128
CHAPTER 34	130
CHAPTER 35	132
CHAPTER 36	137
CHAPTER 37	149
CHAPTER 38	151
CHAPTER 39	157
CHAPTER 40	160
CHAPTER 41	166
CHAPTER 42	169
CHAPTER 43	173
CHAPTER 44	177
CHAPTER 45	179
CHAPTER 46	190
CHAPTER 47	194
CHAPTER 48	201
CHAPTER 49	208
CHAPTER 50	213

CHAPTER 51	217
CHAPTER 52	223
CHAPTER 53	227
CHAPTER 54	232
CHAPTER 55	234
CHAPTER 56	241
CHAPTER 57	246
CHAPTER 58	249
CHAPTER 59	262
CHAPTER 60	265
CHAPTER 61	271
CHAPTER 62	273
CHAPTER 63	274
CHAPTER 64	281
CHAPTER 65	283
CHAPTER 66	287
CHAPTER 67	289
CHAPTER 68	291
CHAPTER 69	295
CHAPTER 70	298
CHAPTER 71	304
CHAPTER 72	308
CHAPTER 73	312
CHAPTER 74	315
CHAPTER 75	321
CHAPTER 76	325
EPILOGUE	329
About the Author	333

Bentley

My faithful and loyal companion.
At my side throughout the writing of *The Cross*.
Your unbridled joy of life will never be forgotten.
This one's for you.

March 9, 2014

ACKNOWLEDGEMENTS

Dylan, who kept me focussed on the word count.
Ted and Clara, who instilled and encouraged my love of books.
MaryJane, Nicky, Stephanie, Mark and Mike
for their critiques of the manuscript.
Many good friends and family members
for their continued support and encouragement.

B.R. Bentley
Eagle Harbour 2015

PROLOGUE

[The month before the present day]
Hamilton, Bermuda – Thursday, April 26, 2012

"Exhume the body! With all due respect and reverence, Eminence, are you out of your mind? Do you really expect me to be part of a process to exhume my mother's body, and I quote, 'to serve the greater good of the Church'?"

Peter Alexander, Barrister & Solicitor, of the firm Whyte, Alexander & Hodgkins, stared at the cardinal sitting in front of him in absolute amazement. He had been surprised when asked by the Vatican to meet with Cardinal Weiler - even more surprised when the cardinal informed him that his mother was involved in a matter concerning the Church – and finally, absolutely shocked at this last suggestion.

"Let me summarize the problems with your request," he said slipping into his standard legal jargon. It felt safer there while his mind toiled away behind the scenes.

"Firstly, there is no legal rationale for this request based on what you've told me so far. Secondly, you would need both my father's and my sister's approval and she is off sailing, excuse me Eminence, God knows where. And lastly, but most importantly, my mother never really cared for religion, and I don't believe she would want to suffer this indignity for the bizarre reason that it, and again I quote, 'would serve the greater good of the Church'."

Seemingly unfazed by Peter's outburst, Cardinal Weiler smiled wearily. "Let me try and explain," he said.

CHAPTER 1

[Present Day]
Tucker's Town, Bermuda – Sunday, May 13, 2012

Anthony Fallon snatched up the telephone on its first ring. He hated that noise.

"Fallon."

"Fallon, it's Howard Alexander. I'm sure you've read that my daughter Sarah is missing and presumed drowned. With no evidence of any debris from her boat, the Rescue Centre crews have decided to end their search. They say they've gone as long as they can. I realize after all that's happened between us I have no right to call on you but, quite frankly, I don't know where else to turn for help. I'd like to continue the search."

"No need to explain. I'd be glad to assist."

"You would?" Howard struggled to keep his voice from breaking. "Thank you, Fallon. My son Peter can be at your home within the hour to give you the details, if that's okay? We all, and I know Kat would have wanted to be included in this, really appreciate your help."

#

Within a half-hour of receiving his father's call, Peter Alexander, twenty-seven years old and one of Bermuda's most eligible but unassuming bachelors, was on his way to Tucker's Town. As he drove along the narrow winding south coast road, his thoughts turned once again to Cardinal Weiler's visit the previous month.

Despite having experienced his fair share of unusual events, the proposal had shaken him to the core. Recovering from his initial shock, and notwithstanding his immediate and instinctive resistance, the cardinal's arguments had ultimately prevailed and, before long, both he and his father succumbed to the strange request.

Secure in the belief that Sarah would ultimately agree with their decision, his father had started the process to have Kat's body exhumed while Peter attempted to make contact with his sister by radiophone. They needed her to return and sign the necessary documents. How he now wished he hadn't reached her. If it hadn't been for his call, Sarah wouldn't have risked sailing a direct Atlantic course and he wouldn't be on his way to Fallon's house.

Anthony Fallon. Now's there's an enigma, Peter thought.

He often wondered what had transpired between his parents and the Fallons, but as neither of them would ever speak about it, the mystery remained. In fact, the only time he had raised the Fallons' names and received a satisfactory response was when he and Sarah suggested inviting them to their mother's funeral. They knew the four had once been good friends, and both he and Sarah had hoped that the Fallons would be of some comfort to Howard after their mother's death. Death, it seemed, always had a way of putting past sins into perspective. Although, in this instance, nothing seemed to have developed from that earlier initiative.

#

Freshly showered and barefoot, Fallon was dressed in his usual morning attire of a red T-shirt and calf-length white shorts. Coffee cup in hand, he stared through his living room window at the Atlantic Ocean beyond. It stretched, brilliant blue as far as the eye could see. Somewhere out there was Sarah Alexander and her boat. There really was no time to waste. The rescue crews had been searching for almost two weeks and found nothing to identify her last location.

Pushing aside the almost certain knowledge that no one could have survived for that long in these waters without some trace being found, he reached for his charts. He knew the area well and he was going to need every bit of that knowledge, and a great deal of luck, to succeed where the others had failed. Peter could give him the exact details of Sarah's route when he arrived, but in the meantime, he had best get ready. He scowled at the thought, and it was only then that his youthful face, below short-cropped dark hair, gave any indication that he had reached his sixties. Of slight build, he had remained lean and very fit; not that fitness was going to be the key issue in this exercise. This was all about knowledge of the sea and the prevailing currents. Even the best marine information did not adequately document the idiosyncrasies of the currents around the local reefs.

Turning from the window, Fallon walked over to a large corner table and stared at the pile of charts laying on its surface. Where should he start?

"At the bottom, dummy," Kat's voice echoed in his head. "It's always the last one we find, so start at the bottom."

How he missed her, he thought as he pulled out the bottom chart.

\#

Other than the occasional casual greeting in passing, Fallon had really only spoken to Katherine Alexander once after their falling out. It took place almost a year after the theft of the *San Pedro* cross. Walking into the reception area unannounced, Kat closed and locked the outer door behind her before striding into his office and dropping into a chair in front of his desk as she had done so many times before.

"Howard's off the island," she said, "and we need to talk."

Fallon sat dumbfounded. Inwardly he was delighted to see her but said nothing and remained outwardly calm as he waited for her to continue.

"I'm going to die, Fallon, and there are questions I need answered."

Fallon started to speak, but Kat cut him off.

"Wait, let me finish. It's terminal. The drugs will keep it at bay for a time, but eventually it will win. For now, if my luck holds, I'll be good for several years but at some point things will apparently deteriorate and, when that happens, it will be quick."

"How's Howard taking this? I assume he knows?"

"Not yet. I've only just heard the news. I'll tell him when he returns. It's not the sort of thing I want to do on the telephone."

"I'm sorry, Kat."

"Me too," she replied, before breaking into a familiar smile. "But that's not why I'm here. I need some answers, and I think you owe me that."

Fallon's mind raced. Finally, he could tell her of Howard's "arrangement" with him. Before he spoke though, he realized that in so doing he would once again jeopardize the remaining happiness of the only woman he had ever really loved.

"I believe I know the question," Fallon said at last. With that, he relayed the events leading up to the ultimate, and disproportionate, sharing of the proceeds from the sale of the *San Pedro* cross which had led to their falling out. Only in this version, after Howard approached him, politely of course, about moderating his relationship with Kat, he had decided on his own how to achieve the required result. "Howard," he said, "was completely unaware of my final plan."

"Moderate your relationship," Kat repeated. "You mean Howard knew we were sleeping together?"

"No, he knew we were close and may have suspected that we were, but he didn't want any details. He just wanted me to end my seemingly obvious attraction to you. I think it unsettled him."

"So who came up with the plan to screw me out of my fair share of the proceeds?"

"I did," Fallon lied. "I didn't know how else to cool our relationship. I thought it was a good idea at the time because you and Howard were financially secure, my business needed the money, and I hoped in time you would get over it. Sort of blew up in my face so to speak," he finished ruefully.

Kat stared at him for a long time before speaking.

"Thanks for telling me the truth. For some reason, I always thought Howard had a hand in it. It seemed too convoluted for you; no disrespect intended. I guess I'll live and learn. Oh, perhaps that should be die and learn."

"Don't say that," Fallon said, his voice harsher than he intended.

"It's okay, Fallon. You know me. If I don't joke about it, I'll break down. This is how I cope."

"I guess so. Can I say one more thing?"

"Sure, go ahead. It's time we cleared the air."

"Fine, but first I have a request. Can we agree to keep this conversation between the two of us? No reason to stir things up after all this time."

"Agreed. What was the other thing you wanted to say?"

Fallon paused, and then without moving from behind his desk looked directly at Kat. "I love you, you know. Always have, always will."

Kat stared back at him. After a few quiet moments, she spoke. "That's what made it so hard to accept. It just didn't make sense that you would behave that way. Even now it's hard to believe, but I know you wouldn't lie to me, not this time."

Fallon's hands, hidden below the top of his desk, clenched uncomfortably. He wanted to leap up, tell her the truth, and take her in his arms. Instead, he sat motionless. He was not going to hurt her again. Not now. Not ever again.

"You've no idea how hard it was to give up all that freedom and become the dutiful wife," Kat continued. "Talk about itches that needed scratching. The children made a huge difference but every now and again, I long for the freedom just to be myself. I guess it may actually be easier now with this fucking disease. For one, the medication will apparently slow me down."

Kat stood. "Well, I'm off. It was good to see you Fallon. I'd like a hug before I go though. I assume that's all right."

Fallon rose and moving around the desk gently took Kat in his arms. They stood, not speaking, holding each other tightly before kissing and finally moving apart.

"I'll let myself out," Kat said turning, but not before Fallon had seen the tears in her eyes. "Look after yourself Fallon."

#

Still standing with the chart in his hand, Fallon forced the images of his conversation with Kat from his mind. His thoughts drifted instead to the last time he had seen her. How he had stared into the coffin at her pale face, surrounded by its frame of dark hair, and realized yet again how beautiful she had been. Then, as he painfully tore himself away and turned to leave, there was the key. Around her neck was a simple gold chain to which was attached a small ornate gold and silver key. He had almost missed it in the folds of her clothes.

The sight had stopped him in his tracks. He stood frozen in front of the coffin, Maggi at his side. He couldn't take his eyes off the key and wondered whether Maggi had noticed it. Then, as they were ushered away and Howard and the children stepped forward, the coffin lid was slowly closed.

Maggi's voice broke into his thoughts.

"Fallon, I'm heading out to church. Any chance you'd like to come? What are you looking for this time?" Margaret Fallon walked into the room, the questions continuing to tumble out before he could answer the first.

"You mean this?" Fallon held out the rolled-up chart in his hand.

"Yes, I haven't seen you look at those in ages."

"Howard just called. He wants me to help search for his daughter."

"Howard Alexander? After all this time?"

"Yes. I said I would."

"I'm glad. It's about time you two settled things. What was it all about anyway?"

"I really can't recall," Fallon lied. "It was so long ago it's probably best forgotten. I think I'll pass on church though, if that's okay. His son will be here shortly with all the details and I need to get ready. I may be gone before you get back. If so, I'll call later."

"That's fine. Let me know what transpires when you can."

With a kiss on Fallon's cheek, Maggi left and Fallon, seemingly not distracted by his wife's pale good looks and striking red hair, returned to his charts.

Perhaps he should take Charlie and Ben, he thought. *Who knew if Peter Alexander was any good at sea, or if he even planned to come along for that matter?*

#

As Maggi drove away from the house she and Fallon shared, she recalled the last occasion she had seen Howard and his children. It had been several months earlier at Katherine Alexander's funeral. Despite her misgivings about Kat's relationship with Fallon, Maggi had not been able to avoid liking her and, if their brief elevator encounter many years earlier was any indication, the attraction might well have been mutual.

Kat's funeral was also the first and only time she had seen the key. She had noticed it immediately they reached Kat's coffin and knew, instinctively, it was the key Cardinal Kwodo had been after ever since they found the cross. She wondered at the time whether Fallon had also seen it, or if she should tell him. In the end, and despite hardly being able to contain herself, she had decided to wait and see what he said first. It had certainly been an unexpected turn of events.

They had driven back to the house from the funeral in total silence, each lost in their own thoughts. Finally, as they turned into the drive, Fallon had spoken. "I think I know where Cardinal Kwodo's key is," he said.

"Me too."

"Really?"

"Yes, I noticed a small key on the chain around Kat's neck," Maggi replied.

"Why didn't you say anything?"

"I'm not sure. Wrong place, wrong time, I imagine. I thought I would speak to you once we got home."

"Funny," Fallon answered, "I felt the same way. Do you really think it's the right key?"

"Absolutely. I'm not a big believer in coincidences and this would be far too much of a coincidence for it not to be the same key. How on earth do you think Kat found it, and why didn't she ever say anything?"

"That's what I don't get. I've been thinking about it all the way home and for the life of me I don't know when she could have discovered it without saying anything to any of us, and now she may have taken that secret to her grave. I have to assume Howard knows nothing about it otherwise why would they bury Kat wearing it?"

"Maybe they had no idea of its value? I know I haven't said anything to anyone about Cardinal Kwodo looking for the key. Have you?"

"No," Fallon replied. "I was hoping we would find it and then sell it to the Church. He said it was extremely valuable; remember? Worth as much, if not more, than the *San Pedro* cross."

"What do we do now?" Maggi asked. "We should probably let Cardinal Kwodo know what we suspect. I suppose there is the outside chance that it's the wrong key, although that seems very unlikely. It's too late to recover it now I guess. I'm sure he'll be very disappointed unless Howard can tell him where Kat's key came from, and that it wasn't from the *San Pedro*. I wonder just how valuable it really is."

"I'll e-mail the cardinal today," Fallon said. "Perhaps there's still some way for us to get a bit of a fee out of all of this. I'll try and word it accordingly."

CHAPTER 2

[Three months before the present day]
Boston, U.S.A. – Wednesday, February 22, 2012

There were times, Brother Peter Nuttall thought, *that he would never understand the Church.*

Father Jacob Despic had been old and in failing health. He expected only to be told to make the necessary arrangements for the burial and to await the arrival of a suitable replacement at a future date. Instead, the tone of the telephone conversation had rapidly changed and he was still not sure what had transpired. Things were moving along smoothly until he, almost in passing, had noted the apparently shocked expression on Father Despic's face.

"Describe to me again exactly how you found him," the cardinal's voice on the other end rasped. "Don't leave out a single detail."

As he once again described the scene he had found, Brother Peter felt somewhat uneasy about mentioning what the old priest had been looking at when he died. What if there was some secret association between this Mrs. Alexander and Father Jacob?

Better get it all out, he thought. *He would just say it was the Bermuda Obituaries without any further detail.*

Unless he was imagining things, the conversation became even more strained only this time it occurred when he mentioned Bermuda.

"Listen to me very carefully now," the cardinal said, "I want you to do exactly as I say. Have the body prepared for burial. Do not turn off the computer. Lock the room and do not touch or remove anything. Before you do though, make a careful note of the web address on the screen. Do not say anything to anyone about this and await my arrival instructions. We can discuss this further when I get there. Is that clearly understood?"

After confirming his understanding, Brother Peter hung up the phone.

Now that was a very strange call, he thought. *There was definitely a lot more here than met the eye.*

Father Despic's body had been taken to the funeral home a short while earlier so there was little else to be done on that front. He hoped no enterprising soul had decided to clean up the place in the interim. As he walked back to the room, he kept thinking about the magnifying glass in the old priest's hand. In all the excitement, he had forgotten to mention it.

Arriving at the room Brother Peter entered, closed the door and walked over to the desk. No screen saver on the computer he noticed, it was still on the same web page. He could merely print out the page and the address would be on the top.

Taking the mouse in hand, he selected "Quick Print" and waited. Moments later, the printed page ejected from the colour printer. Brother Peter picked up the magnifying glass and looked at the printed version of the two pictures he had seen on the screen.

Definitely a very attractive woman, he thought looking at the now enlarged image of Mrs. Katherine Alexander in her thirties. Different clothes and hairstyle, but wearing the same chain necklace in each picture. On the chain, a small gold key with a single bow and shank and one silver and one gold bit just after the collar, each coming off the pin at ninety degrees to the other. Almost like a combination of the two keys used in the papal coat of arms. Intriguing. It made an attractive necklace pendant and he wondered what it could possibly fit that she had worn it around her neck for all those years.

Vatican City – Wednesday, February 22, 2012

Cardinal Paul Cressey leaned back in his chair, the telephone still in his hand buzzing like some irritated insect as it tried unsuccessfully to alert him to the fact that his call was disconnected. Either he or Cardinal Kwodo would have to travel to Boston on the next available flight. They needed to examine what Jake Despic had been looking at when he died. This was not something to be delegated. He could only pray that Brother Peter would do precisely as instructed and that everything would be exactly as it had been when Jake died. He would never have expected to outlive his one-time protégé. His age was beginning to tell on him. Maybe he should leave it to Cardinal Kwodo; he was both younger and in better health.

Hanging up the telephone at last, the old cardinal slowly rose from his chair and went in search of his colleague.

\#

"I agree," Cardinal Bernard Kwodo said. "I can leave tomorrow. This is not something we should delay. I also suggest we say nothing to the Silenti until I return and we have had an opportunity to discuss this further. No reason to stir things up unnecessarily. For all we know there is nothing new to be found. I'll call you from Boston once I have looked further into this matter."

"Yes," I believe that would be best," Cardinal Cressey replied. "God be with you."

CHAPTER 3

[Two months before the present day]
Vatican City – Friday, March 30, 2012

No one it seemed was entirely sure who had called this unscheduled meeting of the Silenti. The five cardinals, the most trusted and senior advisors to the Pope, sat uneasily each waiting for the other to speak. They were all present and yet the great wooden door remained open as the hands on the clock face crept toward the appointed start time.

At precisely nine o'clock, the Pope entered and took his seat. The door of the meeting room was closed and the meeting came to order. The cardinals' surprise at the Pope's presence was evident on their faces. Not only was his attendance at a meeting of this august group a rare event, but it was also the Holy Father's first day back in the Vatican after a lengthy trip to South America.

Without preamble, the Pope swore the Silenti to secrecy before announcing his intention to resign effective February 28, 2013. Not because he was ill, he said, but at eighty-five, he was experiencing the fragility that comes with old age.

He advised the five stunned cardinals that he would make the announcement to the public on February 11, 2013. In the interim, they were instructed to maintain silence even from their colleagues in the College of Cardinals. With that, the Pontiff rose and departed the room leaving the Silenti to their own deliberations.

#

Cardinal Lucien Weiler was ambitious but this was almost unbelievable. The last pope he could recall having resigned was Pope Gregory XII in 1415. Nothing like this had happened in almost six hundred years!

Pope Benedict XVI had been seventy-eight years old at the time of his election and was already resigning due to his advancing age. The College of Cardinals was unlikely, once again, to choose a pope from among the more elderly in their ranks. Cardinal Cressey was over eighty and therefore ineligible to be a candidate, but the Pope's resignation due to age might also effectively rule out any opportunity for the more senior members of the Church like Cardinals Vilicenti and Kwodo.

Although one of the youngest, Cardinal Weiler realized that in these unusual circumstances, even he could be elected the next pope. He needed to elevate his reputation and increase his popularity. Recovery of the missing key from the *San Pedro* cross could make all the difference. As of now, only the Silenti and the Holy Father were even aware of its existence. He could already imagine the response from the College of Cardinals when they heard the news, particularly if it occurred as they waited to elect a new pope. They would be awed, as had he and his colleagues, by both the story and the recovery of such a sacred relic.

First, the unusual tale of the *San Pedro* cross and its missing hidden key. Then the fact that the key opened a secret compartment in the historic Chair of St. Peter allowing access to the very first papal ring. A ring belonging to none other than St. Peter himself. The person delivering the key, or perhaps even the ring, would undoubtedly be accorded the grateful thanks of the entire College; thanks which would more than likely translate into votes.

He must speak with Cardinals Kwodo, Vilicenti and Cressey in private. There were deals to be made. He had to get involved in finding the key, and in a hurry!

#

"I fear you need to travel yet again Bernard," Cardinal Cressey whispered to his colleague as they walked together down the long corridor leading from the meeting room. "We need to speak with the Alexanders. The key is far too valuable to lose. Its recovery is paramount, especially now."

"I will make the necessary arrangements," Cardinal Kwodo replied. "I had planned to head to Bermuda shortly anyway. With these developments, I believe sooner rather than later is the order of the day. Perhaps it is time to bring the Silenti into our confidence?"

Before Cardinal Cressey could answer, a voice rang out behind them. "Eminences...a moment, please."

Simultaneously stopping and turning, they were greeted by the sight of an obviously excited Cardinal Weiler hurrying to catch up with them.

"Eminences," he repeated, "I have just spoken with Cardinal Vilicenti regarding the outstanding matter of the missing key from the *San Pedro* cross. It has been a while since there has been any further information and I wondered if I might offer my help in updating matters for the Silenti. With this morning's news, I am sure you both have more important matters which require your attention and, I must add, it is a mystery which truly intrigues me."

The two clerics looked at each other without speaking and it was several moments before Cardinal Cressey replied.

"Thank you Lucien. Let me discuss your offer with Cardinal Kwodo and then we can get back to you. Perhaps you are right. Perhaps we need some younger legs at this time. No offence, Bernard," he added.

"None taken," Cardinal Kwodo replied. "You may be right. We shall discuss it and get back to you shortly Lucien," he said, and then smiled. "There is indeed a lot to be considered at this time."

#

Safely back in the confines of Cardinal Cressey's office the two elderly cardinals sat facing each other across a gleaming, polished heavy brown desk.

"So, what do you think?" Cardinal Cressey asked. "Divine intervention, blind luck or nefarious intent."

"If I had to choose," Cardinal Kwodo replied, "it would be either the first or the last. The timing is simply too precise to be luck."

"I must agree. As Cardinal Weiler seems to have surmised, the successful recovery of the key would undoubtedly enhance one's reputation. What about you, Bernard? You're eligible for election and, I imagine, a front-runner. The recovery of the key could make all the difference."

Cardinal Kwodo smiled serenely. "I prefer to leave that in God's hands," he said. "If he wishes me to fill that role he will provide. And with that in mind, I will go with my first choice for Cardinal Weiler's request; divine intervention."

"Well you are definitely a better man than I. For what it's worth, my opinion is that either Cardinal Vilicenti or Cardinal Weiler, or both for that matter, plan to try to use finding the key to their advantage at the upcoming election. Although to be fair, neither yet knows of the developments regarding Mrs. Alexander. What's more, I suppose there is always the remote possibility that this is not the key from the *San Pedro* cross and that matters could unfold to their disadvantage." Cardinal Cressey sat back and rested his hands on his ample stomach.

"So what do you think we should do?" Cardinal Kwodo asked.

"I will go with your preference, but we need to watch them carefully if you agree to include Cardinal Weiler in our confidence.

Before you decide though, let us recap for one last time the sequence of events that got us to this point. I'd like to be sure we haven't missed anything."

"Fine. To the best of my recollection, Brother Peter made the first call to you the day Father Despic died. As we agreed at the time, I travelled to Boston immediately we received the news. I was in Boston when the later e-mail about the key arrived from Mr. Fallon."

"That must have been something of a shock," Cardinal Cressey said.

"More than that," Cardinal Kwodo replied. "In truth, at the time I had not noticed anything amiss. Brother Peter had done as asked and kept both the room and the computer exactly as he had found them when Father Despic died. There was nothing remarkable about the scene. What was clear though was that Father Despic had been studying the obituary for Mrs. Alexander at the exact moment he died. What is even more interesting was that he apparently had found the need to examine something in the obituary notice with a magnifying glass. Quite frankly if it hadn't been for Mr. Fallon's e-mail I may have missed it entirely. His e-mail set me on the right track initially, and Brother Peter inadvertently completed the puzzle."

"Brother Peter?" Cardinal Cressey asked with a mystified expression on his face.

"Yes indeed, Brother Peter. Mr. Fallon indicated only that he believed he had discovered the location of the key but could not be sure of his ability to recover it. He wondered whether we had considered a finder's fee for such an eventuality where the possibility of its ultimate recovery would be left in our hands."

"So he didn't tell you where it was right away?"

"No, he did not. I was curious about the timing of his e-mail and indicated I would get back to him once I had consulted my colleagues about his proposal. It was around that time that Brother Peter mentioned he had printed out a copy of the computer screen Father Despic was looking at and that he had a magnifying glass in his hand at the time of his death."

THE BERMUDA KEY

"And why hadn't he told you about the magnifying glass earlier?" Cardinal Cressey asked.

"He had no idea it was relevant and thought only that Father Despic was perhaps looking at some detail he couldn't see clearly without magnification."

"Well, as far as that is concerned, he was absolutely correct."

"He was, but again, he had no reason to appreciate its relevance. As he told me, he only mentioned it because he had noticed a small key pendant around Mrs. Alexander's neck, which resembled the papal keys. From that, he thought she may have had some relationship with the Church."

"Unbelievable," Cardinal Cressey exclaimed. "And how did things go with Mr. Fallon after that?"

"Not well, I'm afraid. I realized at that point that the key might have been lost or misplaced after Mrs. Alexander death. This, of course, was why Mr. Fallon was seeking a finder's fee but could not facilitate its recovery. After several e-mail exchanges we finally reached the point where I was forced to concede that I knew Mrs. Alexander had it as I had seen her wearing it in her obituary notice photographs. It was only then he admitted that, to the best of his knowledge, it had been buried with her. He had, however, no way of being able to confirm whether or not it was actually the key from the *San Pedro* cross."

"Was it then that you enquired of Mr. Alexander as to the origin of the key in the photographs?"

"Correct. And while he had no idea where his wife may have acquired the key, he did confirm it had been buried along with her at her specific request."

"A great pity. Only one way to find out now."

"Yes, sadly, I believe that is the only choice we have. We must seek to have Mrs. Alexander's body exhumed."

"And it is for this task that you now suggest we enlist the aid of Cardinal Weiler?" Cardinal Cressey asked.

"Indeed it is," Cardinal Kwodo replied.

CHAPTER 4

Mangrove Bay, Bermuda – Sunday, May 13, 2012

Andrew Jensen sat on his veranda looking out over Mangrove Bay and the assortment of boats already anchored offshore in anticipation of the day's activities. As he sipped on his morning tea, he kept thinking back to the Alexanders. First Katherine's death, and now it seemed her daughter Sarah was missing and may have drowned.

He had known the family for many years and had really liked Katherine. On her first visit to his jewellery store with her parents, her nose barely reached to top of the glass counters but, even at that young age, the many and varied items on display had captivated her. In the intervening years she had become, and remained, a valued customer and friend right until the time of her death. In fact, it was only about a year ago that she had asked him to make a duplicate of her key pendant for her daughter's birthday. The same Sarah who was now missing off the Bermuda coast.

Strange, he thought, *he could have sworn Katherine said her daughter was in Africa at the time. Why would she be missing off the coast of Bermuda?*

CHAPTER 5

South Road, Bermuda – Sunday, May 13, 2012

Maggi smiled as she pressed the speed dial on her mobile phone. "Hands free" was all the rage and she was right up to date. Bless Fallon's heart. He really could be a pain at times, but on this, he had been adamant.

"You're going to get killed talking on that phone while driving," he said. "I'll get it all installed. You don't have to do a thing. We can switch cars for the day. With all the rotten drivers out there, the least we can do is try and keep you alert."

Try as she might to convince him that she was so seldom on her phone while driving that it wasn't necessary, he could not be swayed. Now, she had to give him his due. She did use it and she did feel safer.

"Hello?"

"Hi, Rhiannon, it's Maggi. I'm heading out to church and then I'm probably free for the rest of the day and evening. Fallon is getting involved in the search for Howard Alexander's missing daughter. Are you doing anything later?"

As she listened to Rhiannon's reply, Maggi thought back to how this all started several years earlier. Rhiannon had come to see her about the investigation into the disappearance of the *San Pedro* cross. Unlike previous meetings, this time the two women were alone and somewhere along the way their mutual attraction had surfaced.

It had taken many months of meeting for the occasional lunch or drink before Rhiannon fully accepted that Maggi and Fallon had no intimate relationship and that their marriage was indeed a carefully disguised sham. In fact, the more Maggi discussed it with Rhiannon, the more certain she became that Fallon was not even aware of her sexual preference.

"What was that?" Maggi asked. "Sorry I got distracted. Okay then, I'll see you around three."

\#

Hamilton, Bermuda – Sunday, May 13, 2012

Assistant Inspector Rhiannon Thomas hung up the phone and looked out at the harbour. It was another idyllic day on the island. She should clean up before Maggi arrived. The place was a mess. Maybe they could head straight out to the restaurant. As she had told Maggi, she was famished after her workout and looking forward to an early dinner at one of the restaurants along Front Street.

Fallon joining the search for Sarah Alexander was news to her. He couldn't be joining the official search party; she would have heard about that. Perhaps Sarah's family were organizing their own search.

Hearing about Fallon and the Alexanders working together brought back memories of the investigation into the theft of the *San Pedro* cross from the Bermuda Maritime Museum. Her failure to find the thief, or thieves, still irked. She wondered if the illustrious Dr. J. Bruce Gordon, the insurance investigator and her associate in the investigation, felt the same way.

His last report had been brief. He had learned nothing more from Father Despic, the priest who visited Bermuda to confirm the identity of the cross after its discovery, and his enquiries of Monsignor Alonso, the Vatican archivist with whom Maggi had been in contact, had borne no fruit. Only one frustrating lead remained. He had heard that a certain goldsmith, Signor Ugo Panzini, often did work for the Vatican, but his investigation had come up short when Signor Panzini was tragically killed in a truck accident before he had time to visit him. His interview with a distraught Signora Panzini regarding her husband's work, had failed to reveal anything. Before leaving though, Dr. Gordon had apparently given Signora Panzini's son, an apprentice in his father's business, a photograph of the *San Pedro* cross. The son had promised to let him know if anything regarding such a cross ever surfaced in his father's working papers. Rhiannon had heard from Dr. Gordon once more before he retired but, at the time, he had still not heard from the Panzinis. Perhaps she should give him a call.

"Enough," she said aloud looking at herself in the living room mirror, "just time for a shower and then I'm going to clean this place up before Maggi arrives." Having given her reflection these instructions, Rhiannon strode down the hall to the bathroom, stripping off her clothes and dropping them along the corridor as she went. Entering the bathroom, she looked at her full-length naked reflection in the bathroom mirror.

Not bad, she thought, *the workouts were paying dividends.*

CHAPTER 6

[The month before the present day]
Heathrow, U.K. – Sunday, April 22, 2012

Bruce Gordon stepped from the sanctity of his British Airways business class cabin into the bustle of Terminal 5 at Heathrow Airport. His well-earned holiday had ended and here he was once again back in the throng of one of the world's busiest airports. Tuning out the noise of the jostling crowds, he headed straight for the Paddington Express, which, if the advertisements were to be believed, would take him into the heart of London within fifteen minutes. Purchasing his ticket en route to the train, he boarded quickly and settled back in the relative quiet of one of several coaches prohibiting the use of mobile phones.

Idly watching the advertisements displayed on the internal television system, his eye was drawn to a perfectly coiffured model with a jeweled gold cross around her slender neck. As he stared at the advertisement, he realized that it had been seventeen years since he was first contacted about the theft of the *San Pedro* cross. To make matters worse, no sign of it had surfaced in all that time and all his leads seemed to have dried up.

Shortly before his retirement, he had contacted Sergeant Thomas in Bermuda only to find that she, like him, had heard nothing further.

THE BERMUDA KEY

Nonetheless, she was able to report that despite the lack of success in this particular case she was now Assistant Inspector Thomas. Her career it seemed had not suffered along with the investigation. She also advised him that the Fallons were still active on the island and that, other than the recent death of Katherine Alexander, nothing was different on the local front.

Several hours later, arriving at his home in the Cotswold's, Bruce Gordon used his foot to sweep aside the unanswered mail lying inside his front door as he struggled in with his luggage. On the top of the pile, and easily legible, was a distinctive post office notification. It appeared that a package was available for pick-up at his local post office outlet on production of suitable identification at that time. There was only one package. It was from Italy and the sender was identified by a single name printed in block capitals - PANZINI.

His luggage forgotten, Bruce Gordon hurried into his study and poured himself a glass of his favourite single malt scotch. Could this be the long awaited lead, and after all these years? To hell with retirement, he thrived on this stuff. Why did these things always come at the end of the day? The post office didn't open until nine o'clock tomorrow and he could barely wait.

CHAPTER 7

[The month before the present day]
Atlantic Ocean, 32° 26' 25.03" North;
64° 50' 00.41" West – Monday, April 30, 2012

Still struggling with the grief of her mother's recent death, Sarah Alexander was sailing a circuitous course to Bermuda on *Silk II*, when she received her brother's strange and brief radiophone call asking that she agree to the exhumation of their mother's remains.

With her urgent need for more information overcoming any natural caution, she immediately changed direction and selected the shortest route to her destination; sailing directly into a severe and unexpected Atlantic storm. Confident in her abilities and preparations to handle the weather she was, nonetheless, unprepared for the catastrophic results of a collision with an enormous metal shipping container, unmarked and adrift in the ocean.

Severely injured, Sarah soon recognized that the combination of damage to the boat and her injuries offered no chance of survival. It was either hypothermia or sharks. One or the other would get her, and she didn't like the thought of either. With desperation overriding her pain, she cut her spare anchor line a few feet from the end and tied it around her waist. She knew her body would rot with time but she had to try to preserve her identity. Her family would want to know what had happened and there was no way of telling how long it would be before she was found, if ever.

Removing a gold chain from around her neck, Sarah tied the chain around the anchor ring and her wrist, her hands moving of their own accord as if guided by some strange intuition. That final act complete, she curled fetal-like around the anchor and began to pray.

#

For hours, the raging wind and sea swept the remnants of *Silk II's* hull before it, Sarah's small broken form lying lifeless and unaware on the deck. Then, in one final furious surge, the sea hurled the hull against a huge protruding rock spilling the last of its contents into the ocean below. Torn at last from the deck, Sarah's body tumbled into the water, pulled ever-downward toward the jagged reef by the weight of the anchor to which she was attached.

By the time the sea claimed Sarah, her previously tanned face was already purple and waxy and her lips, fingers and toes were white with loss of blood. Dark purple-black stains were evident on her side and hip as the blood pooled at the lowest parts of her body. Her hands and feet were blue and her eyes had sunk into her skull. And, as rigor mortis set in, she stiffened into her fetal position; the anchor clasped firmly to her chest.

Within twenty-four hours, Sarah's remains were at the temperature of the surrounding water, her face no longer recognizable. Her head and neck had turned a greenish-blue colour, which gradually spread to the rest of her body. The strong smell of rotting flesh emanating from her corpse was undetectable underwater to all but the nearby foraging marine life.

Several days later, still held underwater by the weight of the anchor, Sarah's entire body was bloated and swollen. Blisters covered her skin and crab and lobster fed on what remained of her flesh. Rigor mortis having now fully dissipated, she drifted loosely on the surface of the sharp coral that continued to tear at her clothing and rip her apart whenever it touched.

    Ten days later, any skin, hair and nails still attached to Sarah's few remaining bones were loose and easily removed by scavenging fish. What little was left of her body lay undisturbed by the wash of the boat passing above or the soft thud of its anchor as it settled into the sand only a few hundred feet away.

CHAPTER 8

Hamilton, Bermuda – Sunday, May 13, 2012

Peter Alexander stood on the dock alongside Fallon's boat totally engrossed in the text displayed on the screen of his mobile phone. Thank God, the thing was actually working. Bermuda's high humidity had been playing havoc with his reception. Probably time for another he imagined. It would be his third mobile in as many years, all failing for the same reason. The message was from Sean Patterson, Sarah's fiancé. He planned to leave Canada in a few days and hoped to arrive in time to join them in the search.

Peter decided to speak to Fallon about that later. For now, he needed to focus on the task at hand. The initial meeting with Fallon had gone well. Any concerns he may have had about his parents relationship with the Fallons had been dispelled within minutes of arriving at their home. Fallon was genuinely welcoming and all business when Peter arrived. Within an hour, he was back on the road with instructions to collect his gear, and the few additional supplies requested, and meet Fallon at the dockside at two o'clock sharp.

Well, he was five minutes early and there was no sign of Fallon yet. The boat's cabin door was open but no sound came from inside. Deciding to start loading up, Peter took one last look along the dock for Fallon, then threw one of his bags aboard. Turning to pick up another, he was about to heave it onto the boat when he looked again at the cabin door. Sitting unmoving, staring mournfully at him with a pair of dark brown eyes, was an all-white boxer. Peter stopped mid-throw.

"Hi boy," he croaked.

Not a flicker of change in the dog's expression signaled it had heard, or intended to respond to, his greeting. He tried again. Firmer this time.

"Hi boy."

"Hi yourself," came an unusually accented female voice from inside the cabin. "What time is it?"

"It's two o'clock. Sorry if I disturbed you, I thought this was Anthony Fallon's boat. I'm Peter Alexander. I was due to meet him here at two with a couple of other fellows. I must have the wrong boat. I thought his was named *Maverick*."

"No mistake. You got it right. This is his boat. Who were these other two?"

"I don't know them," Peter replied, finding it somewhat disconcerting to be talking to some unseen person inside the cabin. "Their names are Charlie and Ben."

"Oh, those two," the voice replied through her laughter. "Hang on a moment and I'll be right out. I'll just finish up in here. You might as well get your stuff on board in the meantime."

"What about the dog?"

"Don't mind him. He won't move unless you try to come inside. He'll watch you carefully though, so don't be nervous."

"He's doing that already," Peter replied, carefully watching the dog whose expression hadn't changed at all throughout the whole exchange, his eyes never leaving Peter for a second.

He had just finished loading the last of his things on board when Fallon strolled leisurely down the dock.

"Ah, right on time I see," he said. "Good start, let's get out of here. I'm all set and Charlie offered to get the boat ready earlier, so we're probably good to go."

"Those two don't seem to be here," Peter said, "and there's someone else on board at the moment."

"Which two?"

"Charlie and Ben, I think you said.

"Oh them," Fallon replied smiling. "Don't worry, they'll turn up."

As Peter and Fallon stepped aboard the dog exploded into life. Its stump-tail wagging so furiously that its whole rear-end shook uncontrollably from side to side while it leapt into the air, bouncing and turning with every jump; its feet scrabbling for traction as it landed.

"Damn, that thing is spring loaded," Peter exclaimed as Fallon crouched on the deck to be bumped and nuzzled by the dog. "Good thing you have outdoor carpeting."

"I don't normally," Fallon replied, "it's only when the dog's aboard. There should be another piece on the forward deck as well. It comes in handy when we're out at sea and can wash it off. You'll see why in due course."

Finally finished with Fallon, the dog moved over to Peter and stood alongside him its weight leaning into his leg.

"Can I move?" Peter asked warily.

"Sure. Now that he knows you're one of us."

"What's with the leaning?"

"He has no left hip ball and socket."

"Really!"

"Yup, it's a long story. Charlie will tell you later if you ask."

"Okay, and who's the woman inside."

"Oh right, you haven't met."

"I'm Maggi's niece, Charlotte Leigh," said a petite dark-haired woman emerging from the cabin, "otherwise known as Charlie. You must be Peter. I see you've already met Ben," she said looking down."

Peter dropped his eyes to where Charlie was looking, the boxer still leaning comfortably against his leg, unmoving. He was glad of the opportunity to look away. He was sure he was blushing. He had heard all the nonsense over the years about love at first sight but had never experienced anything quite like the feeling that engulfed him at that moment. He was, to put it quite simply, smitten. He couldn't speak or even think straight. Mumbling something unintelligible he managed to hold out his hand in response to the one she had offered in greeting. As their hands touched and he looked directly into the greenest eyes he had ever seen, he was hard pressed not to snatch his back at the shock of their contact.

This is ridiculous, he thought. *I'm not some pimple-faced teenager.*

After what seemed an interminable time, Peter finally composed himself and managed to look directly at Charlie, "I think I'll try moving now," he said.

Both Charlie and Fallon laughed at this remark before Charlie said, "Come on, Ben. Move. Leave the nice man alone."

At this last instruction, the boxer moved away from Peter and, after turning in several circles, lay down on a thick brown corduroy pillow carefully placed off to one side of the deck and out of harm's way.

"Okay, now that Ben's ready, let's get underway shall we," Fallon said shaking his head. "You might as well get used to Ben, Peter, he and Charlie are inseparable."

Peter, thankful for the interruption and the further opportunity to compose himself, hurried to comply.

Charlie, with movements that exposed some form of dance background, gracefully curled herself into the forward passenger seat. "Over to you two," she said, "I've done my bit for the moment. Boat's ready to go."

CHAPTER 9

Hamilton, Bermuda – Sunday, May 13, 2012

Although Sarah was still missing, Howard felt an enormous sense of relief. Despite their history, his faith in Fallon's maritime expertise and knowledge of the Bermuda coastline was undiminished. Like him or not, the man was a local legend.

He didn't really know why he had waited so long to ask for Fallon's help. Ego? Faith in the authorities? All he knew now was that he felt better having asked. It helped too that Fallon hadn't hesitated to assist. Not a single question about why now. Just, "I'd be glad to help". Typical of the man. Perhaps it was time to make peace.

Looking around his desk, Howard's eyes fixed on a pile of documents in the far left corner. Reluctantly he reached out and pulled them towards the leather desk pad on which he worked. It was time to finish the submission and set a date for Kat's exhumation. With only himself and Peter now involved, the application would move ahead quickly. He hated what they were doing to Kat and promised himself that neither he nor his son would look at her remains. They would leave that to the undertakers. He was determined that both he and Peter would remember Kat as they had last seen her.

What an exercise this exhumation process had been, he was glad he had done it himself. Peter had sailed through his undergraduate degree and law school before joining the firm, yet Howard was never quite sure how much he enjoyed the practice of law; let alone dealing with something so personal. Although Peter had, as expected, followed his example, there was another Peter somewhere inside the young lawyer. Something raw and unpolished but tightly controlled.

Must be a Kat streak, Howard thought.

He looked down at the short list of documents he still needed to submit, his earlier notes in parentheses alongside each heading.

> a) Licence to exhume human remains: *(Correctly signed by Peter and myself as Kat's next of kin. Exemption for Sarah.).*
>
> b) Consent of the grave owner: *(Cemetery owners surprised but very accommodating with the request. First time they had been asked for such a thing!).*
>
> c) Completed form from the burial authority: *(Nothing else needed.).*

The standard processing time was apparently twenty days, however, after a few well-placed calls, the government authorities had agreed to fast-track the request within a few days of receipt.

Howard sighed and looked at the list again. It was all there. Not even a government fee. That was a first. He could only assume it was because the event was so rare, and so traumatic, that even governments shied away from inflicting further pain or indignity on the participants, willing and unwilling alike. No reason to delay now. It was time to get this done. He would also alert the Vatican once he had a definitive date for the exhumation. He needed Peter to return for that and wondered how long Fallon planned for them to stay at sea this first time out.

#

Howard stood on the Church Street sidewalk outside the government offices, the approval for Kat's exhumation firmly clasped in his hand. He knew this was an unusual event in Bermuda, but somebody, somewhere, had briefed the staff on what to expect and how his application was to be handled. Even priority applications normally went through a pedantic process barely faster than a non-priority event. This time things had been different. Almost as if the documents themselves were too hot to handle.

He had submitted the completed paperwork and then been asked to have a seat and wait. His attempt to leave, with the intention of returning when the processing was complete, had failed when he was once again asked to wait while the documentation was checked. With that the clerk had disappeared into a back office. Barely fifteen minutes later, she had returned and handed him the requisite approval for exhumation duly stamped and signed. Reluctantly he had taken the papers, muttered his thanks and left. As he exited the building he looked over at the Anglican Cathedral looming alongside and wondered what they would think about all this.

Despite the compelling and persuasive arguments from Cardinal Weiler, he still found the idea of exhuming Kat's remains deeply disturbing and wondered again why she had never mentioned the key. Perhaps she had found it during a dive and not thought it had any significance. Perhaps she just saw it as a beautiful old artifact. Had she mentioned it to Fallon? Surely he would have known Kat had found it. It was a pity he and Fallon were not on better terms when he was first approached by the Vatican; he would certainly have appreciated Fallon's usual forthright opinion. Well, he wasn't going to raise it now. This was between him, Peter and the Vatican, and he intended to keep it that way.

Even the island's usual rumour mill appeared to be silent on the impending exhumation, although Howard found the idea that nobody was talking hard to believe. Bermuda's cloak of confidentiality had more holes in it than Swiss cheese. Perhaps anyone who heard anything was just making sure not to mention it to him. The only other reason he could think of was that it was not a topic anyone in this God fearing paradise wanted to have anything to do with, irrespective of the circumstances.

#

Back in his office, Howard looked down at the certificate in his hand. It was time to make the calls. First the cemetery owners, then Peter, then Cardinal Weiler. The Vatican would have to hurry if they wanted to be here for the exhumation. Despite their insistence on being present he wasn't going to wait very long for them to arrive. Having come this far he wanted it over as quickly as possible.

CHAPTER 10

Coast of Bermuda - Monday, May 14, 2012

Two weeks had passed since the sailboat, *Silk II*, sank. Thirty feet below the surface of the ocean, Sarah Alexander was no longer recognizable. The continued abrasion of the reef and the frenzied feeding of marine life had exacerbated her body's natural decomposition until only her jawbone, teeth, and several small bones remained relatively intact. The former two due to their composition, the latter attached limply to an anchor ring, held in place by Sarah's tightly wound necklace chain, a small gold and silver key dangling from its end.

CHAPTER 11

[The month before the present day]
Broadway, U.K. – Monday, April 23, 2012

Bruce Gordon was disappointed. Arriving at his local post office promptly at nine o'clock, he found he was already third in line. Even a trip to deal with their mail was a major event for the elderly residents of this quaint English village. He had experienced similar queues when having his routine blood tests. The medical office, which opened early to accommodate anyone who had to get to work at normal business hours, was full of pensioners. They, it appeared, had commenced lining up at dawn for this major event in their obviously otherwise dull lives.

After what seemed to be a lengthy wait, it was finally his turn. His hand shook with anticipation as he handed over the required requisition along with his driver's license that he assumed would be sufficient evidence of the legitimacy of his claim.

"Good morning Dr. Gordon," the woman behind the counter said, peering intently at the name on his licence as she spoke. "One moment please."

With that, Pat, which according to the tag on her blouse was her name, turned and commenced rummaging through an orderly row of letters in a box positioned on a table immediately behind her.

THE BERMUDA KEY

"I believe it's a parcel."

"Oh, no, it's a letter. You can tell from this code," she replied without turning.

"But the parcel box is ticked."

"It may well be," she replied sternly turning to look directly at him, "but I have been doing this for twenty-three years and this code means letter."

Suitably chastised and somewhat disappointed, Bruce Gordon waited impatiently.

Finally, with a triumphant smile implying "I told you so", Pat placed a large brown envelope on the counter.

"Here's your letter," she said enunciating the last word with considerable care. "Next please." As she spoke the last two words, Pat stared over his shoulder at the next person in line, and he was dismissed.

Taking the envelope, Bruce Gordon hurried from the post office and commenced the short walk back to his home. It wasn't very thick; it felt like only a few pages at most. Finally, unable to control his anticipation, he wiggled one chubby finger into a corner opening and tried to slide it like a letter opener along the flap. Whether it was the weakness of the paper or the thickness of his finger he would never know, but the envelope tore open across its middle spilling its contents onto the ground. As the pages fluttered around in the light morning breeze, Bruce Gordon scrabbled around on his hands and knees trying to collect them.

"Here let me help."

Before he could gather the last remaining sheet, a black clothed arm swooped down, plucked it from the pavement, and then held it out to him to retrieve.

"Thank you," Bruce Gordon puffed. "Much appreciated."

"My pleasure," the priest replied. "Seems appropriate," he added with a smile as he looked down at the sheet in his hand. "Have a pleasant morning."

Puzzled, Bruce Gordon stared at the departing back before looking down at the sheet of paper handed to him by the priest.

It's the cross, he thought. *It's a scale drawing of the bloody San Pedro cross.*

#

Back in the sanctity of his home, Bruce Gordon laid the contents of the envelope on his desk. There were five pages in all. Three were scale drawings of a cross with detailed Italian notations alongside, the fourth a shaded drawing of the same cross without any notations but a set of numbers inscribed in the bottom right corner, and lastly a note in poorly crafted English.

Signor Gordon, he read. *Forgive the writing but I have done the best I could. We have cleaned the shop and find nothing from my father but some papers from my grandfather. Maybe they are interesting to you, no? There is none else. I do not keep any copy so you can make with these what you wish. I hope you are well.* The note was signed *Raffaele Panzini.*

Bingo! Could this be the break at last? He needed to review these in detail. He needed an Italian translation. There were numbers there as well. Maybe only measurements? He couldn't be sure. Moreover, what was this shaded version? He needed some help.

#

Oxford, U.K. – Monday, April 23, 2012

"I appreciate your seeing me at short notice Stuart."

"Not a problem," Professor Stuart Shandro, of the Faculty of Medieval and Modern Languages at Oxford University, replied. "Always glad to see you. You should have stayed in academia you know. It's a good life and well suited to your temperament. All the same, you probably earn more than we do so perhaps you made the right choice when we graduated."

THE BERMUDA KEY

"Who knows," Bruce Gordon said. "At least we both seem to have enjoyed our respective careers, which is more than I can say for a number of our classmates."

"True. Anyway, I know you're in a hurry so down to business. What have we here?"

"I received these drawings today related to a case I was working on before I retired. They probably don't tell us much, but they've piqued my interest. One small problem, the notes are in Italian, which of course is where you come in. You're the best person I know to make sure any translation I get is accurate."

"Are you still working on the case?"

"Not really, I'm supposed to be retired, but as they were sent directly to me from an old lead I thought I'd follow through. If there's anything interesting in it, I'll let my former employer know. After all, they do still pay my pension. It's worth a shot anyway."

"Okay, let's see what we have then."

Bruce Gordon watched closely as his friend shook the contents from the torn, and now taped, envelope, the note from Raffaele Panzini resting securely in the inside pocket of his jacket. Without speaking, Professor Shandro studied each of the drawings in turn.

"Well nothing really remarkable here," he said at last, "just detailed measurements of a cross and specific materials for the metals and stones."

"You mean gold and emeralds, right?"

"No. There is no mention of either gold or emeralds. Well, that's not quite correct. It does mention gold plating, but not solid gold, and there's certainly no mention of emeralds. What it does refer to, and which you may have thought was emerald, is antique cut green glass."

"Really? Cut green glass?"

"I'm afraid so, old boy. No emeralds here to make you rich."

"Well, that's too bad," Bruce Gordon said his heart racing. He was sure he was onto something. "Any chance you could give me a full translation over the next short while so that I can report back and close this file?"

While Bruce Gordon felt badly about deceiving his old friend, he consoled himself with the thought that until he knew where this was going the fewer people that knew about it the better. Besides, he was doing no harm.

"Absolutely. I'll have one of my students run it off as an exercise and then return it to you once I've had a chance to review what they've done."

"Perfect. Would you be able to work from a photocopy? I'd like to take the originals back to Broadway with me, and that way it would save me coming back out. We can always complete this by phone and fax or scanned copy."

"That's certainly not a problem. Let me make a copy of this set and I'll take it from there."

#

Broadway, U.K. – Monday, April 30, 2012

A full week had passed before Bruce Gordon received the translation. The final product though, was far better than he could have hoped. The student assigned the task was obviously a high achiever. He, or she, had removed the panels in Italian and attached an English translation making each document a full English version of the original.

As he went over each detail in the drawings, Bruce Gordon soon realized that what he held in his hands were the blueprints for an exact replica of the *San Pedro* cross. But for whom had it been made, and why? If he could match these drawings to the results of a detailed appraisal of the fake cross in the Bermuda Maritime Museum, he may be able to use them to track down the goldsmith who made the fake. If he could do that, he would be a long way to catching the thief, or thieves. His excitement was palpable.

#

THE BERMUDA KEY

Despite his retirement, the name Bruce Gordon still carried sufficient goodwill within the fraud investigation department of his old firm, Anstey's Insurance, to bypass any red tape. After several days, a full copy of the appraisal of the fake *San Pedro* cross was on its way to his home by prepaid courier.

His initial impulse had been to ask for a copy directly from the Bermuda Maritime Museum before realizing that the request would bring unwanted attention to what was fast becoming his own private investigation. The successful conclusion of which could perhaps even prove to be the start of a very lucrative "JBG Retirement Fund".

By the time he had finished his comparison of the appraisal report and the drawings, Bruce Gordon was convinced. These were the scale drawings for the fake *San Pedro* cross. Everything matched. It had taken him longer than he expected, and he still planned to check his findings with Andrew Jensen, the Bermuda goldsmith who had done the original appraisal, but there was no doubt in his mind as to what he had uncovered. He had only three unanswered questions regarding the drawings. Who had asked grandfather Panzini to make them? What was the significance of the shaded cross drawing? And lastly, what were the numbers without any reference on that page? He would also make one last call to Raffaele Panzini to double check that he did not know anything further.

He was exhausted. Tomorrow was soon enough. Besides, it was Sunday evening. It would be far better to start things early on Monday morning. He glanced at a nearby calendar. Almost mid-May, nearly three weeks had passed since he had received the letter.

CHAPTER 12

Hamilton, Bermuda – Monday, May 14, 2012

Andrew Jensen arrived at his store at precisely ten a.m., exactly as he had done every weekday for most of his adult life. His wife, before her passing, had often remarked that she could set her clock by his schedule. Although now alone, he hadn't bothered to alter his habits. They had stood him in good stead for all these years so why change now. Besides, his disciplined approach had helped make him one of the finest and most sought after goldsmiths in Bermuda. He was proud of that fact and determined to maintain his reputation for as long as he could still work. He had barely finished putting out the window displays that had been carefully locked in the safe overnight, when the telephone rang.

#

The elderly goldsmith had never met Bruce Gordon in person, but his orderly mind responded immediately to the concise manner in which Dr. Gordon presented the recap of events to him in their brief telephone conversation. He had no computer in the store on which he could receive scanned copies of the offered drawings, but was able to provide his personal e-mail address and agreed to download the material that evening.

THE BERMUDA KEY

Dr. Gordon had requested his confidentiality and Andrew was happy to oblige. He recalled that Dr. Gordon had worked with Sgt. Thomas at the time of the theft, a point that Bruce Gordon happily confirmed. He had also advised that he would keep the Bermuda police informed as necessary, so Andrew need not worry on that front. As Andrew still had his copy of the appraisal of the fake cross, he needed nothing else to make a comparison with the drawings, which he agreed to do with all haste.

A faint ring of the front door bell signalled the arrival of Andrew's first customer of the day. It was time for business. He would deal with Dr. Gordon's request later.

CHAPTER 13

Coast of Bermuda – Thursday, May 17, 2012

Peter watched with amusement as Ben walked cautiously along the wooden deck to the small section of dull, green, outdoor carpeting at the bow; its colour faded from frequent washing and the ever-present sunshine. On arrival, his pace quickened as he hurriedly circled before selecting the appropriate spot on which to pee. Balanced precariously on three legs on the gently rolling boat he stared into the distance while completing his morning ablutions. That done he returned to the cabin where he promptly leapt onto the bunk and stood over Charlie looking down at the back of her dark head, her face buried firmly in the pillow.

"Ben. Off." The muffled command did little to curb the dog's enthusiasm and served only to increase the wagging rate of his stump tail, while his upturned nose continued to nuzzle firmly against the back of her head.

"Okay, that's enough," Charlie said, pushing Ben's face aside as she tried to get out of the bunk and out from under the dog at the same time.

Finally, with a last shove of encouragement Ben jumped off the bunk, followed moments later by a rumpled figure in twisted sweat pants and T-shirt.

"I know, I know," Charlie said. "It's time for breakfast."

THE BERMUDA KEY

With the single mention of the word breakfast, the dog immediately stopped harassing Charlie and assumed an immobile sitting position facing the galley.

"Good morning," Peter said, cup in hand, looking into the cabin from the outside deck. "There's coffee already made if you'd like some. Hope I didn't disturb you?"

"Hi. Not a chance, Preppy. I was dead to the world until 'you know who' decided it was time for breakfast. Have you been up long?"

"About twenty minutes," Peter replied smiling at his recently acquired nickname. Apparently, his attire and mannerisms had reminded Charlie of some old classic movie and, after announcing that the combination of the use of his full name and the way in which he was dressed "just wouldn't do old boy", Preppy he had become.

Secretly he was pleased. Although his initial discomfort had reduced, he still wasn't quite used to the effect Charlie had on him and any indication that she might actually like him was certainly welcome. Besides, Fallon had assured him that South Africans only tease you if they like you. He would hang onto that thought for now.

Charlie's irreverent sense of humour had also proved to be a welcome relief from their current task. As if searching for his sister wasn't bad enough, the thought that they were probably really searching for her remains was too hard for him to contemplate. They had been inseparable growing up and despite periodic absences from each other remained in constant contact through the usual slate of electronic communication options.

Right up to that last damned call, he thought.

"Morning," Fallon's voice came from the entrance to the aft berth. "Hard to get any sleep in here with you two babbling away. I knew I should have come alone."

"We were just thinking the same thing," Charlie answered completely unperturbed at Fallon's gruff manner. "You're such a grouch Fallon. Have some coffee and behave."

Peter waited for some response as Fallon stared long and hard at the diminutive figure looking back at him with an exaggerated scowl on her face.

Then, without even a murmur of dissent, Fallon moved into the galley to do as instructed.

Peter, staring at Fallon's back, shook his head in amazement. "What's on the agenda for today?" he asked.

#

It had become readily apparent on their first day out, that any time spent with Fallon would be carefully planned. After anchoring at the same location where Fallon said he and Kat had discovered the cross, they had spread out their own charts and listened carefully as Peter outlined the search information he had gathered. The Bermuda Rescue Co-ordination Centre, or BRCC as it was known locally, had been more than willing to share all they had done since receiving the emergency signal. As they told Peter at the time, there should be no secrets in search and rescue operations.

"On Monday, April 30 at twelve fifty-five," Peter said repeating what he had been told, "the BRCC reported a brief 406 MHz EPIRB signal. They quickly identified it as a local sailboat, *Silk II*, registered to a Sarah Alexander. Attempts to contact her were unsuccessful and, as one of the two emergency contacts listed on her registration, they called me minutes later. After I confirmed she was at sea, rescue operations were instituted immediately based on the location of the original signal."

"I assume that's when the problem's started," Fallon observed.

"Yes. How did you know?"

"Well, there's only one boat based here that's capable of operating offshore for any length of time and that's the *Guardian*. It has twin marine diesels and can cruise at twenty knots for about four-hundred nautical miles. It's also outfitted with the best communication and navigation equipment available."

"Why would that be a problem?" Charlie asked.

"She was on the hard right alongside *Maverick* that day," Fallon said. "Both boats were having their hulls cleaned at the same time. That's why I remember the date."

"That's right," Peter said. "They shut down the cleaning and launched the boat in very short order, but still, quite a bit of time was lost before she was operational."

"Why didn't they use one of the smaller boats?" Charlie asked. "I've seen two of those other rigid hull inflatables around quite often. They're black and grey if I remember correctly."

"Pretty observant for an anthropologist," Fallon replied. "And here I was thinking you only noticed historical stuff. Anyway, you're right, except the RIBs are used mostly for close offshore work. They can't stay out too long as there are no facilities on board."

"They did go out though," Peter interrupted. "They responded immediately and maintained position close to the estimated signal location, and well into a severe offshore storm, until the bigger vessel arrived to maintain ongoing search activities; at which time they stood down."

"I assume they hadn't found anything at that point," Fallon said.

"Nothing," Peter confirmed. "They had hoped to at least have recovered the EPIRB but no such luck. Apparently, visibility was almost non-existent and it had only given one brief signal and then nothing."

"How do they track that thing anyway?" Charlie asked. "My sea-going education fell somewhat short until I met Fallon."

"Really?" Peter said. "You look quite at home out here."

"I am, but most of that is due to Fallon's endless patience, and don't tell him I said that," she continued in an elaborate stage whisper looking directly at Fallon as she spoke.

Fallon smiled. "Enough, you two. Let's get the whole story from Peter, then the questions, and then a plan."

"There's really not much more to tell," Peter continued. "Bottom line, nothing was ever found. I've marked the location of that first and only signal on this chart in blue, and the estimated drift pattern is also recorded there as a dotted blue line. All the search patterns are overlaid in red and marked with the date and time the pattern was run. The search continued with periodic breaks from the time of that first signal until late yesterday, without any success or sign of wreckage."

"What I don't understand is why, if they received one signal, they couldn't find the beacon and why there was no other wreckage?" Charlie asked.

"Look out that porthole behind you," Fallon answered. "Do you see the bracket fixed to the outside of the housing? It has a hydrostatic switch, which will release the EPIRB at a water depth of between three and ten feet. The EPIRB will then float to the surface and begin transmitting. I'm sure Sarah would have mounted hers in the same way so that it could float free if necessary. Any idea of how it was mounted, Peter?"

"Exactly as you said. She was always immaculately prepared, which is what makes the whole thing so strange."

As he spoke, Peter felt the tears well up and his throat tighten. He stood, momentarily unable to speak, until he felt a gentle hand on his shoulder and then a light squeeze. As Charlie withdrew her hand, Peter once again noticed her graceful movements. They were quite mesmerizing and gave the appearance of moving in slow motion.

"So what happens when the signal goes off?" Charlie asked.

"I'm really not sure of the sequence," Peter replied. "Any idea, Fallon?"

"Pretty straight forward really. Either a stationary or earth orbiting satellite, or perhaps both, picks up the signal. These have search and rescue processors, which in turn send a signal to a receiving and processing station; often called a local user terminal. The data generated by these terminals is sent to the nearest Mission Control Centre, which in turn transmits to its Rescue Co-ordination Centre, who then dispatches the Search and Rescue teams."

"So how do they tell the location and, if it's all so slick, why didn't they find it?" Charlie asked.

THE BERMUDA KEY

"GPS data from the EPIRB gives the location, but it's the failure to keep transmitting that worries me the most. As long as it's on the surface of the ocean, the EPIRB will continue transmitting. I've never heard of one failing. It may even transmit if it's just below the surface. Only getting a single signal suggests it was activated very briefly and then deeply submerged through some catastrophic event."

"Like what?" Charlie asked.

"I'm guessing, and this is an example only," Fallon replied looking directly at Peter as if to comfort him as he spoke. "If the boat overturned, the EPIRB may release and then be dragged underwater by the boat itself, or by the sails. Again, this is an example only," he stressed. "I'm not saying this is what happened."

There was silence as Fallon finished speaking, each of the three lost in their own thoughts.

"Maybe I should tell you what the BRCC told me and see what you think," Peter suggested. "Apparently they did follow Sarah's EPIRB signal which, in the absence of any other radio communication, they assumed had self-activated. If they're correct about that," he continued, "then she may not have had time to get into her life raft or grab her panic bag. It contained pre-packed rations and other safety essentials like smoke flares and dye markers. Also, assuming Sarah hadn't changed her habits, her satellite phone would have been clipped to the bag."

"That scenario's consistent with a sudden event," Fallon added.

Peter paused to gather himself. He was choking up again. After a moment he spoke. "All being well, her boat was entirely suitable for a normal ocean passage and her stores and water supplies would have been good for at least two weeks. Sorry," he said, "my mind's jumping. I know that's not relevant to the EPIRB search."

"Don't worry," Fallon replied, "just get out whatever's in your head. It's all useful information and it's far better to have too much than to leave out some detail which may prove to be valuable later on."

"Thanks, Fallon. So back to the search." Without once looking at the notes in his hand, Peter resumed outlining in detail all the activities undertaken by the Search and Rescue teams from the time of the first signal until the end of their search.

As he finished, Charlie blurted out, "Holy smoke, Preppy, how the hell did you remember all that?"

Peter grinned sheepishly. "No idea really, details just seem to stick. I think it's from how I studied at law school. I was never the natural my father thought I was. I always preferred being outdoors, but he wanted so badly for me to follow in his footsteps I just had to see it through."

"What's up, Fallon?" Charlie asked, looking over at Fallon who was staring intently at Peter.

Fallon jerked his head around. "Nothing," he answered quickly, "just thinking about the search."

"Okay, Preppy back to you. What happened after that?"

"That's about as much as I know," Peter offered. "At that point my father asked Fallon to help in the search and here we are. Was there anything else you wanted me to cover Fallon?"

"No. That's a damned fine job. Most people lose functionality under stress. You seem to cope pretty well."

"Always have. Don't mean to sound arrogant but I think it's in the genes."

"Must be," Fallon replied, again lapsing into silence as he studied the charts.

After what seemed an eternity to Peter, Fallon finally looked up and spoke. "Okay, here's what we'll do."

Working from the information Peter had gathered, Fallon outlined the areas where he thought they would be best served by searching again. Recognizing that little was likely to be gained by covering all the same ground as the SAR teams, they had instead focussed on some of the uncharted peculiarities of the Bermuda coastline and currents. Their primary assumption being that any wreck offshore should ultimately result in some debris washing up in one of Bermuda's tidal coves. With an average tidal change of only three to four feet, and Sarah's intimate knowledge of the island, they were reasonably confident that her sinking had not taken place close to land. They were outside hurricane season, so that too was not an issue although the recent offshore storm would almost certainly have played its part. Yet, with Sarah's sailing skills, both Peter and Fallon were convinced there had to have been some other unknown event involved and, with one brief EPIRB signal and no message, the odds were it was both sudden and catastrophic.

As they searched in the days that followed, Peter had been amazed at Fallon's knowledge of the coastline and currents. No wonder his father had asked him for help. Without ever looking at a chart the man seemed to know every current and eddy around the island and yet, days later and despite Fallon's best efforts, here they were lacking even a single sign of wreckage.

#

"I think we should go back in for a day or two," Fallon said. "We've been out here since Monday and are now starting to cover much of the same ground as the SAR people. We need to replenish our supplies and I need to go over the charts and the recent weather reports again. I'm sure we're missing something. No idea what, but there should be some sign and the only thing I can think of at the moment is that we're looking in the wrong place. I can do that ashore while we restock the boat and I'm sure you two could do with a break. Oh, sorry Ben," Fallon said, looking at the dog, "you three that is." This aside was greeted by a leisurely half-wag of the dog's short tail as he continued to lie, otherwise unmoving, at their feet.

"Well, I know I could do with a break," Peter replied, "but I feel guilty about not continuing the search without interruption."

"I understand, but we need supplies and the time will be well spent if we divide up the tasks among ourselves. Charlie can take care of what we need for another few days out on the boat while you check in with the search and rescue group for any news. You should probably update your father as well, Peter."

"Yes, you're right. I'm sure he'd appreciate that. Will you be coming out with us again, Charlie?" As soon as the words were out of his mouth, Peter could have kicked himself. He sounded, well, desperate that she should say yes. As it was, he needn't have worried.

"Absolutely, Preppy. I don't think you and Fallon could cope without me. You're too alike. You'll drive each other crazy. Look at the two of you. You even have the same three small moles in a line on the left side of your chests."

Both men stopped what they were doing and looked, first at each other and then down at their own bare chests, then back at each other, and finally, at Charlie.

"Don't look at me like that," she said, "I'm trained to notice similarities in things. It's part of what I do. Besides, if you two are going to parade around here in nothing but shorts, it's hard not to notice. You have the same toes as well, by the way."

With the last throwaway remark, Charlie turned and walked away. Looking back over her shoulder she said, "I'm off to change. Let me know what the plan is when you're finished."

Peter looked down at his toes and then at Fallon's bare feet. Charlie was right; they were almost identical. He looked up. Fallon was staring at him, a strange expression on his face.

"Okay, let's get this show on the road," Fallon said, seemingly as if to rid whatever thoughts were going through his head. "No sense in wasting any more time. We can be home before lunch and then regroup tomorrow morning at my place. I'll tell her ladyship when she re-emerges. Peter, if you could tend to the anchor, I'll get *Maverick* started up."

As Peter moved to the bow, he couldn't help but wonder at Charlie's observations. They were interesting but not important, yet Fallon seemed disturbed. Oh, well, he had other things to think about rather than worrying about Fallon's idiosyncrasies. Putting aside any further thoughts on the topic, he settled down at the anchor locker and waited for Fallon's command to run the winch.

THE BERMUDA KEY

#

"What's that buzzing?" Charlie asked as they neared Hamilton harbour.

"Oh, hell, it's my phone. I tried checking it this morning but we were too far out to get a signal. I put it on vibrate so as not to disturb you two."

"Very kind, Preppy, but from the sound of things you must be in trouble. It's been buzzing for ages."

"I'll look at it as soon as we dock. If there was anything really urgent I'm sure someone would have radioed us."

CHAPTER 14

Hamilton, Bermuda – Thursday, May 17, 2012

As he walked along the jetty away from Fallon's boat, Peter looked down at the screen of his mobile phone. One call from Sean and eight from his father; two a day starting last Monday. He felt his stomach knot. What could be wrong and, if it was urgent, why hadn't someone radioed the boat? He pressed the number for his father's direct line on his speed dial.

Howard answered after the very first ring. "Good afternoon, Howard Alexander here."

"Hi, Dad, we've just docked." Peter listened for a moment before speaking. "No nothing. What's up?" He listened again. "Thursday the twenty-fourth. Really? So quickly?" He paused. "Okay, I'll come to the house as soon as I've showered and changed. See you then."

#

Later that evening, Peter called Fallon at home. It was a moment or two before he realized that rather than reaching Fallon, his call had gone directly to his voicemail. After waiting for the proverbial beep, he spoke. "Fallon, Peter Alexander here. Look I'm sorry to have to ask you this, but something important has come up which I have to attend with my father. I'll be at your house tomorrow morning as planned but, when we go out again, I need to be back on the island by the latter part of next week. We can discuss the details when I see you tomorrow, but I wanted to give you a heads up as soon as I could. No need to call me back."

Peter disconnected the call. He was not looking forward to next week at all.

CHAPTER 15

Vatican City – Thursday, May 17, 2012

Unlike Peter, Cardinal Weiler could hardly wait for the following week to arrive.

Once Cardinals Cressey and Kwodo had accepted his offer of assistance in the matter of the missing key from the *San Pedro* cross, he had quickly immersed himself in the details. To say that he was astounded with the news of Mrs. Alexander's death and the location of the key would have been a major understatement. He was flabbergasted. He had anticipated being involved in the search for the key, not the very act of its recovery. As far as he was concerned, the news could not have been any better. Within days, he had arranged to visit Bermuda and, a few weeks later, had met with the late Katherine Alexander's son.

The meeting with Peter Alexander had been difficult and it had taken all of his considerable persuasive skills and a great deal of overt religious pressure to get the Alexander family's acquiescence to the exhumation. Howard Alexander had been away at the time of his first meeting with the son, but returned a few days later. After several further meetings with both men, agreement was finally reached. Even then, they had stipulated that their approval remained subject to the daughter's confirmation. This had necessitated further delays while they attempted to contact her in the middle of an offshore sailing trip.

THE BERMUDA KEY

In the interim, and at his urging, Howard Alexander had agreed to commence the necessary documentation and keep him apprised of how matters progressed regarding his daughter Sarah's consent. Of course, the proposed substantial payment had not hurt his negotiating position.

Money does that, he thought.

While it had ultimately cost more than he was originally authorized to offer, Cardinal Weiler still considered it cheap at the price. This was, after all, the key to the Church's most valuable relic. Yet, despite the key's inherent value, it had taken a significant effort on his part to pry three million dollars out of the Institute for the Works of Religion; or the Vatican Bank as it was more commonly known. With over one hundred employees and several billion Euros in assets, the bank still managed to remain highly secretive about its activities, even to someone of his stature within the Church. In this instance, and as often before, he wondered who really pulled the strings inside that stately establishment.

Besides, three million dollars for the key's safe return was not really the only issue. You could not expect a family to agree to the exhumation of a loved one, and the removal of an item she had stipulated be buried with her, without acknowledging the inestimable value to the Church of their agreeing to these acts. The Alexanders wouldn't have bought that. In fact, despite the magnitude of the proposed payment, they remained adamant that only the key was to be removed, and that Mrs. Alexander's necklace would be re-buried with her remains. Attempting to honour a wife and mother's wishes while also satisfying the needs of the Church was as important to them as the money. That said, they were not naive and in the end no less than three million dollars had been necessary to get their agreement on the exhumation and the removal of the key.

What really irritated him at this point, however, was after waiting for several weeks for news of the daughter's approval without success; the Alexanders were now in a rush. With his daughter's loss at sea removing the necessity for her approval, Howard Alexander, even more distraught than before, was now insisting that the exhumation take place "without delay".

In his call the previous Monday, Mr. Alexander advised that the date for the exhumation had been set for Thursday the twenty-fourth. He went on to say that, he was not prepared to wait and, if Cardinal Weiler could not be available to witness the removal of the key, they would proceed without him and hold the key until he arrived. Lucien had paled at the thought. What if the key were somehow exchanged? No, the Church simply couldn't risk that and despite the short notice, he assured Howard Alexander he would be there as arranged. That, he had said, was essential and non-negotiable if their agreement was to remain in place.

#

Cardinal Weiler shook his head as if to rid it of the thoughts buzzing around inside. Where were his colleagues? He had been waiting at least ten minutes for the limousine to arrive. He should never have said he would travel with them. What if they were late? The flight to the U.K wouldn't wait and there was a connection to make. They were to fly out of Rome later that evening and, after transiting to Gatwick from Heathrow, leave Gatwick the following afternoon. Finally, after a seven and half hour flight, they would arrive in Bermuda just after six p.m. local time on the Friday evening.

He certainly wasn't looking forward to such a lengthy journey. Thank heaven the senior members of the clergy travelled in First Class.

CHAPTER 16

Mayfair, U.K. – Friday, May 18, 2012

Bruce Gordon slumped into his seat in the May Fair Hotel bar, realizing for the umpteenth time that he really needed to do something about his weight before it was too late. The walk from the Dukes Hotel, situated at the end of short and narrow St. James Place, had taken its toll. Although only seven minutes from the May Fair, he was puffing and panting. If the Dukes had not been his favorite haunt, and home to one of the best martinis in London, he would have suggested meeting Professor Shandro right here instead.

There was certainly nothing wrong with the May Fair bar. Cloned waitresses in short black dresses, black tights and soft ballet-slipper shoes served smoked salmon sandwiches, champagne and pomegranate juice to the predominantly thirties clientele with the trendy lounge music set at the appropriate decibel level to allow civilized conversation. Not to be outdone, the waiters, in their black slacks, light blue shirts and red ties, generated precisely the correct colour balance while the manager in his all black outfit and red tie provided discreet oversight of the employees choreographed movements among the affluent evening crowd.

He had chosen to stay at the May Fair while looking for a new vehicle at one of the exclusive dealerships near Berkley Square and used the opportunity to meet at the Dukes with his old friend who had been in the city at the same time. Little had been said about his investigation other than once again offering his thanks for the translation and confirming that he continued to work on the case on a part-time basis. Bruce Gordon was still of the mind that the less said about these matters the better.

What remained unspoken, yet foremost in Bruce Gordon's mind, was his ongoing investigation of the Panzini lead with Andrew Jensen. That particular card he kept very close to his chest. He was certain that the plans he had seen were those for the duplicate cross, used to replace the original at the time of its theft.

Independent confirmation from Andrew Jensen was all he needed before leaving for Rome to follow up with Raffaele Panzini in person. Hampered by his own lack of understanding of Italian, coupled with Raffaele's limited command of the English language, his most recent attempt to elicit specific information by telephone had failed miserably. The more he thought about the matter, the more certain he became that the solution, or at least some of the answers, lay in Rome. He had expected to hear from Andrew Jensen by now. He would call him in the morning on his return to the Cotswolds.

With considerable effort, Bruce Gordon re-focussed on the server hovering over his table. "I'm sorry," he said, "my mind wandered. What were my options again?"

CHAPTER 17

Hamilton, Bermuda – Friday, May 18, 2012

Andrew Jensen took one last look at his report. There was absolutely no doubt in his mind that the scale drawings sent by Dr. Gordon were the drawings for the fake cross that now resided in the Bermuda Maritime Museum. Where had Dr. Gordon found them? His curiosity was aroused, but the information had not been offered, and he was too polite to ask.

There were only two items he had failed to resolve. The shaded drawing of the cross, other than appearing to be of similar dimensions, had no other apparent connection to the fake cross. Additionally, the numerical annotation on that page did not relate to any of the materials used in the cross and could just as easily have been a scribbled telephone number. He had made these same observations in the report that he planned to send off later today.

To satisfy his curiosity he had almost dialed the number before realizing that it was very unlikely to be a local number. He also remembered Dr. Gordon's request for absolute confidentiality. Andrew, not one to deviate from his word, had taken this request to heart. Earlier that week he had downloaded the e-mailed information from Dr. Gordon, and then deleted all the files from his computer. It was one of the first steps his son had taught him for removing any spam mail that he might receive. In hindsight, he was glad he had taken the time to learn. Although many aspects of computers were still a bit of a mystery to him, his rudimentary knowledge of e-mails and internet searching worked quite well.

Satisfied that he had not missed anything in his report, Andrew placed it in a large envelope and sealed it shut. He would mail it that afternoon from the quaint Perot Post Office on Queen Street. Not entirely content with his plan of action, Andrew also decided to send a brief e-mail to Dr. Gordon advising him of the mailing before settling down for a quiet lunch alone.

It was at times like this that he missed his late wife, he thought.

#

Due to the difference in time zones, Bruce Gordon was four hours ahead of Andrew Jensen when the e-mail arrived. His mobile, dutifully and wirelessly synchronized with his computer, lay unanswered in his hotel room while he met with his old friend, Stuart Shandro. He would not retrieve it until later that evening after his dinner in the May Fair bar at which time, his frustrated call to Andrew Jensen in response to his e-mail, went unanswered.

Why hadn't the man simply attached his report to the e-mail, he wondered.

Patience was certainly not one of Bruce Gordon's virtues and the resultant sleepless night he endured as he waited for a suitable hour at which to call Andrew Jensen the following morning did nothing to improve his demeanour.

CHAPTER 18

Tucker's Town, Bermuda – Friday, May 18, 2012

Maggi was buttering her toast at the kitchen counter when Fallon walked in.

"Morning, Maggi."

"Morning yourself," she answered turning to greet him. "You're back sooner than I expected. When did you get in?"

"Actually, we got in yesterday but I spent the evening on the boat. I should have called. Sorry. Trouble is there's something we're missing, and it's driving me nuts. I spent the whole evening poring over the charts hoping it would come to me, but no luck."

"So you didn't find anything?"

"Not a damned thing. The bloody boat just disappeared. No wreckage, nothing. It doesn't make sense."

"What will you do now?"

"We're going to meet here this morning and regroup. Will you join us? It wouldn't hurt to have another viewpoint and you know these waters almost as well as I do now."

"I wouldn't go that far," Maggi replied. "I know them from research and charts. You have the advantage of actual time on the water. Don't sell yourself short."

Fallon smiled. "Thanks for that. At the moment I can do with all the moral support I can get."

"How did Peter Alexander turn out?"

"Surprisingly well. I expected him to be a lot more like Howard than he was."

"How so?"

"You know, sort of bookish and detailed. He's certainly detailed, but he's also pretty fit, and tough, and best of all he has an instinctive feel for the sea. I assume he got that from Kat. She was always good on the water."

Maggi flinched at the mention of Katherine Alexander before quickly changing the course of the conversation.

"How did he and Charlie get along?" she asked.

"Now that was interesting," Fallon said. "There's chemistry there for sure."

"Really?"

"Oh yes, indeed."

"What makes you so sure?"

"Just the way they both behaved. Charlie was her usual irreverent self and already has a nickname for him, which he doesn't seem to mind at all. He, on the other hand, acts like a smitten teenager around her. Despite the seriousness of the search, it's actually quite fun to watch."

"My God, Fallon, you're getting soft. Next thing you'll be matchmaking."

"Well I've always liked Charlie, and Peter's pretty easy to get along with. Don't take my word for it though, join us and watch for yourself. She's your niece, so you'll have a better read than I do, but I think I'm right."

"Okay, I will. You've sparked my interest now. How's her research going by the way? I haven't spoken to her for a while."

"Actually, that's one thing we didn't discuss. It may come up next time out though. Sarah's fiancé is supposed to be joining us and although he's Canadian, he spent quite some time in South Africa. How many South Africans did Charlie say were in British prisoner-of-war camps in Bermuda during the Anglo-Boer War?"

"Over five thousand, I think," Maggi replied. "She said they were split between five of the smaller islands, the chosen location depending on their attitude towards the war, believe it or not."

"Unreal. To think that they brought them all the way here, and then repatriated them when the war was over."

"Yes, but not before far too many had died, including children. Apparently conditions in the camps were pretty awful at times."

"I never understood why they would bring children. I assume they were concerned the kids would ultimately become soldiers."

"You should ask Charlie. I'm sure she has a good fix on it even though her interest is primarily physical anthropology. What was it she said her research covered? Something like 'The ultimate effect on the Bermuda population by the assimilation of the South African prisoners of war who remained'; or words to that effect."

"Not bad, I couldn't have said it better myself," Fallon spluttered through his laughter. "I would have said something like 'How South Africans are to blame for the current cultural mess in Bermuda'. After all, it's never our fault. It's always some outside group. Well, I'd best get ready," he said, changing the subject. "They'll be here soon. We'll meet in my study, so join us whenever you like."

"I will," Maggi replied.

#

"Come on in," Fallon said as Maggi appeared in the doorway of his study. "I told Charlie and Peter you might join us."

"Hi, Mags," Charlie said rising on one knee to kiss Maggi on the cheek before flopping back down on the red leather sofa.

"Morning, Charlie." Maggi gave her niece a brief but affectionate hug. "You really should drop in more often. I miss not having you around."

Turning, she held out her hand to Peter who had also risen and continued to stand patiently while she greeted Charlie. "Hello, Peter, very nice to see you again. It's been a long time. I wish it were under more favourable circumstances. I'm very sorry about Sarah."

"Thank you," Peter replied. "It's nice to see you too. Dad and I really appreciate your and Fallon's help with the search."

"Please sit," Maggi said gesturing toward the chair from which he had risen and sitting down on the sofa next to Charlie as she spoke.

Fallon, who had sat silently throughout the greetings, resumed speaking. "Right. To recap for Maggi's benefit, this is what we have so far. All our search patterns have failed to reveal anything. We can either expand the search and continue with the same process or try and think out of the box."

"Are you suggesting something different?" Maggi asked.

"Not as yet, although I'm hoping that with a bit of brainstorming we might come up with other possibilities. Peter has told us that he and Howard have some estate affairs to deal with later next week so our next trip will probably only be a three day stint early in the week."

"How about the Rescue Centre? Have you checked to see if there's any news from them today?"

"No, but that's a good idea. Peter can do that once we break up here."

"I thought they weren't doing any more searches," Charlie said.

"Might as well keep checking," Maggi replied. "If they're anything like the rest of the bureaucratic establishment you never know what they'll do from one moment to the next. Sometimes it just depends on which way the political wind's blowing."

"Damn, Maggi, that really pisses me off," Fallon exclaimed, while three shocked faces stared back at him. "I've been racking my brains for days without success, wondering what we've been missing and you've been here for five minutes and found it."

"I have?" Maggi said, looking none the wiser.

"The wind," Fallon replied. "You said it depends which way the wind's blowing."

"And?"

"And that's why we haven't found anything. If Sarah's boat broke up suddenly, which all indications suggest it did, but she managed to hang onto any large piece which didn't sink, her drift would have been significantly influenced not only by the currents, but also the wind."

"And there was a storm offshore at the time," Peter added, his face illuminating with excitement, "so plenty of that."

"Easy Preppy, don't pee yourself," Charlie said.

Both Fallon and Maggi looked at Peter after this last remark, clearly expecting some response, only to be rewarded with an embarrassed half-smile as he quickly looked away from Charlie.

"I think your earlier observation was correct," Maggi said directly to Fallon, who grinned but didn't respond.

"Okay," Fallon said, "time for some real work. Let's get all the weather charts for the day before, and several days after, the storm. I want to superimpose wind directions over the ocean currents and see if we can calculate where a large piece of floating debris may have been moved by the prevailing winds."

"Don't you think the Rescue Centre would have done this already?" Charlie asked.

"Good point," Fallon replied, "but somehow I don't think so. This hypothesis assumes that Sarah's boat broke up and that she somehow managed to stay afloat by holding onto a large piece that remained. It's still worth checking though. Rather than waiting until later Peter, why don't you give them a call now and we can take it from there?"

#

Several hours later, after confirming with the Rescue Centre that they had indeed not computed the drift pattern as now envisaged by Fallon, and making full use of Maggi's access to the Maritime Museum's electronic charts and historical weather reports, the group had completed their analysis.

"Well that puts us pretty far off base," Fallon concluded as he drew a new large circle on the chart, which already showed their completed search grids enclosed in an earlier circle. "Curiously enough if our calculations hold up, because of the unseasonable level and duration of the north-westerlies at the time, it brings us closer to the island than we thought. We've been too far out."

"Let me make sure I understand correctly," Peter said pointing to one of the two circles that Fallon had drawn. "Based only on the one brief emergency signal and prevailing ocean currents, you would have expected to find debris somewhere in this circle. With the addition of the wind-effect on a large piece of wreckage you now anticipate that the debris would be somewhere in here." As Peter made this last observation, he moved his finger to the second of the two circles, which Fallon had drawn.

"Correct."

"That's a pretty big area," Maggi said.

"I'm afraid it's worse than that," Fallon replied. "If our assumptions are correct there's no telling when and if Sarah lost contact with whatever was left of her boat, so she and the debris may be in two entirely different locations."

Peter whistled softly through his teeth.

"There is some good news though," Fallon continued. "If I'm not mistaken, a number of the local Newport to Bermuda race crews are practicing in that area and will cross directly through our new probable location. We could ask the organisers to put out a bulletin requesting all boats to be alert and report the location of, or even pick-up, any debris they see out there. That will give us quite a few extra eyes in the area."

"Brilliant, Fallon, that's brilliant," Peter said. "Will you ask them or shall I?"

"I'll do it. I know some of the crews and if I ask, it may help focus their attention away from their race preparations. We've almost a month before the race commences anyway but I'm not sure when they plan to leave for Newport so I'll get on it right away."

"When does the race start?" Peter asked.

"June fifteenth, from Newport."

"Does the race itself cross through these same areas?" Charlie asked.

"Depends on the wind," Fallon answered. "Historically they're all likely to be further east. Too bad, but as it's still a month away it's not likely to do us much good then anyway."

Realizing the possible effect of the words on Peter as soon as they were out of his mouth, he placed a hand on his shoulder. "Sorry Peter. That didn't come out quite right."

"It's okay, Fallon. I understand if we haven't found Sarah by then the odds on ever locating her are pretty slim."

"Well, no point in delaying any longer," Fallon said. "We need to get out there if we're going to get you back on Wednesday, Peter. I suggest we leave at first light tomorrow. Are you coming with us again Charlie? Ben's welcome too if you are. Where is that dog anyway?"

"Asleep on the sofa in the cottage. It's a dog's life, don't you know. Yes, I'd like to come if that's fine with you two?"

"It's fine with me. How about you, Peter?"

"Certainly, I'd be grateful. The more eyes the better and I forgot to mention, Sean's been delayed so he won't be coming with us on this trip."

"Okay that's it then. We should go over what we'll need for a few days and then I'll see you all at the boat tomorrow. You alright with that, Maggi?"

"Absolutely. I'll hold down the fort here. Charlie, you can leave Ben with me if you want. I'd be happy to look after him."

"Thanks, Mags. I may do that. He's probably tired of being cooped-up on the boat. Can I decide in the morning?"

"Sure. Just drop him off when you leave if you want. I'd enjoy the company."

CHAPTER 19

Mangrove Bay, Bermuda –
Saturday, May 19, 2012

Bruce Gordon's call to Andrew Jensen took place at eight o'clock the morning following his receipt of the e-mail. He knew it was early, but he simply could not wait a moment longer for the information.

Despite the hour, and being barely awake, Andrew's old world manners quickly took hold and before long, he had answered all the pertinent questions resulting from his e-mail the previous day.

Yes, he was certain the drawings were detailed plans for the fake *San Pedro* cross. No, he had not told anyone else of his findings. No, he did not know why there was a drawing of a shaded cross nor did he know what the numbers represented on that page; in fact he thought they looked like a telephone number.

With suitable apologies for his impatience and disturbing Andrew first thing in the morning, Bruce Gordon terminated the call and sat back in his chair.

How curious, he thought, *and that comment about a telephone number? Why hadn't he considered that possibility?*

Reaching into his briefcase, he withdrew his copy of the drawing. Yes, there it was at the bottom right corner of the page.

If it's a telephone number, he thought, *it's more than likely in Italy.*

THE BERMUDA KEY

Speaking aloud he said, "let's see...country code 39...area code 06...number 698...damn, what was it again?"

Finally, with the number entered in his mobile, Bruce Gordon pressed the dial key. After a brief pause, he heard a ring that was answered almost immediately.

"*Buona puliscono, l'ufficio del Cardinale Cressey. Questo è parlare Padre Escoffier,*" the voice at the other end said.

Caught somewhat off guard by both how quickly the call was answered and his lack of knowledge of Italian, Bruce Gordon nonetheless managed to catch both *Cardinale Cressey* and *Padre Escoffier*. Assuming that a cardinal would not be answering the phone on behalf of a priest, he replied.

"*Mi scusi, Padre*...may I speak English?"

"Of course, sir,"

"I'm afraid I missed your last name Father."

"Escoffier."

"Ah, thank you. I wonder, Father Escoffier, if the Cardinal is available?"

"I'm afraid Cardinal Cressey is away at the moment, sir. May I tell him who called and if there is some message?"

Bruce Gordon alert for just such an opportunity, and having planned for this moment before making the call, started speaking. "Yes, if you would be as kind as to..." and then quickly disconnected the call while still mid-sentence. He had learned this trick many years before when dealing with irate callers. Wait until it's your turn to speak and then hang up...no one ever thinks you would intentionally hang up on yourself.

The proof of this strategy was being played out in the Vatican at that very moment. Father Thibaud Escoffier, personal assistant to Cardinal Cressey looked at the buzzing telephone in his hand.

Must have lost the connection, he thought, and I never even got his name. Oh, well, never mind, if it was important the caller would try again. He must know the Cardinal to have this number anyway.

Bruce Gordon on the other hand was beside himself with excitement. The number on the drawing was the office number of a cardinal in the Vatican! He needed to work out his next move. This couldn't be by chance. It was also not something to be approached lightly. The more he reflected on it, the more certain he became that he should follow up his call in person. He would wait for the report from Andrew Jensen to arrive to ensure he had all the pertinent information, and then he would head to Rome.

CHAPTER 20

Hamilton, Bermuda – Monday, May 21, 2012

Shanice Morgan was invisible, or so it seemed based on the behaviour of the dozens of hotel guests whose rooms she passed through on a daily basis. Whether it was the colour of her skin, her unusual accent - she found it impossible to avoid the Jamaican lilt of her birth in whatever language she spoke - or her occupation, she did not know; perhaps a combination of all three. Whatever the reason, the result was usually the same; she was ignored. Very occasionally, someone would smile in greeting but rarely did anyone say anything and, if they did, Shanice's accent on responding soon ended any effort at conversation.

Frequently mistreated while growing up in her native Jamaica, she was ultimately taken from her parents and placed in a series of foster homes. Adopted out of Jamaica by an affluent Italian family at thirteen years of age, she had been home schooled in Italy in relative comfort and had blossomed in that nurturing environment. Progressing from home schooling directly to university she had completed a degree in computer science and, on her twenty-second birthday, commenced plans for a trip to the United States in search of her biological mother. Her mother, from what she had been able to discover, had left Jamaica shortly after her adoption and ultimately settled in South Carolina, USA.

Sadly, her plans had not come to fruition. Her visa to the United States had been denied, although she had yet to be given a clear answer why. It was suggested that the most likely reason related to her biological mother's resident status, or lack thereof. Around this same time, she had discovered through her family contacts that a thriving expatriate Jamaican community existed in Bermuda and, albeit menial, employment could be obtained. All she had to do was get there. Bermuda was also relatively close to South Carolina and perhaps the proximity would help in finding her mother. With this loose but seemingly practical plan in place, she had arrived in Bermuda and found employment in the housekeeping section of an upscale local hotel. It was here that she went about her daily duties while continuing in her efforts to locate her mother.

One of the few benefits to being "invisible" Shanice found, was that one was privy to a great deal of information freely passed between guests in her presence. Every now and again by stringing together snippets of these various conversations, she was able to piece together interesting local gossip, or important meetings taking place. All this information she carefully kept to herself. After all, she had no one she trusted to share it with on the island and, despite their assistance, she wasn't entirely sure about her Jamaican acquaintances. In fact, the only person she felt truly comfortable with was the lawyer who had helped with her initial residency application. He was nice. He did work like this "pro bono" he had said, and never charged her a thing. That was the first time she had ever heard the expression. Besides, he hadn't made an issue of her accent and, unlike many others, had taken the time to let her speak slowly. That way, he said, he could understand exactly what she meant.

Yes, she thought. *He was about the only one she really believed she could trust.*

Knocking on the door of Suite 402, Shanice listened for a reply.

"Come," a voice said from the other side.

Suite 402 was comprised of six rooms. A spacious sitting area and bathroom, flanked by two large bedrooms, each with their own en

THE BERMUDA KEY

suite bathroom. As she entered the sitting area, her arms overflowing with towels, Shanice smiled in greeting and gestured with the towels towards the bathroom.

"Go ahead," a scarlet robed priest, said with a stately wave of his hand. "Perhaps we should continue in Italian," he said to the group seated in the room, "just in case."

"Certainly Eminence," one of the suited men replied, simultaneously switching to fluent Italian.

Shanice smiled, Italian was virtually her mother tongue now. It was all she had spoken for the past nine years. People really did make the most idiotic assumptions. As she worked, moving from room to room, she listened carefully to the conversation. Much of it was unclear.

Not likely things she wanted to know anyway, she thought.

Sounded like church business. Lots of talk about a key that had been lost and then found, but that they hadn't been able to get back. It seemed the key opened a chair. Now it really didn't make sense. That couldn't be right. Despite her fluency in Italian, she must have misunderstood.

She was just finishing the last bathroom when she heard the name Alexander. Could they be talking about her lawyer? They looked important enough. She listened carefully but couldn't make out all that was said; again something about a key. It seems they were having an awful lot of trouble trying to get it back and, if they did, it would somehow enable them to get a fisherman's ring. No, that wasn't it... it was "the ring of the fisherman", not "a fisherman's ring". It was all very confusing.

Why don't they get a locksmith to pick the lock? Shanice wondered.

Her work complete, Shanice gathered up her things and walked across the room to the entrance door of the suite. The group, seemingly oblivious to her presence, continued their conversation in Italian.

The last words she heard as she closed the door were "as long as the Alexanders never find out the real reason for our interest the whole situation should be manageable. Somehow we have to get that key."

Maybe this was her opportunity. Although she did not know what they were speaking about, she had heard enough to know that it somehow involved her only ally on the island. She owed Peter Alexander for his earlier kindness and who knew when she might need his services again. It was payback time and, if the apparent seniority of the members of this group was anything to go by, this matter, whatever it was, must be important.

CHAPTER 21

Hamilton, Bermuda – Wednesday, May 23, 2012

Little was said, as Fallon, Charlie and Peter stepped off *Maverick* and onto the dock. After several days at sea running seemingly endless search patterns, they had ultimately returned empty handed.

With an audible sigh, Fallon spoke. "I'm sorry, Peter; I really thought we were on to something with the wind drift pattern."

"I know how you feel. I was certain something would turn up. That said I really appreciate all you have done. I'm sure my father will want to get together in the next few days. We're busy tomorrow and Friday but perhaps if you have some time on the weekend we could meet somewhere for dinner?"

"That works. Let me know and I'll check with Maggi at the same time. She'd enjoy seeing Howard again."

"Would you like to join us, Charlie?" Peter asked.

"Thanks. That would be nice. Fallon can let me know the time and place once you folks have set it up."

"Anyone need a ride," Peter asked as he hefted his bag onto his shoulder.

"No thanks," Fallon replied. "My car is in the lot. Are you coming with me, Charlie?"

"Yes, if you don't mind. I'll get Ben from Maggi before I go home. See you at dinner, Preppy. Take care of yourself."

Both Charlie and Fallon watched as Peter walked away from the boat clad only in his shorts, his oversized kit bag slung over his shoulder. Fallon was the first to speak.

"Poor sod."

"Yeah. Must be pretty bloody awful looking for your sister's remains. She couldn't still be alive could she Fallon?"

"Outside of a miracle, not a chance. I still think we have a crack at finding her body though. The Newport to Bermuda race crews will be out there practicing for a while yet, and they've promised to watch out for any sign of wreckage."

"What will you do if they find something?"

"We'll use that bearing, and the point where her first emergency signal was picked up, to try and determine a drift route based on past weather conditions. After that it's back to searching along the route to see what, if anything, turns up. I might also try diving at a few spots along the way once we get it narrowed down. Not that I think that will yield any results without a great deal of luck. What are you going to do for the next few days by the way?"

"I really need to get back to my research. This was a good break and I felt it was for a worthwhile cause. I also enjoyed meeting Peter."

"So I noticed."

"Really, it was that obvious? Oh hell, do you think he knew?"

"Probably," said Fallon smiling broadly. "But then again he seemed to feel the same way about you."

"Do you think so?"

Fallon laughed. "Don't sound so anxious…and yes, I really do think so."

In comfortable silence, with Charlie's arm around his waist, the two walked along the dock toward the parking lot and Fallon's car.

CHAPTER 22

Pembroke, Bermuda – Thursday, May 24, 2012

The preparation room at The First Memorial Funeral Home had never been this crowded. Despite the best efforts of Mrs. James, no one it seemed was willing to wait in the privacy room notwithstanding its location right alongside and, to make matters worse, all insisted on being present at the opening.

Gathered around the barely decayed casket were Howard, Peter, Cardinal Weiler and the Vatican's legal counsel. They stood silently, all staring intently at the coffin, which lay on top of a bright blue tarpaulin draped over a stainless steel table. Slightly off to one side, as if waiting for further instructions, were the unlikely looking pair of Mrs. Darby James, the funeral director, and Mr. Elliot Crane, the mortician. The tall, thin and pale figure of the mortician in stark contrast to the dark complexion and ample size of Mrs. James.

The exhumation had been completed much earlier that morning to avoid any unnecessary onlookers although, with the eight-foot high temporary fence erected around the gravesite, little could have been seen by anyone passing by in any event.

Finally, Mrs. James spoke, and the oppressive silence was broken.

"Gentlemen, you can see for yourselves that there is very little room to work in here. It will also take Mr. Crane some time to remove the casket lid so that we may have access to the body of the deceased.

Let me again suggest you all retire to the privacy room until Mr. Crane is ready at which time he will summon those of you who wish to be present to examine the remains.

"In accordance with the instructions which we have been given, he will remove a necklace from the body of the deceased. From that he will remove a small gold key which he will hand to Mr. Alexander senior, replace the necklace on the body and reseal the casket after which it will be returned to the grave. The Reverend Coventry has agreed to be present at that time and will offer a prayer as the casket is lowered. There is no necessity for you to remain until that is complete unless you so wish."

"I'm afraid we will need to be present while the casket is being opened," Cardinal Weiler said.

"Well, if that's the case," Mrs. James huffed, unaccustomed to being challenged on her home turf, particularly by a non-Bermudian, cardinal or not. "I will leave until requested to return by Mr. Crane. Perhaps, Mr. Alexander, you might suggest to the cardinal that only one of each group remain until Mr. Crane has completed the necessary preparations to provide him a little more room to work."

Without waiting for a reply, Mrs. James turned and maneuvered her way from the small room.

"That sounds sensible, Eminence," Peter Alexander said before his father could respond. "Perhaps your counsel and I can stay here while you and my father wait in the privacy room. We can call you when we are ready."

"Are you sure, Peter?" Howard asked.

"I'll be okay, Dad. Go ahead."

Nodding acquiescence, Cardinal Weiler followed Howard Alexander from the room leaving Peter and Signor Gino Vacchelli, the Vatican legal counsel, alone with Mr. Crane.

Stepping forward, the mortician, who had remained silent throughout the earlier exchanges, moved under the large extraction fan suspended over the table. "Gentlemen, could you please stand as far back as possible as I work," he requested.

THE BERMUDA KEY

Needing little encouragement to do as asked, both Peter and Signor Vacchelli quickly complied.

#

It was almost thirty minutes later when the group, absent only Mrs. James, once again gathered in the small room. They stood, carefully distanced, so that Kat's body remained out of sight below the casket edge.

"Does anyone wish to view the remains of the deceased," Mr. Crane asked.

"Eminence," Howard said, his voice unsteady, "unless it is absolutely imperative I would prefer that we leave the removal of the key to Mr. Crane without the necessity for any of us to view my wife's remains. I would like her to be remembered as she was."

Cardinal Weiler looked at Signor Vacchelli who nodded silently. "That will be fine," he replied.

"Please proceed, Mr. Crane," Howard said.

Leaning over the casket, the mortician removed a long pair of forceps from a tray on the table with his gloved hand. Then, moments after reaching into the casket, he extracted a delicate gold chain from which hung suspended a small gold key.

Cardinal Weiler gasped at the sight. This was unbelievable. It was almost in his possession.

Undeterred by the cardinal's gasp, Mr. Crane gently removed the key from the chain before placing it in a small bowl of antiseptic solution that he had already prepared. He then returned the necklace to the casket before covering the entire box with a white sheet, already folded over one end.

Placing the forceps on the table, Mr. Crane removed the key from the solution with his gloved hand and dried it with a small soft cloth. That done, he held the cloth out toward Howard Alexander, the key resting neatly in the middle of its surface.

"Thank you Mr. Crane. We'll leave you now."

"You're welcome Mr. Alexander. Be assured I will take good care of the rest of the arrangements."

"Thank you. Come, gentlemen, let us go next door and finish this business. I'm not sure I can stand much more."

With that, the four men left the preparation room and adjourned to the room alongside, where they were promptly re-joined by Mrs. James. After repeated assurances that all had gone exactly as requested and that Kat's remains could now be re-interred, Mrs. James once again left the group alone to finalize their arrangements.

#

The four men sat around the plain, round, brown table in the privacy room of the funeral home. In its centre lay a red cloth on which rested a small gold and silver key.

"May I take a closer look," Cardinal Weiler asked the anxiety evident in his voice as he reached for the key.

"No."

Cardinal Weiler jerked his hand back as if burned and Peter turned quickly to look at his father seated alongside. He had seldom heard him speak so abruptly.

"I'm sorry, Eminence, but I've had about as much of this as I can take. We've done as you asked, and here is the damned key. I've desecrated my wife's memory for this, and I'm sick to my stomach because of it. So, this is how it ends. We will sit here while you make the promised payment and when that is complete we will leave and you may have the key. I hope it is worth all the pain this has caused."

For a few moments, all was quiet in the room, and then Cardinal Weiler replied. "I fully understand, Mr. Alexander. My sincere apologies for your discomfort. I assure you the key is of great value to the Church for which we thank you and your family. Signor Vacchelli has a bank draft already prepared. If you would be so kind as to take it to your bank, they can confirm the payment and we can proceed with the transfer of the key."

THE BERMUDA KEY

Peter looked at his father. He looked ill. He needed to get him out of here as quickly as possible.

"Tell you what Dad, why don't you make the deposit and call me when it's done. I'll stay here and no one will touch the key until you call. I promise you that."

Howard stood and shook hands with Cardinal Weiler and Signor Vacchelli. He took the offered bank draft and, without even glancing at its face, patted his son's shoulder and left. With Howard's departure, an uneasy silence settled over the room. Peter's several attempts to determine the real significance of the key to the Vatican went nowhere, and any efforts at small talk quickly died out as each of the parties withdrew into themselves. All, it seemed, preferred to sit silently until the process was over and done.

#

Finally, Peter thought as the telephone jangled on the table.

"Peter Alexander," he said as he lifted the receiver.

"Peter, it's Dad. Three million in the bank, son. Give them the key and I'll meet you at home."

"Okay".

Peter replaced the receiver and stood.

"It seems we are done gentlemen."

After shaking hands with both men, he walked out of the room leaving the Cardinal and his counsel to their own devices. The key, resplendent on its red cloth, still lay in the middle of the table.

#

Neither Cardinal Weiler nor Signor Vacchelli moved as Peter made his exit. Immediately the door closed behind him, however, Cardinal Weiler reached across the table and pulled the cloth towards him. After carefully examining the key, he slowly and reverently wrapped it in the red cloth before handing the small bundle to Signor Vacchelli. The latter opened his black leather briefcase, revealing a grey sponge insert with a small square section cut from its centre. Placing the cloth containing the key in the depression he then locked the case before the two men made their way from the funeral home back to their hotel.

CHAPTER 23

Hamilton, Bermuda – Friday, May 25, 2012

"Good Morning, Peter. Welcome back." Anne Taylor, Peter's ultra-efficient assistant walked across his office until she was alongside his chair and reached out to squeeze his arm.

"I hear that nothing has turned up from Sarah's boat yet. I'm so sorry."

After a brief pause, she continued. "Everything's in the pink folder in your basket. I'll be at my desk if you need anything else." With her summary greeting out of the way, Anne disappeared through the doorway where she had appeared only moments before.

Never one to waste words or time, Peter was sure Anne would have indeed put anything of relevance, which had occurred while he had been away, in the folder. Flipping it open, Peter looked at the list of outstanding telephone calls carefully positioned on top, which required his attention. Three were of particular interest.

Sean Patterson arrives today. He wanted to know if you could meet his flight, and whether he could still stay at the house. I said no and yes, unless he heard differently from either you or me during the course of today.

Shanice Morgan called. She will only speak to you. Quite odd for someone in her position. In case you don't recall, you did her immigration work pro bono. I explained you were away and that I would try to set an appointment for some time next week after I had spoken with you.

Charlotte Leigh called. She said it was personal. I don't think I know this one! Didn't leave a number.

Peter smiled. He would call Charlie this evening. Fallon would have her number. Sean knew how to take care of himself. And Shanice? Well Shanice would have to wait until Anne scheduled her in for next week. He turned the page over and looked at the next document.

CHAPTER 24

Tucker's Town, Bermuda – Friday, May 25, 2012

Charlie was exhausted but content. She had used most of the last two days catching up on her work and despite the time she had spent helping with the search was once again almost back on schedule.

It was a beautiful warm evening, no wind and the usual harmony of the tiny tree frogs. Often heard but always hard to find, she once had one jump onto her arm. Her first thought had been that it was a raindrop before she looked down and saw the tiny creature, which quickly hopped off into the nearby foliage as it realized its serious landing error.

Sitting in the corner of the patio sofa with Ben stretched out alongside her with his head on her thigh; Charlie gently stroked his ears as she waited for the telephone to ring. She needed some guidance with her research and Prof. Oosthuizen at the University of Cape Town had not yet returned her call. It was after midnight in South Africa and she now assumed that he was unlikely to call at this late hour and would probably do so later in the week. She had no sooner reached this conclusion than the telephone, lying on the arm of the sofa, rang. She picked it up and held it to her ear without speaking.

"Hello, Charl," a voice said.

"Professor Oosthuizen?" Charlie asked although she would have recognized the strong South African accent anywhere.

"*Naand meisie. Hoe gaan dit in die middel van die oseaan.*"

"That's how you greet your best student in a midnight call, 'Evening girl. How are things going in the middle of the ocean'? Really Prof, you have to become more politically correct."

"And why the hell should I. I like who I am and, quite frankly, after a glass of wine and a lovely *braai* with friends, you're lucky I even called you back."

"Oh, that hurts," Charlie replied. "I've no idea why my mother likes you so much."

"Nor me. Perhaps it's because I married her best friend. Whatever the reason, you are also my best student and my god-daughter so here I am."

"Oh what a treat," Charlie replied.

"Enough joking around, it's late over here. Everything all right, Charl?"

"Sure. I could have waited until tomorrow you know."

"I know, and I'll reply to your questions at length over the weekend and send you an e-mail. I just thought I would check in quickly before we went to bed."

"Thanks Prof, I'll wait for your e-mail. Can I ask one quick question on genetic similarities while you're on the phone?"

"Fire away."

"What is the likelihood that two people from the same small community with certain very similar genetic features are related to each other?"

"Academic answer or a best guess?"

"At this time of night a best guess is fine. I saw something which sparked my curiosity so just thought I'd ask."

"Best guess, I'd say likely that they were related in some way. Send me the details if you like and I'll give you a more reasoned response."

"No, that's fine. As I said, I was just curious. I'll let you go now and call you once I've read your e-mail. Give Marie my love and tell her I think she's a saint to put up with you."

"*Nag meisie, slaap lekker.*"

THE BERMUDA KEY

With that, the telephone clicked and he was gone.

"What a rascal Ben, he's as bad as you," Charlie said pulling on the dog's ear. An almost imperceptible movement of Ben's tail was her only answer before he once again drifted off to sleep.

Moments later the telephone rang again.

"I know. You forgot to say you love me," Charlie said into the receiver.

"Uh, well, wouldn't that be a bit premature?" Peter replied.

"Who is this?"

"It's Peter Alexander. I'm returning your call but I seem to have caught you at a bad moment. Perhaps I should call back."

"Oh my God. I'm sorry, Peter. I thought you were someone else."

"Clearly," he replied sounding somewhat chastened.

Immediately noticing the change in his tone, Charlie laughed.

"Nothing important," she said. "I called yesterday to see if you'd like to have a drink somewhere this evening during Bermuda's infamous happy-hour. There's a really good sushi bar at the Harbourfront, but I think it's likely over by now."

"We could go anyway," Peter replied. "The crowd's probably thinned out and we should get in. What about whomever you thought was on the phone though? Won't they mind?"

"Not a bit. In fact, I think he'd be delighted. I'll tell you more when I see you. Any issues at your end? If not, how about eight at the restaurant."

"No problems at my end. I'll see you there. I'll be the one with the pink flower in my lapel, in case you don't recognise me."

"Don't worry, Preppy. I'd recognise you even with clothes on."

Before Peter had any chance to reply, Charlie hung up the phone and wriggled free of the dog on the sofa. "Sorry, Ben, I'm off to see that cute lawyer fellow. You'll have to look after yourself this evening."

#

Peter's assessment of the crowd at the Habourfront sushi bar proved to be correct and Charlie had no trouble picking him out. Dressed in light-brown Italian loafers, no socks, coral slacks, a white shirt and navy blue blazer he blended easily with the other similarly attired Bermudian male diners. She had to admit she liked the casual formality with which Bermudians approached dining out. His companion, however, looked decidedly less polished and significantly more tired. Several inches over six feet, he towered over Charlie as both men stood in greeting.

"Hi, Charlie, I should have mentioned Sean Patterson, Sarah's fiancé, would be with me when I phoned. He arrived this afternoon from Canada and is staying with me at the house. I hope you don't mind that I invited him along."

"Not a bit. I'm really sorry about Sarah, Sean."

"Thanks, and I'm sorry to butt in on your dinner. I was delayed in Europe for almost a week and after coming here via Vancouver, I'm beat. I also haven't eaten since getting off the plane and I think Peter feels sorry for me. I'll head back to get some sleep after we've eaten and leave you two in peace."

"No need to rush on my behalf," Charlie replied. "I understand we're all having dinner again tomorrow. Other than Maggi and Fallon, I don't know too many people on the island, particularly around my age, and happy hour seemed a good way to end the week with someone that I at least knew slightly."

#

The rest of the evening progressed without incident. Peter and Sean proved to be good dinner companions and both the conversation and wine flowed freely. Charlie also learned that Sean and Sarah had spent a fair amount of time in South Africa, particularly the Cape Province. They had even docked their sailboat in the small harbour at Gordon's Bay, very near her mother's home on the beach alongside the South African Naval College, or the "General Botha" as the locals knew it.

It was almost one in the morning when the three finally oozed their way out of the restaurant. Piling into already waiting taxis, they agreed to meet again the following evening for Howard Alexander's dinner.

#

Saturday's dinner proved to be a cathartic affair. Whatever old wounds existed between Howard Alexander and Fallon had seemingly healed with time and then been further ameliorated by Sarah's tragic disappearance and Fallon's assistance with the search. Before long, the conversation's sombre tone at the dinner's commencement had given way to laughter and good-natured banter as Fallon regaled the group with anecdotes of the early days of diving and their excitement at the discovery of the *San Pedro* cross. Both Maggi and Howard interrupted liberally throughout the story as the trio recalled their own, and Kat's, respective roles, as well as their shock at the subsequent theft of the cross and the unsuccessful police investigation. Carefully omitted from the anecdotes was any mention by Fallon of the Vatican's ongoing interest in a missing key, or any comment by Howard regarding Kat's exhumation two days earlier.

"So who do you three think stole the cross?" Sean asked.

"Honestly, I don't have a clue," Fallon replied.

"Nor me," Maggi added. "Although for the longest time I thought that Father Despic had something to do with it, even though it was still there after he left. I never fully believed his reason for wanting to examine it in private."

"Funny you should say that," Howard said. "Kat never believed him either."

"Really? I didn't know that."

Howard sat quietly, not knowing what to say next and quickly recognizing this was not a topic he wished to pursue.

He looks awfully uncomfortable, Charlie thought. *I wonder why.*

"Ah well, all water under the bridge now," Howard finally said looking at Maggi and Fallon, his composure restored. "There was even a rumour going around the island that you two had something to do with it. I guess we'll never know."

"Well I can assure you it wasn't us," Maggi replied. "I watched that damned thing like a hawk and it disappeared from right under my nose. I'm still mad about that."

"Yeah, I heard that rumour too," Fallon said. "No cigar there I'm afraid. I think it started because Maggi worked at the Museum. The rumourmongers automatically assumed it was an inside job. What were the names of the two investigators again? The local police officer and that chubby insurance chap from the UK?"

"Sergeant Thomas was the police officer," Howard said. I don't recall the insurance fellow's name."

"It's Assistant Inspector Thomas now," Maggi said blushing slightly. "We've actually become good friends," she added as if needing to explain her knowledge.

Defensive, Charlie thought, but chose to say nothing.

"The other one was an insurance investigator," Maggi continued. "Very well regarded in the art world. Dr. Bruce Gordon if I remember correctly."

"Have they all given up on the investigation?" Charlie asked. "From what you've told us it's been quite a few years since the cross disappeared."

"Probably," Fallon replied. "Any better idea Maggi? Maybe you could ask Inspector Thomas. It would be interesting to know."

"I'll do that when I next have an opportunity, although given the time that's elapsed it's probably been shelved by now."

With little more new information to share about the theft of the *San Pedro* cross or the search for Sarah, the conversation turned to the more mundane aspects of island life and inevitably to local politics and issues. Not long thereafter, the group broke up for the evening with Fallon agreeing to take Peter, Sean and Charlie out for "one last look" at some suitable time the following week. As they left the restaurant, the party split into two with the Alexanders and Sean heading in one direction and Charlie, Fallon and Maggi in another.

#

Sitting quietly in the back of Maggi's car, Charlie listened as Maggi and Fallon discussed the evening's dinner.

"That was nice, Fallon. I had forgotten what it used to be like. I'm glad we got together. How about you?"

"Agreed. I thoroughly enjoyed it and it was time we made peace. It's a pity it took this long. I really like Howard's son. Sean as well for that matter, although that's the first time I've met him. What about you Charlie," he added, "do you like him?"

"Yes, he's very nice. I met him for the first time yesterday evening with Peter."

"Nicely dodged, Charlie," Fallon said and then burst out laughing. Turning around in his seat, he looked over his shoulder. "I didn't mean Sean, I meant Peter."

"Oh."

"That's all you can say. Oh?"

By now, both Maggi and Fallon were laughing and Charlie felt herself blushing furiously.

"Okay, enough you two. Yes, I like him. Satisfied?"

"Well almost," Maggi said. "How much do you like him and then we'll stop."

Charlie sat quietly for a moment and then replied with absolute certainty. "I think I'm going to marry him," she said. "He doesn't know that yet, but we'll get there. Satisfied now?"

There was no reply to her question, only stunned expressions on the faces of both her travelling companions.

CHAPTER 25

Vatican City – Saturday, May 26, 2012

The cardinals waited patiently for the fifth, and last, member of the Silenti to arrive. Unusually late, albeit only several minutes after the appointed time, Cardinal Weiler hurried in clutching a bright red cloth in his right hand.

He looks exhausted, Cardinal Cressey thought. He looked at the faces around the table. Expectant, every one of them, but none more so than Cardinal Vilicenti.

Without a word of apology, Cardinal Weiler laid the cloth on the table and silently took his seat. He had barely settled down when Cardinal Vilicenti began speaking.

"Eminences, our colleague has had an exhausting journey so, with his permission, let me acquaint you with the events of the past short while."

"I don't believe it," Cardinal Cressey whispered to Cardinal Kwodo seated alongside him. "Cardinal Weiler has already gone behind our backs and confided to Cardinal Vilicenti. You will recall Bernard; these are precisely the events of which I warned you."

Cardinal Kwodo laid his hand on the sleeve of his elderly colleague. "Easy my friend let us first see how things unfold."

Barely able to conceal his anger, Cardinal Cressey sat back in his chair and listened as Cardinal Vilicenti outlined the recent events leading up to the meeting, including a somewhat malicious reference to the "exchange", years earlier, of the original *San Pedro* cross by Father Despic under the direction of Cardinal Cressey. An exchange that had failed to secure the key and resulted in Cardinal Cressey still being in possession of the stolen original cross; a situation which left them all under the threat of outside exposure.

Cardinal Cressey had to admit the final summary was accurate in all but the extent of the parts played by himself and each of Cardinals Kwodo, Weiler and Vilicenti. Except where their actions could be negatively interpreted, he and Cardinal Kwodo had been reduced to minor participants, while the role played by Cardinal Weiler was elevated above all but that of his mentor.

As he concluded, Cardinal Vilicenti gestured to Cardinal Weiler. "Lucien," he said, his use of Cardinal Weiler's first name in this formal meeting room clearly emphasising his mentorship role, "would you please unwrap the key."

Cardinal Weiler rose from his seat and leaning over the table slowly unfolded the bright red cloth to reveal the delicate gold key therein. The act was met by a collective gasp from the cardinals seated around the table including Cardinal Cressey who, despite his earlier anger, sat suitably awed at the sight of the ancient and valuable relic.

Cardinal Cressey looked carefully at the key. Gold, with a single bow and shank but with one silver and one gold square bit just after the collar, each coming off the pin at ninety degrees to the other.

Beautiful, he thought. The symbolism of the gold and silver bits and their similarity to the crossed keys in the papal coat of arms not lost on him for a second. He continued to stare at the key. It looked perfect and yet he felt something was amiss. He looked at Cardinal Kwodo. Nothing. No change in his expression as he too sat staring at the key.

Cardinal Weiler's voice broke into his thoughts. "If Cardinal Vilicenti will excuse the interruption," he said, "I would like to offer a suggestion as to how we might proceed. Although I have not yet discussed this with any of you, I have given the matter substantial thought.

"You are all aware," he continued, "that during the middle ages it was customary to exhibit the Chair of St. Peter to the public on an annual basis. Each newly elected pope during this period was also enthroned using this same chair. That custom ceased in the early fourteenth century when, in order to preserve this precious relic, it was enclosed above the altar of St. Peter's in Bernini's enormous bronze casing. For over two hundred years, it remained hidden from the public until, in 1867, it was once again, and for the last time, publically displayed on the anniversary of the martyrdom of the two great apostles.

"From details gathered at that time we know that the seat is about fifty-five centimeters above the floor and approximately ninety-one centimeters wide. The height of the backrest is one hundred and five centimeters to the base of the tympanum, while its total height is roughly one hundred thirty-nine centimeters. It is, you will note, of substantial size.

"We also know it is made from framed fragments of acacia wood encased in an oak carcass and reinforced with iron bands. Much of the wood is worm-infested and pieces have been cut from various spots at different times, perhaps for relics. It is, therefore, quite fragile.

"In addition to its size, weight and fragility, the wood is overlaid with ivory plaques depicting various scenes and animals while its back is comprised of four arches whose columns support an ornamental tympanum. All of which suggest that ideally it should not be moved.

"I have recounted these facts only to suggest we may need to unlock the chair *in situ*, which would I'm afraid, unless someone in this room is privy to the exact location of the secret compartment, necessitate involving the Holy Father prior to making the attempt. Which, of course, we have avoided doing thus far."

Cardinal Weiler once again sat back in his seat looking, if that was possible, even more exhausted than he had only minutes earlier. No

THE BERMUDA KEY

sooner had he stopped speaking than it seemed every cardinal in the room spoke at the same time.

"Eminences, please." Cardinal Cressey's voice sounded above the rest and the room quickly grew silent. "I believe without any further discussion that there is no one in this room who would wish to involve the Holy Father unless absolutely necessary, or until we have succeeded in opening the chair and the ring is safely in our possession. Assuming I am correct in this, let us rather examine all the facts at our disposal and see if among us we can determine how to gain access to the chair and furthermore, how best we can determine the probable location of the secret compartment. From the chair's structure and shape there cannot be too many areas that could safely house a compartment whose dimensions we already know."

#

It was a little over an hour later as the cardinals continued to debate the issues confronting them when Cardinal Kwodo, who had been staring at the key with a puzzled frown, spoke.

"Have we compared the key with that in the funeral photographs of Mrs. Alexander?"

"No, there was no need," Cardinal Weiler responded. "I was there when it was removed from around the neck of the deceased. Why do you ask?"

"Something has been bothering me ever since it was unwrapped and, until a few moments ago, I had not realized what it was. The key has no notches cut into the bits. They are entirely square. Why would a secret compartment have such a simple key? Surely, assuming one knew the location, the most amateur of locksmiths would have been able to open the lock if that was the case."

"But I was there when it was removed from her casket," Cardinal Weiler repeated.

"I'm not doubting that at all, or the fact that this is the key worn around Mrs. Alexander's neck as she lay in her casket. I would just like to be sure that this is the same key which we saw in her photographs."

"Do you think it's been substituted?" Cardinal Vilicenti asked. "Why would they have done that? They have no knowledge of its true nature."

"I agree. I would just like us to make sure before we disturb the original Chair of St. Peter or, for that matter, the Holy Father."

"I agree," Cardinal Cressey added, realizing that the absence of notches in the bits was probably why he had not been able to shake the feeling that something was amiss.

"Easily solved," Cardinal Vilicenti replied. "Perhaps, Cardinal Kwodo could arrange for a suitably enlarged photograph of the key to be brought to the meeting so we can all see that we have the correct item in our possession. I suggest we adjourn and regroup in thirty minutes from now to confirm the key and finalize our approach to the opening of the secret compartment in the Chair of St. Peter."

#

Twenty-seven minutes later the Silenti, absent only Cardinal Kwodo, were once again seated around the table. Precisely thirty minutes later, Cardinal Kwodo entered and hurried to his seat carrying with him a legal size brown folder. Placing it on the table, he paused to catch his breath.

"Well?" Cardinal Vilicenti asked.

Cardinal Kwodo did not reply. Instead, he opened the folder and removed two enlarged photographs before passing one to the cardinal on his left and one to the cardinal on his right. "If you would be so kind as to hand these around," he said. "One is a photograph of Mrs. Alexander taken in her thirties while the other was taken shortly before her death. The key is clearly visible in both photographs. You will see she is wearing an identical necklace with a key pendant in each and that the two bits of the key, one of silver and one of gold, are each cut to resemble the shape of a simple Latin cross."

No one spoke as each cardinal examined the photographs before passing them to the cardinal seated alongside. When both photographs were once again in Cardinal Kwodo's hands, he passed them to Cardinal Weiler. "It appears we have a problem," he said.

"I don't understand how this could have happened," Cardinal Weiler stammered. "I was there when the key was removed."

"So you said earlier," Cardinal Cressey snapped still stung by the manoeuvering that had taken place before the presentation of the key. "Unfortunately, it is clear that a substitution was made prior to Mrs. Alexander's burial, and that what we have before us is a fake. A fake for which we have paid a considerable sum of money, I might add."

The criticism hung heavily in the air until the voice of Cardinal Vilicenti finally broke the silence. "Well, at least we have not disturbed either the Holy Father or the Chair of St. Peter with this key. Besides the monetary loss no other damage has been done."

"I wish we could be so sure," Cardinal Cressey responded. "I have today received word that a meeting has been requested with Monsignor Alonso, our archivist, by a certain Dr. Gordon. He is apparently, still involved in the investigation into the theft of the *San Pedro* cross from the Bermuda Maritime Museum many years ago. It appears that our recent activities may have inadvertently disturbed a sleeping dog, which we should have perhaps let lie."

"There is much to consider," Cardinal Kwodo said. "I suggest we do nothing rash and meet again in a few days to evaluate our options. Perhaps at that time, Cardinal Vilicenti or Cardinal Weiler could suggest what should be done about the key and Cardinal Cressey could offer his thoughts on how best to deal with this investigator. I will have my assistant check with each of yours and establish a suitable time for us to meet again."

#

"Angelo?"

"*Si*"

"There is something I would like you to take care of for me."

"Like before?"

"Yes"

"You want me to use the truck again?"

"I'll leave that up to you. It should look like an accident and have no link back to us."

"Of course. The same terms?"

"Yes."

"Okay, give me the details and we'll take care of it."

After a brief conversation, Cardinal Cressey replaced the receiver. By the time he reported to the Silenti, his problem should have already been resolved.

#

Cardinal Cressey had known Angelo Mosconi since his early days as a priest and, while he had initially found the blunt Sicilian's confessions shocking, there had come a time when the services that Angelo could provide proved useful as he manipulated his way up the religious ladder. Ambition was all very well, but hard work and luck alone were not enough. Nothing it seemed was outside Angelo's domain. From the first nudge to get his simple village congregation to increase their weekly tithes, to Signor Panzini's unfortunate accident, Angelo always delivered. While the price had increased, and Angelo's confessions were a lot more difficult to arrange in his current role, the relationship had served them both well and the mutual trust was a great comfort. In some perverse way, it seemed Angelo felt he was assisting in doing God's work.

CHAPTER 26

Florence, Italy – Sunday, May 27, 2012

Dozens of darting tourists continually jostled Bruce Gordon as they dodged the motorized traffic in the pedestrian route to the Uffizi Museum. Despite the road's designation, bicycles, scooters and the occasional four-wheeled vehicle weaved their way through the throng, assumedly with some form of local permission. None of this could spoil his good humour. The museum was one of his favorite places in all of Florence.

His initial irritation at Monsignor Alonso's inability to meet with him early the following week had soon passed as he contemplated a few additional days in Italy soaking up Florence's famed artworks. The city's proximity to the University of Siena, where he had completed a post-graduate degree in Art History before finalizing his studies at Oxford University in the United Kingdom, had afforded him plenty of opportunity to visit before, and he knew it well. As things now stood, he would be here until Wednesday. Plenty of time to absorb the atmosphere while enjoying the local cuisine. The place was a pasta lover's delight.

On Wednesday, he would take the express train to Rome before taking a taxi to the Vatican in time for his morning meeting with Monsignor Alonso. Only then would he attempt to secure an appointment with the cardinal whose office telephone number appeared on the shaded cross drawing. However, he would first see what he could learn from Monsignor Alonso before he asked that loaded question.

While in Rome, he would also pay one last visit to Raffaele Panzini. He had already spoken to Raffaele by telephone and, after telling him of his plans to visit Florence, they had agreed that early Wednesday would be the best time to meet. During the call, Raffaele had confirmed that he had no further information about the sketches or the numbers at the bottom of the drawing of the shaded cross, although he promised to look at them again when Dr. Gordon visited just to make sure. He reiterated that had sent all the material he had in his possession and did not feel there was anything more he could add. In fact, he went on to say, he had not kept a single copy of any of the documents, as they had no value to him in his business. They were also not the sort of memento that he needed to remember his father or grandfather. He had plenty of other working drawings of items that they had produced. If the drawings were useful to Dr. Gordon, he should feel free to use them as he wished.

#

Although Raffaele could not possibly have known it at the time, the decision to pass all the information to Dr. Gordon and not keep any copies probably saved his life.

CHAPTER 27

Hamilton, Bermuda – Monday, May 28, 2012

Peter looked carefully at the young woman sitting on the other side of his desk. Immaculately dressed, she was very different from the unsure and nervous immigrant he had first met when dealing with her residency application. Despite her halting delivery, he had no reason to disbelieve her story or her motivation in bringing it to his attention.

"Let me make sure I understand this correctly," he said. "The conversation which you overheard specifically mentioned a key and my name, and the people having this conversation did not want me to find out their real interest in this key."

"Well not your name exactly," Shanice replied. "They said the 'Alexanders' so I just assumed, given their obvious importance, that you were probably one of the Alexanders. And, if not, you would likely know which Alexanders they were talking about and be able to warn them."

As he listened, Peter wished he had this information before his meeting with the delegation from the Vatican. Sure, they had parted with a great deal of money for the key, but the fact that they were hiding something made him wonder what he and his father had missed. It wasn't so much the money, they were hardly short of cash, but it bruised his ego to think that somehow they had been outsmarted or misled in all of these dealings.

"I don't suppose you overheard what their real interest was in this key or what they didn't want us to know, did you?" Peter asked in as offhand a manner as he could.

"Not really. That part of the conversation was strange. At first I thought my Italian wasn't as good as it should be, but I'm pretty sure I got it right. It just didn't make sense."

"Why was that?"

"Well, it seems the key opens a chair."

"A chair?"

"Yes, and if they can open it they will get to the ring of the fisherman."

"You mean a fisherman's ring," Peter corrected.

"That's what I thought at first, but they definitely said the ring of the fisherman. I suppose it could be a specific fisherman's ring, but I don't know why that would be so important. The only significant Ring of the Fisherman that I know of is the Pope's ring, but it can't be that because he wears it all the time."

"The Pope's ring?"

"Yes, I guess you're not Catholic. That's what they call the ring that each pope wears."

"Really," Peter said, somewhat embarrassed by his lack of religious knowledge, but now interested in the story that had been brought to his attention by a most unlikely source. Talk about paying it forward.

"That's about as much as I know," Shanice said. "It wasn't very clear but I thought I owed you something for helping me get settled in Bermuda."

"Well I'm not sure I understand it either," Peter said, not giving away that he knew who had made the remarks or that he knew anything about a key, "but I do appreciate your letting me know.

"How do you like your job?" he asked, anxious to change the subject.

"Not much, but at least it's work. I'd prefer employment in my field but I understand that is difficult on the island."

"Why don't you send me your resume," Peter suggested. "I didn't know you spoke Italian when we first met and there may be other aspects that I missed. I'll take a better look at it and see if there's anything I can suggest to help you find something different. After all, one good turn deserves another."

"Thank you, I'll do that. I hope I didn't waste your time with the information."

"Not at all. I'm not sure what it's all about, but I'll certainly keep it in mind if anything comes up."

As Shanice left his office and headed to the elevator, Peter turned to his assistant. "Anne, see if you can track down my father for me, please. Tell him it's important."

CHAPTER 28

Florence, Italy – Tuesday, May 29, 2012

Bruce Gordon couldn't be sure, but suspected he was being followed. His trained mind, long used to scanning artwork for the tiniest detail, registered everyday scenes in a similar fashion. His first inkling was becoming aware of a familiar face in the tourist crowds as he moved from site to site. Despite being densely crowded, the various convoluted display routes often resulted in backtracking while the glass display cases allowed for easy scanning of the people passing by. A single male, without the usual tourist trappings of camera or map, caught his attention at the Accademia Gallery, was again spotted at the Cathedral of Santa Maria dei Fiori and finally confirmed after a few hop on and off points on the city bus tour. The only people who knew he was in Italy were Monsignor Alonso and Raffaele Panzini and he found the repeated appearance of this suspected observer disquieting.

Alighting from the bus near his accommodation on Via L.C. Farini, Bruce Gordon walked directly there without looking back. Anyone following would likely assume he was going to the Tempio Maggiori synagogue. Built in the late 1800's, it was only two buildings from his favourite B & B. Unlocking the street door of his building with the electronic key provided to him when checking in, he crossed the entrance hall with a large Star of David patterned in its floor tiles,

THE BERMUDA KEY

and squeezed into the ancient elevator. The elevator, barely able to accommodate someone of his ample girth, still managed to trundle successfully to the second floor. Once through the electronically locked glass doors of the B&B and safely inside his room he pulled out his mobile phone, scanned for Raffaele Panzini's number and made the call.

Far from being surprised to hear from Dr. Gordon so soon before their planned meeting, Raffaele sounded quite relieved. He explained that an Angelo Mosconi, who identified himself as an *Agente scelto* in the *Polizia di Stato*, had visited him earlier the previous day. The police, he had been told, were assisting in the disappearance of the *San Pedro* cross from Bermuda. They had also questioned him at length about any involvement he may have had with Dr. Gordon. Delighted with the attention, Raffaele had happily confirmed knowing Dr. Gordon and having sent him the design papers for a very similar cross that he had found in his grandfather's papers. Unfortunately, as he told the police, he had retained nothing himself. Nonetheless, he was going to meet with Dr. Gordon early on Wednesday to review the drawings once again regarding some numbers on one of the pages. He was also able to give the police Dr. Gordon's itinerary in case *Agente* Mosconi needed to contact him before his arrival in Rome.

Thanking Raffaele for his "assistance" Bruce Gordon sat down heavily on his bed. He did not know whether Angelo Mosconi was really a member of the Italian police. What he did know was that no one from the Italian police had contacted him regarding any assistance in the investigation, and that he was now positive someone was following him. The latter activity hardly the behaviour of any police force with nothing to hide. Besides, he was not committing any crime. Quite the contrary, he was investigating a theft. The only reason he could think for anyone to be following him was someone trying to prevent him from completing his investigation. He was getting too close and they, whoever they might be, were getting nervous.

If it was the police though, or someone with access to their database, tracking his movements would have been easy. Passport registration with the police was required when checking-in at any Italian boarding house or hotel. There was only one way to find out. Bruce Gordon left his room, found the owners and, with profuse apologies for his sudden change of mind, checked out of the B&B a day early before returning to the street and settling into the waiting car he had ordered before leaving.

"Directly to Siena, Signor?" the driver asked.

"Yes please. I'd also like to confirm you have the necessary license to drive right into the centre of the town."

'Yes, sir. The office received your request for an English-speaking driver and a specific vehicle. This vehicle is registered as a taxi in Siena so we will have no problem entering the medieval city walls and travelling right to the centre. Is there a particular address where you would like to go?"

"Right now it's Piazza del Campo, but I may change my mind before we arrive."

"Okay, Signor, no problem. It's about one and one-half hours to get there but I will go as fast as I am able."

"No rush. Just stick to the speed limits and we'll be fine."

As the driver left Florence, Bruce Gordon periodically checked back over his shoulder at the following traffic but saw nothing suspicious. He looked down again at the *Trenitalia* train schedule in his lap. He would keep to his plan, tail or no tail.

Twenty-five minutes into the trip, he was woken from his light sleep by a yell from his driver who simultaneously fought to control the wildly swerving vehicle. "Idiot," he screamed at the unseen driver in the large truck that moments earlier had sped past them on the highway before abruptly cutting them off and nearly forcing them off the road.

"Apologies, Signor" the driver exclaimed, "but that lunatic could have killed us."

Anything else the driver might have been planning to say was cut off by his scream as he slammed on his brakes to avoid the truck which had braked sharply ahead of them before once again speeding off into the distance.

"What does that fool think he's doing," he asked rhetorically before again moving ahead.

As the car accelerated, Bruce Gordon again looked over his shoulder. The black vehicle following looked official. He glanced at the license plate - *Roma* and a series of numbers. It was hard to see the driver through the slightly tinted windshield but he could have sworn it was the same man from Florence. He looked at the digital face of his watch, 12:15. He could almost make the one twenty-eight train from Siena to Rome. He leaned forward and tapped the driver on the shoulder.

"I'd like you to drive through the *Fontebranda* gate, into the walled city and then out *Camollia* gate. You can drop me at the escalator that goes down to the train station. If you can get me there at exactly one fifteen there is an extra hundred Euros for you."

"Consider it done, Signor" the driver replied. "I can make it earlier if you wish. There is a quicker route."

"No." Bruce Gordon replied. "That's the route I want you to follow and I need to be there at exactly one fifteen."

As Bruce Gordon had anticipated, the *Porta Fontebranda* entrance to the medieval city was fully staffed with police ensuring only specifically licensed traffic entered. With the Siena taxi sticker clearly evident, his driver was quickly waved through, while the upraised hand of the police officer stopped large black vehicle with the Rome license plates following closely behind. Within moments, they were swallowed up by the local traffic and winding roads, the black vehicle left far behind presumably still negotiating unsuccessfully to be allowed in, as they weaved through to the opposite side of the city. Emerging from the *Porta Camollia* at twelve minutes after one, Bruce Gordon smiled as he stepped from the car.

"Thank you," he said, "close enough. When you leave, please take the most direct route back to Florence and don't stop until you get there."

Climbing from the vehicle, he thrust a wad of notes at the driver and walked as quickly as he could to the escalator that descended from the walled city to the railroad station below. Still no sign of the black car or its driver. If he could make the one twenty-eight train, he would be long gone before they could determine where he was or which route he had taken. He would need to change trains to get to Rome but that was a small inconvenience in order to avoid the unwanted scrutiny under which he now found himself. Booking into a hotel in Rome would be another story but, for the time being, he was safe.

#

It was almost five o'clock when the train reached Rome *Termini,* the bustling train station in the heart of the city. Bruce Gordon was exhausted. The events of the day and his weight were telling on him as he puffed his way toward the taxi rank located outside. It was only a short local train ride to his accommodation near the Vatican Museum but he was far too tired for any further train travel. A taxi was in order.

CHAPTER 29

Rome, Italy – Tuesday, May 29, 2012

Angelo was not happy. The Englishman had outsmarted him and that was not good for his ego. How could he possibly explain this to the cardinal? Surely, the man must have local knowledge, and what's more, he was lucky. The incident with the truck should have worked. By now, he should have been on his way to the nearest hospital with severe injuries or, if not injured, to his "destination" by the helpful driver of the large black vehicle coincidentally travelling right behind the accident.

Instead, Dr. Gordon had successfully entered the medieval walled city of Siena in a licensed vehicle leaving Angelo fuming at a patrolled entrance gate. To make matters worse, the police had insisted he park and enter the city on foot. By the time Angelo had ascended the nearby bank of escalators up to the city centre, the man was nowhere in sight and he was forced to continue his journey to Rome empty handed.

Once again, it would be necessary to call on one of his colleagues in the police department to locate this Dr. Gordon's whereabouts. Angelo frowned with displeasure. With his forced early retirement for unprofessional conduct, fewer and fewer of his former co-workers were willing to provide assistance when asked, and he was rapidly running out of favours.

There was one thing though, of which Angelo was certain. Dr. Gordon had an appointment with the Vatican archivist the following day and he was supposed to prevent that meeting. He needed to know where the Englishman was staying tonight and he needed the information urgently. If he couldn't locate him before morning, he would have to intercept him on his way to the home of Raffaele Panzini. The goldsmith had said he was meeting Dr. Gordon at nine o'clock on Wednesday morning and Angelo had to assume that was before the insurance investigator's meeting at the Vatican. Nobody in the Vatican started work before nine in the morning.

CHAPTER 30

Rome, Italy – Tuesday, May 29, 2012

"Ah, Dr. Gordon. Welcome back. It has been a while since you last visited. May I have your passport please and we will get you checked in."

The unsuspecting receptionist had no way of knowing that Bruce Gordon did not intend to surrender his passport that night. They knew him here and, with his reputation and a few well-placed lies, he should be able to stay off any local police radar until at least this time tomorrow and after his meetings at the Vatican.

"I'm afraid that's a bit of a problem this evening," he said. Seeing the receptionist's immediate look of concern, he quickly added, "I left it at the Vatican you see, and cannot get it back until after my meeting there tomorrow."

"The Vatican?" the receptionist asked incredulously.

"Yes. Silly of me I know. I had to surrender it to get one of their audio tour handsets and ending up forgetting to return the handset and reclaim my passport before I left. I'll return it first thing tomorrow and bring you my passport then. I was hoping that would be all right, after all, you know me well and who better to be looking after my passport than the Vatican."

Whether it was because he was a known entity, or that his misplaced passport story was so outrageous, Bruce Gordon would never know, however, the next words were the most welcome he had heard in a long time.

"No problem Dr. Gordon. If you could let us have it as soon as you get it back tomorrow, we will get you registered. In the meantime, please enjoy your stay and let us know if there is anything you need."

#

Bruce Gordon sat staring at the telephone in his room. He was feeling decidedly better.

Amazing what a hot shower and change of clothes will do, he thought. *I wonder if I should call Raffaele Panzini.*

After only a moment's hesitation, he stood and left the room without making the call. Someone was trying to stop him reaching the Vatican. He would skip tomorrow's meeting with Raffaele and make his apologies later. He would instead, go straight to his meeting at the Vatican with Monsignor Alonso. He had questions that needed answering whether they were uncomfortable for the priest or not.

In the meantime, he would enjoy his evening dinner. His brain always worked better on a full stomach. He looked at the three flights of stairs leading down to the lobby, paused, and then pressed the buzzer to summon the waiting elevator.

CHAPTER 31

Tucker's Town, Bermuda –
Tuesday, May 29, 2012

"Good Evening, Peter, Fallon here."

Peter smiled. He had developed a certain fondness for this quirky friend of his father's.

"Evening, Fallon. Has something turned up?"

"No, nothing at all I'm afraid, although I was planning on heading out for another look tomorrow. I know it's short notice, but the seas are expected to be dead calm and I don't know how long it will be before we get a better day. No problem if you and Sean can't make it. Charlie and I are going out anyway."

"I know Sean is free and I'd like to go as well. Let me juggle a few things at my office and I'll get back to you first thing in the morning whether it's one or two of us. What time do you plan on leaving?"

"First light if we can. I'd like to use all the daylight available."

"Okay, Sean will be there for sure and I'll be with him if I can make it."

"Fine. Night."

Peter heard the disconnecting click before he had a chance to reply.

#

Peter and Sean arrived at the dock at six o'clock the following morning only to find the lights in Fallon's boat already on.

"Nice work, gents," said the voice from inside the cabin as they stepped aboard. "We've got about fifteen minutes before sunrise and once Charlie and Ben get back we can take off."

"Where are they?" Peter asked. "We didn't see them on our way down."

"Off somewhere along the waterfront. Ben's completing his morning ablutions."

Seeing Sean's puzzled expression, Peter grabbed his shoulder. "Don't worry, it'll all make sense in a while," he said.

#

It was early afternoon before Fallon finally determined that they had done all they could for the day. "Okay, enough," he said. "We've checked, re-checked and searched our patterns several times over and there's nothing there. We need a break. By the way Sean," he added, "good to have you on board. Despite our lack of results, your experience was invaluable."

"Thanks. The British Columbia coastline is dotted with islands, and the Marine Search and Rescue group that I belong to has unit's spread all along the coast. Although we're all volunteers, we work very closely with the regular Canadian Coast Guard. The training's pretty intense and by all accounts, the group does a really good job."

"How long have you been involved?" Peter asked.

"A little over ten years. Started at the bottom and worked my way up. We have some great equipment and the units are getting more and more sophisticated each year. The one I belong to is located in Horseshoe Bay. Same name as one of the beaches here. A lot different though. No real beaches as you know them. We also have car ferries coming and going all day long as well as an active marina. You folks have pink sand, deep-fried tourists and crystal clear water."

"What's your response time?" Fallon asked grinning broadly.

"Pretty good. When we're on call, we have to be on the boat in full gear within fifteen minutes. I've found that I can get there from home in eight minutes by motorcycle which gives me just enough time to dress."

"Another 'crazy Canuck' was how Sarah first described him to us," Peter interjected.

At the mention of Sarah, the brief moment of levity passed and the group lapsed into silence.

"I think I'll get the lunch out," Charlie said. "We need to eat. Preppy can you give me a hand?"

#

Peter looked around the deck. Fallon sat slouched against the cabin wall a water bottle in his hand, his face impenetrable behind both his white cap and black sunglasses. Charlie lay along the bench seat on the other side of the deck her legs stretched out cradling Ben who, covered in a light towel, slept soundly with his head on her bare thigh. Sean, sitting alongside Peter in the stern, stared unblinking out to sea. The remnants of their lunch littered the inside of the blue and white cooler box on the deck between them all. It was a time on board when secrets were shared and relationships admitted.

Finally, no longer able to contain himself, Peter spoke. "Can I ask you a question, Fallon?"

Fallon tilted his head to one side. From his body language, Peter seeking permission to ask a question seemed to have made him more guarded.

"Sure."

"Did you find anything else along with the *San Pedro* cross?"

"Quite a bit. What exactly were you thinking of?"

"Well, anything else that was of significant value, like the cross."

"Lots of it was valuable, and most of what we found is still in the museum. Nothing that was of similar value to the cross though. Why do you ask?"

Peter paused. All three were watching him closely now. "This is going to sound bizarre," he started, "but shortly after my mother's death we were contacted by a cardinal at the Vatican. Apparently, they had been looking for a key for some time that they thought might also have been on the same Spanish vessel. What's more, they suspected my mother had already found it."

"Cardinal Kwodo," Fallon said.

"Yes. How did you know it was him?"

"The way you phrased the question you were asked. Sounded exactly like the question we received from the Vatican shortly after one of their priests identified the *San Pedro* cross. Then, almost three years later, Cardinal Kwodo paid Maggi and me a visit. He told us they were hoping a small gold key might have been found as well. It, like the cross, had also been in the possession of Friar Roberto on board the *San Pedro*. Apparently, it's of great historical value to the Catholic Church."

"Do you know why?" Peter asked.

"No, he was quite reticent about providing any further information. Merely asked us to continue looking, and to keep the information to ourselves. We were happy to oblige. Far too many divers out here looking for things anyway, without us stirring it up further. Do you have any idea why it's so valuable?"

"I didn't when he first asked, but I believe I may have received some relevant information yesterday," Peter said.

"May I say something?" Sean interrupted.

"Can you hold that thought for a moment Sean? There's something I need to get off my chest and if I don't do it now I never will," Peter said. "And this is when its gets really strange. Apparently, Cardinal Kwodo had seen my mother's obituary notice photograph where she is wearing a necklace with a key pendant. He asked my father whether the key was from the *San Pedro* and if it was still in our possession. Neither my father nor I had any idea where my mom got the key, but the one thing we did know was that she had asked to be buried wearing it, and this is precisely what my father told Cardinal Kwodo had been done.

"Scroll forward a few months and a different cardinal arrives in Bermuda and explains that this key is of such significance to the Church they would like our permission to have my mother's body exhumed and the key given to the Vatican. They would also pay a significant sum to the family for this to take place."

"No. You couldn't," Charlie blurted out before she could stop herself. "I'm sorry," she said. "That was uncalled for."

"It's fine," Peter said. "Believe me we took quite some convincing and the money really was secondary. What's more, all three of us had to agree. To cut a long story short, they eventually convinced my dad and me that this was indeed, to quote them, 'for the greater good of the Church'. We were just waiting for Sarah's return to get her signed approval before we went ahead. Once the official search for her ended and it was presumed she had drowned, her approval was no longer needed and the exhumation took place last Thursday."

Peter paused for a moment, seemingly oblivious to the three shocked faces staring intently at him, and then continued speaking. "So they have the key and we both feel like shit for having disturbed my mother's remains. I hope to God it was really worth it to them. It certainly wasn't to us. I guess that's why I asked the question, Fallon. Do you know where she found the key and whether it's from the *San Pedro*? Cardinal Weiler, that's the one who came to see us, seemed pretty sure it was."

"No I don't," Fallon replied. "The first time I noticed the key pendant was at Kat's funeral. She may have worn it before then but I never registered. Then again I didn't see much of your parents in those intervening years."

For the longest time nobody said anything, then Sean, looking directly at Peter, broke the silence. "So Sarah's reason for changing course mid-Atlantic was to get here for this bloody exhumation."

"Yes, I'm afraid so," Peter confirmed.

"That's justice then."

"What? Why would you say that?"

"They've got the wrong fucking key. Sorry for the language. I'm just really pissed that Sarah may have died because of some religious mumbo jumbo."

"How do you know it's the wrong key?" Fallon asked now fully alert.

"Kat sent the original key to Sarah when we were in Cape Town. She also told Sarah how she had removed it from its hidden compartment in the *San Pedro* cross without anyone knowing. Sarah was supposed to keep that information to herself but shared it with me because we were getting married and she didn't want us to start our married lives with secrets. Now that they're both gone, who's going to care if I share it with you. After all, you're all involved in one way or another. The original key is probably at the bottom of the ocean again and, unless we find Sarah, we'll never know. She wore it around her neck ever since it arrived from her mother and never once took it off."

"The *San Pedro* cross had a secret compartment?" Fallon repeated, still stunned by both the revelation and the offhand nature of its delivery.

"Yeah. Apparently the back of the cross comes off and the key was hidden inside."

"Unbelievable," Fallon said. "I never knew."

"So what key does the Vatican have?" Peter asked.

"An inexact duplicate I assume," Sean replied. "The bits are different on the copy; it won't open anything. Other than that, your mother said it looks just the same. Apparently, she had it made here on the island."

"I'll be damned," Fallon said. "That finally explains what Father Despic was really looking for. It wasn't the cross after all."

"Who?" Charlie asked.

"Father Despic. The priest who came to Bermuda to authenticate the cross. We were discussing him at dinner the other evening."

"Right, I remember now."

"So where do we go from here?" Peter asked. "I'm sure my father doesn't know it's the wrong key. He would never have agreed to the exhumation if he had. It's hard to imagine that my mother didn't tell him though."

"I really don't believe she did," Sean said. "When your mother told Sarah about the key she stressed that she had never told anyone else about it; you and your dad included. She didn't say why."

"Well, assuming Sean's correct, I don't think it will be too long before you hear from the Vatican again," Fallon said. "In the interim maybe we should pool our information to avoid any further surprises. Who knows, we might even establish who stole the cross. In any event, let's wrap it up for today. We can get together again in the next day or two and invite Howard and Maggi to join us. This could get very interesting."

CHAPTER 32

Rome, Italy – Wednesday, May 30, 2012

It was nine-thirty in the morning and Angelo was getting impatient. To make matters worse, Raffaele kept pacing around the room.

"Please, Signor Panzini. Sit. You are making me nervous."

"My apologies *Agente* Mosconi but I do not understand why Dr. Gordon is not here. We had arranged to meet promptly at nine o'clock. He said he had other meetings to attend afterwards."

"Do you know where?"

"No. he never said, but I am sure they must be related to his investigation. He asked many questions and I had few answers. I had given him all the papers we had in the shop and I kept no copies."

"So you said before."

"Yes. I am sorry to repeat myself."

"It does not matter. I should probably leave now but I would like you to call me if he does return."

Tearing a page from his pocket notebook, Angelo carefully wrote his phone number on the page and handed it to Raffaele. He was not concerned with anyone tracing the number later. It belonged to a pre-paid mobile phone that he would discard as soon as his current assignment was complete.

#

As Angelo drove away, he watched in the rear view mirror as Raffaele closed the door without giving a second look at the vehicle he was driving.

Good, he thought.

No suspicions seemed to have been aroused in the goldsmith and he had no reason to return. It was clear that Raffaele had no further useful information. The number he had left would be inoperative as soon as he discarded the phone and he could deny knowing Raffaele if ever questioned in the future. It would be his word against the goldsmith's that they had ever met. He was an old hand at this sort of thing and knew he could comfortably deal with such an event. Besides, it was highly improbable it would ever come to that.

His challenge now was to get to this Dr. Gordon before the Englishman got to Cardinal Cressey. His police contacts said that no hotel had registered Dr. Gordon's passport, which made things a little more difficult but not impossible. If necessary, he would pick up the trail at the Vatican. That might not make the cardinal very happy, but he had little alternative at this point.

#

Angelo would have felt far less comfortable had he been able to overhear the conversation Bruce Gordon was having with Monsignor Alonso at that very moment.

"So my friend," Monsignor Alonso said. "You have discovered some drawings which you believe are of the fake cross in the Bermuda Maritime Museum, and with which you think I can help. I'm not sure how or why you think so, but I am certainly willing to try."

"Well, it's like this. The drawings, which by the way are exact working drawings of the fake cross, appear to have been made by the grandfather, or father, of one of your local goldsmiths. I know that doesn't necessarily guarantee a connection but you must admit it would be quite hard to imagine such a thing being mere coincidence."

"And what did the goldsmith say? I assume you have spoken with him."

"That's where it gets a bit difficult. You see, both his father and grandfather are deceased. He apparently had no knowledge of these drawings until he found them in his grandfather's papers and sent them to me."

"Why would he have done that?" Monsignor Alonso asked.

"I had called to see his father during my initial investigation only to find he had been tragically killed in a truck accident shortly before my visit. I left my card and the nature of my enquiry with Raffaele Panzini and his mother in case they ever heard any news about the cross."

"That is the name of this goldsmith, Panzini?"

"Yes."

"And why had you called on his father? There are many goldsmiths in Italy. Surely you did not call on all of them?"

"No, you are correct. I selected only those who might have done work for the Vatican. As the original *San Pedro* cross was a pectoral cross, I speculated that the thieves might have sought out a goldsmith who was skilled in their manufacture to make a copy. My assumption was that someone who did work for the Vatican would likely have those necessary skills. I also assumed that the thief, or thieves, would not likely have admitted the real reason for such a request."

"I see, and how do you think I can help you now that you have these drawings?"

"You'll notice that there's no reference anywhere on the drawings showing for whom they were made. Raffaele Panzini has confirmed that he does not have that information either. What puzzles me most though is this one particular drawing. Well, it's more of a sketch actually."

Bruce Gordon stretched across the archivist's desk and handed him the shaded cross drawing.

"There are no dimensions annotated on this, it's a simple shaded sketch of the same cross."

"What makes you think it's the same?" Monsignor Alonso asked.

"Two things actually. One, the outline is identical and two, it was apparently found together with the other scale drawings of the cross."

"I can accept that, but how can I help?"

"It's this number on the bottom of the page," Bruce Gordon replied. "It seems it's the direct phone number of a Cardinal Cressey and I wondered if I could meet with him to see what he might know about this drawing, or why his phone number is there. I thought you might be able to arrange such a meeting for me."

#

"He wanted what!" Cardinal Cressey exclaimed. The rhetorical question left hanging in the air as Monsignor Alonso struggled to articulate his reply.

"A meeting Eminence," Monsignor Alonso repeated, "but I believe I have dissuaded him from that course of action."

"And how, may I ask, did you achieve that?"

"I assured him that your telephone number written in such a manner on the bottom of a drawing of a pectoral cross would likely be mere coincidence. Perhaps the goldsmith received a call from your office about another matter and merely wrote the number on the nearest piece of paper in order to call back. I believe we have all done that at some time or other."

"Quite correct," a relieved Cardinal Cressey replied, quickly grasping the offered excuse and grateful for not having to directly lie to his colleague. "That is surely what happened. Where is this Dr. Gordon now?" he asked.

"I believe he is touring the Vatican museum, Eminence. I informed him that rather than trying to establish a meeting in your busy schedule, I would check with you that you had no knowledge of these drawings or why your office number was written on them, and give him a call to confirm later."

"And this satisfied him?"

"I believe so, Eminence. In any event, he accepted my proposal and indicated he would visit the museum while he awaited my call."

"Thank you, Monsignor. You have saved me from wasting valuable time with this investigator's speculations. I must say I am surprised he is still looking into the disappearance of that cross. It was stolen many years ago if I remember correctly."

Monsignor Alonso smiled at this last remark before answering.

"Indeed, you are correct. Unfortunately for us, Dr. Gordon has a well-earned reputation as, what the English call, a bulldog. He is quite persistent in his investigations. I thought as he is getting on in years he would have changed his ways by now, but it seems that this is not the case. Thank you for your time, Eminence. I will call him on my return to my office and that should be the end of it."

#

"Angelo?"

"*Si*"

"He is here."

"A thousand apologies, Eminence. It should not have happened but he managed to evade me in Siena."

"Siena?"

"It is a long story Eminence, but I will make sure this time. I am already at the main exit from the Vatican. I will see him when he comes out. He is not difficult to notice."

"And yet you lost him in Siena?"

"As I said, Eminence, it is a long story. He will not get away this time."

"Very well, but you will likely lose him if you stay there. He is at the Vatican museum and may well leave through that exit. It is at least a ten-minute walk from where you are at St. Peter's square. Do you know where he is staying?"

"No. He has not registered his passport yet. He may be staying with friends and, if not, my police sources are checking regularly for its registration."

"Will that not compromise you if something should happen to him?"

"Please, Eminence. Do not worry. I will take care of this matter. I have another plan and there will be no trace."

CHAPTER 33

Vatican City – Wednesday, May 30, 2012

To say that Cardinal Cressey was irritated would have been a major understatement. He had envisaged reporting to the Silenti of Dr. Gordon's unfortunate demise en route to the Vatican to visit with the archivist. Instead, he was forced to reveal that Ugo Panzini's scale drawings of the fake cross not only existed, but also had been found along with what he presumed must have been grandfather Panzini's sketch of the original cross before he removed the black paint. What Cardinal Cressey neglected to mention to the Silenti was that his direct office telephone number was written on the latter document.

He had wondered at the time about the wisdom of going back to Ugo Panzini with the task of removing the paint from the stolen original but ultimately the care required for its removal from such a valuable object had been enough to convince him otherwise. It was Ugo who had suggested that if Cardinal Cressey did not want him to undertake the work himself that it be offered to his father, a retired goldsmith. A suggestion, which Cardinal Cressey readily accepted after Ugo's assurance that he would trust his father with his life to keep the matter confidential. While still a little uncomfortable with the arrangement, Cardinal Cressey had always trusted that the two men would not find it necessary to compare specific details of the respective crosses on which they had each worked. What he had failed to envision was that with their deaths, their papers would have found their way into the hands of Dr. Gordon.

The whole thing was becoming a nightmare, he thought. *Angelo had better not let him down.*

#

Like Cardinal Cressey, Cardinal Weiler had no better news. He reported to the Silenti that there was now no doubt in either his or Cardinal Vilicenti's minds that they had the wrong key. He would need to re-visit the Alexanders to secure the original key or, at worst, have the Vatican's money returned. He had no idea how an exchange could have been made without anyone seeing but, he assured his colleagues, one way or another he would find out.

Happy to distance themselves from what was rapidly becoming a major fiasco, the remaining members of the Silenti agreed to reconvene when either Cardinal Cressey or Cardinal Weiler had something further to report.

CHAPTER 34

Vatican City – Wednesday, May 30, 2012

Bruce Gordon stood looking at the duplicate "Chair of St. Peter", safely housed in its glass case in the Vatican Museum. Unlike the original, it had suffered no damage from either vandals or time. He had chosen this spot, not because the chair held any special significance for him, but rather because its location deep within the museum and well away from the usual hordes of tourists afforded him an unobstructed view of anyone following. From his current vantage point, he could look directly through the glass case and down the only access corridor to this section of the museum. Additionally, to any outside observer he would appear merely as another tourist absorbed in studying an exact replica of one of the most famous relics in Vatican history.

Much to his relief there was no sign of anyone following. Both his visit to Monsignor Alonso, and his stated intention to visit the Museum, seemed to have escaped any unwanted attention.

He had only spoken to two people about his intended visit to the Vatican: Raffaele Panzini and Monsignor Alonso. Of the two, he was confident, based on Raffaele's surprise at the visit from *Agente* Mosconi, that Raffaele was not the reason he was being followed. It had to be on instructions from either Monsignor Alonso or someone he had told. The only other person who, if he wasn't aware of the visit before, would certainly know once Monsignor Alonso made his enquiries, was this Cardinal Cressey.

Bruce Gordon decided he would stay in the museum a little longer. At least to give Monsignor Alonso as much time as possible to call after his meeting with the cardinal. If that took too long and he did leave, he wouldn't go far. Despite the archivist's comments to the contrary, there was always the possibility that the cardinal might wish to meet and, if that occurred, he wanted to be available at a moment's notice.

CHAPTER 35

Vatican City – Wednesday, May 30, 2012

Angelo Mosconi stood alongside the newspaper stand at the exit from the Vatican museum his right hand cupping a mobile phone, which he pressed tightly against his ear. With a sheaf of papers clenched in his other hand he looked just like all the other tour guides trying desperately to gather their loosely gathered groups. Even to a more critical observer his worried expression would only have suggested a lost tour party or perhaps some scheduling issue. In reality the reason for his concern was the report from his partner, still positioned in the street outside St. Peter's Square, that he too had not seen any sign of the Englishman.

"We will give him another hour," Angelo said before disconnecting the call and breathing a deep sigh. He was tired of this cat and mouse game. One more hour and then they would have to assume they had missed him again.

#

Bruce Gordon bustled along the museum corridor. Cardinal Cressey's message, as delivered by Monsignor Alonso, playing repeatedly in his head as he walked.

Yes, the elder Signor Panzini had done work for the Vatican in the past. No, he had no idea why his telephone number was written on a shaded drawing of a pectoral cross and no, he saw no point in meeting Dr. Gordon, as he could shed no further light on the matter.

He wasn't entirely sure why, but the message irritated him. Perhaps it was the terse nature of the response and yet those were the answers to the very questions he had asked. Maybe because they were almost identical to the answers which Monsignor Alonso had suggested earlier. Whatever the reason, he was annoyed and, because of that, distracted as he rushed through the museum along magnificent vaulted corridors toward the Sistine Chapel. Reaching the Borgia Tower he deviated from the traditional tourist route and, hurrying along a little used corridor, exited the building into St. Peter's Square.

#

Had Bruce Gordon not changed his route, he would have passed through the Sistine Chapel and into St. Peter's Basilica, before exiting from the Vatican's main exit surrounded by hundreds of tourists following the same path. Instead, he exited alone and off to one side, unknowingly facilitating his easy identification by *Agente* Mosconi's partner as he hurried from the building.

#

"I have him," was all Angelo heard as he answered his ringing phone.

"He is with you?"

"No, I am following."

"Are you sure it is him."

"Yes. He is alone and carrying an old leather briefcase. We are now at the street."

"Can you get him into your taxi?"

"I can try but there are many tourists. What shall I do if he will not come?"

"Follow him and let me know where he goes. I am on my way to you now. Call me back when you have him."

Replacing his mobile phone in his pocket the two hundred and eighty pound, six foot five inch, man picked up his pace until he was alongside Bruce Gordon.

"Taxi, Signor?" he asked.

"No. It's fine. I'm not going far."

"But, Signor, it is too hot to walk."

"No thank you. I'm fine."

Dino Ricci was renowned for his physical size and strength, not his power of thought. Acutely aware that, rightly or wrongly, failure to get the Englishman into his waiting taxi would incur Angelo's wrath, he did the next best thing he could think of at short notice. He snatched the leather briefcase and ran as fast as he could through the ambling crowds. Despite Bruce Gordon's cries of "stop thief", no one took up the chase of the very large man whose lengthy strides quickly carried him beyond reach.

With the only proof regarding the Vatican's possible connection to the fake cross carefully stowed in that very same briefcase, Bruce Gordon, hampered by years of overindulgence, tried desperately to follow Dino. Two blocks later, still surrounded by dozens of tourists either going to, or coming from, the Vatican, he realized that further pursuit was pointless. The man was long gone and his heart was hammering in his chest. He needed to sit down.

Moving to a nearby low stone bench, he sat on its edge. He wasn't feeling too good. Things were getting out of hand. He should call Andrew Jensen and see if he had kept copies of the drawings. Reaching into his pocket, he took out his mobile phone. Damn...no entry for Andrew Jensen...he hadn't entered Andrew's number. What was the name of the Bermudian police officer again? Thomas. That was right, Rhiannon Thomas. He scrolled through his contacts. There it was. Pressing "dial" he waited and finally heard a distant ringing. Double damn. Voicemail. Finally a request to leave a message, then the beep.

"Rhiannon. Hello. Bruce Gordon here. Listen, I may lose this call. Not feeling very well. Check with Andrew Jensen about some drawings of the fake cross. Must go. Chest hurts."

Cutting off the call, he tried to dial 112. Passers-by were looking at him strangely. He felt a sharp pain in his chest that seemed to radiate down his left arm. Even his jaw seemed sore. Something wasn't right. Forget the cross. He needed help.

He was sweating now and felt like vomiting. His fingers seemed to have minds of their own. It was hard to punch the keys. As he slumped from the bench, Bruce Gordon saw people moving towards him and then, thankfully, all went dark.

#

Angelo stood off to one side looking at the crowd forming around the Englishman. Something had happened to the man. He was lying on the ground and seemed to have had an attack of some sort.

No wonder, Angelo thought, *he was very overweight.*

He pressed forward. There were several people bent over Dr. Gordon. One of whom kept shaking his head. Then the man stood and announced "*E' inutile. Lui è morto.*"

Angelo was stunned. Dr. Gordon had died. This was not good. Too many trails led back to him and his questions. He had to find Dino and ask what had transpired. Reaching for his phone, he walked quickly away from the growing crowd.

#

Angelo entered the confessional in the small church located just outside the Vatican walls and placed an old brown leather briefcase on the seat. The church was closed when he arrived, although he had no trouble opening the large entrance doors that remained unlocked as if expecting his visit.

"It is done," he said looking at the privacy screen.

"Without trouble?" was the enquiry from the other side.

"Yes, he seems to have suffered a heart attack."

"He has died?"

"Yes. I have his briefcase."

"What is inside?"

"I have not looked. It is here with me. I will leave it behind."

"You have done well, my son. Go now and I will be in touch."

Angelo rose and left both the confessional and the church without once looking back. As he exited the main doors, a scarlet robed figure emerged from the other side of the confessional booth, retrieved the briefcase, and left the church through a side entrance.

CHAPTER 36

Hamilton, Bermuda – Friday, June 1, 2012

Fallon looked down at the construction site directly across the road below. Like his own office, the window of the conference room of Whyte, Alexander & Hodgkins faced directly toward the inner harbour from its location on the fourth floor of the Belvedere Building on Pitts Bay Road

"Looks like you're losing your view, Howard," he said.

"Yes. Too bad really. Ever since they demolished the Waterloo House, I've been waiting to see what would go up in its place. You must have a similar issue from your office."

"I do, but the angle is different. I'm hoping they leave a view corridor so I can still see the water."

"Pity, isn't it. Waterloo House had been there since about 1812. I thought they'd knock down our building before that one."

"Me too," Fallon said before switching topics. "The others should be here any moment now. Is there anything we should cover off before they get here?"

"I don't think so. This meeting is a good idea. I don't plan to hold anything back. Peter filled me in on the discussion you had on the boat. After hearing that, I can't help but think that if it hadn't been for my demand that you break off your relationship with Kat, things would have turned out a lot differently."

"Perhaps, but who could have known," Fallon replied. "Your motives were understandable at the time. I don't think we need to air that issue at the meeting, do you?"

"No, you're right. Thanks for that. Is Maggi coming?"

Before Fallon could answer, the elevator, located directly outside the glass walled conference room, opened to disgorge the ebullient threesome of Sean, Charlie and Peter. With identical Buzz coffee cups in hand, they entered the conference room all trying to speak at the same time.

"Whoa," Howard said. "Slow down, please. What's got you lot so excited."

"They found Sarah's survival suit," Peter blurted. "Maggi just called us."

"Maggi?" Fallon repeated. "How would Maggi know that? And why wouldn't she call me?"

"She tried, and so did they," Charlie replied. "You didn't answer the marine radio in your office when they called or your mobile phone when Maggi tried. They had reached her on the marine radio at your house."

Fallon reached instinctively for his mobile remembering as he did so that he had left it on his desk when he joined Howard in the conference room. "Damn, my phone's on my desk. Who called Maggi?"

"Some banker from his boat," Charlie said. "Mags said you would know him. The boat's called the *Osprey*. He's on his way to Newport for the start of the Newport Bermuda race. Mags was on her way here when she called us, she should be here momentarily."

"This is good news, right?" Peter asked.

"Not necessarily," Sean said looking at Fallon, his eyes pleading for support.

"It certainly is in helping us find her," Fallon said trying to find some way of gently lowering everyone's expectations. "Nevertheless, I have to agree with Sean; Sarah's survival suit by itself raises other concerns as to why she wasn't wearing it. We really need to speak to the *Osprey* crew."

"Why don't we all move to your office and call them now, Fallon?" Howard suggested. "We can reconvene here when we're done."

"Okay," Fallon replied. "As soon as Maggi gets here we'll get whatever other details she has and make the call to the *Osprey*. The boat belongs to Barry Smythe now. She used to belong to his father. Do you know him, Howard?"

"I do. He has a bit of a cavalier attitude to things in general. Would you trust the information he gives you?"

"In this case, yes. He's an ass in many ways but I'm sure on this one he'll go out of his way to be accurate. Besides, one of his crew, a fellow by the name of Ivor Thomas, used to be a New York detective. I'm really hoping he'll be able to give us whatever critical details are available. Barry will be fine for location coordinates, but what I really want are any observations Ivor may have about the suit."

The door to the conference room opened and Maggi walked in. "Sorry I'm late," she said dropping into the first seat she reached before looking directly at Fallon, "I assume you've heard the news by now."

"Yes. We were just waiting for you to arrive before we called the *Osprey*. Do you have any other information besides that they've retrieved Sarah's suit?"

"Nothing. I assumed you would call them as soon as you got the news. Where's your mobile phone by the way?"

"Left it on my desk," Fallon replied. "Sorry about that. I'll get it as soon as we're done here."

#

On board the *Osprey*, Barry Smythe and his crew deliberated their options. While a few hours delay would not materially change their plans, they were anxious to continue on their set course to Newport. It was more than twenty years since they had hired Fallon to whip them into shape for their first ever Newport Bermuda race and their sailing abilities had improved markedly. Weather permitting they could easily make up any lost time if they needed to wait for someone to pick up the survival suit. For the moment though, they were content to let the fifty-foot sailboat sit in irons until Fallon returned their call. Based on their conversation with Maggi they knew that wouldn't be for more than half an hour at the most.

"What do you think, Ivor," Barry asked. "Do they need the suit?"

"Not much to tell from it other than the cuts," Ivor replied. "If her name hadn't been written on the collar we wouldn't even have known it was hers."

"There's some jagged tearing there as well," Barry said.

"Yes, I noticed that. It's a wild guess, but I'd say her suit snagged somewhere and she had to cut herself free. I can't imagine any other reason you'd abandon your best chance of survival. Hell, it's both warm and it floats."

"If that's the case, what about blood? There's none on the suit."

"Even if there was initially," Ivor replied, "the sea would have washed it out pretty quickly, and it's been in the sea for weeks now. Don't give up your day job, boyo; banking's definitely more your style."

The discussion terminated as their marine radio suddenly squawked to life.

#

Fallon and the group were once again assembled in the conference room of Howard's law office. Their call with the crew of the *Osprey* was over and, between Barry Smythe and Ivor Thomas, they now had the exact coordinates of where Sarah's survival suit was found and a detailed description of the damage to the suit itself. They had also arranged to have a nearby fishing vessel retrieve the suit from the *Osprey* and return it to the Bermuda Marine Police. Ivor Thomas would wrap it up to avoid any possible further contamination. This mid-ocean pick-up would allow the *Osprey* to resume her journey in plenty of time to make the start to the Newport Bermuda race and get the suit into the hands of the appropriate authorities as quickly as possible.

"I know it's your office, Howard," Fallon said, "but perhaps I could kick things off."

"That's probably appropriate," Howard replied. "After all you found the cross in the first place."

"Let's deal with this morning's news first and then I think we should go over all the events leading up to where we are now. If Sean's correct, and Sarah has the key which the Vatican want, there may be others equally keen to find her."

"But why wait?" Peter asked. "Surely we should be out searching as soon as we can. We can't afford to waste time."

"Steady, son," Howard interrupted. "I think we all know that only a miracle would have kept Sarah alive up to this point. I'm as anxious to find her as you are but we'll need a careful review of winds and currents to work backward to where her survival suit might have gone overboard before we start searching again. A few hours at this end won't make much difference. Correct, Fallon?"

"Correct."

"I agree," Sean added. "I want to find her as much as you do Pete, but your dad's right. In my experience, detailed analysis is definitely necessary before we go out again. Sad to say, but a few extra hours delay won't hurt Sarah at this point."

"Okay," Fallon said. "Let's get on with it. First this morning's news. Once we are done here, I suggest Sean and I go over the charts and all the historical weather data we can lay our hands on to see if we can come up with a probable drift route for the suit. We should, by a series of plots, also be able to determine where the suit was abandoned on the day Sarah's emergency signal was received. Starting there, we can search along the probable route and even dive some of the more likely spots as we move along."

"What do you want me to do in the meantime?" Peter asked.

"If you're available and don't have to work, and this goes for you too Charlie, I'd like you to get the boat ready for another trip. When

Sean and I have finished, we'll call everyone and arrange to go out. I don't think there's too much to be done on the boat so, if you finish early, come and join Sean and me at my house."

Fallon looked at Peter and Charlie as he finished speaking. Both nodded in acquiescence at the proposed plan.

"Right, second item," Fallon said. "I know it's hard given the recent news but, if we can all try to put that aside for now, let's go over what we know. As we go through feel free to jump in with any information you have that might be of interest to the group."

Four faces stared at Fallon without speaking.

"How about I start," he said. "It was 1985, and the diving business was barely breaking even. Howard was the company's lawyer even back in those days and Kat had joined after university. She and I were out searching an area where our anchor had fouled on an earlier trip. It always intrigues me if the anchor snags unexpectedly. My first thought is that it's debris from a wreck."

"Ever the optimist," Maggi said smiling.

"Well this time it was justified. Kat was on the boat when I brought up the *San Pedro* cross and I don't recall it ever being out of my sight after that."

Fallon paused, thoughts of Kat naked in the boat cabin running through his head.

"Well anyway, not for more than a few minutes at most," he corrected. "After we docked, I took the cross home and gave it to Maggi. She, or the museum, have pretty well had custody of it ever since."

"Not so fast," Maggi said. She looked over at Peter, Sean and Charlie. "In case you three don't know, I worked for the museum at the time and the cross was in my custody until we sold it to the Bermuda government. After that it was in the custody of the museum although, as the curator, it was still ultimately my responsibility."

"So when did it disappear?" Charlie asked.

"Actually, that was part of the problem. It never really disappeared at a specific time," Maggi replied. "Sometime in the next nine years, between 1985 and 1994, a fake was substituted for the original. The switch wasn't discovered until the Queen's visit to the island when Fallon was asked to show her the cross."

"So where's the original and where's the fake?" Sean asked.

"The original's still missing," Maggi replied, "and the fake is on display in the museum. I should add that I was paranoid about it being stolen and had all sorts of security and cameras to help protect it, but to no avail."

"She wouldn't even let Jacob Despic, that's the priest who came to authenticate it, look at it alone," Fallon added. "Maggi didn't seem to trust him. Not sure why." He looked at Maggi as if waiting for her to comment on this observation.

"No I didn't. Just a feeling," Maggi said blushing slightly as she recalled Father Jake Despic, respected Vatican representative and, unbeknown to anyone present, her former lover. "But I never did let him look at it alone, so I'm pretty confident it wasn't him. Besides, priests are not usually also thieves."

"Are you absolutely sure, Maggi?" Howard asked. "Kat said she had a plan to help Father Despic get to look at the cross in private. She always said she didn't believe his story about secret markings and felt that there must be another reason he needed to see it without anyone else being present. Now that we know from Sean that Kat had found its secret compartment, maybe she had already opened the cross and removed the key. If my assumption's correct, she would also know that he wouldn't find it when he looked."

"Why would she want to help him without telling us?" Maggi asked.

"Money," Howard replied without hesitation. "He offered Kat a significant amount in order to get access to the cross alone." While Howard also knew that Kat had encouraged Jake's offer, he deemed it prudent to say nothing about it at this time.

"Did you know what she was doing?" Fallon asked.

"No. She insisted I stay out of it and, as you know, she was pretty strong-willed. All she told me was that the priest wanted to examine it by himself, and she had a plan to help him. I didn't know then about any secret compartment, or that she may have taken the key out of it. I must now assume that she already had the key when she spoke to me. That's why she was so certain that the cross was in no danger and that all Father Despic wanted to do was open it and take the key; which of course she had already done."

As Maggi listened to Howard, she remembered her own breathless encounter with Kat in the elevator, which, to her knowledge, was the only time the priest could have had brief and unobserved access to the cross alone. Could that have been Kat's plan all along? Although, if she remembered correctly, even then its display case had been partially locked.

"I can only think of one occasion when I was with Kat that there might have been an opportunity," Maggi said. "Nonetheless, even on that occasion, the display case containing the cross was locked with one of its two keys. The priest would have had to have had access to that key to get into the case."

Perhaps he did, Howard thought, remembering how he had told Kat of Montell Lightbourne's keys hanging below his desk.

"Wow, this is getting pretty interesting," Peter said, "and here I was thinking you lot were a staid bunch of senior citizens."

"Permission to keelhaul the cabin boy, Captain," Howard said.

"Granted," Fallon replied, grateful for the lighthearted interruption.

"Okay. Seriously though," Peter said, "what I now understand is you three think that my mom opened the cross and took the key sometime before Fallon gave it to Maggi. Once Maggi had the cross, my mother is supposed to have helped this priest get to see it in private. When he was alone, she assumed he would try to steal the key from the secret compartment. Which, of course, we now suspect she had already done. At that point, the priest would find it was already gone and leave empty handed. As well as a few dollars short."

"That about sums it up," Howard said.

"If the priest was prepared to steal the key from the cross," Peter said, "what's to say he wouldn't steal the entire cross, especially when he discovered the key was missing?"

"Nothing," Maggi replied, "but to do that he would have had to come already prepared with a fake cross."

In a plain, brown, paper wrapper, she suddenly thought, remembering how Jake had explained away the image of the cross on a brown wrapper she picked up from the floor of the display room. Caused by him holding the original to examine it earlier, he had said. He had also been very quick to retrieve the wrapper from her. Although she had dismissed any suspicions she may have had at the time, things were taking on a very different perspective now. Besides, what about Kat helping the priest? That was a surprise and probably explained her unexpected behaviour in the elevator.

"So where do we go from here?" Sean asked, breaking the silence. "I know the information Sarah got from Kat is fact, but the rest sounds like a fair amount of speculation."

"Not entirely" Fallon said. "Let's look at the things we know for sure. One, the original *San Pedro* cross was stolen. Two, it was replaced with a very fine replica. Three, based on what Sean has said, Kat found a secret compartment in the cross and removed a key that she wore around her neck for many years. Four, the Vatican was willing to pay Kat so that Father Despic could have access to the cross alone and yet, to my knowledge, they have never commented on the subsequent theft or that there was something missing from the cross. Five, and finally, they seemed pretty sure that the key which Kat wore around her neck was, to use their words, of great significance to the Church."

"If those assumptions are correct," Howard said, "we should be hearing from them pretty soon."

"Why is that?" Charlie asked.

"*Cui bono.*"

"Thanks." Charlie smiled. "That's helpful."

"Sorry," Howard replied, "just showing off, but the Latin phrase says it best. It means 'to whose benefit'. If we take Fallon's point, the Vatican have made no comment about paying Kat for access to the cross even though we assume they found nothing there that they wanted. If that was you or me we would probably have complained bitterly."

"Unless you took the cross in exchange for your payment," Fallon said.

"Exactly," Howard replied.

"But that's stealing," Charlie protested.

"True," Howard said, "but as the payments were substantial in both cases I have to assume there's much more at stake here than that of which we are aware and, whatever it is, it's important to the Vatican. Consequently, this time, once they find they have the wrong key, I believe they will be back."

"What will they want?" Charlie asked.

"Either the right key or their money back, I would imagine. Option one is, of course, not possible, the other I'm still considering. I also need to discuss that option with Peter alone, but I don't plan to do anything until we hear from them. It's really their move now. I just wish we knew more about the value to them of both the cross and the key."

"I think I can help on the latter question," Peter said. I know you're going to find the source of this is hard to accept, but hear me out before making any judgement."

#

It took quite some time, but eventually Peter felt he had covered most of the highlights of his association and conversation with Shanice Morgan. In particular, how she came to overhear the discussion regarding the key and why she had taken that information to Peter.

Fallon sat quietly throughout Peter's delivery. He thrived on this stuff. Seemingly oblivious to the unbelievable odds of what he had just heard happening, he was content to accept the events simply as the hand of fate. After all, this was how he had made most of his important diving discoveries, hard work and then a stroke of seemingly blind luck. He was just about to air these thoughts when Maggi spoke.

"Well, I don't understand the part about the key opening a chair, but my Catholic roots suggest that the Ring of the Fisherman is, as your informant says, either this, or a former pope's ring. Every pope has an episcopal ring made on his election, known as the Ring of the Fisherman. They wear it until their death when it's destroyed and their successor has their own ring created."

"I assume that's the one everyone kisses," Charlie added.

"Correct."

"But what about the chair?" Peter asked.

"This is a real guess," replied Maggi, "but the most significant chair that I know of within the Catholic faith is the Chair of St. Peter. However, it's unlikely to be that one, as it's on display in St. Peter's Basilica in Rome. It's also enclosed in an enormous bronze sculpture designed by Gian Lorenzo Bernini in the 1600's."

"Wow. I'm impressed," Charlie said. "How did you know all that off the top of your head?"

Maggi laughed. "Some from childhood and some from my general research work," she replied, "but thanks for the compliment."

"Even if we ignore the part about the key opening a chair," Fallon interjected, "it seems reasonably certain that the key is somehow linked to some serious artifact within the Vatican."

"That's the first thing that went through my mind when Peter told me about Shanice Morgan's visit to his office," Howard said. "Although I didn't have the information then that Maggi has now given us, Shanice's comments and the importance that Cardinal Weiler placed on retrieving the key from Kat's necklace made me realize it probably has far greater significance to the Church than we originally believed."

"Or were led to believe," Peter suggested. "So what now?" he asked.

"It's my guess that if the key doesn't fit," Fallon said, "Cardinal Weiler will be back. He doesn't know you don't have the original and will probably assume you switched the keys for some reason or another. I suggest you don't say anything and wait to see what he does. In the meantime, we can continue our search for Sarah. There's nothing more we can do about the key at this stage anyway, unless we find Sarah first."

"I agree," Howard said with barely a pause between Fallon's last words and his own agreement. "I'd also like to add," he continued ruefully, "that despite the circumstances it is nice to all be working together again."

#

After making the necessary arrangements to resume the search, Fallon rose to leave and looked around the table. Howard, Peter and Sean were still actively engaged in a discussion while Charlie sat quietly off to one side, her eyes fixed on the group. Maggi sat immobile staring straight ahead and seemingly lost in thought.

"I'm off, Maggi," Fallon said. "See you at home. Do you need a ride Charlie, or will you go back with Maggi?"

At the mention of Charlie's name, Peter broke off from his conversation and looked over at her. "I can give you a ride home if you like," he offered. "We're almost done here."

Charlie smiled and nodded at Peter, before replying to Fallon.

"Thanks anyway, but don't worry about me. I'll get a ride from Peter."

CHAPTER 37

Hamilton, Bermuda – Friday, June 1, 2012

Maggi walked along Pitts Bay Road toward Rhiannon's downtown apartment her mobile phone pressed tightly against her ear in an effort to reduce the noise of the passing traffic. She wanted to talk to Rhiannon while the details were still fresh in her mind. It was already difficult trying to recall what she may have told her about the key in the past. These were the moments that she hated her double life. Maybe she should follow Fallon and Howard's example and come clean about their relationship. Everything would be much easier once the truth was out.

What's more, as the recent group discussion with Howard and his family had proved, when all available information was shared it was amazing what might be revealed. In that particular case, it had been a veritable jigsaw puzzle where each one of them held several pieces. Only by sharing in its assembly did they get to see the whole picture.

Ten minutes later, Maggi arrived at the apartment and knocked. Her hand was still raised from knocking when Rhiannon opened the door. "I came as soon as I got your message," she said. "I was only a couple of blocks away. What's wrong?"

"Nothing's wrong. It's just that I heard an amazing series of seemingly unrelated events which when pieced together might give you a completely new avenue for your investigation into the disappearance of the *San Pedro* Cross. I wanted to speak to you before I forgot something."

"The *San Pedro* Cross, really? That was eons ago."

"Yes, I know, but wait until I tell you what I learned. After that, you decide what, if anything, you want to do with the information."

"All right. I'll make a couple of calls and free up some time right now, then we can talk. Why don't you pour us something to drink in the meantime? I'll meet you on the patio in a couple of minutes."

#

Maggi was well into passing along the new information about the cross and the key before she remembered that the woman she loved and trusted was also a Bermuda police officer, sworn to uphold the laws of the country. What if Rhiannon felt there was something criminal in the potential sale of the key Katherine Alexander had removed from the cross? Her fears were quickly alleviated when, on raising the topic, Rhiannon responded in a thoughtful but dismissive manner.

"That did concern me at first but, as far as I can tell, no one really knows whether Katherine Alexander's key is in fact another ancient relic or something else entirely. At this point, all we know is that the Vatican bought a key that belonged to Mrs. Alexander. Nothing wrong with that. I'm more interested in the Vatican's possible connection to the theft of the cross. I'd like to get Bruce Gordon's opinion and I'll call him first thing tomorrow. He's four hours ahead of us so he'll be well into his day by that time. It will also give me more time to go over the facts with you again so that I don't inadvertently divulge anything about the key. Satisfied?"

Maggi smiled her agreement and the conversation quickly turned back to the details that she had learned earlier in the day.

CHAPTER 38

Hamilton, Bermuda – Saturday, June 2, 2012

Rhiannon stretched lazily. With her eyes still firmly shut, she moved her arm around the bed. No Maggi. God, she was tired, she hadn't even heard Maggi leave. They had spent hours going over the details surrounding the theft of the cross, each doing their best to recall all that had happened over the intervening years. By the time they had finished talking it had been too late for her to go back to her office, and Maggi was free for the remainder of the evening. Seizing the opportunity for some unexpected time together they scrambled into bed furiously groping each other until, temporarily satiated, both had fallen asleep.

Assuming Maggi must have woken and left, while she had slept right through to morning, Rhiannon finally opened her eyes and looked around the room. Not a sign of Maggi, or her clothes. She looked at the clock. Ugh, Saturday. Despite it being the weekend she decided she had better go into the office and see what, if anything, had carried over from Friday afternoon and needed to be dealt with this morning.

#

Bermuda Police Headquarters was almost deserted when Rhiannon arrived. The few officers on duty went about their business with little personal interaction. Nobody, it seemed, had much interest in working on what looked like a perfect morning. Unlike the previous weekend, which followed the Bermuda Day holiday, today looked to be very quiet.

For the public, Bermuda Day sparked the annual rush to get one's boat back in the water and the men to, once again, start wearing Bermuda shorts as formal business attire. For the police, while it provided a clear signal that summer had started, it was still too early in the season for the heavy tourist inflow and the associated summer party-crowd problems.

Rhiannon looked at her desk. Not much had changed since the previous day. One lonely fax left in the centre of her desk blotter appeared to be the only new item. She picked it up and started reading as she flopped into her chair.

Within seconds, all thoughts of a lazy summer day had vanished. The fax was from the *Direzione Centrale Della Polizia Criminale*. She knew them well. The Italian Criminal Police Central Directorate, dealt with both the coordination of criminal police investigations in Italy, and facilitated international police cooperation with their domestic police divisions. What could they possibly want?

As Rhiannon continued reading, her initial interest in the fax turned to disbelief. It concerned Dr. Bruce Gordon. Given her conversation with Maggi the previous evening, the coincidence was unnerving. Disbelief and coincidence soon turned to melancholy as she found that the good-humoured and sharp-witted Dr. Gordon had succumbed to a massive heart attack while in Italy. It appeared from the report that he had been seen chasing a pickpocket when he collapsed and died on the sidewalk outside the Vatican. The Italian police were contacting her as the last call from Dr. Gordon's phone was to her number in Bermuda. While they were able to obtain her name from his mobile phone listing, there was apparently no answer to the associated number, which immediately deviated to voicemail. This had prompted their fax to Bermuda Police Headquarters requesting that she contact them as soon as possible.

Picking up the telephone Rhiannon checked her messages. Nothing. It didn't make sense. She sat down and stared at the fax. What number had Bruce Gordon called? Oh shit, it was her old number, the one she had before her promotion. That telephone was now on a spare desk in the general office.

Hurrying into "the pit", as it was known within the detachment, she looked around. Every desk but one was covered with the usual office debris. Off to one side, on the only unused and uncluttered brown wooden desk, a red light glowed like an angry eye on the single black telephone in its centre.

Rhiannon strode over to the desk and snatched up the telephone. Pressing the voicemail button she was rewarded with a metallic voice. "Please enter your password".

With a silent prayer, Rhiannon entered her password. She hadn't changed it in ages. Would it still work on her old telephone? Praying that the telephone service was its usual inefficient self and that nothing had changed, she punched in the numbers.

"You have two new messages. To listen to your messages press one."

Before the voice could offer any further options, Rhiannon hit the one button.

"Rhiannon. Hello. Bruce Gordon here. Listen, I may lose this call. Not feeling very well. Check with Andrew Jensen about some drawings of the fake cross. Must go. Chest hurts."

The telephone beeped and the metallic voice said, "Press seven to delete this message. Press nine to save it."

Rhiannon pressed the nine button.

"You have one saved message and one new message. To listen to your new messages press one. To listen to your saved messages press two."

Rhiannon pushed the one button and this time was rewarded by a heavily accented request from the Italian police to call them regarding Dr. Bruce Gordon as soon as she received the message.

Saving the second message as she had done the first, Rhiannon impatiently went back through the message process and listened to Bruce Gordon's message for a second time. Grabbing a pen and paper from a nearby desk, she copied down the message verbatim. Then, replacing the receiver, she hurried to her own office and retrieved her digital voice recorder. Returning, she recorded both messages before deleting them from the telephone system. She would get the answering message on the spare desk telephone disconnected first thing on Monday. In the meantime, she had all she needed. Things were definitely getting stranger by the minute.

Back in her office, Rhiannon typed up a quick fax to the Italian police giving them her correct contact details including her e-mail address for any future communication. With that complete, she read her handwritten copy of Bruce Gordon's message once again. He wanted her to check with Andrew Jensen about some drawings of the fake cross. She knew Andrew's store on Front Street was open on Saturdays. She would walk down and pay him a visit this morning.

#

Andrew Jensen was behind the counter at the right rear of his jewellery store when Rhiannon arrived. Perched on a stool with a cup of tea at his elbow he looked decidedly like some character from an early nineteenth century novel. A pair of magnifying glasses pushed up on his brow and the ornate gold broach in his hands only serving to exacerbate the initial impression.

Looking up from his work as she entered, Rhiannon could almost see the cogs of his brain turning as he tried to place where he had seen her before. Then, as the proverbial penny dropped, his face lit up and a huge smile appeared.

"Sergeant Thomas, I believe," he said standing and holding out his hand in greeting.

"Correct, Mr. Jensen, you have a good memory, although it's Assistant Inspector now."

"Oh my. Congratulations. I'm sure it's very well deserved. How can I help you? Are you looking for something specific or are you just browsing? I assume as it's Saturday you're not working."

"Sadly, it's the latter, and I'd like to ask you a couple of questions if you don't mind."

"Certainly, always glad to assist the police. Please have a seat," he continued while bringing a stool for Rhiannon from behind the counter. "Nobody local is likely to be shopping this early so we shouldn't be disturbed. Also still a bit too early for tourists," he added.

Despite Andrew Jensen's welcome, as Rhiannon started asking questions about his relationship with Dr. Gordon, his affable manner and ready smile were gradually replaced with a failing memory and an anxious expression. Finally, as if the old man couldn't bear the strain of trying to avoid her questions, he sat back, sighed, and then sat forward again and spoke.

"I'm really not trying to be uncooperative Inspector but it's like this you see, although I have not met Dr. Gordon in person I was aware he worked with you on the *San Pedro* cross case. We have been corresponding recently and he did seek my assistance in a matter that he asked me to keep confidential. In fact, now that I think of it he said I need not worry about sharing any information with the police, as he would be doing that himself. The questions that you are now asking leave me in a very difficult position, as it appears Dr. Gordon has not yet spoken to you. If I did so now I would be breaking his confidence. Unless this was a matter of life and death," he said smiling once again, "which, of course, would be quite different."

Although she had been trying to keep her questions very general, Rhiannon had a hunch that it was time to come clean with the elderly goldsmith. Pulling the handwritten copy of Bruce Gordon's message from her pocket, she handed it to Andrew Jensen.

"I'm sorry to have to tell you this," she said, "but Dr. Gordon passed away a few days ago. He left this message on my telephone shortly before he died."

With a slight tremble to his hands, the goldsmith read the message. Then, rising from his stool without speaking, he walked over and closed the door to the store. Picking up a small wooden "CLOSED" sign, he hung it on the glass of the door.

"We won't be disturbed now," he said. "I have quite a bit to tell you."

#

Rhiannon's mind was racing as she rose to leave. Maggi's story of the possible Vatican link to the theft of the cross seemed even more likely now. How she wished she had a copy of the drawings that Dr. Gordon had sent Andrew Jensen. Keeping confidentiality was one thing, but deleting all his computer correspondence and files, that was overkill. She would have to ask the Italian police if Dr. Gordon had any papers with him when he died. She really wanted the shaded drawing with the annotation that Andrew Jensen thought might have been a telephone number. How she would love to get her hands on that!

On reaching the door, Rhiannon turned back to a now obviously relieved Andrew Jensen. "One last question, but a bit off topic. I wondered if you recall making a key pendant for Katherine Alexander. I saw it once and loved it. I wouldn't mind getting one made for myself."

"I do," he beamed. "I copied it from an original she had, but it wasn't for her as far as I recall, it was for her daughter's birthday. She lived in Africa at the time you know."

"Could you make another?" Rhiannon asked.

"Close I think. I have no pictures or drawing so I would have to make it from memory. It looked a bit like those pictures you see of the papal keys."

"Really, that's interesting. Perhaps I could think about it a bit more and then get back to you."

Andrew Jensen was still nodding his agreement as Rhiannon exited the store and walked quickly back toward her office.

It looked like the papal keys, she thought. *How curious.*

CHAPTER 39

Vatican City – Sunday, June 3, 2012

The Silenti rarely met on Sundays. Today, however, they were meeting at the specific request of Cardinal Cressey who had new information to impart regarding the investigation into the disappearance of the *San Pedro* cross.

Once all members were present, Cardinal Cressey wasted no time on preliminaries and instead moved directly into the circumstances surrounding the unfortunate but opportune death of the insurance investigator Dr. Bruce Gordon. He also assured the group that with Dr. Gordon's death, he was confident any investigation into the theft of the original *San Pedro* cross was now at an end and it could remain safely in his care.

Although the ensuing discussion revealed some scepticism on the part of his colleagues, all it seemed were equally anxious to put the matter behind them. After some brief questioning they readily agreed that, absent any further outside enquiry, the matter would no longer remain on their agenda.

With that item disposed of attention turned once again to Cardinal Weiler and his plans for the recovery of the original key, or the return of the money. Without any specific plan in mind and not wishing to appear unprepared, another visit to Bermuda to meet face to face with the Alexanders was the best he could muster. To his relief the group accepted his proposal and the meeting adjourned on the understanding he would report to them on his return. Although no specific timing was discussed, it was clear that the members of the Silenti wanted the issue resolved sooner rather than later.

#

As they walked back from the meeting together, Cardinal Kwodo turned to Cardinal Cressey.

"That seemed a particularly well-timed event."

"Indeed," Cardinal Cressey replied. "I confess I was having Dr. Gordon's movements monitored after his visit to the archivist, but his sudden death was certainly not of our making. I understand he was severely overweight and the attack which he suffered was brought about by heat and over-exertion."

"Something we too should be careful of at our advanced age," Cardinal Kwodo replied. "What do you think will happen when Cardinal Weiler re-approaches the Alexanders?" he asked.

"Hard to say. I can't imagine they would be agreeable to returning the money. It all depends on whether they still have the original key and this was a genuine mistake, or if they somehow managed to make a switch for some other reason. I must say though that, in hindsight, I'm glad Lucien made the offer to handle this in the beginning. It's becoming an awkward issue."

#

Unlike his more senior colleagues, Cardinal Weiler had little option but to remain clearly focussed on the issue of the wrong key. He had arranged the transfer of three million dollars for its payment and so far had only managed to obtain an inexact copy of the original. Despite this setback, he was confident he had done nothing wrong and yet he remained concerned.

The Vatican was going through a difficult time. A senior cleric in the Administration of the Patrimony of the Apostolic See, or APSA, the section of the Vatican Bank that handles its treasury activities, was suspected of laundering money by using accounts within the bank. To make matters worse, the Pope had recently established a special commission to examine the bank's activities, including the accounts of many clerics who worked in areas where organized crime was rife.

No easy task, he thought. Officially known as the Institute for the Works of Religion, the bank, with over one hundred employees, assets in excess of five billion Euros and almost twenty thousand accounts, is also one of the world's most secretive financial institutions.

Despite the legitimate intentions of his purchase, a three million dollar expenditure for what transpired to be a fake key was not good for its reputation and would not be favourably received. The quicker he could address matters with the Alexanders the better it would be for all concerned. Besides, and as far as he was concerned more importantly, he did not intend to become yet another casualty in the Vatican's financial purge.

CHAPTER 40

Southampton, Bermuda – Sunday, June 3, 2012

Sean snapped awake. Unsure what had disturbed him he listened intently for any strange noise. The house was quiet. Far below, he could hear the waves breaking on Horseshoe Bay beach. Not moving he strained to hear any slight sound from within the house. He and Sarah had spent enough time together at Peter's house that he felt quite comfortable here. There it was again, the sharp clink of crockery. Either Peter was awake or there was someone else in the house.

Sliding from the bed, Sean pulled on the shorts he had left hanging over the arm of a nearby chair and padded quietly out of the bedroom and down the stairs. An intruder was unlikely yet if Peter was up, he had rarely been this quiet in his own home on Sean's previous visits. It was almost sunrise and the house, high on the bluff above Bermuda's spectacular south shore, was a dubious target for random burglary. As he neared the ground floor landing Sean heard the outside kitchen door open.

"Finished?"

Sean stopped moving. It was a woman's voice. He headed toward the kitchen. All was in darkness, the only illumination provided by the early morning sky as it lightened with the approaching sunrise.

As Sean inched forward, the kitchen was suddenly flooded with light from an opening refrigerator door. Satisfied that this was not the behaviour of a thief, Sean peered around the corner. Sitting patiently in front of the open refrigerator was Charlie's dog, while she stood at the kitchen counter mixing an assortment of leftovers into a large bowl.

"Morning," Sean said. "Certainly didn't expect to find you two down here."

Startled, Charlie looked up. "Sorry, I tried not to wake anyone, but Ben needed to go out."

Then, realizing that standing in Peter's kitchen wearing one of his large old T-shirts as a dress was hardly the height of decorum, blushed furiously to the tip of her upturned nose, while focussing all her attention on the mixing bowl in front of her.

Sean laughed. "Don't mind me. Sarah and I spent a lot of time here. I know she's gone but I still feel like part of the family. Hell, I can't believe I said that. It's so surreal. At times I think she's just out there sailing."

"I'm sorry. It must be terrible just waiting and not knowing."

Neither spoke for a few moments while Charlie finished feeding Ben, turned on the kitchen counter lights, and eased carefully onto one of the counter stools. "There, at least we can see a little better."

"That we can," Sean replied looking intently at her. "Peter's a lucky guy."

Blushing furiously all over again, Charlie said, "I'm making coffee. Would you like some?"

"Yes please. No offence intended by that remark. I think you two are really well suited. He needs someone like you in his life. He's a great guy despite being a little stuffy at times, which I think is pretty understandable growing up on this island."

"I know what you mean." Charlie replied. "Very polite old world-culture, isn't it?"

"Sure is. What did you think about yesterday's events?"

"Fascinating. I felt like a fly on the wall listening to everyone share everything they knew about the cross and the key."

"Do you really think they shared everything there is to know?"

"What else could there be? It was all pretty revealing."

"I don't know. There were moments when I felt certain details were omitted. Maybe it was because they were too personal, but at times I felt there was more to be said."

'What could be more personal than exhuming your wife's body? That really shocked me,' Charlie said.

"Yeah. Me too, but I guess you're right."

Charlie handed Sean his coffee and the two lapsed into silence looking out at the turquoise expanse of the Atlantic below as the sun's early rays lit up the stunning vista. Ben, his breakfast finished, walked over to Charlie and laid his head in her lap.

"Oh, Ben," she said pushing him off. "You're a mess."

Sean watched as Charlie stood up, took a wet cloth and wiped a mixture of drool and breakfast residue from her T-shirt and then the dog's jowls. That done, she plopped back down on the stool and picked up her coffee.

"That's exactly what I mean," Sean said smiling broadly and pointing at her wet front. "Peter would probably have gone up and changed. Having you around is definitely good for him. How long have you two," he paused as if searching for the right words, "been an item?"

"About two days," Charlie replied self-consciously, "It's all a bit sudden." Then, as if anxious to change the subject, "tell me about yourself. Where do you live? How did you and Sarah meet? That's if you don't mind speaking about her?"

"No, I don't mind at all. We met at University in Canada. I was a law student and football jock; she was an arts major and tomboy. The perfect match," he said cynically. He smiled. "It was our mutual love of sailing where we really connected. I'm Canadian and my parents live in a quaint bay called Eagle Harbour in West Vancouver, British Columbia. We're all members of the local yacht club, and it's where I learned to sail. After graduation, Sarah and I came back here for me to meet her family and pick-up her mother's boat, *Silk II*. When we left Bermuda it was the start of our round the world sailing trip. Kat was already quite ill by then but refused to let us put off the trip. She wasn't going to let Sarah sit around and wait for her to die."

"Sounds like quite a woman."

"She was. I'm glad I met her. Getting to know her also helped me feel closer to the rest of the family. Sarah was a lot like her mom, you know." Sean's voice broke and he looked away and stared out of the window at the sea. "What about you?" he finally asked.

"What about me?"

"Where's home? You told me about your research the other evening, but you never said where you were from, other than South Africa; and that you were Maggi's niece."

"Home is Gordon's Bay in the Cape Province. Very near where you and Sarah docked your sailboat. I didn't say anything about it at the time, but our family home is right alongside the Naval College. My father passed away some years back so my mother lives there alone now. I have an apartment in Rondebosch near the university but spend as much time out at my mother's as I can."

"What about school and university?"

"Pretty normal really. I was a good student and a reasonably good ballet dancer and gymnast. Those things took up most of my time."

"No serious relationships?"

"One, once, but that's over now. He was more interested in the family textile business than he was in me. So here I am, free as a bird."

"Not if Peter has anything to do with it," Sean countered.

"Not if Peter has anything to do with what?" Peter said walking into the kitchen.

"Leaving you behind while we continued the search," Charlie replied, adroitly changing the topic.

"Why would you do that?" Peter asked.

"Well, maybe you have work to do. The two of us don't have any day-to-day tasks. Not while we're in Bermuda anyway."

"True. Nonetheless, I plan to check in with the office and see whether I'm needed or if I can spare some time away for a few days again. Did you and Fallon decide when and where we would search, Sean?"

"We did. By the way, we were a little surprised you two didn't turn up on Friday evening. Fallon assumed readying the boat took longer than expected. Recent observations suggest that may not necessarily be accurate."

Both Peter and Charlie looked suitably embarrassed while Sean burst out laughing. "It's okay," he said. "Your secret is safe with me. Just try not to look so goddamned guilty will you two. It's actually kind of cathartic in the middle of this mess."

"Thanks," Peter replied. "The boat is ready though and Charlie planned to go over and see Fallon this morning. We assumed when nobody tried to contact us on Friday, or yesterday for that matter, that going out today was not in the cards."

"You're right. The weather is against us for now, but the good news is that we've narrowed down the search area quite extensively. We reverse engineered the drift patterns based on wind and tides and Fallon is confident about where we should pick up the search. The Rescue Centre is apparently doing the same thing so it'll be interesting to see where they decide to focus their efforts."

"Seeing as we're all up, why don't we rustle up some breakfast and then Charlie can head over to see Fallon," Peter replied.

"Sounds good," Charlie said. "I'll call you two once I've seen him."

#

As the trio settled into creating a quick communal breakfast, Charlie marvelled at the easy familiarity of the two men during what was obviously still a very emotional time for them both. Different in many ways and yet so similar in others. Each accepting without judgement the strengths and weaknesses of the other. As an only child she had limited experience of family ties of this nature and, although Peter and Sean were technically not family, the strength of their "almost brother-in-law" bond was obviously formed well before Sarah's death.

CHAPTER 41

Rome, Italy – Thursday, June 7, 2012

Agente Alessio Barone looked at his watch. His shift was about to end and still no word from his former partner. It had been a week and not a single message from that creep. Angelo Mosconi may not have been the perfect colleague but, since leaving the department, his one redeeming feature had been his absolute reliability in paying promptly for information. Now this, a week of silence and a not in service message from Angelo's mobile phone.

He had kept his enquiries as discreet as possible but the questions were starting. Angelo paid well for the occasional use of police resources, and who cared if Alessio made a little money on the side. No one was getting hurt and the work usually needed doing anyway. A police officer's salary could do with all the help it could get. Everything cost more these days.

Then, two days ago a new cadet, fresh out of training school and obviously wanting to impress someone, started with the questions. What's more, the stupid little bitch had gone through the regular channels. Not a quick courtesy call to him to satisfy her curiosity, but rather a formal approach through the official channels. Just trying to be helpful regarding his investigation the memo said. Well, it wasn't fucking helpful at all, and now his boss wanted to know why he had been asking questions at Passport Control about an Englishman who had turned up dead.

Merda. Where was that fool, Angelo? He was getting sloppy. If he didn't pay in the next few days, Alessio would simply admit to doing a former colleague a small favour. Moreover, if asked why Angelo needed the information, he would merely say it had to do with surveillance for a wife or mistress or something like that, and that he hadn't pressed for any details. He would probably be reprimanded but that was okay. If Angelo was up to no good, he wanted nothing to do with any of this. Besides, if Angelo wanted him to keep his mouth shut he should pay his bills.

#

Unbeknownst to Alessio, far from getting sloppy, Angelo had been trying desperately to cover his tracks. The services that he provided to Cardinal Cressey were extremely lucrative and while circumstances had ultimately, and fortuitously, fulfilled his assignment with respect to Dr. Gordon; things had certainly not gone according to plan.

Having lost contact with the Englishman he had, in a moment of desperation, contacted his former partner and asked him to check the passport records. Unfortunately, the Englishman's death so soon after his enquiry could now very easily provoke questions. Questions which, if followed to their source could, albeit unlikely, lead back to him. And, while there was no obvious link between him and Cardinal Cressey, that was not something he wished to risk. The Cardinal was all too powerful and, as Angelo well knew, ruthless when it came to matters concerning himself and the Church.

The only positive aspect, Angelo realized, was that he had not once used his regular mobile phone to call either the police department or Raffaele Panzini. Once he rid himself of the pre-paid mobile, there would be no record of him making contact with either of them. It would take a very thorough investigator to track down the records from such a phone. Even if they were successful, they would still need to establish a link between him and anyone to who calls had been made; and why would they bother? No crime had been committed. He had simply been seeking information on a visitor to the country, who had subsequently died while running after a thief. Angelo was sure any investigation would end almost as soon as it began.

As he walked to the train station, he had dismantled the pre-paid mobile and periodically tossed the various components over the bank into the river Tiber. No one would ever find them there. The number that he had provided to both Raffaele Panzini, and his former partner, would cease to exist. He would arrange for Alessio's payment in a couple of weeks, but for now, he planned to disappear from the city. His friends in Sicily would vouch that he had been there the whole time Dr. Gordon had been in Italy. After all, wasn't that the reason for well-paid friends?

#

Little did Angelo realize that his offhand dismissal of Alessio Barone's expected payment, despite his genuine intention to pay it a few weeks later, would prove to be a case of too little, too late.

CHAPTER 42

Coast of Bermuda – Friday, June 8, 2012

For the first time in many years, Fallon was about to break a cardinal rule. He was going to dive alone.

They had spent the better part of three days earlier in the week searching for any sign of Sarah's boat without success. With no material discrepancies between their calculations and those of the Rescue Centre, the two groups had each covered the entire probable drift path of Sarah's survival suit until, they were as sure as they could be, that all likely scenarios had been covered. Whatever remained of *Silk II* had either been taken further out to sea, or buried in the depths below.

Fallon had spent the previous day alone, poring over the charts until he was satisfied that all the peculiarities of the local currents had been taken into account. Barring one small eddy around a sharp reef outcrop which was only visible at extremely low tide, he was satisfied nothing had been missed. Besides, for it to have any effect would have taken an unusual combination of wind and waves. The wind would have had to push an object against the current and around the reef outcrop before it could be caught in the eddy.

The estimated drift path also indicated that whatever happened to Sarah's boat had occurred fairly far from the coastline. From that information and the lack of distress communications, the most likely case remained some catastrophic event. If these assumptions were accurate and *Silk II* had broken-up a long way offshore, anything too heavy to float would have sunk in waters too deep to dive. The only chance of finding wreckage was if it had remained afloat and, allowing for an unusual combination of wind and currents, had broken up against the rocks several hours later. As far as Fallon was concerned, the only place that could have happened was this one reef.

He manoeuvred *Maverick* into the eddy and dropped anchor. He was far enough away from the reef not to have any issues with the current and the anchor would hold against any changes. It was half an hour before slack tide and he only planned to be in the water for about forty minutes. A single tank dive was all he was allowing himself. Ideally, twenty minutes on either side of slack. He wanted one good look at the area around the outcrop after which he too would be calling off any further search efforts.

#

There was almost no movement in the water as Fallon eased his way around the submerged section of the outcrop. Despite the warmth of the water, he was wearing both gloves and a full wetsuit. The reef was too sharp to take chances. He looked at his gauges. Only twenty feet down and he was already at the reef's surface. Jagged rocks in every direction interspersed with small pockets of sand and intermittent spots of colour from the various forms of marine life attached to the reef.

As he hovered above the ragged surface, Fallon's body, in perfect suspension, rose and fell ever so slightly in time with his breathing. Thirty minutes later and, according to his gauges, now well into his tank of air, Fallon was almost back to the point from which he had started his circumnavigation of the outcrop. It was then that the fluke of an anchor imbedded in a small sand pocket caught his attention.

Probably a tourist's, he thought. *Looks new. Maybe it snagged and they had to cut it free.*

Not seeing any attached line Fallon drifted over and grasped the exposed fluke. Pulling it free of the sand, he inhaled sharply. Fastened to the anchor ring were several small bones, all held in place by a tightly wound gold chain with a small gold and silver key dangling from its end.

Expelling air from his BCD, Fallon settled onto the reef and felt the sharp edges pressing through the wetsuit into his flesh. Removing his gloves, he carefully untied the necklace chain while holding it over the open end of a small pouch he had removed from his dive belt. As the chain came free, the bones dropped neatly into the bag. Fallon pulled the bag strings tight and reattached it to his belt. Holding the necklace with the key still attached, he peeled open the bright yellow Velcro top of the pocket on his BCD and placed the necklace inside before pressing it closed. Then, with the anchor in one hand and his gloves now firmly wedged in his dive belt, he headed for the surface.

As Fallon started his ascent, the casual kick of his fins raised a swirl of sand and with it a white object. Tumble turning in the water he again descended and moments later grabbed what appeared to be a portion of a jawbone. Placing it under his arm, Fallon, with a brief burst of air into his BCD, re-assumed his ascent.

#

Half an hour later, *Maverick* was moving steadily back towards the harbour with Fallon at the helm. Despite having no expectation that Sarah would have survived this long, finding the jawbone had shaken him badly. She had been such a beautiful young woman. How the hell was he going to tell Howard?

First things first. He would take the bones to the police so they could run whatever tests they needed to establish identification. Once he had finished with them, he would go and see Howard but only tell him that he had found a few small bones and an anchor. He would leave out the finer details. That should be sufficient. As far as identifying Sarah was concerned, he assumed they would have to wait for some sort of DNA test on the bones before they were sure.

The necklace and the key were another matter altogether. Howard had already sold Kat's key to the Vatican and been paid; he wasn't expecting to now retrieve the original. As for the Vatican, if they had bought the wrong key that was their problem.

Perhaps he should just tell everyone about the necklace but not the key, he thought.

No, that wouldn't work. There was no way anyone would believe that he had only found one and not the other. He wouldn't have believed it himself. He either had to admit to finding both or none at all.

Realizing he needed more time to think things through, Fallon decided to say nothing about either the necklace or the key for the moment. The anchor and bones would be sufficient to keep everyone fully occupied. He would decide what to do about the key later. He could always "find" it on another dive if need be.

He suspected there was probably no way to identify the anchor, which looked generic. Fallon moved it around the deck with his bare foot as he steered the boat. Certainly no markings on the outside surface. Some sort of stamp-mark on the inside of the one fluke was all he could see. Most likely a manufacturer's mark. Deciding to look more closely once he was on dry land, he turned his mind once again to the problem at hand. All he knew for sure at this point was that he had better get his story straight before he reached Hamilton. You never knew who might be around when you docked.

CHAPTER 43

Hamilton, Bermuda – Friday, June 8, 2012

"Excuse me Inspector, there's a wet man at the front desk asking to speak with you."

"A wet man?"

"Looks like he's been swimming. His hair and shirt are quite wet. He says his name is Fallon. I assume it's his last name."

Rhiannon felt a momentary rush of anxiety. Then, realizing that even if Fallon had discovered her relationship with Maggi he was very unlikely to approach her at police headquarters, quickly regained her composure.

"Show him in please."

On the few occasions Rhiannon had met Fallon, he was always relaxed and unruffled. Today, he looked decidedly different. His white long sleeved shirt was untucked and, as the constable noted, rather wet, as was his hair. There were also patches of damp on his jeans and his loafers had dark water spots on the light tan leather.

"Mr. Fallon, good to see you. How can I help?"

"I'm not sure you're the correct person," Fallon replied, "but if not, I'm sure you will know who should get this."

Rhiannon looked down at the black pouch that Fallon held out to her as he finished speaking. It too was wet she noticed, as water dripped from the bag onto her desk.

"Sorry," Fallon said wiping the desk with his sleeve. "Came straight from the boat without cleaning up first. Quite shaken by the whole thing actually."

"Shaken by what Mr. Fallon?" Rhiannon asked, taking the pouch at the same time.

"Before you open it let me explain."

Rhiannon placed the pouch on her desk blotter. "Have a seat," she said. "Take your time."

Rhiannon watched Fallon closely as he sat down, caught his breath and then gave a prolonged sigh before speaking. "I'm sure you know we've been looking for Sarah Alexander's boat," he began.

As Fallon described the search he and the Alexanders had undertaken, Rhiannon marvelled at his detailed recollection despite having been visibly upset when he arrived. As he spoke, he regained his composure and by the story's end appeared quite calm.

"So, if I understand you correctly, other than Sarah's survival suit which was picked up by the *Osprey*, nothing more was found until your dive today when you picked up an anchor and some small bones."

"Right."

"And what makes you think they belong to Sarah Alexander?"

"Well, as I said before, we had calculated the probable drift path of any wreckage and our calculations were materially the same as those of the Rescue Centre. This particular spot was fairly close to that path. I know there are a few unusual currents around that rock that don't show on any marine charts, so I thought I would have one last look. If it had just been the anchor I probably wouldn't have thought much of it, but the bones…that's different. They really shook me up."

"So why did you come to me specifically and where are the bones and anchor now?"

"A couple of weeks back Maggi and I were discussing the theft of the *San Pedro* cross with the Alexanders when your name came up. She mentioned that you two had become friends. I wasn't sure how I would be received by the police when I turned up with a bag of bones and thought, given your friendship with Maggi, I might have the chance of a little more credibility coming directly to you."

"Why do you need credibility?" Rhiannon asked, puzzled.

"That's probably the wrong word. I really just wanted to be sure that Sarah's remains were properly treated and that any testing required was completed before they became more contaminated than they are already. If anyone doubted my story who knows how things would be handled. No disrespect intended," he added.

Without answering Rhiannon rose from behind her desk and walked out of her office. "Back in a second," she said.

Returning moments later, Rhiannon placed a large plastic bag on the desk. "Evidence envelope," she said while opening Fallon's black diving pouch and shaking the contents into the clear plastic envelope.

"Oh." Rhiannon cringed at the sight of the jawbone with its neat row of teeth.

"Had that effect on me too," Fallon said. "If it's okay with you, I'll go and get the anchor. It's in my car. I didn't want to lug it in here if you were going to send me somewhere else."

"That's fine. Why don't you do that and then we can let you go. Just leave me a contact number where you can be reached. I'll take care of the rest and let the Rescue Centre know what you've found. They may want to send divers to the same spot, so we'll need you to give us the coordinates."

"I'll make sure I have them available before you or they call," Fallon replied. "They won't want to dive until the next slack tide which isn't for a while yet."

After Fallon left, Rhiannon stared down at the package on her desk. Although this had not been her case before, it certainly would be going forward. She would have preferred to have DNA testing done on the bones before any news leaked out of what Fallon had found but it was probably too late now. Once she advised the Rescue Centre, news of a break in the search for Sarah Alexander would be all over the island before evening.

Rhiannon looked up at the knock on her door. Once again, Fallon stood at the entrance to her office, this time with an anchor in his hand.

"I've just thought of something," he said.

He held the anchor out toward her. "There's a stamp on each fluke. At first, I thought it was a manufacturer's mark, but it's quite precise and seems to have been added after the anchor was cast. Manufacturers don't usually go through the time and expense of doing that, they're more likely to incorporate theirs at the time of casting."

"What do you think it is then?"

"I think it might be someone's initials. My guess would be Sean Patterson. I plan to ask him as soon as I leave here."

"Who's he?" Rhiannon asked.

"Sarah's fiancé," Fallon replied. "I'll call you as soon as I know."

"Wait." Rhiannon held up her hand as Fallon made to leave.

"I'd like to keep this as quiet as we can until we have a positive identification. Have you spoken to the Alexanders yet?"

"No. I left a message for Howard when I docked but haven't heard back. I thought I'd get hold of his son, Peter, and Sean Patterson once I leave here. I'd rather they heard the news from me than anyone else."

"I understand, but I'm going to need a DNA sample from Howard Alexander. I'll wait until you've spoken with him before I call, but please let me know as soon as you two have talked."

"Okay, will do. Thanks for personally taking care of this. I know Howard will appreciate it."

"One last question before you go. You didn't find anything else, did you? You know, personal effects, jewellery, anything like that."

"Nothing," said Fallon over his shoulder as he walked out of her office.

As Fallon left for the second time, Rhiannon looked at the package. She might as well get the process started. The DNA testing would take some time and as soon as any information about Fallon's discovery leaked, the press would be all over her.

CHAPTER 44

Vatican City – Friday, June 8, 2012

Finally, a reply. Cardinal Weiler stared at the screen of his computer. It had taken him days to draft a suitable letter to Howard Alexander. His first thought had been to telephone but he feared that might not allow him to explain fully his reasoning for requesting a meeting to discuss the return of the money; in exchange, of course, for the key that he now held. After all, he had written, he had paid to receive the key in the photograph of Mrs. Alexander and not for the key which had somehow been substituted, and which he had received. Despite his irritation, he had taken great pains with the letter and phrased it in a most sincere manner without suggesting that any intentional deceit had taken place. Now here, after some delay, was the reply.

Your Eminence:

Please accept my apologies for responding by e-mail rather than by letter; suffice it to say, I am away from the office on business and will not be back for some weeks.

While I appreciate your sentiments, I am afraid I cannot agree with your proposed solution. My family and I have endured a great deal in order to provide the key that you now have in your possession. Under the terms of our agreement, you specifically sought the key that my late wife was wearing at the time of her burial. You have that key.

For greater clarity, and as a sign of good faith, I can confirm that neither my son nor I are in possession of the key, which, as you have pointed out, my late wife was wearing in her obituary photographs, and which you have advised is different to the one that you now hold.

Yours truly, Howard Alexander.

From the tone of the reply, Cardinal Weiler sensed that it had taken a significant degree of control for Howard Alexander to compose his e-mail response. What's more, with his reference to neither he nor his son having any other key, he was effectively cutting off any further discussion on the matter. One did not have to be a lawyer to recognise that when he spoke of the "terms of our agreement", that he was prepared to defend the transaction in court if necessary. Howard Alexander, however, had not mentioned his daughter and Cardinal Weiler's instinct was to press further on that front despite recognizing that the last he had heard she was missing and presumed drowned.

Deciding that, for the time being at least, a softer approach was in order he carefully drafted a response to Howard Alexander. In it, he suggested that at some future date, he might seek to visit to discuss the possible location of the key in the photographs and, if by some chance it appeared before that date, perhaps Mr. Alexander could contact him.

In the near term, Cardinal Weiler realized that he might have to accept responsibility if the oversight group of the Vatican's financial affairs had questions. After all, he assured himself yet again, he had done nothing wrong or illegal. Given the magnitude of the problems reported in the press regarding the Vatican Bank, the expenditure for the key should be the least of their worries.

CHAPTER 45

Tucker's Town, Bermuda –
Saturday, June 9, 2012

Fallon was exhausted.

I'm getting too old for this crap, he thought to himself as he slid out of bed, standing only once his dangling feet touched the floor. Yesterday had disturbed him far more than he expected. This was not the first time he had found skeletal remains, but not those of someone he knew, and who had been so young and vibrant.

To make matters worse, Howard was off the island and he had the unpleasant task of telling both Peter and Sean the news. He had asked them to meet him together and from their expressions when he arrived at the house, they seemed to expect the news. He had been careful to generalize what he had found, referring only to some small bones and the anchor.

Sean had quickly identified the anchor and confirmed that he had stamped his initials on it for Sarah. While they all believed that the proximity of the bones to the anchor, and the anchor itself, almost certainly indicated they were from Sarah and her boat, Peter, in the absence of his father, readily agreed to provide the police with the necessary sample of his DNA for positive identification purposes.

As he recounted the events of the dive, at no time did Fallon mention the necklace and the key. For now, uncomfortable as it might be, he was saying nothing to anyone, not even Maggi. That in itself was unusual. As far as he was aware, they had few real secrets from each other and yet something in the way she had described her relationship with Assistant Inspector Thomas, and the Inspector's parting question the day before, was causing him to have second thoughts. Her enquiry had startled him and he hoped his lie hadn't been too obvious. He wondered what she knew. Had Maggi told her about the key? Surely not. That was confidential among the six of them.

If he now told Maggi about the key, was her relationship with Rhiannon Thomas such that she would immediately share the information? He couldn't take that chance. For the moment, the necklace and key would stay hidden.

Hearing Maggi coming down the hall from her bedroom, Fallon slipped on a pair of shorts and headed to the kitchen.

"Morning. How do you feel today," Maggi asked.

"Pretty crappy. I can't recall ever having felt this disturbed about an underwater find before."

"Understandable. Sarah was such a gorgeous, young woman. I only saw her a couple of times in passing after Kat's funeral, but she was always bright and cheerful. Such a pity. How is Howard taking it?"

"He's off the island. I met with Peter and Sean yesterday instead. Peter said he would call Howard with the news. The police wanted DNA for a positive identification. In Howard's absence, Peter will provide the necessary sample. I didn't have an opportunity to mention it to you yesterday, but your friend Assistant Inspector Thomas is handling the identification process."

"Really? How did she get involved? I thought this would have gone through the Rescue Centre first."

"I took the anchor and bones directly to her. I remembered you mentioning you knew her at our little group meeting. I figured we needed somebody we knew and trusted. I didn't want the samples contaminated by some rookie cop. It's too important to Howard."

Maggi smiled. "You two have certainly become close again. I must say it's good to see. You have few enough friends as it is. No offence meant."

"None taken," Fallon replied smiling. "Don't leave me will you. I need you for the naked truth. Speaking of naked, you're looking trim these days. Someone I should know about?"

Maggi blushed furiously the colour quickly spreading over all the exposed areas of her body. While she and Fallon had no intimate relationship, clothing had always been optional in the humid island climate and after many years together, neither seemed to notice. Fallon's comment was, therefore, both unusual and perceptive because she had indeed been working out regularly to keep up with her younger lover.

"Sorry, didn't mean to strike a nerve," Fallon said. "It's a genuine compliment. Not really prying," he mumbled.

"Thanks," Maggi replied quickly regaining her composure. "Just trying to stay in shape. Nice of you to notice."

The tense moment passed and the two settled into their individual morning routines. After some time, Fallon spoke. "What's the name of the priest at your local church?" he asked.

"Father Edward Baird. Why do you ask?"

"I'd like to visit with him. Any chance you could introduce us? I think I met him on one of the few occasions I attended a service with you, but I'm sure he won't remember."

"What on earth are you up to Fallon? It's not like you to go to church, let alone speak with a priest."

"Actually I just want to ask him some questions about the Catholic Church hierarchy. I have an idea that I'd like to explore."

"Couldn't I help? I think I'm reasonably up to date, and anything I don't know I can always look up or find out for you."

"Thanks, but no. I'd like to run this idea to ground myself and not waste your time if I don't have to. It's pretty far-fetched and I don't think you can look it up. You'd have to be part of the Church infrastructure to answer this question."

"Now I'm really intrigued but I'll do as you ask. Promise me one thing though. Please don't do or say anything to get me thrown out, or excommunicated, or anything like that. You know sometimes you can be a little rough around the edges and pompous."

"Who me?" Fallon asked. Then, before Maggi could respond, "okay, I promise. Set it up though, will you. The sooner the better."

#

It had taken several days but, true to her word, Maggi had arranged the meeting with Father Baird. As Fallon travelled along South Road from his home in Tucker's Town, he reflected on his impromptu decision. The priest would probably think he was crazy, and perhaps he was, but there was definitely something odd about this whole business and one way or another he planned to find out the truth. For too long in this affair of the *San Pedro* cross and its hidden key he had been a passive observer while others manipulated events. That was about to end. After all, he had found the cross and as far as he was concerned, and with all due respect to Kat, both the cross and the key were rightfully his.

As he drove, he reflected on the events that had led to his current rationalization. The Bermuda government, under regulations that they had drafted themselves, had claimed ownership of the cross while paying him only half its value. A cross that he alone had found after it had been lost under the sea for almost four hundred years. No matter which way he examined it, it was completely unfair. They had invested neither time nor money in any search and yet they claimed half the prize.

Then there was Kat. What had he really owed her? Although he could accept that he had treated her unfairly, she, on the other hand, had somehow manipulated Father Despic who paid her to help him gain access to the cross in private. Or perhaps, as it now appeared, steal it for the Vatican. To make matters worse, Howard, in reality acting on Kat's behalf, was paid yet another sizeable amount for the key that Kat had secretly removed from the cross. A key that was rightfully his and, if not his alone, at least fifty percent his. In his mind, these events made them all square. Once again, just as it was when he first started diving, it was everyone for themselves.

Last, but by no means least, was the possibility that the Church may actually have sanctioned the theft of the cross. That really irked him. Finding something and keeping it a secret was one thing. Stealing something that did not belong to you, even if it once had several hundred years earlier, was another matter altogether.

It was only while he was speaking with Maggi after finding Sarah's remains that it had suddenly struck him. What if this was not a conspiracy by the whole Church, but rather of a few people within the Church? If that were the case, the Pope may know nothing about what had happened. Of course, if the whole Church was involved, well then he was screwed anyway.

#

Father Baird met Fallon at the entrance to his church. A serious, square-jawed man, he looked to be about forty-years old. With his neatly trimmed grey-flecked brown hair, receding hairline and rimless gold-metal glasses, he could have passed for a senior bank executive. Far from being intimidated, Fallon warmed to the priest immediately.

Looks like a no bullshit kind of guy, Fallon thought, *I can deal with that.*

"Mr. Fallon," said the priest, smiling and holding out his hand in greeting. "Margaret said you would be on time; and so you are."

Fallon glanced at his watch. Two o'clock exactly. As usual, and as noted, he was right on time.

"Good afternoon, Father. Old habits die hard I'm afraid. Never could stand tardiness. It always seemed presumptuous to assume that the other person's time was less valuable than my own and that they should wait."

"Indeed," the priest replied. "Although I fear most people don't really give it that much thought. Come inside. We'll go to my office where we can speak in private. Margaret said that you were looking for some clarification on the Catholic Church hierarchy. Is that correct?"

"More or less," Fallon replied, lowering the volume of his voice as they entered the church; its brightly lit panels of green, yellow and white glass providing a cheerful contrast to the more somber church interiors with which he was familiar.

They continued in silence down the left side of the main hall before entering a large well-appointed office about halfway down the aisle.

"So, Mr. Fallon," Father Baird said as they sat down in his office. "How can I help you?"

"I'd prefer if you just called me Fallon. It's how I'm known to most people, even Maggi."

"Sounds a bit harsh to my ear, but if you prefer, Fallon it is."

"Thanks. So let me ask you this first, Father. Can I assume that everything we discuss here is governed by your rules of clergy-penitent privilege and will be kept entirely confidential?"

"My word. That is not what I was expecting. I assumed you were only seeking certain information. This is entirely different and you are not even a member of my congregation."

"If my understanding of the law is accurate, I don't believe I have to be a member of your congregation for this to apply. We could try and proceed without the background information that I want to share, but that may make it very difficult for you to appreciate and assist me with my request."

"Well then, let's start there. You ask your questions and if we get stuck we'll reconsider the confidentially aspect."

"Fair enough," Fallon replied. "If you don't mind though, perhaps you could begin by giving me a brief overview of the existing Church hierarchy."

"In very broad terms, there are three levels of clergy. Bishops, who normally lead a specific geographical area of the Church called a diocese; priests, like myself, who serve the bishops by leading local parishes; and deacons, who serve the bishops and priests in a variety of administrative and religious roles. The ultimate head of the entire Church is the Bishop of Rome or, more colloquially, the Pope. There are also a variety of other smaller religious orders and institutions within the Church that function autonomously and which sometimes report directly to the Pope."

"Where do cardinals fit in?" Fallon asked.

"Cardinals are the most senior members of the clergy and are appointed by the Pope, usually from among the bishops, although it is not a requirement that a cardinal must be a bishop. The various cardinals also make up the College of Cardinals, whose responsibilities include electing the Pope's successor."

"Does that mean there are different levels of cardinals?"

"Yes. There are cardinal bishops, cardinal priests and cardinal deacons. The former two, despite their misleading titles, are normally chosen from among ordained bishops whereas cardinal deacons are often chosen from among officials of the Roman Curia."

"It's already getting complicated," Fallon said. "What's the Roman Curia?"

"It's the administrative group for the whole Catholic Church. Its structure is like that of many governments with different departments and staff members. It's presided over by the Cardinal Secretary of State who reports directly to the Pope."

"Without going into further detail, would that cover the major structure of the Church? No other senior Church administrators or cardinals lurking in the weeds?"

Father Baird smiled. "Funny you should say that. There is in fact one other form of cardinal, although little is ever written about them."

Fallon's ears pricked up at this unusual piece of news. "And what is that?" he asked.

"A cardinal *in pectore*."

"A what?"

"A secret cardinal. *In pectore* in Latin means 'in the breast'. Keeping it close to your chest in modern terms."

"And what do they do?" Fallon asked, now very interested.

"It's not so much what they do but rather from what they are being protected. Usually, only the Pope knows who they are, and it's even possible that they themselves do not know of their appointment. Of course, they cannot function as cardinals while they are *in pectore*. These selections are often made to protect them, or in some case their congregations, from real or perceived danger. Once the Pope deems it safe to make the position public, he may do so at any time. The cardinal in question then ranks in precedence based on the date of his appointment *in pectore*. However, if the Pope dies before revealing any cardinal nominated in this way, the appointment expires."

"So to be clear, anyone chosen in secret like this couldn't be going around dressed and behaving as a cardinal until his position was made public."

"Rather a simplistic clarification, but yes."

That rules out Cardinals Kwodo and Weiler, Fallon thought. *For a while I imagined they might have been part of a secret group.*

"So, Father, two more questions. Given the complex organization of the Church, do you think it would be possible for several senior members to conduct business without it being brought to the attention of the Pope?"

"I would think so. Like any very large organization the details of the majority of Church business rarely reaches the upper echelons. Information is continually prioritized and synthesized. This enables the senior administrative or religious leaders to evaluate it and make appropriate decisions within their delegated authority. Operating outside their authority is another matter entirely, just as it would be for any senior corporate executive who operated outside their delegated authority. Why do you ask?"

"Let me ask you this one last question before I answer. Who are the most senior clerics to have visited Bermuda as far back as you can remember?"

Father Baird laughed. "Believe it or not, that is really easy to answer. In the fifteen years that I've been here the island has, despite our best efforts, only managed to attract two very senior members of the clergy and, to make matters worse, neither was available to attend any functions while they were here."

"Holiday?"

"Heavens no. The first was Cardinal Kwodo, who apparently had some insurance matters to attend to on behalf of the Vatican, and more recently Cardinal Weiler, who I understand was here to arrange some banking."

"Did you meet either of them?"

"Unfortunately neither of their schedules allowed for attendance at St. Patrick's nor any other Catholic Church on the island. Nor any social engagements, for that matter. A pity really. It's not often that a priest in my position gets an opportunity to spend time with such senior members of our Church. But again, why do you ask?"

Fallon stared long and hard at Father Baird. The priest responded in a similar fashion, his open expression free of any guile or concern.

He's clean, Fallon thought. *Not a twitch when he mentioned the names of both cardinals and, unless he bluffs better than any gambler I've seen, absolutely no idea about their real reason for visiting.*

"Here's where it gets tricky," Fallon replied. "A group of friends and I have been dealing with some very senior members of the clergy on certain matters relating to the Church. I'd like to ask for your assistance, but I need to be sure that anything which we discuss is covered by your confidentiality parameters."

"Is this business legal?"

"It certainly is on our part. I can't speak for the Church."

"Let me worry about the Church," Father Baird said smiling. "I'm sure that side is fine."

"We are agreed then?" Fallon asked.

"Agreed. Given that your wife Margaret is a member of my congregation, I'm satisfied that the rules of clergy-penitent privilege will extend to my conversation with her husband. Now how can I help you?"

"I'd like you to arrange for me to meet with the Pope."

"Are you serious?"

"Absolutely. Let me explain why."

#

Father Baird asked very few questions as Fallon recounted the discovery of the *San Pedro* cross, its subsequent theft, and the Vatican's interest in a key originally secreted within the cross itself. In recounting the story, Fallon omitted mentioning several important details. In particular, Kat's removal of the key from the cross and that she was wearing a key pendant in her obituary photograph; his suspicion that the Vatican was involved in the theft of the cross; and the sizeable payments made to Kat and Howard by the Church. However, he did inform the priest that Cardinals Kwodo and Weiler had each indicated that the key was of significant value to the Church.

"You mean that's the real reason they were here?" Father Baird asked at last. "To try and locate this key?"

"I believe so," Fallon replied.

"And why then do you wish to meet with the Pope?"

"I suspect that Cardinals Kwodo and Weiler are not necessarily operating in the best interests of the Church," Fallon said, trying to phrase his answer as delicately as he could.

"Why would you say that?"

"For your own sake Father, I believe it is best that you do not know the answer to that question."

"But without that information what reason could I possibly give to try and arrange a meeting for you with a senior Vatican representative."

"Simple," Fallon replied. "You see Father I have discovered the key to the missing cross."

"You mean you now know where to find the cross and the missing key?"

Fallon looked puzzled, and then realized his choice of words had confused the priest but still served his purpose. "More or less," he replied. "But Father, I don't want to meet a senior representative. You've already indicated that Cardinals Kwodo and Weiler are senior members of the Church and we've met with them before. I need to get to the top, and if not the Pope, then someone very senior who I can be sure is not directly involved with either of those two. Can you arrange that?"

#

It was almost an hour later when Fallon made his way out of St. Patrick's. The visit had gone better than he had hoped. Father Baird, although not agreeing to try to arrange a meeting with the Pope, did agree to make discreet enquiries into the specific duties of Cardinals Kwodo and Weiler at the Vatican, and who might be an appropriate senior contact for Fallon in the Pope's stead.

Whether the offer of assistance arose from a genuine desire to help, or from some deeper resentment felt by Father Baird resulting from his exclusion in the Church's real activities in Bermuda, Fallon did not know. Whatever the reason, he was pleased with the result.

CHAPTER 46

Hamilton, Bermuda – Wednesday, June 13, 2012

Rhiannon stared at the DNA results. There must be some mistake. Perhaps she had rushed them to complete the testing. She looked at the calendar. Two samples were submitted on the evening of June 8. Howard Alexander was off the island at the time but his son Peter had provided a sample of his DNA instead. The other sample was taken from the bones Fallon had found. They had said three days but June 8 was a Friday, maybe they worked all weekend. Realizing that her compulsive analysis of the procedures at the DNA lab was pointless, Rhiannon read the report again.

Using polymer chain reaction or PCR technology, the lab identified any genetic relationship between the two samples she had provided. As an additional step, they had also examined the results with the explicit assumption that the two samples were taken from related siblings with the same parents. The report also contained a summary of the DNA process in plain English. Presumably, Rhiannon imagined, to prevent unnecessary questions from confused police officers like her. She read the summary again to make sure she understood the process correctly.

"*During conception, the father's sperm cell and the mother's egg cell, each containing half the amount of DNA found in their other body cells, meet and fuse to form a fertilized egg, called a zygote. The zygote contains a complete set of DNA molecules in a unique combination from both parents. Eventually, the zygote divides and multiplies into an embryo and ultimately, a full human being. At each stage of development, all the cells forming the body contain the same DNA; half from the father and half from the mother. This allows a variety of different cells to be used for sampling purposes in relationship testing.*

Although a significant amount of DNA contains information for specific functions, some, called junk DNA, is used for human identification. At specific locations in the sequence, predictable inheritance patterns are found along with specific DNA markers. These are useful in determining biological relationships and identifying individuals, respectively.

In a DNA paternity test, the markers used are short tandem repeats, or STRs, that occur in highly distinct repeat patterns among individuals. Each person's DNA contains two copies of these markers. One copy inherited from the father and one from the mother. The markers at each person's DNA location could differ in length, and sometimes sequence, depending on the markers inherited from the parents. This combination of marker sizes found in each person makes up his or her unique genetic profile. When determining the relationship between two individuals, their genetic profiles are compared to see if they share the same inheritance patterns at a statistically conclusive rate, resulting in a match".

The summary concluded with a highlighted note.

"The attached report shows the genetic profiles of each tested person. Utilizing the markers shared among the tested individuals, the probability of a biological relationship was calculated to determine the likelihood of the tested individuals sharing the same markers due to a blood relationship".

Conflicting Results. The opening words jumped out at Rhiannon as she read the attached report. She was flabbergasted. The Mitochondrial DNA, apparently only inherited from the mother, was identical in both samples. A positive indication that the same person, presumably Katherine Alexander, was the biological mother of both Peter and Sarah. The problem, it seemed, arose with the remaining DNA that showed an only approximately twenty-five percent overlap between Peter and Sarah's DNA and, accordingly, a high degree of probability, that they were only half-siblings. Same mother, different fathers!

Now more than ever Rhiannon needed a sample from Howard Alexander to compare the results. Besides, she also faced an ethical dilemma. Her job was to determine if the remains were those of Sarah Alexander, not to raise questions about the paternity of the Alexander's children. If Howard was the father of Sarah then, as far as Rhiannon was concerned, the matter should rest there. While she would not deliberately mislead anyone, she could see no reason why any question regarding Peter's paternity need be disclosed, unless absolutely necessary.

She would call Howard again to request a sample. She would use the fact that all men have one X-chromosome that they pass on to all their daughters as the only sure way to establish beyond any doubt that the bones were Sarah's. The fact that all men also have one Y-chromosome that they pass on to all their sons, and would assist her in establishing whether Howard was also Peter's father, she would keep to herself.

#

Howard Alexander was in Boston when he received Rhiannon's call. While initially a little surprised at the need for an additional test, he listened carefully to her explanation before agreeing to attend at whatever location Rhiannon could arrange to provide the necessary sample.

As many of Bermuda's advanced medical requirements were already carried out in hospitals and clinics in Boston, Rhiannon had little concern that she could quickly make the necessary arrangements for the test to be completed in that city. Howard was not returning to the island until the following Monday and she didn't want to wait that long for a positive identification. Despite her trying to keep Fallon's find as quiet as possible, the press were all over the story. If she could get the sample taken today, she might even have a match by the time Howard returned.

Rhiannon had barely finished the call when her telephone rang. She glanced down at the display. "Reception" was all that showed. Picking up the receiver she listened; the Italian police were returning her earlier call. If she would stay on the line the main reception would transfer the call to her now.

Good, she thought. *She had a number of questions for them.*

CHAPTER 47

Hamilton, Bermuda – Friday, June 15, 2012

Maggi loved sunset in Bermuda. The warm evening breeze and gentle whistling of hundreds of tiny tree frogs surrounded her as she sat on the outside patio of Harry's Restaurant and Bar. The ice-cold lime margarita and appetizer-sized portion of crispy-fried calamari didn't hurt either. She sat back contented, Friday evenings were definitely her favorite time of the week.

Maggi had arrived early for her usual get-together with Rhiannon. There was a growing tension in their relationship and she needed some time alone to think. For her part, she was fine with their current arrangement. She and Fallon had led essentially separate lives for so long that they were more like two close siblings who happened to live in the same house. Rhiannon, however, lived alone and Maggi knew the younger woman was anxious for them to establish a home together. Despite the significant adjustment such a move would require, Maggi was ready, although she worried about raising it with Fallon. After all the years they had spent together, she had little appetite for hurting him unnecessarily. To be fair to Rhiannon though, it was time she made a decision; one way or another, it was time.

Maggi was on her second drink and halfway through the plate of calamari by the time Rhiannon arrived. It was clear from her clothes that she had gone home to change before coming down to

Harry's. The skimpy, pale yellow, beach dress and flat string-sandals were hardly the normal dress code for an Assistant Inspector in the Bermuda Police. An observation confirmed by the admiring stares from diners at nearby tables. With a brief kiss on Maggi's cheek, Rhiannon dropped into an adjoining chair, the flimsy dress serving only to accentuate her striking features and lithe body and once again causing the heads of most men and several women in the vicinity to turn.

"Hi girl," she said, the colloquial Bermudian greeting rolling easily off her tongue.

"Hi yourself," Maggi replied. "You look amazing."

"I do?"

"You know you do. If you look around slowly, you'll see that the other thirty or so people on the patio agree with me. They're literally drooling into their drinks."

Rhiannon laughed. "Speaking of drinks, I'll have one of those." She pointed at Maggi's drink.

"Here," Maggi said. "Sip on this while I order another, it's my second anyway. I got here a while ago. Why did you go home first? Did you finish work early?"

"Sort of, I had some calls to make and, seeing we were meeting here after work, I decided to make them from home so I could change first. Judging from your expression that seems to have been a good idea."

Maggi nodded and smiled. "Let's order," she said looking around for a server. "You can tell me about your day while we wait. What's new in the world of Bermuda skulduggery?"

#

The dessert plates had been cleared away by the time Rhiannon finished updating Maggi on recent criminal activities on the island. Ignoring official protocol, she, like many couples in strong personal relationships, held little back from her lover. Police confidentiality was disregarded, and anything shared was understood and expected to be kept between themselves.

"It's hard to believe that so much crime takes place on this tiny island," Maggi said.

"It's mostly gang related," Rhiannon replied. "Unfortunate and really stupid, but with so many young people on the wall, crime just escalates."

"I've heard the same thing from some of my former colleagues at the museum. When their children can't find work and don't have that natural social connection, they do actually spend their time sitting idly on the stone walls along the main roads. In their boredom, they then often join in whatever street activity is taking place. Sadly, as you said, it's mostly gang or drug-related; a disastrous decision for many of them."

"Speaking of disastrous decisions, and I know this one's a bit close to home, but can we discuss the *San Pedro* cross theft and Sarah Alexander?"

"Wow. That's going back a bit. Sure we can, but what does one have to do with the other?"

"Nothing really, two separate topics. It's just that I've received some strange information on both that I'd like to run by you. The one item is very sensitive though, so you can't breathe a word about it to anyone."

"I never would. You know that," Maggi said.

"I know, but this is really sensitive, so swear you'll keep it to yourself."

"Okay I swear, but now I'm really intrigued. What is it?"

"First things first," Rhiannon replied. "Let's order coffee and I'll tell you about the cross. I'll save the best for last."

Maggi scowled lightheartedly at Rhiannon as she caught the eye of a nearby waiter and ordered coffee. No sooner had he left than Rhiannon started speaking again.

"Do you remember what you told me about Katherine Alexander's possible involvement in helping Father Despic get access to the cross alone, and how you now thought he may have in fact stolen it?"

"Of course."

"I don't know how well you remember Bruce Gordon, the insurance investigator."

"You mean the chubby chap. I thought you liked him. You said he's quite brilliant, if I remember correctly."

"You're right, I did like him. And yes, he was brilliant. Anyway, it seems that he was in Rome around that same time. The morning after we spoke I picked up a voicemail from him suggesting I contact Andrew Jensen about some drawings of the fake cross."

"Our Andrew Jensen? The goldsmith on Front Street?"

"The same."

"Did he say why?"

"No, that was it. The only other thing he said was that his chest hurt and that he had to go."

"Have you spoken to him since?"

"No. There was one other message on my phone. The Italian police called to say that a Dr. J. Bruce Gordon had died from a heart attack while apparently chasing a pickpocket. The last number called from his phone was the message to me."

"Oh. That's awful. The poor man."

"Sit tight; this is where it gets really weird." Rhiannon paused as the coffee was served.

After what seemed an inordinately long time, the waiter finally left. "Go on," Maggi said. "What happened then?"

"I visited Andrew Jensen. He not only confirmed that Bruce Gordon had sent him specific drawings of the fake cross which we now have in the museum, but that after reporting back to Dr. Gordon he had deleted all his files at Bruce Gordon's specific request. It's my supposition that Dr. Gordon had the original drawings with him when he was robbed in Rome."

"Maybe that's what was stolen from him," Maggi said.

"Very sharp," Rhiannon said smiling. "I'm convinced that's the case and the reason why he left the message he did. I spoke to the Italian police today and they confirmed that there were no papers in his possession and none in his luggage. Which took them some time to locate by the way because, somehow, he had managed not to register his passport when he checked in at his hotel. Made up some story about leaving it at the Vatican.

"I don't know if they were feeling bad about it, or why they offered the next piece of information, but apparently a former police officer by the name of Angelo Mosconi, who now works as a private investigator, had been asking questions about the whereabouts of a Dr. Gordon only days before he died. Something about a wife or mistress wanting him followed."

"Bruce Gordon, really? He didn't seem the type," Maggi said.

"I agree. It struck me as odd too. Frankly, it seems a bit of a red herring. I'd like to speak to this Angelo Mosconi though. I'd also like to know if Bruce Gordon has any copies of the drawings at his home in the U.K. I'm going to get in touch with Scotland Yard to follow up on that. Andrew Jensen says there is a number on one of the pages that looked like a telephone number. I'd give my eye teeth to get my hands on that page."

"The whole thing is unbelievable," Maggi said.

"I'm not finished. I did something else. I casually asked Andrew Jensen if he had made a key pendant for Katherine Alexander as I had seen hers and thought of having something similar made."

"And?" Maggi said, her eyes widening.

"He did."

#

It was several hours later when Maggi rose from the bed and looked down at Rhiannon's sleeping form. Not a peep, just steady even breathing. She was pulling on the last of her clothes when a sleepy voice asked the question she had been dreading all evening.

"When are you going to move in so we can stop all this creeping around?" Rhiannon asked without any apparent rancour.

"Soon," Maggi replied, surprising herself with the commitment in her voice. "I know it's time. I just need to find the right moment to speak to Fallon. I'd really like to soften the blow as much as I can."

"Fair enough," Rhiannon said. "By the way, I almost forgot I had one other question about Katherine Alexander."

"What was that?"

"Do you know if she was seeing anyone else besides her husband around the time she and Fallon found the cross?"

"I don't think so," Maggi said, her face turning a bright red. "Why do you ask?" was all she could manage to say as she walked briskly to the bathroom keeping her face turned away from Rhiannon.

"Bit of a question on the DNA samples from the bones Fallon found. I'll call you tomorrow. I'm too tired to even think straight now."

"Okay," Maggi said, still curious but relieved. "Go back to sleep. I'll let myself out."

#

As she drove back to the house in Tucker's Town, Maggi realized that after all these years things were finally coming to a head. By now, her relationship with Rhiannon was an open secret. The island was too small for it to be anything else and it appeared most people either knew or suspected. Only Fallon, it seemed, was completely out of the loop. How like him. Totally preoccupied with either one adventure or the next. Her affection towards him had not diminished in all the years and their sibling-like bond had endured. They were probably happier than many other conventionally married couples on the island. Why rock the boat?

Because Rhiannon needed it, she thought. *It was time to make a greater commitment. That was only fair.*

In that same instant, her mind jumped tracks. What was this new mystery? What did Rhiannon mean by some issue with DNA?

Why was she asking whether Kat had another relationship besides Howard? She wouldn't have known but, of course, Kat had another relationship, a relationship with Fallon.

Maggi had always wondered about the extent of their involvement but had never pressed. Was this a paternity question? The anticipation was unbearable but she would have to wait for Rhiannon to call tomorrow to find out more, and she would have to be careful. While she'd prefer not to involve Rhiannon any more than necessary in this affair, she did want answers to her long outstanding suspicions.

CHAPTER 48

Tucker's Town, Bermuda –
Saturday, June 16, 2012

Charlie was still in bed when there was a light knock on the front door of her cottage. Ben, who had abandoned his location on a very large six-inch thick cushion lying on the three-hundred year old hardwood floor in favour of Charlie's bed, exploded into life.

Charlie's coffee cup, balanced precariously on her knees and held lightly with her free hand, the other holding several sheets of her research paper, went flying. Coffee spilled all over the cream coloured duvet cover where it was rapidly absorbed leaving a spreading trail of light brown streaks.

"Ben," Charlie screamed, her protestations wasted as the boxer headed for the door, his feet slipping on the highly polished floor.

Thank God, it's so old and hard it won't scratch, Charlie thought as she leapt from the bed naked. She looked down. Despite his scrabbling feet, Ben's claws had barely left any marks on the dark wood.

"Be right there," Charlie shouted, searching frantically for something to wear while simultaneously pulling the wet duvet from the bed onto the floor.

Finally, with some sense of order and dignity restored, the now semi-clothed Charlie looked through the glass of the front door to see

Maggi, wearing a full-length grey and white striped nightdress slit on either side to the hips and carrying a bright red cup, standing outside.

Opening the door chaos again erupted as Ben, his body wiggling uncontrollably, twisted and turned in front of Maggi in greeting. Maggi, for her part, tried desperately to satisfy the dog's exuberant request for attention without spilling her own hot tea.

"Good grief, Mags, what's the time? Is everything okay?" Charlie asked.

"Fine," Maggi replied. "I saw the cottage light was on so I assumed you were up. I can come back later if you like its only seven-thirty. Am I disturbing you?"

"No, no problem. Come on in. I woke with the sunrise and I was just lazing in bed going over some research material. I love the early summer mornings. The air's so still and warm. Besides, I have to get up now anyway. Ben sent my coffee flying when you knocked. Let me put the duvet cover in some water to soak and I'll meet you in the living room in a minute."

Maggi watched Charlie's back as she returned to the bedroom, images of her sister flashing into her mind. How similar their mannerisms and, like Charlie, her sister had always been the cute one.

"How's your mom doing, honey?" Maggi asked, raising her voice so Charlie could hear from the room alongside.

"Good thanks. I spoke to her a few days ago and she sends her love. She said you should go out and visit her."

"She's right, or she could come here, but it's a long way for either of us. Why don't you suggest she visits while you're still here?"

Charlie reappeared laughing. "You two are exactly the same. Neither wants to travel. How long since you've seen each other anyway?"

"Almost three years. Too long, I know. I guess we got used to living away from each other after we left Ireland and I came here and later she took off to 'visit' South Africa," Maggi said, adding quotation marks in the air with her hands. "Then she met your father, the good-looking doctor, and that was that."

"What about you and Fallon? Seems to me both you and my mother did the same thing."

"I guess you're right. Almost right, anyway."

"What do you mean almost? You both married and stayed in the countries you were visiting. Until my father died, I'd say your circumstances were the same. Both married to men you loved but living in a different country from your birth."

Maggi paused. "You like Fallon don't you?"

"Yeah, I guess so," Charlie said. "Actually I think it's closer than that. He's become a sort of surrogate father to me over here. He's a good man Mags, you're very lucky. I was surprised at first by your seemingly independent lifestyles but, in the time I've been here, I've come to realize it works very well for the two of you. Not what I'll expect from my husband though," she smiled, "nor he from me I hope, but it certainly seems to work for you two."

"I understand," Maggi replied. "But things are not necessarily always quite what they seem. I did wonder if you'd noticed but I guess it's difficult not to, living in a cottage on the same property separated only by the pool."

"Not exactly a hardship living here is it," Charlie said. "But what do you mean about things not being quite what they seem?"

Maggi looked at the younger woman curled into the corner of the sofa, her ever-present dog snuggled up right alongside her, his head on her lap, fast asleep.

"They must have put something in the water," she said. "There seems to be a sudden need for disclosure. First, all that shared information about the cross and the key, and now me feeling the need to share yet another private matter with you. Hardly the norm on this secretive little island."

"Another secret? If its half as good as the earlier ones I can't wait." Charlie said now fully alert.

"Different, but equally confidential. Before we get to that, I'd like to ask you a couple of questions. Is that okay? The reasons will become clear later."

"Absolutely, I've got nothing to hide. Well almost nothing anyway," Charlie said looking sheepish.

Maggi burst out laughing. "I think you can safely assume any secrets you think you have about you and Peter Alexander are spread all over the island by now. The burgeoning relationship between one of the island's wealthy and good-looking bachelors and the beautiful, visiting academic has been the centre of the gossip grapevine for weeks."

"Really?" Charlie cringed. "Oh, shit. I hope Preppy doesn't get too embarrassed. I don't know many people here and I'll be gone in a couple of months; but he knows everyone and he's here forever."

"Why don't we let the future take care of itself," Maggi said. "Things have a way of working themselves out."

Charlie looked contemplatively at her aunt. "I guess so," she said. "Anyway, enough of that, what did you want to know?"

"How much do you know about DNA, and is your research broad enough to enable you to obtain a DNA test from a specific sample without revealing the person's identity?"

Surprised, Charlie stared at her aunt in silence. Despite the nature of the question, Maggi looked quite at ease.

Almost relieved, Charlie thought.

"Forget I asked," Maggi said, mistaking Charlie's silence for disapproval. "Just thought it may be something you could do for me. It's nothing criminal; nothing like that," she added by way of explanation.

"I'm sorry. I wasn't saying no, you just caught me by surprise. It's the last thing I could possibly have imagined. I don't know why. It just seems so... so unexpected; and yes, I think I could. I've had to do it before. I had some bone fragments and needed to be sure of their origin. Is this similar?"

"Actually, it's paternity. If you can do this test, I'll give you two samples and ask that you give the result only to me. I would prefer not to give you the names. I'd also need you to promise not to tell anyone about this request and, by no one, I really mean no one. Not your mother, not Fallon, not Peter Alexander…no one. Could you promise me that?"

"This involves Fallon, doesn't it?"

"Yes. That's why I asked how you felt about him. I suspect that we both love him in our own way, and wouldn't want to hurt him. It's essential to me that he does not know about the test. If you don't feel that you can keep it from him, then I won't do it."

"And if I can?"

"Then we will go ahead and, other than withholding the names for the samples, I'll tell you the rest of the story. Some of this may one day be public and some may never see the light of day. That will not be my decision but rather the decision of those involved."

"You mean the people whose DNA we test?"

"Yes."

"And what if there is no match?"

"Then it ends."

"No follow up, no further testing, nothing?"

"Nothing," Maggi repeated.

"Can I ask what sparked this sudden need to know? I assume it's something you've wondered about for some time."

"They're doing DNA testing on the remains Fallon found," Maggi replied. "You know that don't you?"

"Yes. Peter told me they had taken samples from him and were waiting to get a sample from his father as well. I'm not sure when they expect to get the results. Is this related to your request?"

"No," Maggi lied. Although feeling extremely guilty about the lie, this was not something she wanted to share with her niece. Not yet anyway, and maybe not ever. "But it did make me realize there was a way I could get an answer to a long outstanding question."

"But there's no connection between the two?" Charlie asked again.

"No, none," Maggi said. The second lie coming a little more easily than the first.

"Then I'll do it."

Despite not knowing who or what was involved, Charlie knew Maggi was right. Neither of them would do anything to hurt Fallon and, if this helped both him and Maggi, or at least Maggi without hurting Fallon, she would do whatever she could to assist.

"I'm not sure who I'll use or how best to do this," Charlie said, "but I promise to look into it on Monday and get back to you later in the afternoon. Now what's the rest, or are you going to keep me in suspense forever?"

#

Reaching all the way back to her arrival on the island and her first meeting with Fallon, Maggi recounted her story. The delivery a mixture of copious detail and lengthy contemplative silences as she described their growing relationship and subsequent marriage of convenience to circumvent Bermuda's very restrictive immigration laws. Like a faulty faucet, Maggi's story coughed and spluttered along as she tried to get it all out. Finally, the relief of confession, particularly to a family member who reminded her so much of her sister, unclogged the last elements of resistance and, like the faucet, her story finally flowed and then gushed.

Charlie listened attentively, asking gentle probing questions throughout. Then, just when she was sure there couldn't possibly be any further surprises, Maggi, in a final emotional admission, and for the first time in her life to anyone other than Rhiannon, admitted to her own sexual proclivity. Charlie sat stunned and silent, looking at her aunt sitting quietly at the other end of the sofa, her face slightly flushed.

"There," Maggi said, "it's all out in the open. I should go now." With that, she stood and leaning over kissed her niece on the cheek and walked slowly out of the cottage.

#

It was almost ten o'clock by the time Maggi left the cottage. Charlie watched through the window as her aunt walked across the manicured lawn along the edge of the sparkling blue pool, her shoulders back and lightness in her step. She looked content. Drained but content, if one could be both at the same time. Charlie, in contrast, was anything but content. Maggi's heartfelt disclosure had left her emotionally exhausted. What was she supposed to do with what she now knew? All this information. She hated secrets. They clouded one's life and cluttered the brain.

"Ben, Ben, Ben," she muttered aloud to the still sleeping dog. "What on earth do I do now?"

CHAPTER 49

Hamilton, Bermuda – Monday, June 18, 2012

"Morning, son."

Peter Alexander looked up from the document he was reading to see his father standing in his office doorway. "Hi, Dad. Good to see you back. When did you get in?"

"Landed at around eleven. I took the direct Delta flight. Anything urgent going on or can we catch up over dinner this evening? Assuming that suits you?"

"Sure, that's fine."

"Anything new about Sarah?"

"No. No DNA answers from the police either."

"They called me while I was in Boston. No confirmation," he added quickly seeing Peter's anxious expression. "I'll fill you in over dinner. I gather Sean's still here. Why don't you both come over at seven?"

"He is, and I'll check with him later. Plan that he's coming, unless you hear differently before you leave the office today. Good to have you back."

"Good to be back. See you this evening."

Peter looked back down at the document. He had been glad of the brief interruption. He simply could not concentrate. Normally he breezed through legal documents, readily grasping the pertinent points. Now they just wouldn't stick. It wasn't only today either. He'd been having this trouble ever since Sarah first disappeared.

No, that wasn't quite right, he thought. *It had been ever since that first trip with Fallon looking for Sarah's boat. That was the tipping point; that first day out on the ocean searching.*

He had felt different being out there with Fallon. He felt alive. For the first time in recent memory, he really felt alive. He had experienced moments like that before, usually diving or sailing with his mother, but always deferred to his father's steady guidance and the path laid out for him. He was destined it seemed, to follow both the law and in his father's footsteps.

Things were different for Sarah. The spitting image of Kat, both in looks and behaviour, she had always been allowed the freedom to follow her passion and ultimately, the sea. Not that anyone could have stopped her anyway. Fiercely strong-willed, once her mind was set on something, nothing short of a major catastrophe could stop her. Besides, there had been no adverse pressure on Sarah from Howard. He was satisfied as long as his son moved steadily along the path laid out for him and ultimately assumed what Howard believed was his rightful position in the law firm alongside his father.

It had all worked, Peter thought, *until now.*

Now, both his mother and Sarah were gone and here he sat, paralyzed with indecision. Knowing how he felt and yet not knowing how to move forward without hurting his father. Besides, if he gave up the law what in hell's name would he do and, furthermore, how would he support a wife and family.

Peter smiled. A wife? What was he thinking? He had never before contemplated such a thing. He also knew instinctively it wasn't any wife; it was Charlie. He couldn't get her out of his mind. At times, he thought they weren't even remotely compatible, but then there were those other times. He smiled again.

"Excuse me Peter"

Peter looked up to see Anne Taylor staring at him, a puzzled frown on her face. "What's wrong?" he asked.

"You're asking me? Since when did reading a settlement agreement make you smile?"

"Oh," he said sheepishly. "It's not this. It was something else."

"I see," she replied, clearly not seeing at all. "I thought you should know we've managed to find a permanent job for Shanice Morgan."

"Who?" Peter asked.

"Shanice Morgan. Really Peter, are you all right? This is not like you. She's that young woman you asked to submit her resume. I didn't know what you wanted us to do with it, and you haven't been around too much of late, so I took it upon myself to do some investigating. She's quite talented you know. Anyway, she now has two roles with the firm."

"She does?"

"Of course she does. Why would I make something up? Are you sure you're all right? She works full time in IT but also does some part-time work doing Italian translations from the international correspondence."

"Where?" Peter asked, obviously still on some other wavelength than his trusted assistant.

"Here of course. Really, if I didn't know you as well as I do, I'd say you were in love or some other silly thing." With this last statement, Anne turned on her heel and left.

Peter watched her leave without speaking.

Yes, he thought smiling again. *Maybe that was it. Maybe he was in love. Wouldn't that be a turn up for the books? Steady Peter Alexander, madly and crazily in love.*

#

It was nearly three o'clock and Peter had not been in his office since one-fifteen. He had not known where he was going when he left, only that he needed to get out of there to think. Leaving the Belvedere Building, and following his established daily path, he headed for the buffet at Miles Market. Located behind and below the building diagonally across from his office, it was his usual lunchtime stop. There were two ways to get to the market. One either went down a flight of stairs on one side of the building, or along the roadway on the other. If one took the latter route, Miles, as it was known, was accessed by turning right at the junction a short way down. Failing to turn right led directly to the waterfront wharf.

It was hot, and Peter, his tie pulled down and his collar unbuttoned, strolled lost in thought along the road. When he finally stopped, it was at the edge of the wharf. He had no idea what he had passed along the way, or whom he may have slighted by failing to greet them as he walked. His concentration had been unbroken. Turning left, he continued along the concrete wharf toward the fuel dock at the end. He would get lunch later.

Peter was halfway along the wharf when he stopped. With the marina now behind him and the open water of the inner harbour in front, he sat down on the hot concrete and leaned back against a nearby bollard. The harbour, as was usually the case, was busy with passing vessels. Small boats of every description bustled back and forth; either engaged in some commercial activity or filled with people out enjoying the typical Bermuda weather. This was more like it. He looked back over his shoulder across the construction site at the Belvedere Building and his office windows four floors up.

Call it what you like, he thought. *Early-life crisis, trauma, whatever, he was done. Not next year, next month or even next week. Today, done, finished, kaput.*

A wave of relief sweep over Peter as he reached his decision and then, as if to prove that despite this epiphany life continued as before, his disciplined mind took over. What would he do? Did he have enough to live on? He knew by most standards he was wealthy, but was it really enough to live well or would his lifestyle have to change? Realizing that his fears were pulling him back into the past, he took off his tie, unbuttoned his shirt and lay back in the sun. He had decided.

#

"Dad, do you have a moment?"

"Sure, Peter. Come on in."

Peter closed the door behind him as he entered his father's office. He didn't want to be disturbed.

"Looks serious," Howard said, pointing at the door.

"Sort of," Peter replied. "I don't want us to be disturbed."

"Not bad news I hope. I've had about as much as I can take, as I'm sure you have."

"Well, not really bad. I'd like to make some changes and wanted to give you a heads-up first."

Howard sat very quietly as Peter relayed all that had been going through his mind that day. Not by a single question did he interrupt. Finally, when it was clear Peter had nothing further to say on the matter, he spoke. "Are you sure you wouldn't prefer to take a leave of absence? Maybe take a year off before deciding, something like that?"

"No," Peter said. "I appreciate the offer but I'm sure. I'm really sorry to disappoint you Dad, but I think this is best for me in the long haul. I know I said immediately but, obviously, that would be after getting someone else to take over my clients. I have no intention of leaving you or the firm in the lurch. Quite frankly, I'm surprised you seem to be taking this as well as you are."

"The last few months have made me look at things a lot differently," Howard replied. "I've changed, as have you. I'd like to speak to the other partners before deciding how best to proceed. Can you wait for that before making any announcement?"

"Absolutely."

"Fine. Let's talk later. It's a lot to absorb at the moment."

Peter stood to leave the office. As he reached the door, his father spoke again. "You really don't have any idea what you plan to do?"

"Not a damned clue," Peter said with a huge smile on his face.

CHAPTER 50

Vatican City – Monday, June 18, 2012

Little had disturbed the sanctity of Cardinal Cressey's daily thoughts since the unfortunate death of Dr. Gordon.

After retrieving the doctor's battered old brown briefcase from Angelo Mosconi and familiarizing himself with its contents, he had carefully shredded the offending papers. In doing so, he was astonished to see his private telephone number written alongside a shaded sketch of the *San Pedro* cross. A timely reminder of how a small, and apparently insignificant, action could prove the undoing of all the work that had gone into the recovery of that ancient relic.

He had also found and destroyed a small laptop computer he located inside one of the zippered compartments. Unclear of what exactly was critical or not, he had taken it apart and then carefully discarded the various pieces in sundry garbage bins within the Vatican. Anyone finding a single piece of broken computer would surely pay it no heed.

He had not shared any of this information with his friend and colleague Cardinal Kwodo, preferring, as always, to keep matters to himself unless it proved absolutely necessary to do otherwise. Cardinal Kwodo, in turn, seemed perfectly satisfied with the assurances given by his good friend Cardinal Cressey that the matter was now behind them. It appeared that from Cardinal Kwodo's perspective, the less he knew about how things had been taken care of, the better. Besides, the Silenti had agreed to remove the matter from their agenda and that was good enough for both of them.

#

Cardinal Weiler's thoughts were another matter entirely. The original key remained missing and the fake key, for which he had paid an exorbitant sum, lay in the top drawer of his desk. An irritating daily reminder of this unfinished business.

To be fair, none of his colleagues had raised the issue again, either as a group or in private. Unfortunately, as he later came to realize, by their very silence they were, as best they could, removing themselves from any political fallout surrounding the fake key and the payment. Even Cardinals Cressey and Kwodo, the originators of the search for the key, remained distant. Cardinal Vilicenti too, up to now his mentor and staunchest supporter, was conspicuous by his absence.

As each day passed, it became clearer to Cardinal Weiler that, as far as the search for the key was concerned, he was now on his own and that he needed to get the matter settled as soon as he could. His approach to the Alexanders had yielded nothing. No key, no refund, and no offer to meet. He had tried to leave that door open with the suggestion that at some future date he might seek to visit with Mr. Alexander to discuss the possible location of the key in the photographs. Alternatively, if by some chance it appeared before that date, that Howard Alexander might contact him. He had however, heard nothing further. No response to his suggestion, and no new information about the location of the missing key. Other than what he had learned from Howard Alexander's original e-mail, he was at a dead end.

Picking up the e-mail, he read it again.

If the truth were told, he thought, *this was the seventh time he was reading it.* Hoping, as if by some divine intervention, the contents would be different. But, as before, nothing had changed. Not even that final paragraph about Howard and his son with its implied threat of litigation. What did it say again? Cardinal Weiler read it out aloud to himself.

"For greater clarity, and as a sign of good faith, I can confirm that neither my son nor I are in possession of the key, which, as you have pointed out, my late wife was wearing in her obituary photographs, and which you have advised is different to the one that you now hold."

Why had Howard Alexander only mentioned himself and his son and not included his daughter? Although she had recently died, was it an intentional omission? After all the man was a lawyer. Perhaps he was being particularly careful in case the matter went to court. A court may frown upon omission, but lying would be another matter entirely. Howard Alexander would not want to be caught lying. That would jeopardize his position and perhaps even his career. Was it possible that the daughter may have had the original key and that was why he had omitted to include her in his statement?

Cardinal Weiler could feel his excitement rising. Maybe there was something to this theory. Perhaps he should try to get Cardinal Vilicenti involved again. He could certainly use his guidance right now.

#

While Cardinal Vilicenti had not deliberately been avoiding his protégé he had, as suspected by Cardinal Weiler, purposely receded into the background on the matter of the key. His issue was not the key itself, but a possible examination of the payment. While it was a legitimate payment made in good faith for the procurement of what was, at the time, thought to be a genuine relic, it raised the possibility of reviews of other payments he may have authorised. The Pope's special commission, established to examine the affairs of APSA, was also examining the accounts of many clerics. He did not intend to become a potential victim in this process for some obscure facilitation payment he may have approved in the past.

After listening to an obviously excited Cardinal Weiler, and then carefully reading the e-mail himself, Cardinal Vilicenti had to agree. The closing paragraph was almost too precise. Granted the man was a lawyer, but his view was the same as that of Cardinal Weiler. There was more here than met the eye. A return visit to Bermuda to meet with the Alexanders was definitely in order.

"What do you think will happen when you re-approach them," Cardinal Vilicenti asked.

"That will depend on whether our suspicion is correct and the daughter did actually have the original key. If she did not, then it is all about the return of the money and we are no wiser than before about the location of the original. If she did, it then begs the question as to whether or not this was a genuine mistake or they somehow managed to make a switch."

"Why would they make a substitution? They have no idea of the key's use or its real value."

"That's what bothers me most," Cardinal Weiler replied. "If the daughter had the original key, why not then merely exchange it for the one we now have. After all, they have been paid and, as you say, they have no knowledge of its real value."

"Unless," the elderly cardinal said, "they know she had it but they don't know where it is."

"Of course," Cardinal Weiler scowled. "You are right. Why didn't I think of that?"

Cardinal Vilicenti smiled. "It does not matter," he said. "We are only speculating at this stage. The sooner you can arrange to meet with the Alexanders the better. At least then we should know where we stand."

CHAPTER 51

Vatican City – Monday, June 18, 2012

Father Baird's request had finally reached Monsignor Jacques Gaudin, the Pope's personal secretary. Born into an ancient and aristocratic French family, Jacques Gaudin could trace his roots back to the second last Grand Master of the Knights Templar, in 1291; a connection that proved to be of quite some interest to his fellow seminarians during his early years of training. He and they, among whom was a certain Edward Baird, spent many an evening arguing over the merits or otherwise of the Knights Templar. A topic sparked on most occasions by some earlier reference to his last name.

Monsignor Gaudin had not heard from Father Baird in many years, the last he could recall being in late 2004; a date he would not soon forget. That was the year in which an Italian paleographer published her report outlining how she had discovered, what later became known as, the Chinon Parchment in the Vatican Secret Archives. Of specific interest to Jacques was the confirmation contained in the document that in 1308, Pope Clement V had absolved Jacques de Molay, the last Grand Master of the Knights Templar, and other leaders of the Order, from the fictitious crimes with which they had been charged.

In a burst of satisfaction for the years of teasing he had endured about the Templars conduct that had caused the Church to behave as it did in arresting them all on that infamous Friday thirteenth in October, 1307, he had sent a copy of the report to all his classmates from the seminary. He had received many light-hearted letters in return, including one from Edward Baird, most of which offered their congratulations on his family's "posthumous absolution".

Sadly, the group had long since lost their tenuous communal connection and, like the arrival of Father Baird's letter today, it was only when their widely differing paths accidentally crossed that they exchanged any news. Besides, his own accelerated progression through the ranks had served only to exacerbate the growing distance between him and his fellow classmates, many of whose company he had thoroughly enjoyed. Jacques imagined that his current position as papal secretary did little to alleviate this detachment.

If only they knew the whole truth, he thought, *the separation would be even worse.* For, unbeknown to anyone but him and the Pope, he was in fact already a cardinal *in pectore* and, if their plans progressed as expected, almost certainly a future pope.

Yes, there was an election process and yes, it appeared these things were left to chance and politicking, but behind this facade lay the careful plans of generations of popes; the line of succession carefully established and protected long before any elections. In a process that bypassed even a pope's most trusted advisors, each chosen heir received secret resources and information that would one day prove invaluable in facilitating their own election to this most exalted position within the Church. A position, whose very power and influence could not, for the sake of the Church's continuity, be simply left to chance.

Only a few times in history had the system failed. "Caretakers" the chosen called them; each such head of the Church serving only long enough to make way for the rightful heirs. One only had to look at the historical records to identify them. Stilted progress and discord seemed to be the hallmark of their papacies.

Still, Monsignor Gaudin thought, *it was nice to be remembered by a fellow seminarian. I wonder what he might want. Perhaps a visit to the Vatican?*

Picking up a small but beautifully crafted letter opener, in the form of a military officer's ceremonial dress sword passed down by his family through the generations, he withdrew it from its scabbard, slit open the envelope, and removed the letter.

My Dear Jacques:

I apologise for the circumstances under which I make contact after all this time and trust that this letter finds you well. If you are unable to provide me with the necessary guidance on who to approach in this matter I will understand, and there it will end.

I write to you in rather strange circumstances and in the strictest of confidence but, frankly, I am at a loss as to how I should proceed. I believe you may well be the only colleague with whom I am personally acquainted that might have access to the required information and resources to deal with this request. Furthermore, as I learned so well in the seminary, your integrity is without question and this matter, if my source is to be believed, is quite possibly of significant benefit to the Church.

The husband of one of my parishioners has approached me with a request for an audience with the Holy Father, or if not the Holy Father, one whom is sufficiently senior within the Church to recognize the importance of the information which he holds. His request, however, comes with a very specific caveat. He has identified two very senior members of the clergy and has indicated that whatever transpires, neither they nor any of their known close associates may know of his request. He has refused to share the reasons for this with me, preferring only to advise that, in his opinion, it would be in my own best interest not to know.

He has also indicated, in somewhat of an ultimatum I'm afraid, that should we fail in meeting these requirements we will not hear from him again, and access to the information will be lost to the Church forever. In this, he is adamant.

I have enquired as discreetly as I could into the specific areas of responsibility of the two members of the Church in question and have found no commonality in their responsibilities and no possible way of identifying all their close associates.

Mr. Anthony Fallon, for that is the name of my parishioner's husband, has provided a somewhat obscure reference that he indicates should make sense to an appropriate senior member of the Church with whom he could meet. Furthermore, he advises that recognition of this reference will also substantiate the authenticity of his information.

Notwithstanding the unusual nature of this request, I have complete faith that my parishioner would not have directed her husband to me had she any doubts as to his sincerity. I have known Margaret Fallon since my arrival in Bermuda and can attest to her deep faith and love for the Church. Mr. Fallon assures me that while his wife is aware of many of the details he has shared with me, she is unaware of his current request or, for that matter, that he has possession of this secret information.

Without any intended disrespect on my part, the senior members of the clergy who may not know of this request are Cardinals Kwodo and Weiler. The recognition phrase, which Mr. Fallon has provided, is that "He has the San Pedro key". While he was very specific with respect to this phraseology, from my limited information I assume it to mean that he has access to the information to locate the missing San Pedro cross.

Please let me know if there is any further information that I could provide to aid in your consideration of this matter.

I look forward to receiving your guidance as soon as you are able.

Respectfully yours in Christ,

Edward.

Monsignor Gaudin placed the letter on his desk. It was happening again. He could scarcely believe it. His entire life seemed filled with secrets. Secrets about his own family's association with the Templars; secrets about his bloodline; secrets about his appointment as a cardinal to protect him from other groups within the Church; and now this.

Had Father Baird asked, he could have saved him the time and told him that his discreet enquiries would discover little overlap between the affairs of Cardinals Kwodo and Weiler and, when it came to their known associates, any investigation was almost ridiculous. Given the disparity in ages between the two, their associates would probably include most of the members of the College of Cardinals. It was no wonder Father Baird had failed.

Monsignor Gaudin was, on the other hand, privy to information that the majority of his colleagues, including Father Baird, were not. He knew that both cardinals were members of the Silenti. He was also aware of the details that the Silenti had shared with the Holy Father regarding the discovery of the *San Pedro* cross. Although, to the best of his recollection, there had not been any additional reports since its theft many years before. The known associates of the two cardinals, to whom Mr. Fallon unknowingly referred, were certainly the remaining members of the Silenti,

Unlike Father Baird, Monsignor Gaudin found no ambiguity in Mr. Fallon's message. He knew about the key contained in the cross. What was more, he was aware what it opened and what lay inside. He also knew that it was of paramount importance that he meet with Mr. Fallon immediately.

Despite his privileged position, Monsignor Gaudin did not relish the idea of addressing the matter with the Pope himself and certainly not while things were still somewhat obscure. If he were going to help Father Baird in this affair, he would have to handle it himself, at least in the early stages. Before he did so though, he needed to make a few calls.

#

Father Thibaud Escoffier was not surprised to receive a call from Monsignor Gaudin. Raised in similar circumstances the two shared many of the same interests, occasioned in no small part by their early privileged upbringing and current roles within the Vatican. While not quite at the lofty position of his colleague, Father Escoffier nonetheless served in a role that afforded him a great deal of influence without the inflexibility of association that restricted his more senior colleague. The two had over the years formed a tight and useful bond and could often be seen walking together, one of slight build with black, neatly-combed hair, the other several inches taller, his hair prematurely grey, his reading glasses dangling from a gold chain around his neck. The chain, Monsignor Gaudin had once confided, a present from his paternal grandfather.

Recognizing in each other the next generation of the Church's most senior clergy, they frequently shared pertinent information that would not normally have come their way through regular channels. Today, it appeared from the call, was to be one of those days.

CHAPTER 52

Tucker's Town, Bermuda –
Monday, June 18, 2012

Charlie knew she would miss the cottage when it came time to leave. Located at the corner of Maggi and Fallon's large and beautifully groomed property, it was an amazing sanctuary. Several hundred years old but completely modernized, with two bathrooms, a kitchen with all the latest appliances, air conditioning throughout and large French doors leading to a private red-bricked patio off the spacious living room. It also had both the usual stored rainwater and Watlington water, the local piped water supply; an unlikely but worry-free alternative for any long, hot summer water shortages.

Hidden by hedges on three sides, it had been freshly painted a soft grey colour before Charlie arrived which, together with Bermuda's ever-present white limestone roof, reflected the sunlight in such a way that it seemed to sparkle among the magnificent colours throughout the spacious gardens.

"Privacy is paramount for Fallon," Maggi said when she first showed Charlie the cottage, and she was right. Despite sharing the same gardens as the main house, it was completely private, and Charlie loved it.

Therefore, it was no surprise when there was a knock at the door without Charlie hearing anyone approach. What was a surprise though, was that there was no response at all from her dog. Charlie opened the door to find both Maggi and Ben on the porch. The latter's mouth was open, his panting tongue hanging from one side, his butt wiggling in greeting as he pushed past her and into the living room.

"Thought you might like him back," Maggi said. "We've been playing catch. I'm not sure who's more exhausted, him or me."

"Thanks Mags. I hope he wasn't a nuisance?"

"Never."

"Actually your timing's pretty good. I was going to call you later, but as you're here anyway can we have a quick chat about that test you wanted me to do."

"Sure, but as I said before there's no problem if it's not possible."

"No, it's still okay. I checked with my regular contacts and I can do it with unidentified samples. I'll just include them as part of my research requests and label them A and B or something equally innocuous. What I do need to do though is to give you some sterile containers for the samples so they aren't contaminated. What form do you think they will take?"

"What form?" Maggi looked at her niece, her face a picture of confusion."

"Yes. You know, what will they be? Hair, teeth, bones, blood, whatever."

"That sounds so sinister. What works best?"

"Saliva or nails would be fine. Can you get a sample? Oh," Charlie said, suddenly thoughtful. "They are both alive, aren't they?"

"Yes," replied Maggi. "They're certainly both alive. Can we assume the sample will be something small? I don't know what at this juncture, but I'll do my best. Can they be done at different times? I've no idea if I can get them together."

"Sure, but we won't be able to get the answer until we have the results of both tests."

"Of course. I understand." Then, as if uncomfortable with the current subject, "how are you coping without a car? Okay?"

"No problem," Charlie replied. "It's working out just fine."

"I still feel a bit guilty," Maggi said. "If you were a regular expat, we would probably have included the assessment number in the lease so that you could buy and use a car. We've sort of taken advantage of you so that we can continue to use both our cars ourselves."

"Nonsense. I've been quite happy to share cars with you two. Fallon explained all this to me when I first arrived. I had no idea cars were such an issue. He said that the cottage provided you with an additional assessment number for a second car. Apparently, if I remember correctly, in an effort to reduce traffic congestion Bermuda's automobile regulations allow only one four-wheeled vehicle per household. In order to have two vehicles, you built a separate cottage on the property that both generates income when rented, and qualifies for an additional house assessment number and hence another vehicle. He said it was a godsend."

Maggi laughed aloud. "Godsend is right. We never seemed able to coordinate our travel with only one car. When we first got together, he spent most of his time riding his ratty old scooter. I got the car."

Charlie smiled. For all his perceived grumpiness, Fallon was certainly soft when it came to Maggi.

"I'd better go," Maggi said. "Do you have the containers? I can take them now and return them when I get the samples."

"I'll get them," Charlie said. "You can get them back to me when you can. There's no rush from my side."

"Thanks. I'll be as quick as possible."

#

Charlie jerked awake. She looked around, unsure of her surroundings. Then slowly, as if struggling through a brain full of thick fog, reality returned. She was still in Bermuda. She had fallen asleep on the sofa, with Ben snuggled in beside her, in front of some mindless television show. Picking up the remote, she turned off the flickering screen, kissed Ben on the head, and staggered toward her bedroom.

She had been dreaming of bells. Her recollection was unclear, but she was almost sure the bells had woken her. Switching the wall light off as she left the living room, Charlie continued toward the bedroom, her path lit by a pulsing red glow, her foggy brain finally registering that the intermittent red message light was flashing on the telephone.

That must have been what woke me, she thought, *the telephone ringing.*

Charlie looked at her watch. It was only nine-thirty, almost too early for bed but she was exhausted. Her research was moving along nicely and she was all caught-up from the breaks she had taken while searching for Sarah.

Maybe Peter called, she thought. *I should check the messages but I'm so tired.*

She had only seen Peter a few times in the past week and, when she had seen him, he seemed preoccupied. She had tried not to take his preoccupation personally, rationalizing that with all that had happened and Sean's continued presence at the house, things were anything but normal at the moment. Still, she missed their newly established intimacy. Ignoring the pulsing red glow from the telephone, she pulled the covers up to her ears and within seconds was fast asleep.

CHAPTER 53

Salt Kettle, Bermuda – Monday, June 18, 2012

Howard had received the call from Assistant Inspector Thomas during dinner. The DNA test results were back and there was a positive match. The remains found by Fallon were Sarah's. The Inspector had apologized for not delivering the news in person, but thought Howard would appreciate receiving the information as soon as it was available.

#

Dinner had been over for quite a while. The three men sat quietly around the huge unlit fireplace in Howard's home, each preoccupied with their own thoughts. Finally, Howard rose, walked over to a large oak cabinet, took out three glasses, filled each with a generous measure of his favorite vintage port, and handed a glass to each of Peter and Sean. "Gentlemen," he said, "a toast."

Both Peter and Sean immediately rose to their feet, glasses at the ready.

"To Sarah. Much loved and forever missed," Howard said.

"To Sarah," Peter said, followed immediately by a similar toast from Sean, his voice choking.

"To Sarah."

The three men sat down and silence once again enveloped the room.

"I think we all expected this result," Howard said at last. "I know it doesn't make it any easier but I think we knew." He stopped, unable to continue for the moment. Then steeling himself, spoke again. "Sarah wouldn't have wanted us to mope you know. She wouldn't like that. Therefore, in her honour and despite how difficult it may be to begin, I'd like to go back to where we were at dinner before the call. Looking to the future and what in hell's name the three of us plan to do now. To make it easier, I'll start."

"Maybe you should tell Sean what I told you today," Peter interjected.

"That's probably as good a place as any," Howard replied.

"Know any good lawyers who want to work in Bermuda, Sean?"

"What?"

"I'm only joking. Well, almost only joking. Peter decided that he's leaving the firm. I haven't told the partners yet, but earlier today he seemed reasonably certain." Howard turned back to Peter. "Still of the same mind, son?"

"Afraid so, Dad. Somehow it seems like the right thing to do at this time."

"What will you do?" Sean asked.

"Don't really know," Peter replied shaking his head. "Probably something outside an office. What about you? Back to Canada and the same routine?"

"Yeah, I guess so. I'm not very excited about moving back into the house Sarah and I bought. West Vancouver's nice, but it won't be the same without her." Sean lapsed into silence.

"What about my dad's question?"

"What question?"

"About knowing any good lawyers who want to work in Bermuda. Why don't you come and work here with him? You're a lawyer and, if my sister is to be believed, you're good. He may have been kidding, but I'm not. You're just like one of the family and we both practice in similar areas of the law. He needs somebody to take my place and you're reluctant to go home, so who better than you? It's a great place to live and I'm sure the pace is a less intense. The change will probably be good for you at this time anyway."

Before Sean could answer, Peter turned to his father. "What do you think, Dad? Could you swing it?"

"I don't think you've given either of us enough time to think it through," Howard replied, his tone and manner suddenly serious. "No offence Sean, but I'm sure you appreciate this is something I would need my partners to agree on and unless you were fully committed to moving here, probably not something we would consider. That said, from my personal perspective I would be delighted if you could join us so perhaps it is something you may want to give some further thought."

Sean looked from Howard to Peter and back again. "I'm sorry guys but this is all a bit too much to take in right now. Don't misunderstand me. What you have offered is very generous, but it's not something I had contemplated. At least not in the near term. My focus has been to try to become a partner in the Vancouver law firm where I work, although that's probably still a few years off. As you know, it's a large firm and partnerships are doled out slowly and very carefully. I'm confident it will happen; it's just a matter of timing. Coincidentally though, before she set sail, Sarah and I did discuss the possibility of moving here someday. We both understood that if I were offered a partnership in Vancouver, we would need to make a firm decision at that time. Acceptance would pretty much have locked us into staying in Canada for the foreseeable future."

"Certainly nothing wrong with that," Howard said

"I know, but if we'd had children, Sarah really wanted to raise them in Bermuda. If that happened after I'd been made a partner in Vancouver, we'd have a problem."

Then, as if suddenly realizing the futility of the topic with Sarah's death, Sean stopped speaking and sat numbed and silent, his eyes filled with unshed tears.

"I think," Howard said, "that perhaps this wasn't such a good topic after all for tonight. Let's put this on the back burner and discuss it over the next few weeks. There's no rush and we have plenty of other details to take care of in the interim. Why don't we pick up the discussion before you leave at the end of the month, Sean?"

"Thanks, I'd appreciate that."

"Is there any more of that port available, Dad, or are you keeping it for posterity?" Peter asked. "I think we could all use another. After that, I suggest Sean and I take a cab back to my place. No sense in having two bumbling lawyers pulled over for driving under the influence."

#

Peter replaced the receiver and looked at his watch. Nine-twenty and there was no answer at Charlie's cottage. He had called as soon as he and Sean arrived home. He wanted to let her know about Sarah, but wasn't about to leave that information on a machine. With a quick message that he would give her a call the following day, he replaced the receiver and headed straight to bed. Sean had gone to his room as soon as they arrived and Peter couldn't blame him. It had been a tough day for all of them.

#

Unlike Peter and Sean, Howard remained motionless in his chair for hours after the boys, as he thought of them, had left.

First Kat, now Sarah. Nobody should have to go through this, he thought.

For their sake, he had tried his best to stay positive this evening. Sean's emotions were very close to the surface but Peter seemed to have his locked tightly away. Other than his sudden decision to get away from work, he showed little indication of the depth of his feelings about Sarah.

Strange, thought Howard. *They were so close.*

He wondered in what other ways the loss would manifest itself in Peter's behaviour. Perhaps they ought to consider counselling. He had always tried so hard to protect his family. Thank God, Peter was safe; he couldn't imagine life without both his children. Sean too, Peter was right; Sean was like one of the family. Maybe it would be good for all of them if Sean came to work on the island. He would approach his partners first thing tomorrow.

Rising from his chair, Howard returned to the liquor cabinet and poured his third port. Only one more and then he would go to bed. It was almost midnight and tomorrow promised to be a long day.

CHAPTER 54

Hamilton, Bermuda – Tuesday, June 19, 2012

Howard stared at his computer screen as it flickered to life. He had arrived at the office early and, despite getting little sleep the previous night, was determined to make the day a productive one. He had employed this tactic for more years than he cared to remember. When in doubt or just unsure of what course he should follow he had focussed on the details and simply started moving, one small task at a time.

He could still hear his father's words ringing in his ears from early childhood and, while he could not remember the occasions on which they had been delivered, he certainly remembered the intent.

"Son," his father had said repeatedly, "there are men in the ranks who will stay in the ranks, simply because they lack the ability to get things done."

Well, he had definitely received the message. He was not one of those men. If there was one thing Howard could do, and do well, it was to get things done.

Ignoring the available coffee from the office kitchen, where the finest blends in china cups were readily available, he had chosen instead to buy his coffee in its paper cup from the delicatessen on the ground floor of the Belvedere Building. Aptly named Buzz, it seemed appropriate for how he planned to start the day.

THE BERMUDA KEY

Deciding to check his e-mails before tackling the first task, Howard opened his Outlook mailbox. As the inbox filled with its dozen or more new messages, a subject line about half way down the overnight list caught his attention. "Visit" was the only word, the sender identified as Cardinal L. Weiler.

Despite his earlier intention to avoid distractions, Howard opened the e-mail. The Cardinal it seemed was anxious to visit and discuss the possible location of the missing key in person. While he had clearly understood from Howard's earlier correspondence that neither Howard nor his son had the original key, out of a sense of duty to the Church, he would appreciate an opportunity to discuss its possible whereabouts with Howard face to face.

Howard smiled grimly. It appeared that the cardinal had seen through his attempt to close this particular door and recognized that his omission of Sarah from the statement may have been intentional rather than a mere oversight. He did wonder at the time about the value of including that particular closing sentence in his e-mail. Well, no use worrying about it now, Sarah was gone and the key with her. Let Cardinal Weiler come. He wouldn't see him alone though. He would have them all present, Peter, Fallon and himself. Sean too, if he was still on the island. He would check their respective schedules before he replied.

Might as well have one last meeting, he thought, *after which, hopefully, the whole matter could be put behind them for good.*

Determined not to be distracted any further, Howard quickly sorted his e-mails into their respective priority folders before choosing the first item on his list and getting down to work.

CHAPTER 55

Tucker's Town, Bermuda –
Wednesday, June 20, 2012

Father Edward Baird pulled into the drive of Fallon's home.

This is nice, he thought. *Treasure hunting obviously has its rewards.* From his earlier conversation, Father Baird understood that although Fallon was in the salvage diving business, his passion, his *raison d'être*, was searching for old wrecks. Moreover, while he apparently spent less time diving with each passing year, from the looks of his and Maggi's home it was obviously something at which he had been very successful in the past.

Yesterday's call from the Vatican in response to his earlier letter had been a surprise. Jacques Gaudin was not your average priest. Even in their early years at the seminary, his treatment was different. While he took a lot of ribbing from his fellow students about the autonomy accorded him, he usually managed to shrug it off with a self-deprecating smile.

"I don't see it," he had said. "We are all treated the same way."

Father Baird knew better. There was definitely something unusual about his colleague. Whether because of his Knights Templar ancestry or his aristocratic upbringing and connections, he was definitely unlike the rest of them.

Monsignor Gaudin's career path had done nothing to dissuade Father Baird from these early observations. While others may have been appointed cardinals at a younger age, there was no more influential position in the Church than being the personal secretary to the Pope. Yet despite his ascension to such a lofty position, Jacques had responded to Father Baird's letter in a most timely manner and further, had done so by way of a personal telephone call. What is more, such was the measure of his relationship with Father Baird, he said, he would see Mr. Fallon himself.

Although Father Baird was delighted to hear from Jacques Gaudin after all these years and could have happily talked for hours, the conversation had, before long, turned to the contents of his letter. While Monsignor Gaudin agreed with his assessment that a papal audience was out of the question, he had assured his colleague, and thereby he hoped Mr. Fallon, that by personally meeting with him he could maintain the requested secrecy while dealing with Mr. Fallon's request. In fact, he promised Father Baird, the discussions would remain between himself and depending on the particulars that emerged, only a trusted colleague or two. There had been only one stipulation from Jacques Gaudin. The meeting needed to take place on the upcoming Saturday.

#

"Father Baird. How nice to see you. This is quite a surprise."

"Hello Margaret. It's good to see you too. I'm here to see Anthony. He is expecting me."

Maggi's spontaneous burst of laughter caught Father Baird unawares and he stood looking extremely perplexed as she struggled to contain herself.

"I'm sorry Father," she gasped at last. "It's just so strange to hear Fallon called Anthony. I've heard a few people call him Tony, which sounded strange enough, but not Anthony, that's a new one. You should probably just call him Fallon. I'm certain that would make him feel more at ease; whatever it is you two are going to discuss."

"I'll certainly try if your response to my calling him Anthony is any gauge as to how he will feel. I do recall that he did ask me to call him Fallon before, so Fallon it is. Is he home?"

"Yes, of course. I didn't mean to be rude. Please come in. He's in the living room. I'll take you through."

As Maggi and Father Baird entered the living room, Fallon turned from a corner table where he stood looking down at a chart of the Bermuda coastline and strode forward hand outstretched.

"Father Baird," he said in greeting. "Good to see you."

"Thank you for agreeing to meet at such short notice," Father Baird replied, "but the message I have is a bit time sensitive." He paused, glancing back at Maggi still in the entrance to the living room. "Is this a convenient time to talk?"

"Sure. Maggi won't mind giving us some privacy. She's used to my idiosyncrasies by now."

"Certainly," Maggi said from the doorway, "I'll leave you two alone. Give me a call if you need anything. Nice to see you again, Father."

As Maggi left, Fallon resumed speaking. "You said this message you received was time sensitive, Father. What exactly did you mean?"

"Well, since we last spoke I did some investigating of my own and, if I may say so, the results have surpassed my wildest expectations. Let me explain…"

#

As Father Baird outlined what had transpired, Fallon could not believe his good fortune. He had known that requesting a meeting with the Pope was outrageous, but then again he hadn't any better idea as to where he should start. Either the meeting with the Pope's private secretary was an incredible stroke of luck or he was on to something sinister within the Church. Although he had no idea whether the meeting could successfully insulate him from the activities of Cardinals Weiler and Kwodo, at least he would have the opportunity to chase down his own crazy idea. Besides, what was the worst that could happen? They couldn't throw him in jail for trying to give something back to the Church. It was what he wanted in return that might cause some upset.

#

"There is, however, one immediate problem," Father Baird concluded. "You need to be at the Vatican on Saturday. According to Monsignor Gaudin, he has information which leads him to believe that it is better that you talk sooner rather than later. He was not at liberty to share this information with you, or me, at this time but stressed the need for an early meeting."

"That's not a problem," Fallon replied. "I can leave tomorrow. There is nothing that I'm involved in that can't wait for a few days."

"I must say," Father Baird offered. "I find this all quite strange and exciting. I truly never believed that your request, notwithstanding my best efforts, would generate much traction within the Vatican. I do hope that someday you will be able to share more than these cryptic details with me. Until then, as promised, my lips are sealed."

"Thanks Father, I hope so too. You have been of inestimable help thus far. I trust the Church will think the same. Before you go though, can you give me some guidance on dress and protocol at the Vatican? I wouldn't want them scared off by an erroneous first impression. Why don't I rustle up some tea or coffee and then you can fill me in."

#

By the time Father Baird left, Fallon felt he was as prepared as he could be for his visit. He would arrange flights and leave tomorrow. No sense in waiting for the evening flight via London, he would fly through the US and then on to Rome. What was he going to tell Maggi? Probably nothing, better not to lie. Maybe just one of those "trust me, I'll tell you all in due course" statements. This sure was an interesting turn of events. He'd better not forget to take the key.

With this last thought, Fallon's face paled. The key! It was still in the pocket of his BCD. How could he have been so bloody stupid? Petty theft was rife on the island and, although he had locked the boat and almost everyone knew it was his, you could never be sure.

"Maggi. Back in about an hour," he yelled as he hurried from the house. Forget the car his scooter was quicker and, although a few minutes either way was not going to make any difference now, he couldn't wait.

#

As he hurried along the dock, Fallon wondered what had been such a distraction that he had forgotten to remove the key from his BCD pocket. Then he remembered the bones. That was it, he had been so preoccupied with reporting his finding of Sarah's remains he had forgotten the key. Not forgotten that he had it of course, simply that he had forgotten to put it somewhere safe. Not only that, he hadn't even rinsed his dive gear. As far as he could recall, that was a first. He had never forgotten to do that before. He had simply dumped it on the floor of the shower cubicle and taken off for the police station.

Arriving at *Maverick's* moorage, Fallon looked carefully at the cabin door. The combination lock was intact and the door still closed. Hurrying aboard, he spun the combination, opened the door and looked inside. All appeared unchanged. It had been almost two weeks since he had last been aboard, what in hell's name had he been thinking. Opening the cubicle door, Fallon looked at the hooks fastened along the inside wall. All his diving gear, including his BCD, was hanging, rinsed and dry, on the various pegs. Someone had been here.

The bright yellow flaps of the storage pockets in Fallon's BCD were turned toward the wall. He spun the jacket around, ripped one pocket open and felt inside. Nothing. He heart sank. He ripped open the other and fished around inside. Right in the bottom corner, he felt something hard. Squeezing gently with two fingers he grasped what felt like the links of a fine chain and gradually withdrew his hand. It was definitely a chain and, as the last links of gold appeared at the top of the pocket, a key.

Fallon slumped down on the toilet seat. The key was still here, unharmed. He turned it around in his fingers. Small and exquisite, its double bit made of gold and silver with cross-shaped patterns cut out of each. Fallon went to put it in his shirt pocket, then stood and looking in the mirror, fastened the chain around his neck, the key dangling on his chest beneath his shirt. Closing the door as he left, Fallon climbed out of the cabin and locked the door with its large combination lock before stepping onto the dock.

"Well, look who's here Ben," said a voice behind him. Fallon reached instinctively for his neck. The key was safely out of sight.

"Hi Charlie, what are you doing down here?"

"Just thought we'd take a walk and check on the boat. I've been well trained you know and it seems that the skipper is preoccupied these days. Even left his gear lying around inside."

"So it was you who cleaned up," Fallon said. "Thanks. I was a bit shaken up the other day and left in a hurry."

"I guessed as much. I was looking for one of my books that I thought I'd left on the boat. When I saw your gear on the floor, I gave it a quick rinse and hung it up. I was in a bit of a rush and didn't do a very good job I'm afraid, just sprayed it down. Didn't flush out the pockets or anything, I assumed you'd be back sooner. Sorry about that."

"No need for apologies. I certainly appreciate what you did; everything's perfect. I must go though, I promised Maggi I wouldn't be long," he continued without waiting for any response from Charlie. "Stay on the boat if you like. Goodbye Ben." With a brief rub of Ben's head, Fallon turned and walked quickly away leaving Charlie, puzzled by his abrupt departure, still standing with Ben on the dock.

#

Fallon was putting the last of his things into his suitcase the following morning when Maggi walked into the room. He travelled light and couldn't recall the last time it had proved necessary to check baggage. Along with an ever-present briefcase, the same battered carry-on had been his only luggage for years. He could quite easily last for two weeks from this one small suitcase as long as it didn't have to accommodate two opposing seasons in one trip. It also housed spares of most small personal toiletries he had collected at different times.

"Have you seen my toothbrush?" he asked as Maggi entered.

"Why would I have seen your toothbrush?"

"Well it's not here and I don't know where else I'm likely to have put it. I'm too anal for that."

"Don't you have a spare? I thought you always did?"

"Probably, but it bugs me that it's missing."

"Maybe you already packed it. It'll probably turn up. Stop fussing. By the way, this is your last chance to tell me what you're up to and then I'm off. Are you sure you don't want to change your mind?"

"Trust me on this will you. I'll fill you in as soon as I can and I promise not to do anything to embarrass you."

"Okay, travel safely. See you when you get back." With a quick peck on his cheek, Maggi left.

CHAPTER 56

Hamilton, Bermuda – Thursday, June 21, 2012

"It's really nice having you here," Rhiannon said. "How long will you stay?"

"Just until the end of the weekend," Maggi replied. Then, seeing the expression on Rhiannon's face, quickly added, "I still plan to move in permanently early next month. Will that be okay?"

"Okay? You have to be kidding me. I've wanted that for years. Of course, it's okay. Are you sure?"

"Yes, I'm sure. There are a couple of things that I'd like to get sorted out before I move, but it's not critical if I don't. That's what I'm waiting for right now. Unfortunately, Fallon's taken off to Rome and I'd prefer not to move until I've at least had a chance to talk to him. He won't be able to change my mind, but I still feel I owe him at least a face to face explanation before the move rather than after."

"Rome? What on earth is he going to do there?"

"That's the weird part. He won't tell me. Just say's it's something he needs to do. I assume it involves the Catholic Church because he asked me to introduce him to our local priest. Fallon went to see him a short while ago and then, lo and behold, Father Baird visits Fallon at the house yesterday. Then, first thing today, Fallon's packed and off he goes. He wouldn't even wait for tonight's BA flight to London. He took the JetBlue flight to JFK this morning instead."

"Do you think this has something to do with the theft of the *San Pedro* cross?"

"It must have. I've no idea what else could have got him all fired up like this. Speaking of the cross, did you ever hear anything from the UK police about Dr. Gordon's drawings?"

"Nothing yet, apparently his executor is going through all his papers with a fine-toothed comb to try and help us, but no luck to-date."

"What will you do if they find them?"

"Assuming they include the one that Andrew Jensen thinks has a possible telephone number on it, I'm going to track it down. That theft has been in the back of my mind for years. Despite how tenuous this lead is, I'm not giving it up easily."

"No surprise there," Maggi said. "I'd be more surprised if you did. I can't recall you ever giving up on anything once you set your mind to it."

"Another thing I'm not giving up on is the gym. I'm running behind. If you're staying here, can I take your car? I assume its outside. Mine's in the underground parking and I'm already late."

"Sure. Keys are in my bag. Help yourself."

Gathering her things, Rhiannon picked up Maggi's bag and fished around inside for the keys. Moments later, she withdrew a clear plastic tubular container with a bright blue screw top containing a purple toothbrush. "I see you packed to stay over," she said, before noticing the laboratory label attached to the outside.

"What is this for?" Rhiannon asked, suddenly serious.

Maggi, who only moments before had been lounging on the sofa, sat forward, her face tense. "You weren't supposed to see that," she said.

"Well I wasn't exactly looking," Rhiannon replied. "I still haven't found your keys and it was right on top."

"You're right. It's my fault. I should have been more careful."

"What is it anyway? It looks like a laboratory sample tube. I used several of them recently for the Alexander DNA tests. Are you having a DNA test done?"

Maggi looked guilty. "Yes," she admitted.

"Whose?" Rhiannon asked her tone sharper than intended. Any thoughts of getting to the gym on time now forgotten.

"Fallon's."

"Why? Does this have anything to do with what I told you the other day about Peter Alexander?"

Maggi nodded, not quite trusting herself to speak.

"Really? Fallon?" Rhiannon asked. "You think he…and Kat?" Leaving the sentence unfinished, Rhiannon put down Maggi's bag and joined her on the sofa.

"I think so. After all these years, I just had to know. Besides, Fallon always wanted a son and maybe if there's a match he should know."

"If you're right, how will you tell him and how can you check anyway? You don't have Peter Alexander's sample, or the results."

"I still have to find a way to get a sample from Peter," Maggi replied. "I haven't really thought it through. Fallon was still packing this morning when I saw his wet toothbrush. I just scooped it up and took off while I could. I didn't want to wait until he got back."

"And who's going to do the tests? You can't just stroll in and ask for them, you know."

"I know. I've already asked my niece, Charlie. She sometimes needs DNA testing in her research. She said she would get them for me without me having to identify whose samples they were. We agreed I didn't have to tell her who they were from, although she guessed Fallon was involved."

"Why didn't you just ask me? You know I already have the DNA results from Peter Alexander."

"I don't know. A bit embarrassed I guess, and I didn't want you to think I was taking advantage of information I got through your work. Well, not directly anyway."

"I'll tell you what," Rhiannon said sighing, "if you really need to do this, and if you tell me how you plan to deal with it once you know, and then only if I'm satisfied no one gets hurt, I'll send the sample to my lab."

"You will? But who will you say it's from?"

"Leave that to me. I'll think of something. For now, you just tell me what you plan to do once you know."

#

"We're agreed then?" Rhiannon asked.

"Yes. I think you're right. I'll only tell Fallon if there's a positive result and, if I do tell him, it's entirely up to him what he does with the information. If there's no match, we'll let the whole matter rest. It's not up to me to interfere in Peter Alexander's life."

"Nor me, any more than we will already have done. You realize that I'm only agreeing to this because I know you'll try to do the tests through your niece anyway if I refuse. There's a lesson here for me too about information that I might share. I really shouldn't have said anything to you."

"You weren't to know there might be a connection," Maggi said.

"I know, but that's exactly my point. One never knows when and how there may be a connection. Anyway, lesson learned, so let's finish this."

"But you haven't told me how you'll submit the information?"

"I'm inventing a male Alexander relative," Rhiannon said. "Initials AF. I'll ask that they check the sample against both Sarah and Peter, just to cloud the issue a little. Only I get the original lab reports. Any copies will be filed in the lab and there's no follow up unless we ask. I'll give you the original if it's positive. If it's negative, I'll shred it."

"Won't you get into trouble?"

"Only if this ever leaked out. The wild card is Fallon and what he might do when, and if, he hears."

"He's a clam. I'm confident that he'll be very careful, whatever he does."

"You'd better be right," Rhiannon replied with a worried frown. "My career depends on it. I'm only doing this so that we can start the new phase in our relationship with a clean slate."

CHAPTER 57

Vatican City – Thursday, June 21, 2012

Jacques Gaudin looked decidedly pensive; something that Thibaud Escoffier was quick to point out.

"Why the long face my friend?" Father Escoffier asked.

"There's a lot at risk here and the worst part is we don't know how much this Mr. Fallon knows."

"Whatever it is, he is unlikely to be much better informed than you and me."

"I accept that, but who knows what we have missed? We are not part of the Silenti and we have gathered our knowledge like scraps from the table. We may know what they have eaten but we have not seen the whole dish."

Father Escoffier burst out laughing. "Where do you come up with these expressions, Jacques? Perhaps you have missed your true calling."

"Laugh if you will, but I tell you the Silenti did not reach their positions without a great deal of careful planning. We should not dismiss them so lightly. If it wasn't for our pooled knowledge, even the individual scraps we have would not yield a coherent story."

"If it will make you feel better, why don't we go over all the definitive information and also what we speculate Mr. Fallon might know. At least that way you will be better prepared when he visits on Saturday."

"That would certainly make me more comfortable," Jacques replied. "From what you have told me, Cardinal Cressey was actively involved in trying to obtain the *San Pedro* cross for the Church after its discovery."

"That is correct. He assigned Father Despic, a priest based in the United States at the time, to authenticate the cross. I believe from the odd bits of information I managed to gather that something went wrong. After his return from Bermuda, and a meeting with the Silenti, Father Despic was transferred from Boston to Port Elizabeth, South Africa. His relationship with Cardinal Cressey also changed. From what I saw, his visits and calls became far less frequent. I believe, although I can't recall who told me at the time, that Cardinal Vilicenti had taken him under his wing, whatever that might mean. All I know for sure is that it was several years before he returned to Boston and his communications with Cardinal Cressey resumed; although far less frequently than before."

"That sounds ominously like he served some sort of penance"

"I agree, although I never saw or heard any proof of that. The matter is of course now moot as Father Despic passed away some years ago."

"And you are sure the cross has since been stolen?"

"Oh, yes. It was in the news at the time. Disappeared right from the museum in Bermuda. It seems strange that Mr. Fallon now wishes to see you about this same cross."

"Yes. I found that surprising myself," Monsignor Gaudin replied. While he disliked not being entirely candid with his colleague there were some things he could not afford to share, including anything related to the key originally contained within the *San Pedro* cross. The Holy Father had told him its secret in absolute confidence and that was how it would remain.

"But, as he was the one who discovered it, I thought it appropriate to encourage the visit and see what he has to say," Monsignor Gaudin explained. "I pressed for an early meeting after you mentioned that Cardinal Weiler's assistant had requested some information on Bermuda accommodation from you. I must assume the cardinal is visiting there for something related to the cross. I have found no indication of anything else taking place in Bermuda that might require his attention."

"You are probably correct, and we were lucky to even discover that he was making the trip. If his usual accommodation at the Hamilton Princess had been available, the trip might have gone unnoticed. In this case though, his assistant knew I had visited the island in the past and asked for my advice on alternative places to stay. I informed him of a suitable hotel immediately across the road from the Princess. It's called the Rosedon."

"Is there anywhere you haven't been?" Jacques Gaudin asked.

"Not many places. Travel is my second passion after the Church. On that note, I had better get back. Cardinal Cressey might need me. I'll let you know if I hear anything further before your meeting."

"Thank you my friend. I'll keep you informed on how things progress."

As the two priests made their way back to their respective offices, Monsignor Gaudin thought again of the recognition message Anthony Fallon had provided.

He must mean he has the key, he thought.

Could it be that the Silenti had somehow located the key and tried to procure it for themselves? Why wouldn't they have informed the Pope? Mr. Fallon's request was starting to make sense, but how could he possibly know about the Silenti? Saturday couldn't come quickly enough as far as Jacques Gaudin was concerned.

CHAPTER 58

Hamilton, Bermuda – Friday, June 22, 2012

Friday it seemed, was clean-up day in several parts of the world. Rhiannon had barely sat down at her desk when she received an e-mail from the Metropolitan Police Service enclosing an electronic copy of a letter from the executor of Dr. Gordon's estate. In it, the executor went to great lengths to assure the police that, after extensive due diligence, he had found no evidence of the documents they and Rhiannon were seeking.

He also went on to report that he had found no evidence at all of any correspondence between Andrew Jensen and Bruce Gordon. If any such correspondence had existed in Dr. Gordon's computer files, he assumed they would be in his laptop, which along with his briefcase was still missing in Rome. All that remained in his home was a docking station. His old desktop computer had apparently been scrapped years earlier for a newer portable option.

Rhiannon was sorely disappointed at this news that threatened to put a serious crimp in her investigation. With neither Bruce Gordon nor Andrew Jensen having a copy of the drawing, she now had only one small thread left to follow. The former Italian police officer who had been asking about Bruce Gordon's whereabouts. Reaching into her drawer, she withdrew a bright yellow binder and read the highlighted name on the copy of an e-mail fastened inside - Angelo Mosconi.

Apparently, he was now working as a private investigator. The Italian police had even provided a telephone number. She didn't for one second believe the story they had offered about Bruce Gordon's wife, or mistress, having him followed. From her recollection, Dr. Gordon was hardly in shape for dalliances of that nature. She also wasn't sure, even if she did manage to contact him, how forthcoming Angelo Mosconi would be about why really he was trailing Dr. Gordon, but she knew she had to try.

Picking up her telephone, Rhiannon dialed the number from the e-mail. After a momentary pause, and then a few clicks, a recorded message announced *"Il numero chiamato non è in servizio."*

Rhiannon tried the number again and listened closely. Even without any understanding of Italian, she managed to grasp the Italian versions of "number", "not" and "service" from the brief message.

Strange, she thought, *the police providing a number that's not in service.*

She would have the main Bermuda police reception track down Angelo Mosconi's number while she finished the rest of the things she wanted to accomplish today. She had sent Maggi's sample to the lab, and she would tackle the other tasks before she made the call. After that, she was taking the rest of the day off.

It wasn't often that Maggi was also free this early in the day and they had a lot to plan. She could hardly wait until Maggi moved in. Besides, this weekend was likely to be busy with police activities, so she might as well get some rest while she could. The Newport to Bermuda race yachts had been coming in since Monday and it was party-time for them. Despite the wide disparity in ages of the crews, they could be rowdy and the police would need to provide some discreet shepherding to avoid any trouble with the locals. She also wanted to see her father. He was, once again, part of the *Osprey* race crew. They had arrived on the eighteenth and she hadn't even seen him yet. Perhaps she and Maggi could pay him a visit. Might as well start that process now; it felt like being a teenager all over again.

#

Sitting on Rhiannon's patio, Maggi looked out at Hamilton Harbour and the myriad of yachts tied up around Albouy's Point and the Royal Bermuda Yacht Club. She was going to like living here. Very different from the house she shared with Fallon in Tucker's Town, but the ease of access to everything downtown would be great. More importantly, there was Rhiannon; they would be together every day. Once she had the results of the DNA test and Fallon returned, she would let him know her plans. The conversation wasn't going to be easy after all the years they had been together. Nonetheless, she was sure that in the end he would understand, after all their friendship had already withstood the test of time and she hoped things would remain as before. There really was no need for that relationship to change.

She did need to call Charlie though and tell her that she no longer needed help with the DNA tests. She wouldn't tell her about Rhiannon; far better that she just offer a small white lie and say that she had changed her mind. She had, she would say, decided to leave things as they were.

She also needed to call Howard Alexander. There was a message on her phone from him. It seemed he was looking for Fallon.

#

Similar to every other lawyer he knew, Howard liked leaving his office with a clean desk on Friday afternoon. Not that every file was complete, merely that the responsibility for the next action was with somebody else for a while. That way, for the weekend at least, his head would be clear of work and he could enjoy his free time. This Friday was no different. He had dealt with all his open legal files, or would have done so by the end of the day, and the only outstanding matters were of a personal nature. Those would certainly remain on his mind over the weekend.

The first of these was the need to respond to Cardinal Weiler. He had checked with Peter and Sean, both of whom had indicated their availability to meet anytime through the end of the month. Fallon, based on his closed and locked office, was still away. True to form, there was no indication at either his office, or on his voicemail, as to where he was, or when he might return. Howard had left a couple of messages but had not had any response. His message to Maggi, left earlier this morning, had not been returned yet either.

Deciding not to wait, Howard sent a quick e-mail to Cardinal Weiler suggesting a meeting in a week's time. If he heard back from either Fallon or Maggi before the day was out, and the date didn't work for Fallon, he would change it at that time. Besides, they didn't have the original key and he did not intend to refund the money. Whatever date they met really wouldn't change those facts.

Of greater concern to Howard, and significantly more personal, was what he should do about Peter; and Sean for that matter. His son seemed determined to leave his law practice and, while Peter's suggestion that Sean fill his place had merit, was it a prudently considered option or merely an expedient short-term solution? His first inclination had been to blame Maggi's niece for Peter's seemingly uncharacteristic behaviour. The two of them were inseparable. While Peter had girlfriends in the past, on this occasion he appeared totally besotted. If he was fair though, Howard recognized that although he had not spent much time with Charlie, on each occasion they had met, he had been increasingly impressed.

Kat and Sarah would have loved her, he thought.

She fitted right in, and damn she was smart. Her frequently mischievous manner successfully hiding a very keen mind. Howard, no slouch himself in the brains department, had debated Charlie on several topics where she easily held her own. He should have realized it sooner; after all, she was completing her doctorate while here on the island.

THE BERMUDA KEY

No, Charlie was not the problem.

Sarah's death perhaps, that was far more likely to be the reason for Peter's behaviour. Her death had affected them all deeply and each of them had reacted in different ways. He had turned to his work; keeping himself occupied so that he didn't have to think about it. Sean had withdrawn. His colourful Canadian personality hidden, albeit temporarily, while he dealt inwardly with his grief. Then there was Peter who seemed to have undergone a complete metamorphosis. The studious, focussed lawyer now wanted to be outdoors, or on the water. My God, Peter was starting to sound like Fallon. Perhaps spending time away would do him some good. He could always come back to the firm later.

Howard looked up, startled by the sharp knock on his door. Shanice Morgan, the newest member of the firm's IT department, stood in the doorway. Speaking slowly to avoid being misunderstood, she quietly informed him that she needed to complete a security update on his computer. It would only take her a few minutes, but she needed to sit at his desk. Already distracted by his concerns over Peter, Howard was happy to oblige. Peter had brought Shanice into the firm and, based on the comments he had heard about her performance, she was doing a stellar job. Apparently, any IT backlog had quickly disappeared since her arrival and she had proved adept at assisting some of their overseas clients with translation issues. She was quite a find among the limited local population and he wondered how Peter had discovered a way around the island's hiring guidelines for temporary residents.

That's another reason I wish he would stay, Howard thought. Manoeuvering through Bermuda's regulatory red tape was a sorely needed talent within the firm.

With time to kill while Shanice worked on his computer, Howard decided to make the short walk from his office to Andrew Jensen's store. He had been meaning to ask the old goldsmith whether he recalled making a copy of Kat's key pendant and this seemed as good a time as any.

#

Andrew Jensen was thinking about Kat, too. Not about her pendant, but rather the famous *San Pedro* cross which she and Anthony Fallon had found. What is more, he was distraught. Andrew could not remember having told a single lie in his entire life and yet it appeared that he had now, albeit inadvertently, lied to an Assistant Inspector in the Bermuda Police Service.

When Assistant Inspector Thomas visited his store, she had asked specifically about the drawings he had sent to Bruce Gordon. Andrew honestly believed at the time, and had assured her of this, that he had deleted all the associated files in his computer and had no copies of any drawings. Last night, after what his son described as a simple virus, that belief had proved untrue.

Neil Jensen, who routinely kept an eye on his father's computer, had arrived to look into the latest problem. After removing the virus, he re-installed the information from a back-up disk he had made for his father a month or so earlier. It was while apologizing to his father that some of the information was dated and that Andrew would need to go through it all once again to get rid of anything he did not want, that Bruce Gordon's files made their reappearance. Without Andrew's knowledge, Neil's last back up had captured the files.

With printed copies of all the drawings now in his hand, Andrew Jensen was about to call Assistant Inspector Thomas with his confession when Howard Alexander walked into the store.

"Andrew, good to see you," Howard said.

"And you," Andrew Jensen replied, hurriedly putting the drawings under the counter and out of sight. "What brings you in today?"

"I wanted to test your memory."

"Really. That's a bit of a stretch these days, I'm afraid."

"Well perhaps this is an easy question. I wonder if you recall making a key pendant for Katherine?"

"Indeed I do." Andrew smiled broadly. "She wanted it for your daughter's birthday. In fact, Inspector Thomas asked me the same thing only a short while back. Seems she had seen it and liked it and was hoping to have a similar one made."

"How coincidental, two similar questions out of the blue after all this time."

"Well hers wasn't quite so coincidental. She was doing some sort of investigation into the disappearance of the *San Pedro* cross and one thing sort of led to the other."

"Investigating the cross? Again, after all this time?"

"Oh dear, I really shouldn't have said anything. It seems the original insurance investigator was in Rome looking into its disappearance and died. That set things off again. I know you won't say anything about this, but please forget I mentioned it, will you?"

"Of course. Well, I should get along. Thanks for telling me about Kat's key pendant. I was thinking about having another copy made," he lied, "but I'll come back when I have more time."

As Howard left the store, Andrew Jensen reached for a nearby stool and sat down. His hands were shaking. Reaching under the counter he took out the drawings and dialed Bermuda Police Headquarters.

#

Rhiannon had barely hung up the phone after a disjointed conversation with an either genuinely puzzled, or intentionally obtuse, Angelo Mosconi when her telephone rang. Her delight in the news from Andrew Jensen quickly overrode any possible irritation with his confusion over his deleted files. A short time later, she sat staring down at copies of the very same drawings that had resulted in Bruce Gordon's trip to the Vatican and there, alongside the shaded cross sketch, was a possible telephone number.

Picking up the telephone, and assuming the number was in Italy, she dialed. There was a moment of silence, and then a single ring before it was answered.

"*Buona puliscono, l'ufficio del Cardinale Cressey. Questo è parlare Padre Escoffier,*" said the voice at the other end.

Without understanding what had been said, Rhiannon grasped at the first name she heard. Replying in English, she identified herself as a Bermuda Police Officer and asked to speak to Cardinal Cressey. Without hesitation, the voice at the other end switched to impeccable English and asked her to hold while he transferred the call. Moments later she was speaking directly to Cardinal Cressey and trying desperately to explain the purpose of her call and how she had come to have his number.

#

By the time Howard returned to his office, Shanice had left. He slumped down behind his desk, his mind spinning, and held his head in his hands. The brief visit to Andrew Jensen to clear up the possibility of a second key had resulted in far more information than he was expecting. He could really do with talking to Fallon. Where the hell was the man?

Finally noticing the light flashing on his telephone, Howard pressed the speaker key and listened to the message. It was from Maggi, short and to the point. Fallon had gone to Rome and wouldn't be back until later the following week. And, she added assuming Howard would like to know, she didn't have a clue why and Fallon had refused to say.

#

Sean Patterson closed the lid on his laptop. Sitting at Peter's black-flecked granite kitchen counter, its surface in stark contrast to the white cabinets and stainless steel appliances, he had been through all his outstanding e-mails. Life it seemed just kept moving along. Like the old adage about putting your hand in a bucket of water and then pulling it out and seeing how little impact it had, Sarah's death, so raw to him and others close to her, appeared insignificant in the bigger scheme of things. Despite being on compassionate leave, his law practice e-mail traffic continued to flow. Life moved on. He was sick of this. Perhaps working for Howard was the answer.

Sean looked out the window. Turquoise sea all the way to the horizon and, of course, there was the weather. Walking to the patio door, he pulled it open and was hit with a blast of hot humid air. It was like a furnace and he loved it. The work would likely be the same, although in a new practice and different culture it would take some time to adjust. And the island was so small, twenty one miles long and only a mile and a half at its widest. Then again, it was a short trip home anytime he felt like it. A brief flight to Toronto and then on to Vancouver. Good old Canada, it was immense; the internal leg of the flight was more than twice as long as the flight from Bermuda to Toronto. Hopefully Howard would make some sort of offer in the next few days, if not, he would ask directly. It was time to start afresh.

With his mind largely made up, Sean decided to seek out Charlie for one last reality check. She had lived on the island for a while and, while she had never intended to stay, her opinion on moving here as a single person would be welcome.

#

Charlie was furiously scrubbing the deck of *Maverick* when Sean found her. Her first indication that anyone was watching was a single bark from Ben. Without moving from his spot in the shade, the dog had merely raised his head and offered one short half-hearted "woof" in greeting to an obviously known entity.

"Serving penance or are you just a very kind guest?" Sean asked.

Charlie, without turning around, stopped scrubbing and sat back on her haunches her head hanging down. "Careful friend. Agitated woman at work."

"Would you rather I left you alone?"

"No, not really." Charlie turned around. "Why don't you come aboard? I, for one, am desperately in need of a drink right now and I don't like drinking alone. There's wine and ice in the fridge. I planned to leave it for Fallon, but seeing as he's not going to be back for a few days we might as well drink it and I'll restock later."

"Are you two heading out somewhere?"

"No. I had a few things on my mind and thought that cleaning up the boat would be good therapy. It seems to work for Fallon so I thought I might as well try. It's nice down at the water anyway. What brings you here?"

"Actually I was hoping to find you. I went over to your cottage and there was no reply so, on an off chance, I thought I'd try the harbour. I had a something I wanted to bounce off you, but if you've too much on your mind it can wait."

"No need for that. I'm sure, whatever it is, it will be a good distraction. You pour the wine and I'll get cleaned up. The deck can wait." Moments later as the door to the aft cabin closed behind her, Charlie called out, "go ahead, start talking. I can hear."

Not needing any further prompting, Sean launched into his dilemma. He was in the middle of his story when he suddenly stopped mid-sentence. "Are you always like this?" he asked.

"Like what?"

"It's so easy to talk to you. I'm not really sure why, it just is. I'm not complaining mind you, it just struck me that I was telling you things that I normally keep to myself."

"I've no idea. I try not to be judgmental. Maybe that's it. Anything I might say by way of opinion is only that; my opinion. Besides, this time there's a chance of a bit of *quid pro quo*. I could do with some advice myself."

"Go ahead. What's up?"

"No, you finish first."

#

Two glasses of Chardonnay later, Charlie and Sean had exhausted the topic of his possible move to Bermuda and, as he so aptly put it, "consensus had been achieved". They both agreed that if Howard offered him a suitable position with the firm, he should take it. Besides, as Charlie noted in a particularly blunt closing observation. "Fuck it, Sean. If it doesn't work out you can always just pack up and go home."

With Sean's future settled, the conversation logically turned to Charlie's earlier agitated state and the advice she was seeking.

"The first one's really quite petty," Charlie said.

"Maggi had asked me to do something for her and after I got it all worked out she called this morning and said to forget it, she had changed her mind. Actually now that I've told you it sounds really stupid. So, that's it. I'm going to forget it right now."

Sean grinned. "Well I'm glad I solved that," he said. "One last glass while we deal with number two?"

"Sure." Charlie held out her glass to Sean who promptly refilled it before repeating the process with his own.

"Okay. Go ahead," Sean prompted.

"Preppy proposed."

"What!"

"Peter woke me up at the crack of dawn this morning with an armful of roses and proposed. He said he had quit his job and would like to marry me. Beyond that he didn't have a clue as to what he was going to do for the rest of his life."

"And where is he now?"

"I think he went to work. He had things to finish up."

Sean burst out laughing. "Isn't that like him," he said. "Even when he's being irrational, he does it in a rational way. Can I ask what you said?"

"I said I couldn't deal with it that early in the morning and needed to think about it. I was still doing that when you turned up at the boat."

"And now?"

"I think I'd really like that. I have no idea of how we sort out the details though. I'm not concerned about his work; I'm sure that will all pan out. What really concerns me is where we will end up living.

I always assumed I'd live in South Africa and Peter…well Peter's so Bermudian. He really belongs here."

"As you convinced me a few minutes ago, Bermuda's not too shabby."

"No, I guess not. It's family and work that worry me. It's much harder for me to get home than it is for you and I'm not sure there's enough work in my field here."

"But you're going to say yes, anyway?"

"I believe I am. I'm pretty sure he's going to drive me crazy, but I know I wouldn't be happy without him in my life."

#

Contrary to Charlie and Sean's expectations, Peter wasn't getting much work done. While he had arrived at the office with the best of intentions, he hadn't been able to stay focussed. In the past few days he had really turned his life upside down. First, he had quit his job and then this morning, at six a.m. to be precise, he had driven over to Charlie's and proposed.

The thought had first occurred to him the previous evening, and after going out and buying two dozen roses in case he didn't change his mind, he decided to sleep on the idea. Fresh roses wouldn't be available again until later the following day and no one could ever accuse him of being disorganized. Impulsive maybe, disorganized no.

Peter wasn't sure what he expected Charlie to say, so he wasn't too upset when she said that she would think about it. Unfortunately, that uncertainty was definitely playing on his mind now. It was no wonder he couldn't concentrate on his work.

The interruption from Shanice Morgan, when it came, was therefore a welcome relief. She needed to upgrade his computer security system and, after a few pleasantries as to how she was doing and discovering that the search for her mother was progressing as well as could be expected, he left her alone in his office. He was glad she had settled in. The information she had provided about the cardinal and the key was extremely interesting. Its value, he was sure, would prove itself over time.

In the interim, he would head down the hall and visit his father. They should really have a serious discussion about the possibility of Sean joining the firm and, if a suitable opportunity presented itself, he might even tell his father about his marriage proposal.

#

"More Champagne, Ivor?" Barry Smythe asked holding out the bottle. "You look perplexed. Still thinking about that survival suit we picked up?"

Replacing his mobile phone on the restaurant table, Ivor Thomas looked around at the faces of his fellow crewmembers from *Osprey*. All were watching him closely.

"No, nothing like that. My daughter tells me they've found some remains. The young woman is definitely dead. Very limited wreckage though. Just an anchor and some bones apparently. Seems that we found the only sign of any floating debris."

"So what's troubling you?"

"Rhiannon wants to have dinner, specifically to introduce me to her friend."

"Sounds like a future son-in law to me," Barry said, happy to provide his opinion without ever being asked. "It's about time she got married anyway, a beautiful young woman like that."

"That's what I thought."

"Then why the worried look?"

"Her friend's name is Maggi."

CHAPTER 59

Rome, Italy – Friday, June 22, 2012

Fallon had arrived at Rome's Fiumicino airport late the previous evening and, after clearing customs, took the Leonardo Express train to Rome Termini. After a brief taxi ride from the railroad station, he had checked into his hotel, a short walk from the main Vatican entrance. His meeting with Monsignor Gaudin was not until Saturday morning and, after a quick meal at a nearby pizzeria, he had turned in for a relatively early night. He wanted to be as sharp as possible by the time of his meeting.

His hurried departure from Bermuda had left him feeling out of sorts and it had taken last night's good sleep and most of today before he finally settled down. He had been brusque with Charlie down at the dock and barely talked to Maggi before leaving. It was as if he was on some sort of adrenalin rush. He knew he was fixated on his idea, but he just didn't seem able to slow himself down. Once he had decided to take some proactive action with regard to the key and the cross, all he wanted to do was to get on with it. He was about to toss a proverbial hand grenade into the Vatican's affairs and then sit back and see what transpired.

Of course, it was possible that his whole plan could backfire and he would scuttle out of the Vatican with his tail between his legs. Cardinals Kwodo and Weiler may have acted with all the appropriate authority and Father Despic may have been completely legitimate and have had nothing to do with the disappearance of the cross. He didn't think so, but time would tell. Whatever the potential outcome, it was too late to back out now.

Fallon fingered the key hanging around his neck. Still there. Well, no matter what they thought about his allegations he did have the key and, whatever else transpired, he knew they wanted that!

#

Angelo Mosconi replaced the telephone on the hall table in his modest house. It hardly ever rang. He preferred to handle all his business on mobile telephones. Preferably those that he could discard if necessary. Yet today, he had received not one but two calls on his home telephone. He had just completed the second call and felt violated. This was his private space.

The first call had surprised him. It was from an Assistant Inspector Thomas of the Bermuda Police. Although his home number was no secret, they must have worked through the local police to locate the correct Mosconi. There were dozens in the directory. Besides, he knew who was to blame for their call. It had to be that idiot Alessio Barone. He was the only one who knew of Angelo's interest in the Englishman, and he was probably angry he hadn't yet been paid. There was a score to settle there, but Alessio would have to wait for his return from Bermuda. If it hadn't been for him, Angelo's impending trip would not be necessary.

Angelo was confident he had given nothing away in the call with the police officer although his attempts to draw her out into why she thought he would know anything about Dr. Gordon proved equally challenging. After several refusals to speak to her of any of his clients and pretending to be confused about her questions or not understanding the language, she had finally cracked. The Italian police, she said, had told her that Angelo was following Dr. Gordon for a client and that it was a matrimonial issue. Grateful to have some plausible excuse for following Dr. Gordon, Angelo grabbed at the offered reason. While her information was correct, he admitted, he had not had any direct contact with Dr. Gordon and, as his client wished to remain anonymous, there was nothing more he could say on the matter.

It was the second call that had necessitated the upcoming trip.

Cardinal Cressey rarely, if ever, needed to call Angelo at home. On this occasion, however, his call was urgent and he was agitated. Neither of these factors appealed to Angelo. Without pausing after his initial greeting, the cardinal put forward his request.

"Angelo," he said, "I would like you to travel to Bermuda. There is unfinished business there which might prove somewhat difficult to accomplish."

By the time Cardinal Cressey terminated the call, Angelo had learned not only of Andrew Jensen and Assistant Inspector Thomas, but also of how the Bermuda goldsmith had provided the police with a copy of the same material that Dr. Gordon had carried in his briefcase. Cardinal Cressey's telephone number was apparently included in this material, which had prompted Assistant Inspector Thomas to call him. The cardinal wanted Angelo to visit the island and "take care of things".

Deeming it prudent to say nothing of his earlier call from the same police inspector, Angelo agreed to do as requested and advised that he would leave for Bermuda as soon as he could make suitable travel plans.

CHAPTER 60

Vatican City – Friday, June 22, 2012

Cardinal Weiler opened Howard Alexander's e-mail minutes after it arrived. After a quick scan of its contents, he grimaced. Despite the lengthy delay in accommodating his request for a meeting, Mr. Alexander was now suggesting they meet a week from today. He would have to make the arrangement work. He couldn't risk a further delay. Several days earlier, on the off chance something might be arranged, he had asked his assistant to check availability in the Hamilton Princess during July, only to be disappointed that they were already fully booked. Summer, apparently, was well underway.

Obtaining accommodation at the Princess, his favorite hotel on the island, for one week from today was probably even more unlikely. Not only did he enjoy its location and the luxurious accommodation, he loved its history. From famous visitors to the hotel, to its use as an espionage listening post during the Second World War, the stories fascinated him.

Sighing, he called out to his assistant. He needed to finalize his arrangements. He would also invite the Vatican's counsel, Gino Vacchelli. After all, both Howard Alexander and his son were lawyers. No point in starting-off outmatched. He couldn't recall the name of the hotel suggestion his assistant had obtained from one of his fellow priests, but hoped it matched the Hamilton Princess in all its pink glory. Maybe there would be a vacancy the following week. He should let Cardinal Vilicenti know of these developments.

#

To say that Cardinal Vilicenti was unexcited at Cardinal Weiler's news would have been a significant understatement. Nothing related to the *San Pedro* cross, or its hidden key, had gone according to plan. If he didn't know better, he would suspect it was cursed. While he was certainly pleased at the opportunity to try, once again, and get the original key from the Alexanders, his confidence in his colleague's ability to achieve that aim had been sorely eroded by past events.

While success would quickly erase any past sins in their efforts to obtain the cross and the key, failure would certainly not yield the same results. It was for this reason that although he encouraged the younger cardinal to do his very best, he continued to insulate himself from any negative fallout should things go awry.

#

Cardinal Cressey, too, was quietly reflecting on the increasing vulnerability of his own position. After years of careful manoeuvering, his ascendency to the highest position in the Catholic Church had been defeated by old age. Not only that, despite being over eighty and at a point where he should be sliding gently into retirement as a revered elder statesman of the Church, he was now being forced to take more and more extreme measures merely to protect and hold on to the power and authority which he had fought so hard to achieve.

He could only hope that with his latest call to Angelo, the issue of the theft of the *San Pedro* cross would cease to exist and it could remain securely locked in his office where it had been for these many years.

After his death, and as he had requested in his will, it was to be placed among the Vatican's own treasures where he hoped it would remain to somehow atone for his own actions. Actions, which he had always believed he took in the best interests of the Church.

The call from Assistant Inspector Thomas had worried him. Was there no end to the consequences of a simple action by Signor Panzini? He had even briefly considered changing his telephone number but decided against it. That would only serve to make him appear guilty.

And what of the key? he thought.

A few days earlier, as he passed through the outer office, he overheard Father Escoffier speaking with someone about accommodation in Bermuda. After Thibaud terminated the call, he had jokingly asked his assistant whether he was planning yet another holiday. He was not, Thibaud had said, the enquiry had been made on behalf of Cardinal Weiler who was having accommodation problems for an upcoming trip.

It had to concern the key, Cardinal Cressey thought. *Yet, as far as he was aware, neither he nor Cardinal Kwodo had been consulted. Another reminder of how he seemed to be losing control over what had originally been his assured path to the papacy.*

Although Cardinal Weiler had failed in his initial attempt to locate the original key, Cardinal Cressey had to assume he was still on its trail. Only this time, he seemed to have abandoned his liaison with Cardinals Cressey and Kwodo.

Perhaps he was strengthening his alliance with Cardinal Vilicenti. What if Cardinal Vilicenti became Pope? Perish the thought. Cardinal Kwodo was more to his liking, but unless they obtained the key themselves, there was no certainty of that. The accolades, which would accrue to the one who recovered it, would certainly enhance their prospects of ascending to the papacy. It was time to speak with Cardinal Kwodo again. Despite his earlier comments about leaving things in God's hands, what were his real aspirations? There should be some way to ensure that if Cardinal Weiler were successful, the glory would be evenly spread, or better still, carefully directed as Cardinal Cressey saw fit.

#

Father Escoffier felt good. The minor secrets he shared with his good friend and colleague Jacques Gaudin did not cause him the least discomfort. Nor did he feel disloyal towards his boss. He had long ago learned that the Vatican was full of secrets and more often than not, even the secrets had secrets. He wondered sometimes how they ever got anything done. Everyone it seemed had a hidden agenda. The only way to move ahead was to choose your friends carefully and play the game. Failure to understand the politics would very quickly leave you isolated and languishing in some godforsaken post. There was something very different about Jacques Gaudin, and Thibaud was confident of his friend's continued promotion within the Vatican. He would continue to foster that relationship and follow along in Jacques' wake.

Father Escoffier's daydreaming was interrupted by the sight of Cardinal Kwodo standing in the doorway, his broad white-toothed smile in sharp contrast to his dark skin.

"Good-day, Thibaud, is Cardinal Cressey available?"

"I believe so, Eminence. Let me check," Thibaud replied looking at Cardinal Cressey's closed office door.

"Don't bother; I shall only be a moment."

With that, Cardinal Kwodo knocked on the closed office door and without waiting for a response from inside entered, immediately closing the door behind him.

Unusual, Father Escoffier thought. *The old African cardinal was seldom, if ever, impolite.*

#

"I thought it best to come down," Cardinal Kwodo said looking at his colleague's startled expression. "You sounded disturbed on the telephone."

Cardinal Cressey looked up at his fellow cardinal. "Disturbed may be too strong a word but, I confess, I am somewhat concerned. Are you aware that Cardinal Weiler is making another trip to Bermuda?"

"No. Did he speak with you about this?"

"No, he did not. Nor with you apparently. Do you think he is doing this on his own volition or do you think Cardinal Vilicenti is pulling the strings?"

"If I were to be charitable I would think he was doing it on his own. After all, the Silenti did agree he should try to meet with the Alexanders, and report to us on his return. However, given our earlier involvement, for him not to advise either of us of his plans seems unlikely."

"Unlikely, unless he has spoken with Cardinal Vilicenti who has sanctioned his plans in such a manner that he feels our support is no longer needed. As I have mentioned before, while locating the key can do little good for my career at this stage, it could do wonders for your own prospects."

Cardinal Kwodo smiled. "Thank you my friend, but as far as I am concerned, and as I too have said before, I prefer to leave that in God's hands."

"So what do you think we should do?" Cardinal Cressey asked.

"Watch and wait. If God requires more of us, I am sure He will find a way to let us know. Now you must forgive me. I should go. I have an appointment to see the Holy Father and Monsignor Gaudin keeps a very tight rein on his schedule."

#

Jacques Gaudin, as suspected by Cardinal Kwodo, was indeed looking at his watch at that very moment. Three minutes before the Pope's next scheduled appointment. He needed to go over his notes for the meeting with Mr. Fallon the following morning but that would have to wait until later this evening. It appeared there would be no time during the day.

Jacques sighed. He hated feeling unprepared. While he would certainly have enough time that evening, there was the possibility he needed to contact someone, or have some point clarified, and a late night review would not allow that.

Deciding he was over-thinking things, he looked at his watch again. Two minutes before the meeting. As he looked up there was a light knock on his door. Cardinal Kwodo stood in the doorway, his smile seeming to light up the room.

"Monsignor Gaudin," he said, "is the Holy Father available?"

CHAPTER 61

Gordons Bay, South Africa –
Friday, June 22, 2012

Sibeal Leigh, (née O'Malley), had, similarly to her sister Maggi's visit to Bermuda many years before, originally left Ireland for a short visit to South Africa. Then, as Maggi often joked, she met the handsome doctor, and that was that. Now, thirty-four years later, here she was sitting on the beach alone, three years after her husband's death.

She looked pensively back at the house perched on the rocks above the small beach. Alongside the naval college in Gordon's Bay, its border on one side was the college's fence that ran far out into the ocean, and on the other, large rocks and pounding surf.

A private paradise was how her husband, one of Cape Town's foremost heart surgeons, had first described it to her. Somewhere to escape the craziness of being on-call at all hours of the day and night. Success in his field had brought the usual accolades and financial comfort, but along with those came the ever-increasing demands on his time. The house proved to be a much-needed sanctuary and, until his death, had been their home away from home.

After his death, the emptiness of living alone in the southern suburbs and the sudden absence of activity had been more than she could stand. Within months, she had sold the Claremont house and moved out here. Besides, as she was prone to rationalize, Charlie had her own place and worse, was now working and living in Bermuda. Albeit only temporarily, she missed her only child.

At least she's with Maggi, she thought. *That was something.*

Sibeal realized it must have been very early in Bermuda when Charlie called. As far as she could remember, they were six hours behind. Despite her surprise at the news, she had to smile. It was not often she heard her daughter unsure of herself. Notwithstanding the dozens of questions she had about the suitability of this chap who had proposed to Charlie, she had tried hard to contain her own curiosity and provide a steady sounding board for her obviously flustered daughter.

In the end, with a final "thanks mom, have to go," Charlie had ended the call with a promise to telephone in a day or two with her decision.

So much like her father, Sibeal thought.

She hoped Charlie was being sensible. From the little she had said it seemed this Peter Alexander was a local Bermudian lawyer, who had recently quit his job. Hardly an auspicious start. Apparently, Maggi knew him and his family. She would give her sister a call once she heard from Charlie again. Perhaps she would say no and the whole thing would blow over. Maybe a trip to Bermuda was in order. Deciding to call her best friends, and Charlie's godparents, before doing anything, she made her way back along the beach to the house. If Marie Oosthuizen couldn't settle her down, George certainly would, the man was a rock.

CHAPTER 62

West Vancouver, Canada – Friday, June 22, 2012

"When's Sean due back, hon?" Chris Patterson asked.

"Not until the end of the month," Carol Patterson replied. "It's so sad. I really loved Sarah you know. She was a perfect match for him."

"I know. It's hard to imagine him with anyone else now. Time will tell I guess."

"Why did you ask?"

"I want to haul *SeaQuill* out of the water to clean the hull. I could do with his help. It can wait until the end of the month though. I'm walking down to the yacht club later this afternoon. Why don't you join me? If the weather holds we can go out for a short sail before dinner."

CHAPTER 63

Vatican City – Saturday, June 23, 2012

Fallon arrived at the *Portone di Bronzo* at the Apostolic Palace precisely on time for his meeting with Monsignor Gaudin. Dressed in a black suit, crisp white shirt, black shoes and black tie, he felt appropriately dressed for his meeting in this magnificent building.

Magnificent and intimidating, he thought as he stared at the two members of the famous Swiss guards in their traditional Medici blue, red and yellow uniforms guarding the front entrance. His escort, another Swiss guard, although this one dressed in his every-day all blue uniform, ushered him forward.

As Fallon stepped into the enormous entrance and past the two guards, a tall priest with, judging by his youthful face, prematurely grey hair and a pair of reading glasses dangling from a gold chain around his neck stepped forward to greet him. His clerical rank clearly indicated by the broad purple sash around his waist.

"Mr. Fallon," he said, his hand extended. "Good of you to come at such short notice."

"My pleasure," replied Fallon and for one of the few times in his life content not to try to correct the formal use of his name.

The place did that to you, he thought.

"I'm afraid this is all new to me. Do I call you Monsignor Gaudin?"

"How about Jacques? It's probably easier and certainly less formal. May I call you Anthony, or do you prefer Mr. Fallon?"

"Actually I prefer just Fallon, but Anthony sounds fine in here."

Monsignor Gaudin laughed. "It can be a bit stuffy," he replied. "Come with me, I'll point out a few things that may be of interest as we walk."

As they walked through the palace, Fallon was awed by both its opulence and cleanliness. The floors, all highly polished marble with scattered richly woven rugs partially covering ornate biblical scenes or checkerboard patterns. The staircase windows with their huge mosaics of St. Peter and St. Paul. The former's robes brilliant blue and yellow, the sash red, all the same Medici colours as the guards. The latter's robes green and red, the sash yellow.

Huge paintings adorned the walls. Even the light switches were elaborate. Shining brass plates, each embossed with the papal crest surrounding the white toggles. Long passages with high, decorated ceilings indicated their path, while delicate white covered chairs lined the way past the huge Ducale and Clementine Halls.

Fallon could barely believe the range of emotions he was experiencing that morning. Standing in St. Peter's Square looking at the Vatican buildings, he had felt embarrassed by his earlier audacity in asking Father Baird to arrange a meeting with the Pope. Who did he think he was? Although neither Catholic nor religious, he certainly knew of the Pope and was well aware of his global standing. Now, walking through the magnificent corridors of the Apostolic Palace he felt intimidated, and his planned request trivial in the face of such great wealth and power. Then, as if a switch tripped, he became angry. Angry that the guardians of all this power and wealth would even consider lying and cheating to achieve their aims.

At that moment, Fallon knew what he was doing was right. No matter how audacious his initial request, or how insignificant he was in the bigger scheme of Vatican affairs, they had something to hide. That was why he was here. Any uncertainty fell away and, by the time they reached Monsignor Gaudin's office, as far as Fallon was concerned they were every bit on equal terms. It was going to be all or nothing. Oh, yes, he would be polite, but with respect to his demands, he was inflexible.

#

A short while later, comfortably seated at a small table surrounded by four chairs off to the side of Jacques Gaudin's spacious office, the waiting coffee was served and traditional pleasantries were exchanged. Jacques Gaudin asked after Father Baird and Fallon's connection with him, and Fallon queried Monsignor Gaudin's role in the Church. Finally, the question Fallon had been waiting for was asked.

"So, Anthony, how can I be of assistance to you?"

"Well, I'd like to tell you a story. Some of it is fact and some of it is supposition. I'm assuming it's of interest to you or else you wouldn't have agreed to meet. It's also going to take a while so I hope you have time?"

"Of course. Take all the time you need."

"It was Thursday, August fifteenth, nineteen eighty-five," Fallon began. "Katherine Shannon and I were diving off the coast of Bermuda when we found the *San Pedro* cross. The cross was originally in the possession of Friar Roberto Esponso who was travelling on the *San Pedro* when she sank in fifteen ninety-six. Can I assume you have heard of the cross or would you like me to describe it?"

"I have heard of it of course, but if you could describe it that would be helpful. I presume its description is germane to the rest of the narrative."

"It is. The cross is three inches in length and two inches across. Handmade in yellow gold, the front is an ornate-bas relief studded with seven brilliant large green emeralds of about fifteen carats each. Two are oval, three are round and one is pear shaped. The back has an engraved floral design. It looks for all intents and purposes like a pectoral cross worn by a senior member of the clergy."

"Very valuable I imagine. Not something an everyday priest was likely to have worn," Monsignor Gaudin said.

"Quite. There is, however, one additional aspect to the cross of which I was unaware at the time of its discovery. There is a secret mechanism which allows the back to be removed and hidden within the cross was a small key."

"And you know this for a fact?" an astonished Jacques Gaudin asked.

"I do. I didn't at the time, but I have since learned that Katherine Alexander discovered it. That's the same Katherine Shannon I referred to earlier; she married Howard Alexander, my lawyer."

"What happened then, or is there more to this story?"

"There is quite a bit more. Before we discuss the key, I'd like to tell you how we authenticated the cross. How it came to be that my wife corresponded with a Vatican archivist about the *San Pedro*. How she then received a call from a Cardinal Cressey, who subsequently sent Father Despic, one of your priests from Boston, to authenticate it. Then how, many years later during a visit to Bermuda by Queen Elizabeth II, it was discovered that the original cross had been stolen and replaced in the museum with a very clever forgery. A forgery which is, in fact, still on display in Bermuda."

"Are you suggesting Father Despic had something to do with its disappearance?"

"I'm not suggesting anything at the moment, but I would like to tell you the whole story in detail and then let you draw your own conclusions as to what is the truth and how we should proceed."

"Very well. I'll pour us each another cup of coffee while you continue."

#

Two hours had passed by the time Fallon finished his story of what he knew, and what he suspected had happened to the cross from the time of its discovery to the day its disappearance was first noticed. He spared no detail in the telling, omitting only what he did not know or suspect.

As Fallon finished, Monsignor Gaudin rose and, walking over to a hidden refrigerator in the paneled wall, returned with two bottles of ice-cold water and two crystal glasses.

"I think we could do with these," he said.

"Thanks," Fallon replied. "Thirsty work all this talking."

"If I could summarize," Jacques Gaudin said. "You believe although you have no proof, that somehow Father Despic and by association Cardinal Cressey may have been involved in the disappearance of the *San Pedro* cross."

"Correct, but the story doesn't end there. Shortly after the discovery of the cross, another cardinal approached us, a Cardinal Kwodo. He wanted to know whether we had discovered a small key from the same shipwreck. Not once did he mention that it was in any way associated with the cross."

Another member of the Silenti, Jacques thought.

Aloud he said, "and what did you reply?"

"The truth; or at least the truth as it was at the time. Neither my wife nor I had any knowledge of a key and we told him as much. As he had asked us to keep the matter to ourselves, we did so until, at the time of her death, a photograph of Katherine Alexander wearing the key around her neck on a gold chain was published. Both we and the Vatican it seems, although in entirely different circumstances, became aware of the key around the same time."

Fallon went on to outline the events from the time of Kat's burial wearing what was assumed to be the original key, through to its purchase from the Alexander family by Cardinal Weiler.

Yet another member of the Silenti, Jacques Gaudin thought.

"Which almost brings us to where we are now," Fallon said.

"Which is where?" Monsignor Gaudin asked, still somewhat puzzled as to where this was all going and ill prepared for Fallon's next words which shook him to his very core.

"The location of the original key which will open the chair to get the ring."

Fallon had stewed over this line for days, massaging the simple words to imply he knew exactly what they meant. In truth, besides for the location of the key, all he had was some third hand overheard remarks from Peter's contact. He couldn't risk using Maggi's supposition that the reference was to the Chair of St. Peter and a specific Ring of the Fisherman. If that were wrong, it would ruin his credibility. As it was however, his guarded words seemed to have done their job. Monsignor Gaudin's face went pale and, as Fallon recalled later, his jaw had actually seemed to drop.

"How could you know of that?" Jacques Gaudin stuttered.

"No matter," Fallon replied, his confidence rising as he witnessed Jacques physical response to his remark. "What is important is that I know the location of the key and, as you can tell," he lied, "we know its real value to the Church."

Jacques Gaudin was still reeling. He could not understand how Anthony Fallon could possibly know of the Chair of St. Peter and the original Ring of the Fisherman. In his shock, he also failed to recognize that Fallon had not specifically mentioned either of these aspects. Fallon had merely painted the outline with his words and Jacques had filled in the blanks. It was this error that prompted his next words.

"Where is this key and what would you want for its return to the Church?"

Fallon, who to an outside observer must have looked as if he could not stop fiddling with his tie, reached between the buttons of his white shirt with his fingers and withdrew a gold chain still fastened around his neck. At its end dangled an exquisite gold and silver key.

"Right here," he said, holding the chain so that Monsignor Gaudin had a clear view of the key. "Let me tell you why I believe it's authentic and what I would like in return. You're familiar with the term a Judas kiss I assume?"

"Of course. Every member of the clergy is aware of its biblical origin. It's an act of treachery disguised as an act of friendship."

"Right," Fallon replied. "Well, here's the Bermuda kiss."

CHAPTER 64

Vatican City – Saturday, June 23, 2012

Jacques Gaudin had listened carefully and said little as Anthony Fallon outlined his proposal. As his old chess mentor would have said, he was now in check; and if he wasn't very careful with his next move it would very likely be checkmate. Then, drawing on an old rugby adage, he did the best thing he could when in doubt; he punted.

Confirming that Fallon was able to stay in Rome for a few more days he requested some time to consider the proposal and to establish what authority was needed within the Church in an attempt to bring it to fruition. Particularly, he noted, as it was based on supposition and potentially not even possible. To his great relief, Anthony Fallon agreed to the delay and then left.

Mr. Fallon had surprised him. Despite coming from a very small island, the man had not been intimidated by the power exuded by his surroundings. Quite the contrary, from the time of their first introduction Anthony Fallon had seemed to grow more confident with each passing minute. Jacques had not once felt they were on unequal terms.

Mr. Fallon's proposal though, was something else entirely. Although it made a number of assumptions, Jacques had to concede it was both aptly named and clever. It also ensured Mr. Fallon would be well compensated for his efforts. Jacques wondered if Anthony

Fallon realized the potential repercussions of his actions on those he believed had not dealt with him and his friends in good faith.

For his part, Jacques was not looking forward to his next meeting. There was only one man who could help him now; he would need to make his own appointment for an official meeting with the Holy Father.

CHAPTER 65

Hamilton, Bermuda – Saturday, June 23, 2012

As her deep pulsating orgasm subsided, Charlie clung tightly to Peter, the intensity of whose climax had matched her own. "Don't move Preppy," she whispered, "it's very sensitive." Peter lay unmoving and silent, his body pressed hard against hers, his face buried between her shoulder and neck. After a while, Charlie spoke again. "If you promise you can do that again, the answer is yes."

"Really?" Peter raised himself up on his elbows and looked directly into her face.

"Really," Charlie said. "There's a lot to consider and a lot to discuss, but yes, I'd love to marry you."

"This calls for a celebration," Peter said, simultaneously rolling off both Charlie and the bunk. "Does Fallon have any champagne on this boat?"

Charlie looked at her future husband standing naked in the main cabin of *Maverick*. "Afraid not. Nor do I imagine he would be too happy about you standing around looking like that on his boat either."

Peter grinned. "Well then it's off somewhere to celebrate. I'm not going to let this moment pass without at least one glass of bubbly. Why don't I give Sean a call and maybe the three of us can go out. At some point I'd like to tell my father, but that can wait for now."

"Sounds good to me, but let's tidy up first. I cleaned the boat for Fallon yesterday while I stewed over your proposal and wasn't expecting to have to do it again today. I'm not sure he'd be too impressed with its current use."

"Don't blame me. You suggested the boat was a good place to talk."

"I said talk, not…well you know."

Peter laughed, while Charlie blushed, grabbed her clothes from the floor, and hurried from the cabin to dress. "Back in a moment," she said over her shoulder as the door closed behind her.

#

"Judging from your expressions and that open bottle of champagne I imagine congratulations are in order," said Sean striding out onto the patio of the Royal Bermuda Yacht Club.

Charlie watched as Peter stood and the two men embraced while shaking hands. Moments later Sean leaned over her as she too tried to stand and, enveloping her in a bear hug, kissed her firmly on the cheek.

"Congrats, Charlie," he whispered in her ear. "He's a good man. I know you'll be happy wherever you live."

"Thanks, Sean," Charlie whispered. Then, in a more normal tone, "you sure got here fast."

"Not really, I wasn't at home when Peter called. I was visiting Howard at his office just down the block."

"On a Saturday," Peter exclaimed. "What's the old man doing at work today?"

"Apparently you two had a discussion yesterday about my joining the firm and he wanted to sound me out before formally approaching the partners."

"And?" Peter asked.

"I agreed that if they wanted me, I would stay. For a trial period anyway. Three-year contract and then a final decision one way or another. That should give me enough time to see if I can stand living in such close quarters to you lot. But enough of that," he continued, "I want to know what you two plan to do. Pour me a drink and reveal all."

As the conversation flowed, Charlie again marvelled at the easy familiarity of the two men and realized, as they shared intimate details of their respective plans, that at that moment she too had become part of this little group and accepted without reservation. That point was reinforced some twenty minutes later when, as Howard Alexander strolled onto the patio of the club, Peter stood and waved to his father.

"Dad," he called, "come on over. I think you might like to congratulate your future daughter-in-law."

As the club members sitting at nearby tables burst into spontaneous applause, Howard beamed and striding forward, gathered Charlie in his arms and squeezed her tightly. Charlie's eyes filled with tears, these men had been through so much recently and yet had welcomed her so warmly into their family.

Oh hell, she thought, *family. I must call my mother and Maggi before they hear it through the grapevine.* Nothing stayed confidential on the island for long. A few more minutes to avoid being rude to Howard and then she would leave. She had calls to make.

#

"How do you think things went with your father?"

Before Rhiannon could reply to Maggi's question, the hands free telephone in Maggi's car rang and "Charlie" appeared on the dashboard display.

"Just one second," Maggi interrupted pressing the speakerphone button as she spoke.

"Hi Charlie."

"Hi Mags. Can you talk?"

"Sure hon. I'm with a friend but go ahead."

"It's a bit personal. I'll see you when you get home."

"Are you sure? If it's urgent, I can call you back a bit later. I won't be back for a few days; I'm staying over while Fallon's away."

"Oh. Okay, call me back when you can. It's not urgent. Bye."

"Bye."

"My niece," Maggi said to Rhiannon by way of explanation. "You'll have to meet her one of these days. She's dating Howard Alexander's son, Peter."

"About as well as can be expected," Rhiannon said, ignoring the interruption and replying to Maggi's earlier question about their meeting with her father. "I think it was a bit much for him to take in all at once. We've never discussed my sexuality, although I would have expected he might have guessed by now. I should also have realized that he might not have spoken to my mother about me. With him living in the States since their divorce he only sees her once a year at most, and even then he's too concerned with the yacht races to get into personal stuff. He obviously liked you though and that certainly helped."

"I think the age difference might have thrown him a bit as well."

"Perhaps. But he'll get over it in time. It's not as though I'm a teenager. I know my own mind. I'm very much like him in that regard."

"So you're still sure about this."

"Absolutely," Rhiannon replied.

CHAPTER 66

Hamilton, Bermuda – Tuesday, June 25, 2012

Rhiannon stared at the DNA test results. A match! Fallon and Katherine Alexander were Peter Alexander's parents. Maggi's suspicions were right. She looked at the results again. No parental connection between A.F., the relation she had invented, and Sarah Alexander, but a definitive result between A.F. and Peter Alexander.

Placing the original A.F. and Peter report in her briefcase, she put the A.F. and Sarah test results through the shredder. The lab would have copies but without any notes in the police file, nobody would ever go to the lab for these missing reports. As far as the police were concerned, Sarah's remains had been identified and the case was closed. Rhiannon would give the original of the A.F. and Peter report to Maggi as promised. What she did with it after that was up to her. Rhiannon had done her part. Besides, she wanted to get back to serious police work including the nagging mystery of the *San Pedro* cross theft.

Despite the lead from a dying Bruce Gordon, her follow-up calls to Angelo Mosconi and Cardinal Cressey had yielded nothing. Perhaps it was time to let it go. Maybe too many years had passed. Who would care anyway? She would of course, but her primary supporter in the investigation was dead and anything he knew, besides what he had left in his message, was gone.

Had Rhiannon been aware of Angelo Mosconi's activities at that very moment, she would have been far less likely to dismiss the old investigation quite so easily.

CHAPTER 67

Rome, Italy – Tuesday, June 26, 2012

Angelo Mosconi smiled at the travel agent as he collected his airline ticket to Bermuda. She confirmed that no visa was required for his visit and that he needed no other travel documents for his planned fourteen-day vacation stay. They would provide the necessary landing cards on arrival in Bermuda, but other than those, everything else was complete. As he paid his bill, she wished him a pleasant trip and advised him, for the second time during their brief conversation, that he would be leaving on the Thursday flight via New York.

Cardinal Cressey would be pleased, he thought.

#

It had taken several days but, true to his word, Jacques Gaudin had been busy. On completion of his investigations, his meeting with the Holy Father had lasted much longer than anticipated and several subsequent meetings on the official calendar had either to be cancelled, or postponed. The matter at hand, he was informed, took precedence over everything.

Shortly after his meeting concluded, he had, on behalf of the Pontiff, summoned Cardinals Cressey and Kwodo. They in turn, left their meetings, eyes downcast and without further comment.

Cardinal Cressey returned to the papal chambers about an hour after his first appearance. He handed a small, white leather box to Jacques with a brief comment that it was to be delivered to the Holy Father and was not to be opened under any circumstances before that time.

By the time Jacques met with Fallon on the Tuesday morning, everything was arranged.

#

"Mr. Fallon, Anthony, it is good to see you again."

"Good to see you too, Jacques. I was beginning to think you had forgotten me."

"Touché. Nothing like that though. It has taken quite a bit of investigation and coordination to meet your request, but I believe we have been successful."

"You have?" Fallon tried but remained uncertain that he had removed all the surprise from his voice.

"Indeed. Here is my suggestion as to how we move forward. It will take some faith on both our sides but I believe by the end of this meeting we will have established the necessary goodwill to allow both of us to proceed as planned. This is what I propose."

As Fallon listened to the plan, his mind boggled. How naive was he to think he could possibly go up against the Vatican and win. They made cunning look like a stroll in the park. Jacques Gaudin's proposal was simple but Machiavellian in its elegance. This was a real Judas kiss. If things worked out as they suggested he could be on the Thursday flight home. He took the necklace from around his neck and removing the key, handed it to Monsignor Gaudin, who in turn handed him Cardinal Cressey's small, white leather box in exchange.

CHAPTER 68

Vatican City – Tuesday, June 26, 2012

Without any prior notice or fanfare, St. Peter's Basilica was closed for the evening. Swiss guards stood at every access point looking outwards, their backs to the inside of the building. If asked, all would have offered the same reason. A valuable artifact was being repaired. To gain the necessary access other artifacts needed to be moved and, to avoid the possibility of anything going wrong, security had been temporarily increased. They knew nothing more than that.

At precisely seventeen minutes before nine, the Chair of St. Peter was carefully removed from Bernini's sculpted gilt bronze casing, and gently lowered onto its back on a prepared stand. The four men involved in its extraction then left the building. At five minutes before nine, two figures, both in the traditional long dark cassocks of ordained priests entered from an inside passage at the darkened end of the Basilica and made their way across the great hall in silence.

The younger man offered a small gold and silver key to the elder, who slowly shook his head.

"Go ahead, my son," he said. "It is in the right front leg. There should be a keyhole at its base." He smiled. "You are the first, outside of an unbroken line of former popes, to be aware of its location," he said. "This knowledge has been held sacred for centuries to avoid anyone attempting to open the secret compartment by picking the lock. Although hidden in plain sight, without knowing exactly where to look it would be very difficult to find. Of particular concern, and hence the confidentiality of this information from even the most senior papal advisors, was that any attempt to open it without precisely the right key would trigger a mechanism that renders the compartment permanently inaccessible without destroying the chair; itself an ancient and valuable relic."

The younger priest, for it was obvious from their clothing now fully revealed in the light illuminating the chair, that the two were indeed priests, stooped forward and, taking the glasses held on a thin gold chain around his neck, placed them on his face.

"It appears to be filled with something," he said. Removing a small pocketknife from inside his cassock, he gently scraped at the bottom of the chair leg while the elderly and somewhat stooped older priest looked on. "Perhaps wax," he muttered, "but I think it is now all removed," he said at last.

"Try the key."

Inserting the key, the younger priest twisted it clockwise. Nothing, no movement. He tried anti-clockwise. Although very stiff, there was a slight movement. He applied more pressure. With a muted click an inside section of the front right leg of the chair slid open. Inside this miniature drawer lay a simple gold ring secured on what, from its shape, appeared to be a fabric covered piece of round wood; a twig perhaps.

Involuntarily both priests crossed themselves as they looked in awe at the artifact.

"The first Ring of the Fisherman belonging to St. Peter himself," the elder breathed, his tones hushed. "After all this time."

Delicately, he inserted two fingers into the cavity and removed the ring on its cloth-covered holder. Sliding the ring from the badly decayed material, he handed it to the younger man as he attempted to unfold the crumbling cloth and then gasped at the sight. A bone, a small bone.

"A fragment of a finger?" the younger man asked.

THE BERMUDA KEY

"Perhaps," the elder replied. "Perhaps even from his finger." The awe still evident in his voice, he continued, "we should go."

Gently pressing the previously hidden and now empty compartment back in place, the younger priest turned the key locking it as it had been before. Removing a vial from inside his cassock pocket he scooped out a small quantity of dark brown putty, which he pressed firmly into the keyhole; once again rendering it invisible to all but a very careful observer. With that, the two men turned and left the Basilica through an inside passage, taking their treasure with them. Only the light, occasionally reflecting off the bright red shoes of the elder, marked their path, as they once again disappeared into the darkened recesses of the enormous hall.

At nine-thirty, the four men returned and replaced the Chair of St. Peter in its gilt bronze casing before leaving the building. As far as they could tell, nothing had been disturbed although they assumed, incorrectly, that the small repair necessary to be made to the casing had been completed as scheduled.

At ten o'clock the guards, save for the usual building security, were discharged. The Basilica would once again be open to the public the following morning.

#

"Thibaud." Jacques Gaudin said as soon as Father Escoffier answered his ringing telephone. "My apologies for calling at this late hour, but I now have the key we discussed. If I deliver it to you tonight, do you think you can get it to the son of that goldsmith Cardinal Cressey has used in the past? I think you said his name was Panzini. Despite being later than we anticipated, we still need a duplicate for Mr. Fallon by Thursday morning as originally planned."

Jacques listened briefly, and then replied. "Good. I am on my way."

A short time later after dropping off the key with his friend and colleague, Jacques was safely on his way back to his apartment in the Vatican. The only difficult moment of the evening having occurred when Thibaud innocently asked why he was dressed as a priest with nothing to signify his clerical rank. He hoped his response that he had dressed in a rush was accepted without any further thought.

CHAPTER 69

Vatican City – Thursday, June 28, 2012

Fallon rose early and, following the directions he had been given the previous evening, took an early morning walk around the extensive and enclosed Vatican gardens. His earlier delight at being offered accommodation in one of the Vatican apartments had abated somewhat along with the realization that he was, without any locks or bars, effectively a prisoner in this place. Nonetheless, he had enjoyed his two-night stay although he was pleased to be heading back to Bermuda at last. Returning to his room some thirty minutes later he was surprised to find Jacques Gaudin and another priest already waiting.

"Good morning, Anthony, did you enjoy the walk?"

"I did. It's somewhat surreal when one realizes that these magnificent private gardens are essentially in the centre of Rome. You are very fortunate to live here."

"Thank you. I assure you we realize that, and rarely take it for granted."

Jacques gestured to the priest standing alongside him. "Let me introduce you to Monsignor Escoffier."

"Monsignor," Fallon said, extending his hand.

"Mr. Fallon," Thibaud Escoffier responded. "But I fear Monsignor Gaudin has made a mistake. It is Father Escoffier or Thibaud if you prefer."

"No mistake," Jacques interjected, "the appointment is effective today. I have the Holy Father's permission to pass on the news and, I must confess, I am enjoying this moment of surprise immensely. Congratulations Thibaud, it is well deserved. Besides, your new rank will provide better camouflage in the next phase of our little deception."

Before either Thibaud Escoffier or Fallon could make any comment, Jacques outlined the plans for the remainder of the morning. The three men would meet once more shortly before noon, when a limousine would be standing-by to take both Fallon and Monsignor Escoffier to the airport. There they would catch a flight to New York, before continuing on to Bermuda. Although surprised at the arrangements, Fallon could not help but smile at the audaciousness of the plan that had been put in place to facilitate their agreed transaction.

#

The boarding line for Delta flight DL 245 to JFK airport in New York that afternoon proceeded without incident. Among the passengers was Mr. Anthony Fallon, around whose neck hung a small gold and silver key on a gold chain, and whose luggage included an empty, white leather box. Travelling with Mr. Fallon was a Catholic priest, Monsignor Thibaud Escoffier, his clerical standing evidenced by a brilliant purple sash and ornate gold pectoral cross hanging from his neck. Several passengers behind the two was a swarthy individual who, despite the coolness of the airport buildings, was sweating profusely. There were two reasons for this. The first, Signor Angelo Mosconi had been late and consequently had hurried all the way from security to the boarding gate. The second, he really hated flying.

#

THE BERMUDA KEY

Cardinal Weiler, too, was en route to Bermuda. He, however, had left the previous evening accompanied by the Vatican's chief counsel, Signor Gino Vacchelli. All things being equal, they would arrive in Bermuda late on the Thursday evening, but well in time for his meeting with Howard Alexander the following day.

Unbeknownst to Cardinal Weiler, who was incommunicado while travelling, Fallon had finally made contact with Howard Alexander. The latter, on learning of Fallon's late departure from Rome, had left a message at the Rosedon Hotel for Cardinal Weiler. In it, he apologised for the last minute change of plans but nonetheless, rescheduled his meeting with Cardinal Weiler for the following Monday. He hoped Cardinal Weiler would understand and take advantage of the delay to enjoy an extra few days on the island. The weather, he advised, was expected to be sunny and hot throughout the weekend.

CHAPTER 70

St. George's, Bermuda – Friday, June 29, 2012

Delta flight DL 485 landed at L.F. Wade International Airport at precisely noon and right on time. Some twenty minutes later, Fallon and Monsignor Escoffier made their way down the stairway, across the tarmac, past the cheerful reggae band and into the arrivals hall where they separated. Fallon to the "Residents" line and Thibaud Escoffier to the "Visitors".

Having disembarked from the business class cabin and thus ahead of the majority of his fellow passengers, Fallon had only moments to wait before he was ushered forward to the first available customs officer. After a brief discussion, he signalled to Thibaud, who by this time was surrounded by chattering holidaymakers, to leave his place in the line and join him at the customs desk.

"Are you traveling with Mr. Fallon, sir?" the customs officer asked.

"Yes, a brief visit. I leave again on Monday."

Taking the offered landing cards and passport from Monsignor Escoffier, the officer gave them a cursory glance, stamped the passport and handed it back to Thibaud.

"Enjoy your stay, sir. Please go ahead."

As Fallon and Thibaud walked past the desk pulling their carry-on bags behind them, Fallon whispered to the priest.

"One more check."

Avoiding the luggage claim area, they strode directly towards the exit doors and yet another customs officer. Once again presenting their passports, they waited while he looked them over.

"Only carry-on baggage, gentlemen?" he asked.

They both nodded.

"Fine, welcome back Mr. Fallon. Enjoy your stay, Father."

They were only a few steps past the officer heading towards the exit doors when his voice rang out again.

"Father…your cross."

Thibaud stopped dead in his tracks. He and Fallon both half-turned and looked back at the customs officer in concern.

The customs officer smiled. "I think you mistakenly put it on backwards before you disembarked. A bit of a rush was it?" He smiled again. "You may want to fix it before you go out in public."

Smiling his thanks, Thibaud reached for the gold chain around his neck as he and Fallon resumed walking toward the exit doors. There had been no mistake. He had purposely reversed the brilliant gold cross for the entire trip. The floral design on its back was far less conspicuous than its ornate bas-relief and emerald-studded front.

#

Unlike Fallon and Monsignor Escoffier, Angelo Mosconi had travelled in economy. While his connections were the same, his journey had been far less comfortable. By the time he cleared customs, it was almost two in the afternoon. He badly needed a shower and a drink. He had local contacts to meet but they could wait. It was hot and he was tired. As far as he was aware, both the goldsmith and the police officer were still on the island. He would arrange to meet his contacts later today and finalize his plans on the weekend. Now that he was here, there was no immediate rush.

#

Maggi was standing at the door of the house as Fallon pulled into the drive. If she was anxious about her planned conversation with him, it didn't show. While he had said he was bringing a guest from Rome for the weekend, she had no idea what to expect. What she, in her wildest dreams did not anticipate, was the sight of the purple-sashed priest who emerged from the passenger side of Fallon's vehicle, the sun glinting off a modernistic sleek silver cross hanging from around his neck on a sparkling silver chain.

"Hi Maggi," Fallon said kissing her on the cheek. "I'd like you to meet Monsignor Thibaud Escoffier. He's staying with us until Monday. I thought you might like to introduce him to Father Baird sometime this weekend. I think they'd get along."

Maggi stared dumbfounded at Fallon.

What, on earth, had he been up to? Who was this priest? How was she going to tell him all her news while they had company?

None of these concerns showed on her face, however, as she walked forward and greeted the priest. "Monsignor Escoffier, welcome to our home. I'm Margaret Fallon."

#

In her cottage at the far corner of the Fallons' property, Charlie, lying on the sofa with her bare feet resting lightly on her dog's side, heard the car enter the drive.

"Guess who's back, Ben," she said.

A few cursory wags of the dog's short tail acknowledged her spoken observation.

She was glad Fallon was back. She wanted to share her news with him. More importantly, if she were honest with herself, she wanted to know what he thought about her decision to marry Peter. He would have an opinion for sure. One thing about Fallon, right or wrong, he always had an opinion. She would wander up to the main house and visit.

Perhaps tomorrow, she thought. *He probably had plenty to catch up on with Maggi today.*

#

It was late by the time Monsignor Escoffier finally retired for the night. The guest room, which stood ready and waiting for months on end without any visitors, had taken only moments to prepare for his stay and, to his obvious delight, afforded him a magnificent ocean view as well.

Maggi was in the living room when Fallon returned from showing Monsignor Escoffier to his room.

"Are you tired?" she asked.

"Somewhat," Fallon replied. "No jet lag though. We slept over in New York. Something on your mind?"

"Quite a bit. Perhaps it should wait until tomorrow. We could meet here after I drop Thibaud off with Father Baird. Does that work for you?"

"Why not now?" Fallon replied. "It must be important. You would normally have peppered me with questions about my trip by now. Other than your discreet probing over dinner, you haven't pressed at all. Something serious must be afoot."

"Sometimes you surprise me Fallon, despite your often apparently distracted attention to whatever is going on, your intuition when you choose to use it, is often spot on."

Fallon appeared to ignore Maggi's comment. "Do I need a drink?" he asked.

"Perhaps. How about getting us each a liqueur?"

As Fallon poured their drinks, Maggi steeled herself. She had no idea how he would respond to her news. She would deal with the Rhiannon news first, the paternity could come later. Even then, that would depend on how Fallon responded to her initial announcement.

As Fallon placed the liqueur glass on the table beside her Maggi spoke.

"You know how much I care for you, don't you?" she said.

"But," Fallon replied.

Maggi stopped short, then seeing the faint outline of a smile on Fallon's face continued. "But, there is someone else."

"Assistant Inspector Thomas?"

Maggi went pale. "How could you know?" she asked trembling.

Fallon rose from his seat and knelt beside her. "It's okay Maggi. The island's too small for any real secrets and I think I understand." He placed his arm around her shoulders and squeezed, before returning to his chair. "Why don't you take your time and tell me what you think I need to know. Whatever it is we'll work it out. It was sure to come to this someday. We've had a good run. No, I retract that. We've had a great run, and in my own way I love your dearly. As I believe, you do me. Between us, I'm sure we can get through this. I'll shut up now and you go ahead. It's time."

Maggi felt an enormous wave of relief come over her and the tears spilled freely from her eyes as she finally let it all out and shared her innermost secrets with the man who as he had said, had loved her dearly in his own way for almost as long as she had been on the island.

#

It was almost two in the morning when Maggi, exhausted from her self-imposed confessional finally said, "I think we've covered it all. I had no idea we would get this far but thank you, Fallon. You made it easier than I could ever have imagined. What's more, thank you for the offer of the house. I'll speak to Rhiannon. If she's uncomfortable with the idea, we'll pass, but I really appreciate the thought.

Fallon slumped back in his chair.

He looks exhausted, thought Maggi. *This probably took more out of him than he was prepared to let on.*

She was about to suggest they turn in for the night when he spoke.

"Anything else? Might as well get it all out. No more surprises tomorrow. I don't think I could handle that."

Maggi thought of the DNA report in her bedroom drawer.

"No," she answered looking at Fallon, exhaustion oozing from his every pore. "Nothing more."

CHAPTER 71

Hamilton, Bermuda – Saturday, June 30, 2012

It was late afternoon when Angelo Mosconi completed his arrangements. His last visit having been to a local store specializing in Italian hand-made tiles. His "samples", pre-wrapped for convenience, were handed to him in full view of the other customers.

"Please return them when you have decided," the middle-aged man behind the counter requested, his thick Italian accent sharply at odds with the Bermudian décor of his store. "You can pay the full cost of the selected tiles at that time."

Angelo left the store with his "tiles" and looked around. *Merda*, it was hot, he needed a drink. Unsure of the location of the nearest bar, he asked the way before heading off as directed.

#

Justis Small, convicted felon and frequent abuser of women, looked at the retreating figure of the swarthy, squat tourist. The man stood out like a sore thumb. What was he doing on Court Street? Justis, on the other hand, looked right at home. With his white baseball cap askew, plain while T-shirt hanging loose, his low-hanging jeans and loosely fastened high-topped runners, he looked just like every other member of his gang. This was their turf, to be avoided by locals and tourists alike. To make matters worse, the fool had asked for him directions.

Ever the opportunist, Justis had swaggeringly pointed the way deeper into his territory before whipping out his mobile and calling for back up. Cowardice was high on his list of priorities and despite feeling the comfort of the four-inch knife blade in his pocket he wasn't about to take on the squat tourist alone.

#

Angelo walked up the hill sweating, the package in his hands awkward to carry. Looking around, the street appeared empty and somewhat residential. He hoped that arrogant little shit hadn't given him the wrong directions on purpose. He would go one more block and then head back down the hill towards the harbour. It was quite a few blocks in the opposite direction, but he knew there would be a bar on the main street. He had just wanted something closer.

The package was an irritation. He tore open the brown wrapping and checked the gun concealed inside the cardboard box. A box that could easily be mistaken as containing a few tiles. The stubby revolver was loaded and ready. Slipping it into his pocket, Angelo crumbled the paper into a ball and threw in the gutter. The box went the same way. Still no sign of anyone else. He was almost at a corner. He would check there for a bar and then turn back.

#

Justis Small had made many errors in his short and unappealing life but none more so than that Saturday afternoon. As Angelo arrived at the corner, Justis and two of his cronies stepped out from where they had been waiting. All were dressed alike. Braver now with his support in place, Justis stepped forward, the knife in his hand pointing upward at Angelo's face.

Years of instinctive survival governed Angelo's next move. He didn't hesitate for a second. Pulling the gun from his pocket, he pointed and fired, shooting Justis right in the centre of his spotless white T-shirt, the 38-caliber bullet tearing through vital organs as it travelled. With an enormous expulsion of air, Justis fell to the ground, his shirt turning bright red as it soaked up his blood. His two partners in crime, meanwhile, fled in panic along the street, and as far away from the crazy tourist as they could get.

Angelo turned and walked quickly away. He could hear doors opening behind him but didn't look back. Everything had changed. He no longer cared about being hot or thirsty. All he could think about was how to get out of Bermuda as fast as he could.

#

Angelo was asking directions for the second time that day. Ignoring his earlier return ticket on Delta, he had booked a seat on BA flight 2232 to Gatwick, leaving at eight-fifteen that evening. It was the first available flight out of Bermuda on which he could obtain a seat. He was unfortunately cutting short his visit, as he told the ticket agent, to attend a seriously ill family member. All he now needed was a taxi to the airport from his hotel in Mangrove Bay.

Mistakenly thinking it would be easier to flag down a taxi on the street outside the resort, he stood looking at the empty road, a lone elderly male walking along its edge. After hurriedly questioning the old man, and being advised that the quickest way to obtain a taxi was to return to the resort hotel and have them call, Angelo rushed back along the route he had travelled only minutes earlier.

Andrew Jensen continued his walk, shaking his head at the distraught tourist. The man really needed to slow down and smell the roses. He had barely listened to Andrew's advice as he hurried away.

Angelo, worried about his own safety, and how he was going to explain things to Cardinal Cressey, had no idea of the opportunity that had crossed his path. That realization would come during his flight to London when he finally opened the package delivered earlier to his hotel containing the photographs and addresses of both Andrew Jensen and Rhiannon Thomas.

#

Safely in his seat on flight BA 2232, Angelo stared at the photograph of Rhiannon Thomas, carefully shielding it from the view of the passenger alongside, while she, at that very moment, was standing alongside the morgue technician, staring down at the body of Justis Small. Still in its same bloody clothes, the body lay in an open drawer, one of the nine available in the Bermuda morgue. A post mortem would come later, but for now, here it would stay.

"Any leads?" the technician asked. She had been doing this job for three years and gang violence was not new to her.

"Nothing yet," Rhiannon replied. "You know what it's like on Court Street. Nobody saw or heard anything. Just a gunshot and then some male hurrying away. Not even clarity as to whether he was white or black. Sort of dark skinned seems to be the best description. Although one of the people interviewed said he looked older, whatever that means. Probably that he looked older than the usual gang members."

She stopped speaking and took one last long look at the body. "Thanks, you can close up now. I can't say I'm surprised about this one."

"I know what you mean," the technician replied with a resigned sigh as Rhiannon left the morgue. "I wish they could see where it all ends."

CHAPTER 72

Hamilton, Bermuda – Monday, July 2, 2012

It had been one of those meetings thus far. The parties arranged on either side of the law firm's boardroom table were clearly adversaries in the discussions. On one side sat Howard, Peter and Fallon. On the other, Cardinal Weiler and his counsel, Signor Gino Vacchelli.

Howard opened the discussions with an apology for the change from the previous Friday, noting that Fallon had been unavoidably delayed while traveling offshore, and only returned to Bermuda late that day. He was careful not to mention exactly where Fallon had been for two reasons. One, because, other than Rome, he was not entirely sure where Fallon had been, and two, because he had absolutely no damn idea what Fallon had been doing there in the first place.

He then summarized his e-mail exchanges with Cardinal Weiler. In his summary, he stressed yet again, that he had acted in good faith regarding the sale of the key worn by his late wife and, while it may not have been the key wanted by Cardinal Weiler, it was indeed the only key known to be in her possession by him and his son.

Peter nodded his agreement but said nothing.

Signor Vacchelli then spoke on behalf of Cardinal Weiler and the Vatican. Their position, he noted, was that despite everyone's good faith bargaining, at the end of the day a considerable sum had been paid for the wrong key. The Vatican should not suffer a loss for this shared error and, if the correct key was not readily available, then at least the payment should be returned.

The discussion went on for some time, neither party giving ground, merely repeating several different versions of their original opening remarks. The only truly tense moment coming after a suggestion by Signor Vacchelli that perhaps Howard's daughter had been in possession of the original key and that the family should look through her things more carefully.

Howard, incensed at the insensitivity of the remark in light of Sarah's recent death, turned pale and was about to lash out verbally when Fallon, recognizing where things were going, interrupted and suggested a brief recess. Taking Howard by the arm, he led him outside.

"Steady friend," he said.

"Thanks. I was about to tear a strip off that prick."

Before Fallon could reply, his telephone rang. Excusing himself, he listened carefully a puzzled expression on his face. Walking away from Howard, he sat down in a nearby chair and continued listening as Howard and Peter stood nearby talking quietly to each other. It was several minutes later before he terminated the call still without saying a word.

"Do you think we could take a break?" Fallon said. "I need to speak to Maggi. She's moving today and something has come up."

"Moving? Where to?" Howard asked.

"It's a long story. I'll fill you in later. I'll call her from my office. Why don't you suggest we regroup in an hour?"

"An hour? What more is there to say? We don't have the bloody key and even if Sarah did have it," Howard said, "it's gone now."

"Just give me an hour...please. It's important."

"Fine. An hour, no more. Honestly, Fallon, I don't know what you're up to, as usual I might add, but this is a sensitive issue for me. I'd like to get it over with as soon as we can and believe me; I have no intention of refunding their damned money. They had us dig Kat up for God's sake. I still can't get over the fact that I agreed. What the hell was I thinking?" With that, he turned and headed back into the boardroom closely followed by Peter.

As Fallon walked across the elegant law firm lobby to his own office on the same floor of the building, he looked grim. "Pocket dial" he believed it was called. That awful moment when someone unintentionally activates their mobile phone. Well, Maggi had pocket dialed him while engaged in a conversation with Rhiannon. It appeared she had not been entirely truthful about having nothing else to discuss. She was in possession of some DNA results which she had seemingly changed her mind about sharing. He wanted to see them for himself and he was going to get her to bring them over. Not later either, he wanted to see them right now.

#

Fallon walked slowly back to the boardroom DNA results in hand. As he resumed his seat at the table, Howard Alexander looked up.

"You okay, Fallon?" he asked. "You don't look so good."

"Fine," Fallon replied his speech slow and trance-like.

As the conversation resumed around the table, Fallon removed all the papers from the folder in front of him and replaced them with a single sheet containing the typed DNA results with some hurriedly scribbled comments he had added below. Reaching into his pocket, he removed a plain white envelope, also covered with his handwriting, containing Sarah's original necklace with a key pendant and placed it on top of the test results in the folder.

Cardinal Weiler was mid-sentence as Fallon rose from his chair and, with slow deliberate movements, walked around the table until he stood alongside Peter Alexander. By the time he reached Peter, all conversation in the room had ceased. Howard looked as if he were about to speak but Fallon's upraised palm stopped him before he had uttered a single word.

Placing the folder in front of Peter, Fallon spoke. "I think Kat would have wanted it to go this way," he said. "There's a deal to be done that will long survive Howard and me. I believe Peter is the best person to make that deal. Howard, if you would join me I think we need to go for a drink. We have a lot to discuss."

Stunned at the turn of events but trusting Fallon knew what he was doing, Howard stood. Peter started to rise as well but Fallon held him down with a hand on his shoulder.

"No Peter, you stay. Everything you need is in that folder."

Peter sat open-mouthed at this turn of events as Fallon turned to Cardinal Weiler and his counsel. "Gentlemen, thank you for your time," he said. "Come Howard, we should go. Trust me on this one."

As Fallon turned to leave the room, he patted Peter on the shoulder.

"Good luck my son," was all he said.

CHAPTER 73

Hamilton, Bermuda – Monday, July 2, 2012

Peter read Fallon's hand-written notes for a second time while Cardinal Weiler and Signor Vacchelli waited. Still dumbfounded by the contents, he re-read them for a third time while simultaneously trying to grasp their full significance.

A comparative DNA test had been done using the sample he had provided for Sarah's identification and he and Fallon were related. Not only related but also, according to the notes, Fallon was his father. Fallon, so he had written, did not intend to tell anyone, Howard included, and was leaving any disclosure entirely in Peter's hands. Equally astounding, the envelope that he had yet to open was supposed to contain his sister's original necklace and key pendant.

Where did Fallon get it? What was Peter supposed to do now? The man was mad. He couldn't drop all this in Peter's lap and just walk out. Then again, he had, and not only that, he had taken Howard with him. Peter, unless he arranged another meeting, was well and truly on his own. He looked over at Cardinal Weiler who was watching him very closely. Talk about being dropped in the deep end.

Then it struck him. Even though he would be flying by the seat of his pants, he trusted Fallon's instincts. He knew the right thing to do.

"Eminence," he said, "I believe there is a solution."

THE BERMUDA KEY

#

In one of his last legal acts in Bermuda, the document drafted by Peter was as simple and straightforward as he could make it. Even Signor Vacchelli, despite his best efforts to modify it, had finally agreed it would suffice unchanged. Besides, as Peter in a moment of frustration pointed out to him, what real choice did he have? Any alternative options he might think he had were, biblically speaking, definitely founded on sand rather than rock.

Even Cardinal Weiler had enjoyed the religious simile and, after carefully examining the key and comparing it with the one in an enlarged photograph of Kat, had suggested to his counsel it was time to agree. They would sign the document as prepared. The Alexander family would give them the key, which Peter now held. No money would exchange hands. Any payments made in the past, for the key received at that time, would constitute full payment for both that key and the key now received, without qualification. There would also be no further effort on the part of the Vatican to recover any funds from the Alexanders.

"But what if, once again, it is not the correct key? Signor Vacchelli asked one last time before signing the document on behalf of the Vatican.

"One, I believe it is," answered Peter. "Two, after examining my mother's old photograph and comparing that key with the one here today, Cardinal Weiler believes it is. Three, we have no better information. And finally, we still believe you have no cause to ask for any of the earlier funds back. If you want this key, you sign today and we are done. Don't sign, and we will keep the key and it will be forever lost to the Vatican. The choice is yours."

Signor Vacchelli, locked eyes with Peter who stared directly back at him. Looking away at last, he turned, looked at Cardinal Weiler who inclined his head ever so slightly. Signor Vacchelli signed.

#

By the time the meeting concluded that day, Monsignor Escoffier was well on his way back to Rome, the camouflage services of his priestly apparel no longer needed. The Fallons had proved to be gracious hosts and the short sightseeing trip arranged by Father Baird had been just sufficient to ensure he would want to visit this charming island again.

Sitting quietly in his seat, contemplatively fingering the silver pectoral cross hanging from around his neck, his only regret was that he would not see the remainder of Anthony Fallon's plan unfold.

CHAPTER 74

Hamilton, Bermuda – Friday, July 13, 2012

It had been a little over a week since Maggi moved in with Rhiannon. They had talked at length about Fallon's offer of taking over the house she and Fallon had shared, before finally deciding it would potentially be too uncomfortable a location in which to start their new life together. On telling Fallon, Maggi was once again surprised at his understanding.

He had taken her initial announcement well, even graciously. It was her decision to withhold the DNA results that had unsettled him. Damn those mobile phones. Her telephone, which had been in her jeans pocket, had re-dialed the last number she had called, which just happened to be Fallon's. After hearing her conversation with Rhiannon and her decision to withhold the results, he had flipped. She had rarely heard him so angry. Having stepped out of a meeting with Howard Alexander at the time he had insisted…no that wasn't right…demanded she bring him the results immediately.

Feeling as guilty as all hell about her actions, she had done as he asked. Their conversation was brief and to the point. She simply told him the truth about the results and when asked why she hadn't told him earlier, had confessed that after his gracious acceptance of her relationship with Rhiannon, she had not wished to cause him any further pain and decided it was best to leave things as they were.

They had said little after that, but after a few days silence, he had called her and made peace. He had told Peter he said, and would leave it at that. Any further moves were up to Peter. He asked that she and Rhiannon respect his decision and his privacy. Maggi had assured him they would.

Then, this morning, Fallon had called again. Would they reconsider the offer to take over the house? He had an alternative plan. Rather than move in right away, they could live at Rhiannon's while undertaking a complete renovation of the house, moving in only when it was finished. Then it would be theirs, both practically and emotionally. He would have Howard draw up the necessary legal transfer. Fallon had spoken to Charlie and he would be moving into the cottage on a permanent basis once she left. Between it and *Maverick*, his minimalistic needs would be entirely satisfied.

Maggi was thunderstruck. Bermuda's property prices had skyrocketed. The house was worth a fortune and its location stunning. She shook her head. The man was an enigma, always had been. She wanted to call Rhiannon and tell her the news but decided to wait. It was Friday and Rhiannon's practice was to try to clear as much of her desk as she could before the weekend. This idea deserved more than a hurried telephone conversation. She would definitely wait.

#

Despite her usual Friday habits, Rhiannon's attention was not on a pre-weekend clean-up, but on the investigation into the death of Justis Small and had, momentarily at least, been distracted. As a normal procedure, Bermuda's entry and exit landing card information, along with the associated passport information, was regularly scanned for any anomalies; drug trafficking being the most obviously expected crime. Today, there was one such anomaly. A tourist, whose landing card information indicated a two-week stay, had left one day after arrival and on a different airline. Coincidentally, the departure date was the same day as the Justis Small murder and the tourist's name was Angelo Mosconi.

The name seemed to jump off the page and Rhiannon visibly recoiled. She had a million questions. Could this be the same man she had spoken with in Italy? Was he connected to the murder? What could he and Justis Small possibly have in common? Was he a frequent visitor to Bermuda?

She needed to check. She didn't believe in coincidences. There was something very strange here; maybe it even linked back to the missing cross. Rhiannon had no idea how this would all develop. All she knew was that every instinct she had was screaming. It was going to be a long weekend. She was going to dig and dig until she found something, even if it meant going to Rome to do it.

Poor Maggi, Rhiannon thought. *It was their first real weekend together and she was going to be distracted. She knew she would be, no matter how hard she tried.* Oh well, if things were going to work between the two of them, Maggi would have to understand. Besides, if it involved the cross it might pique Maggi's interest as well. It would be nice to have someone at home to discuss things with at last.

#

What a difference a couple of weeks make, Howard thought. Once again, it was Friday and here he was clearing his desk before the weekend. Only this time, no pending meeting with the Vatican. What a day that had been.

He'd had no idea what was going on when Fallon first pulled him from the meeting and then, while Peter stayed to deal with Cardinal Weiler and his counsel alone, had told him how he discovered the key along with Sarah's remains. Not only discovered the key, but that he had given it to Peter inside an envelope as they left the meeting. At the time, Howard didn't know whether to be relieved or angry. All his posturing with the Vatican about how they didn't have the key while Fallon sat quietly knowing where it was all along. He even had Sean waiting in his office on standby, ready to tell Cardinal Weiler about Kat giving the key to Sarah and, how it was presumably lost when she drowned. Howard's first impulse had been to rush back into the meeting to clear things up but Fallon had insisted they both remain outside and let Peter play out the hand. "After all," he had said, "you've already been paid and I'm sure Peter will do the right thing." Which, of course, he had. After signing the release document Peter had prepared, and with the key clutched securely in Cardinal Weiler's sweaty palm, the two representatives of the Vatican had hurried from the law firm of Whyte, Alexander & Hodgkins to pack and catch their flight back to Rome. He, Peter and Sean had left the office together shortly after that, leaving Fallon alone. As they walked away, he realized that he had never asked Fallon what exactly he had been doing in Rome. Quickly recognizing that whatever the reason it probably no longer mattered, he turned his attention to the boys. They had a lot to discuss. With the issue of the key behind them, they could focus on Peter's marriage plans and Sean joining the firm.

Howard sighed and sat back in his chair. Despite their recent loss, things were getting back to normal. Sean was excited about the move to Bermuda and Peter, notwithstanding his distracted behaviour ever since the meeting, finally appeared to be caught up in the excitement of his impending marriage.

He's probably still worried about his career, Howard thought.

#

The furthest thing from Peter's mind immediately after the meeting was his career. Even his marriage plans with Charlie were pushed to the back of his mind.

Fallon was his father!

He didn't know how he felt about that. Days went by and he still didn't know what to do or how to respond. He could tell his distraction was starting to affect those around him. In turn, each of Charlie,

Sean and Howard had asked if something was wrong. Finally, he had decided he needed to meet with Fallon.

It had been a strange meeting. Two men, each not sure of the other's position, dancing around a topic without revealing their true feelings.

Fallon finally broke the logjam. "Look," he said, "I know the delivery and its timing was appalling but you knew within fifteen minutes of my being told. Frankly, I didn't know how to tell you and decided to throw everything at you all at once. Impulsive I know, but I thought you could handle it, and you did."

"I seem to have inherited that streak," Peter said in the first sign of recognition of his true parentage.

"Here's what I think you should know," Fallon said. "Once I'm done, I'll answer any question you ask. Now or later. I owe you that. Okay?"

"Okay."

"I loved Kat. Our time was before she and Howard married. I didn't know that you were my son until now and somehow I don't think Kat knew either. The tests on our respective DNA samples shouldn't have been done; at least not the way they were, but neither you nor I had any part in that and we cannot change the truth. I will never tell Howard and if I were you, I wouldn't either. No good can come of it. He's a decent man and loves you without reservation. Why hurt him now. For my part, I'm delighted just knowing, and will take our secret to my grave, if that's what you want. Maggi and Rhiannon have made the same promise. The rest is up to you."

For a time the two sat in silence. "I'll tell Charlie," Peter said at last. "Not immediately, but at some point before we get married. I'll know when the time is right. I won't tell Howard. For now though, I'd like you to tell me more about you and my mother."

#

Fallon's memories of Kat had been kept tightly bottled up for years. As he spoke, more and more flooded out. Trips on the boat, diving together, her irreverent sense of humour; the memories as fresh as when they were made. Peter asked few questions throughout until Fallon finally reached the time of the discovery of the *San Pedro* cross.

"Tell me more about its discovery," Peter said. "I'd like to know as much as I can right up to your finding Sarah's copy of the key."

"Not the copy," corrected Fallon, "the original."

"Right." Peter smiled. "I almost forgot. I have the copy." Reaching into his pocket, he withdrew a small gold and silver key.

"Where did you get that? I thought Howard sold it to the Vatican?"

"He did, but the unwritten part of my arrangement with Cardinal Weiler, was that he returned to us the key which he had purchased the first time. It was my mother's and I wanted it back. Selfish I know, but I thought they may have it with them and it turned out I was right. He was more than happy to exchange it for the original."

"Now that sounds like a deal I would have made," Fallon replied. "I'm sure he'll be welcomed back at the Vatican with open arms."

He sounds cynical, Peter thought, *I wonder why.* Deciding that enough personal information had been shared for one day, he chose not to ask.

CHAPTER 75

Vatican City – Friday, July 13, 2012

The Vatican was rife with rumours of a major reorganization. No one appeared to know what exactly had sparked the resignations, reassignments and appointments.

It had started the previous week. An unnamed senior member of the clergy had apparently made clandestine arrangements to access the Chair of St. Peter, for undisclosed reasons. While the motives of an anonymous caller were unknown, he had alerted the Commander of the Swiss Guard who, in turn, detained the culprit. The only clue to the caller's identity was that the telephone number was a public phone located inside the Vatican City walls.

The following day, many insiders noticed that the papal schedule had been hurriedly rearranged and a succession of very senior cardinals met with the Pope, each meeting lasting quite a bit longer than usual. Shortly thereafter, the announcements started.

#

Cardinal Weiler was the first casualty. He had arrived back in Vatican City the previous week secure in the belief that the key which he now held would unlock the Chair of St. Peter and provide him, not only access to the original Ring of the Fisherman, but with a significant advantage at the next papal election.

There were several things wrong with this plan.

First, and foremost, the key that he had obtained from Peter Alexander was yet another fake. To be fair to Peter, he was unaware of this, a fact which both Fallon and Monsignor Gaudin thought best to keep to themselves. In Cardinal Weiler's case, he only became aware of the true nature of the key after his detention by the Swiss Guard. It was then that the same tools used in the destruction of papal rings were used; symbolically it seemed, to destroy the beautifully crafted fake that Jacques Gaudin had given to Fallon. The original, which Fallon had delivered and which had been used to open the chair, was now securely locked in the Vatican archives along with an, as yet, unidentified ring finger bone fragment and a simple gold ring. Only the three unmoving security cameras focussed on their location in a bulletproof glass case, gave any indication of their potential value.

Secondly, in his ambitious haste, Cardinal Weiler had forgotten who had brought him to the dance in the first place. Cardinal Kwodo, a man with an enormous capacity for forgiveness, was not unduly perturbed at the behaviour of his younger colleague, who effectively cut him and Cardinal Cressey from any possible accolades for the recovery of the key. Cardinal Cressey, less so, and he had a mean streak.

A few weeks earlier, Cardinal Cressey had been summoned to an uncomfortable meeting with the Holy Father. There, after hearing the Pope's suspicions carefully compiled by Jacques Gaudin, he had admitted to still being in possession of the stolen original *San Pedro* cross. At the time, and in an effort to mitigate his own past behaviour, he offered up the name of Cardinal Weiler as the architect behind the Silenti's current clandestine efforts to secure both the key and the Ring of the Fisherman without papal involvement, or permission. A short time later, and as instructed, he had delivered the cross to Jacques Gaudin in a small, white leather box marked for the Pope's attention.

He would, he thought at the time, *need to remove all references to the cross in his will. No point in leaving that apparently magnanimous gesture there for posterity now. Even after death that would really be embarrassing.*

Cardinal Weiler had also taken Cardinal Vilicenti's support for granted. This assumption, while certainly correct had his mission been successful, was woefully incorrect with its failure. Cardinal Vilicenti was too old and too cunning to rely on any but his own devices when it came to protecting his reputation. He had, during his younger colleague's absence in Bermuda, been expressing his grave concerns about Cardinal Weiler's strange behaviour to the one remaining member of the Silenti. This reserved cardinal, the only member in the Silenti's history to have come from Argentina, was a modest, straightforward man who completely understood his colleague's concerns. His support later proved invaluable when, on being questioned about the affair, he was able to point to Cardinal Vilicenti's expressed concerns about Cardinal Weiler's past behaviour.

The announcement itself was terse. The Pope had accepted the resignation of Cardinal Weiler, one of the Vatican's youngest and most promising cardinals, who was resigning due to ill health. Cardinal Weiler would resume a strictly private life with no further participation in any public, religious or civil events. The many questions as to the nature of his illness remained unanswered.

#

Cardinal Cressey was the second casualty. He was, it was announced, stepping down from his roles within the Vatican. While not resigning, he would be re-assigned to a position more in keeping with his advancing age and increasing infirmity. Many of the cardinal's colleagues expressed surprise. He had hidden any signs of his advancing age and condition well.

Cardinal Kwodo almost escaped unscathed but, in the end, he too fell victim to the purge. To many observers, his appointment as the Apostolic Nuncio to South Africa was an unusual posting based on his historic progression in the Church.

#

Cardinal Vilicenti, thanks in no small part to the support of his Argentinian colleague in the Silenti, escaped untouched. The absence of his name from any announcements was not noticed by any, other than his former colleagues in the Silenti who had not been as fortunate. They, it should be said, were not surprised.

Despite his apparent success in protecting his own reputation and hence his ambitions, Cardinal Vilicenti had made one serious long-term tactical error. He had failed to recognise the possible future challenge posed to his goals by his reserved and highly respected Argentinian colleague in the Silenti.

#

There were two further announcements made, both on a more positive note. The Secretariat of State of the Vatican, would be honouring the newly appointed Monsignor Thibaud Escoffier with the traditional formal diploma the following Wednesday; and Monsignor Jacques Gaudin's appointment as a cardinal was revealed. No longer *in pectore*, he would take over all responsibilities and positions formerly held by Cardinal Weiler. Monsignor Escoffier, previously assistant to Cardinal Cressey, would move to a new position as his assistant.

The two remaining members of the Silenti now at least knew who one of their new colleagues would be. They did wonder, however, who would be appointed to the two remaining newly vacated seats.

CHAPTER 76

Claremont, South Africa –
Sunday, September 9, 2012

It was a simple ceremony at a small church on the corner of Church Street and Main Road, Claremont.

In attendance were Charlie's mother, her godparents, Howard, Sean, Chris and Carol Patterson, Fallon, Maggi and Rhiannon. Immediately the ceremony was over the newlyweds headed straight to the airport for a flight to Mossel Bay, and then a short drive to Hunter's Country House Hotel. Most of the celebrations had occurred during the preceding two weeks as the various groups arrived from Bermuda, and elsewhere.

"Hunter's", nestled in the forest between the Tsitsikama Mountains and the Indian Ocean was, as their tour operator had told them, once nominated as the best family-run hotel in the world. Everything about it lived up to their expectations and, after settling in and a magnificent dinner, they were finally alone in their room.

Charlie turned to Peter. "Well, that's done. What now? I can't imagine you wanting to live here and practice as a lawyer. Perhaps we should go back to the island. You could work with Fallon. He'd like that."

"Someday," Peter replied. "Not sure what we'd live on though. I can't see us making too much money unless we get lucky and have a find like he and my parents did."

Strange, he thought. *Still can't get used to knowing Fallon is my father.*

Maybe someday that would change. For now though Howard was, and would remain his father whenever he thought about it, or whenever anyone asked. It seemed that both he and Fallon wanted the same thing. Neither of them wanted to upset Howard, and he was certainly none the wiser unless one of them told him.

"Anyway, for now I'd like to stay here and soak up as much of this beautiful country of yours as I can. Speaking of which, what was in that box Fallon gave us as a wedding gift?"

"I don't know. He was quite secretive and told me to put it away very safely and not look at it until everyone had gone home and we could open it together."

"Want to do it now or in the morning" Peter asked, smiling.

"Let's do it now," Charlie replied. "Unless there's something you would rather do instead."

Had anyone been near the door of the otherwise perfectly sound-proofed suite, the exuberant female shriek, fortunately muffled by the heavy wooden door, would have quickly provided Peter's response to Charlie's question.

#

Breakfast was served on the patio of their suite the following morning. It was shortly after sunrise and only the gentle sounds of the doves indicated they were not alone on this magnificent morning.

"Is it always like this in summer?" Peter asked.

"Almost every day, Preppy. Still want to go home?"

"Not when it's like this. It's not even humid. I could really learn to like this."

"I see you brought Fallon's package," Charlie said. "Do you think he wrapped it himself? Unusual wrapping for a wedding present; bright red."

"Yes, I recovered it from the front desk. They had put it in the office safe as you asked."

They both sat looking at the package, its bright red colour in sharp contrast to the white starched linen tablecloth and silver cutlery of their breakfast setting.

"I know he gave it to me but I really think you should open it. After all, he is…" Charlie's voice faded off.

"I know. I can't quite get used to saying it myself. I'll probably always think of Howard as my father even though I now accept that Fallon is my biological one. Perhaps I should just consider myself lucky to have two fathers in my life, both who seem to want the best for us."

"I couldn't agree more. Now open the damned present before I burst."

"You sure you want me to do this?"

Charlie nodded.

Peter picked up the package and gently tore open the red wrapping. Inside was a plain white leather box with an elastic band around it and a folded piece of white notepaper underneath.

"Now that looks more like Fallon," Charlie said before bursting out laughing.

Peter unfolded the paper and looked at it blankly.

"What is it?"

"It seems to be a typed list of some sort. Names and addresses. They're all private individuals as far as I can tell. I recognise a couple as being part of the world's rich and famous crowd, but not the others. Here, you take a look."

Charlie took the offered single sheet of paper Peter held out to her.

"Oh," Peter said looking over at Charlie while she read. "There's a handwritten note on the back. I didn't see it before."

Charlie turned the page over. "Typical Fallon. It's cryptic as hell. Here, I'll read it out loud."

Dear Peter and Charlotte, by now you two are married and we are all en route to our respective homes and have left you in peace. I don't know what your plans are for the long-term but here are two things for you to consider. I've always wondered what would happen to my business after I died. I couldn't see Maggi running it and, as things have turned out, she has a new life of her own. Then again, I now also have something special in my life... a son... and a daughter-in-law.

So here it is. I plan to leave everything I own to you two when I die; not that I plan to do that anytime soon. I'd be delighted if you kept the business but that's up to you. I think you'd be good at it, Peter. It's in your genes. If you'd like to join before I've turned to dust, I'd be elated, but again I leave that up to you. Look after Charlie, my son, she's a gem.

Speaking of gem's, the attached list contains all the buyers of exotic jewellery that I know. They can afford to be. They are all very wealthy and not too concerned with documentation. I've met most of them in person at one time or another and those I haven't will know my name. Use it to gain access as and if you wish. Love, Fallon

P.S. Yes, it's the original.

"Wow," Peter said. "He almost read our minds about working with him, but what the hell are we supposed to do with the list?"

"Perhaps he gave us something we could sell if we wanted. Maybe it's from an old wreck. Wouldn't that be fantastic? Open the box Preppy, but do it carefully. He said it's the original."

Peter removed the elastic from around the box and lifted the lid.

"Oh my God," he said holding out the box to Charlie. "It's the *San Pedro* cross. The original bloody *San Pedro* cross."

EPILOGUE

Sean and Howard left South Africa together the morning after the wedding. They had been in Cape Town for almost two weeks and there was a lot to be done back at the office. Fallon, it appeared would be staying a while longer.

Howard had received an e-mail shortly before the wedding advising that Shanice Morgan was leaving the firm. She had located her mother and would be making an extended trip to the United States to try to rebuild her own family life. While he was disappointed, both at losing a good employee and because of the work Peter had done to accommodate her stay in Bermuda, he understood her motives.

He had received one further piece of news from the island. Andrew Jensen had passed away, and a home-going service was to be held two days after he and Sean returned. He decided to keep both pieces of news from Peter. There was nothing to be gained from upsetting what had been a truly wonderful event.

Rhiannon and Maggi could not have been happier; their union was accepted by everyone in the group. Not a single frown or question had ruined their stay. This, coupled with the wedding and a brief excursion to the magnificent Shamwari game reserve just outside Port Elizabeth, had made it an occasion to remember. Maggi could have stayed on indefinitely, but Rhiannon was getting restless. She wanted to check up on Angelo Mosconi. Something didn't feel right about his hurried departure from Bermuda. She was convinced he was somehow involved in the disappearance of the San Pedro cross and the deaths of both Justis Small and Bruce Gordon. She would follow up on her return. She did not intend to let this one go.

Sibeal was ecstatic. Her only daughter was married to a man who appeared to be everything she could possibly have wanted. She liked his father too. In fact, she had thoroughly enjoyed the entire Bermuda contingent. Particularly Fallon, there was something about him that stirred things inside her. She hated to be disloyal to her sister, but Maggi had chosen a different lifestyle now. Sibeal hadn't felt this way in years. She wondered if she should invite Fallon to stay for a few weeks. Just to be sociable of course. After all, he was still her brother-in-law, for the moment anyway, and it was his first trip to South Africa. Besides Bermuda was such a long way away and he might not get another chance to see the country. She would bounce the idea off George and Marie Oosthuizen, and see what they thought.

Carol and Chris Patterson left South Africa the morning after the wedding. They had two long flights to get home to Vancouver. While they had enjoyed meeting Sean's Bermudian friends, they were understandably disappointed in his decision to stay on in Bermuda and work with Howard. Carol, in particular, was concerned at how little she would see of her son. She was only partly mollified by the thought that getting to Bermuda from Vancouver was not too bad a journey and would ensure, for a few years at least, that she and Chris would get away regularly on vacation. She could live with that.

Deciding that there was no pressing reason for him to return to Bermuda immediately, Fallon accepted the invitation from Maggi's sister to stay on in Gordon's Bay for a few weeks. They seemed, as Maggi remarked to Rhiannon, to get along inordinately well.

THE END

About the Author

The author has lived in Bermuda, Canada and South Africa while enjoying a successful global career as a banker and corporate executive. An avid scuba diver, sailor and occasional art collector, B.R. Bentley draws on the knowledge gained from his international travel, business career and recreational pursuits to facilitate his writing. He currently lives on the coast of British Columbia, Canada with his wife and several family pets.

For more information, visit the author's website at **www.brbentley.com.**